# Praise for **AFTI**

~

*"This book reels you in and doesn't let go until you're seduced by the compelling characters. Rivera moves past the well-trodden JFK conspiracy tropes and gives us a glimpse into the intimate struggles of those who are caught in the wake of historical events. He offers us a front-row seat into a chess game of moral compromise and conflicting ambitions. A thought provoking debut novel – riveting and relevant."*

**M. Stolper, Unsinkable Productions New York, New York**

*"The characters in this novel took up residence in my head and made themselves at home. After Dallas is seamlessly woven into the fabric of history, delivering a gripping narrative that packs a powerful dramatic punch. Rivera's literary touch borders on the poetic while also providing timely insights into the dark undercurrents that can influence our political landscape—insights that linger long after the final page."*

**Kevin Carroll, Paramount Global**

*"After Dallas eases you into the mind of a tormented assassin and just when you think he's redeemed himself, Rivera upends everything with a shocking twist. Trust me, you'll never see it coming."*

**Julie R. Houston, Texas**

*"A captivating, technicolor thrill ride…richly painted characters weave together the darkest chapters in our collective history…a tale of unchecked power and questionable intentions that resonate far too well with today's political climate."*

**Lauren C. Hingham, Massachusetts**

# AFTER DALLAS

*A NOVEL*

LOUIS A. RIVERA

LYNDON PRESS

First Edition: 2024

LYNDON PRESS

ISBN: 979-8-9912753-2-3

Cover design & interior formatting:

Mark Thomas / Coverness.com

*For my family, whose love and support*
*tether me to all those who came before us,*
*and for Ariana and Kristen,*
*who fill me with joy, inspiration, and hope*
*for the future.*

*"So, let us not be blind to our differences—but let us also direct attention to our common interests and to the means by which those differences can be resolved. And if we cannot end now our differences, at least we can help make the world safe for diversity. For, in the final analysis, our most basic common link is that we all inhabit this small planet. We all breathe the same air. We all cherish our children's future. And we are all mortal."*

*President John F. Kennedy*
*Washington, D.C. – June 10, 1963*

# PROLOGUE

In a modest dwelling nestled in the Muslim quarter of the ancient city of Jerusalem, a short distance from the revered Dome of the Rock and the sacred Garden of Gethsemane, where it is said that a Jewish carpenter-turned-rabbi looked into the future and sweat droplets of blood, sat a little girl and her mother, their eyes fixed on a flickering TV screen.

Amal, a precocious ten-year-old, snuggled close to her mother Asima, as they watched the somber funeral rites for the fallen president of the United States. It was a mere three days since the tragic assassination.

The little girl's gaze was drawn to a veiled figure cloaked in black mourning attire, barely discernible amidst the shadowed hues of grief. The woman appeared dignified and strong, reminding the child of her own mother when she wore similar garments in the aftermath of heartbreaking loss. Flanking the lady in black were two children, one of whom, a young boy, tenderly offered his departed father a military salute.

Three hundred million homes joined together in collective mourning, witnesses to the savage outcome that hate had unleashed upon the innocent and guilty alike. Now Asima's tears flowed freely, mingling with the devastating anguish cascading around the world. Amal reached out to her mother, her small hand resting gently against the damp cheek.

"Who are they, Mamma? Why are you so sad? Do you know them? Are they family to us? Are you sad because we must leave here and move to France?"

"Be still, Amal!" her mother implored, struggling to control her sobs. "We are all connected by such sorrows. I feel her suffering. She is a mother, I am a mother. She lost a husband, I lost a husband. We all must live in the same broken world, we all want the same things for our children, and this man did not deserve such a fate. We are all bound by grief and suffering, and by the pain we feel over the senseless violence that surrounds us."

Amal felt the comforting rhythm of her mother's heart beating against her own; she held her mother very close for a very long time, the lines between them blurred by their shared grief and solace.

As they hugged, Asima whispered, "Blood of my blood, I pray to our merciful God that we may never be apart."

"I don't understand, Mamma."

"You will."

# 1

# COLLATERAL DAMAGE

Tony De Castro hated his job.

He loved fine Scotch and a full-bodied Rioja. He loved playing dominoes under the shade of the black walnut trees in Little Havana. He loved the inspiring prose of Hemingway and Mario Vargas Llosa. He loved the rhythmic cadence of waves as the evening tides moved toward darkening horizons. He loved listening to the tender melodies of his youth played by old men on worn guitars.

Above all else, he loved his gifted young daughter, Raquel.

But Tony De Castro—a survivor of the Bay of Pigs, an expert in covert operations, entrusted by the most powerful man in the world to do what needed to be done—hated his job.

He hated killing.

The job had already cost him everything he loved.

The savory aroma of a recently cooked meal filled the room. Toys and clothes were scattered across the floor, an unfinished chocolate bar in its crumpled foil wrapping lay deserted on the kitchen table.

*Something's not right, he should be alone.*

Tony moved cautiously through the Parisian apartment, puzzling out why his target had broken safehouse protocol. A woman's blouse hung limply from the shower curtain. In the bedroom he stumbled on a small tennis shoe, scuffed white Keds abandoned among a child's playthings. He froze in mid-stride, his breath trapped in his throat, his heart surging with apprehension. His daughter, the one he may never see again, owned an identical pair.

*A child staying in a safehouse? How could this be?*

A torrent of emotion swelled within him, threatening to derail his attention. *Not now*, he urged himself, clinging to the fragile thread of resolve that tethered him to the present moment.

*Not good, too many unknowns.*

Spikes of adrenaline triggered fight or flight impulses. The inner voice, the doubt creator, demanded attention, insisting he reconsider what he was about to do. He paced back and forth, compulsively rubbing his sweating hands over his trousers.

*A child*, the voice insisted, *about the same age as your daughter.*

*There must be another way.*

*Steady!* he admonished himself. *The mission comes first, the target must be eliminated. Today. No exceptions. Regardless of Aaron's contribution. Everyone on The List must be dealt with. They must be erased.*

The voice offered a compromise. *You're done with this business. When this is over you get out and you disappear. For good.*

Tony retrieved a towel from the bathroom and wrapped it tightly around his sweaty hand, the hand now clutching a gun. He focused on steadying his heart rate, wresting control from the unsettling inner turmoil.

No room for distractions, he rationalized. No time to dwell on his daughter.

*Remember, this is for her. Even if you never see her again, you know what must be done, you have a vital role to play. It's imperative you do everything you can to make the world safer for her. Whatever it takes.*

He continued arguing with himself, reciting age-old justifications. *Collateral damage is inevitable in war.*

Approaching the end of this harrowing mission, he recommitted to concluding it swiftly and vanishing into obscurity. Erased from history, along with the rest of them.

He fixed the suppressor onto the High Standard HDM—the silencer to muffle the noise, the towel to mitigate flash and residue. *Wait until the target turns on the TV or radio, providing cover with background noise, clean kill, this is no place for a firefight. One to the back of the head or through the heart, exit the scene at a normal pace. Must be executed flawlessly, no room for error, and absolutely no witnesses.*

Moving in and out of shadows, probing for optimal leverage, he inadvertently tramples the white tennis shoe. He shudders.

*Focus, goddammit!*

He settles on the small alcove near the front entrance and waits, a purveyor or lethal corrective measures lurking in the dark.

Ideally situated, the safehouse was located in a bustling Parisian neighborhood at the heart of the Latin Quarter with cafés, bakeries, student housing, and jazz clubs thick on the ground. A quiet side street leading to the lively Boulevard Saint-Michel, with the Odéon at one end and a popular bookstore at the other. Easy for a stranger to blend in amidst the usual Parisian throngs. Students, professors, artists and hippies wandered the streets, blissfully unaware of the perilous brink the world teetered upon.

From his concealed vantage point Tony meticulously surveyed every doorway, every egress, his gaze tracing potential escape routes, his mind exhaustively exploring every conceivable contingency. The target, Aaron, an accomplished Mossad asset, a stand-out among the most elite covert operatives in the world, would be formidable if backed into a corner.

Mossad didn't tolerate incompetence; you either excelled or you perished. Tony vetted him carefully, he traveled to Israel to meet him and his family— he had to be sure he was reliable. Twenty-two from The List had met their fate at Aaron's hands, dispatched with unfaltering precision. At the end of this night, only two operatives would remain privy to the dark secret behind the mission. And, if the plan unfolded as designed, only one would be left to carry the burden of truth.

*One more, then you disappear.*

Veiled in darkness, he continued to wrestle with relentless deliberations. *Was it perverse to have met Aaron's wife, knowing the inevitable outcome of this assignment?* Aaron wasn't a thrill-seeking mercenary. Soulless guns-for-hire were common in this line of work, motivated solely by the thrill of wet-work and the allure of blood money. Tony had no tolerance for them; they were unreliable, their allegiances transient. He had encountered their ilk at the Bay of Pigs— men unable to grasp the nobility of sacrificing everything for a cause they believed in.

Aaron was cut from different cloth; his motives transcended monetary gain. A significant portion of his family had perished in Nazi concentration camps. He witnessed first-hand the relentless tug-of-war between good and evil, and comprehended the unwavering will resistance demanded. Aaron recognized that prevailing in this eternal battle occasionally required deeds of unspeakable cruelty.

He brandished a tailor-made CV. Too young to make a difference in '42 or '43 when his ancestors were being slaughtered throughout Germany and Eastern Europe, he dodged a brutal fate. As a young boy the underground resistance smuggled him out of Germany while the German Wehrmacht sliced through Europe. In 1950, at the age of twenty-two, after the Israeli Knesset passed the Law of Return, he moved to Israel as a citizen of the Jewish state. He joined the Israeli Defense Force and quickly rose through the ranks, distinguishing himself as an expert in special operations. He retired from the military and operated as a private contractor, taking covert assignments for the Israeli government. Well known in certain circles as a discreet, effective, no-nonsense operative who got things done.

Aaron and his wife were good people. His wife Helen was a wise, capable and compassionate partner. There was a quiet strength about her he admired. As husband and wife, they shared a partnership buttressed by a fierce sense of duty.

*Why would he invite a woman to stay with him in a Paris safehouse? Aaron didn't do things on the fly.*

Maybe he wasn't getting sloppy at all. Maybe this was how he blended in. What Frenchman didn't have a woman on the side? He turned the safehouse into a pied-à-terre. Maybe the setting wasn't as crazy as it seemed. Maybe she needed a place to stay; maybe she was cheating on her husband. But what about the kid? Maybe Aaron would walk through the door alone. One shot. Done. Slow walk out of the building and down the street, textbook elimination.

*Please God, let him be alone.*

Uncertain of God's intentions, Tony chose to no longer harbor doubts about his own.

Outside, the Eiffel Tower glimmered against a moonlit sky. The city of Paris remained a testament to beauty and human potential, a magnet for dreamers and wanderers drawn to its labyrinthine streets and bustling brasseries. A spellbinding achievement of civilization that even the callous Nazis could not bring themselves to destroy. Yet the enchantment of the City of Lights held no sway over him now. He had a job to do.

*Soon you will leave Paris and forget all this blood and madness.*

*Quiet now!* He reprimanded the badgering inner voice and reviewed exactly how he would execute the hit. He would not wait for his target to get settled, even if it meant risking whatever noise might escape his dampening agent. *Just get it over with!* He secured the towel around his hand and gun and waited in the small alcove beside the door. A close-range hit. Aaron would enter, close the door and it would be done.

The reasons and rationalizations sufficiently parsed, doubt yielded to certainty. With each passing moment, his heartbeat slowed, his nerves steadied, and the persistent inner voice fell silent. He waited, surrounded by shadows and the palpable presence of death.

The sound of a turning lock triggers his hyperawareness; sounds of shuffling of feet, the rustling of bags, hushed conversation at the door. The specifics elude him—now irrelevant details to the matter at hand. The jingling of keys, latches echoing in the hallway, a bolt sliding away, his own heartbeat accelerating, amplifying the rising anticipation. The door groans, swings open and then quickly closes, sealing them inside with an ill-fated thud. A woman's voice, another voice, a…

He fires three shots in quick succession. POP. POP. POP. One shot each. Clean. Efficient. Fatal. Stepping over the target and two other bodies lying face down, he moves toward the unlocked front door, avoiding the oval-shaped pools of blood.

Tony turns on the TV, exits, and gently closes the door behind him. Maintaining a slow pace, he strolls out of the building into the embrace of a warm Paris evening.

The image of a spilled bag of groceries, a stuffed animal soaking blood from a child's head, the Eiffel Tower glistening through an open window, permanently imprinted in memory. He would carry it like a scar, a curse, a sin, a wish that he too could lie beside them in darkness, in the pain-free nothingness of oblivion.

The memory weighed him down, pulling him further into dark places he was ill-equipped to visit.

His wife Helen should hear of Arron's fate directly from him. He resolved to visit Israel and sit Shiva with her, he owed him at least that. Aaron died a noble death in the service of a higher cause.

He had to convince her of this.

He had to convince himself.

His sanity depended on it.

\* \* \*

"It is done."

"Good," said the voice on the other end of the phone, distorted by the crackle of a poor connection. The anticipation of what came next, predictable and unwelcomed, added to Tony's surging dread. "Then it is over, comrade, as I too have completed my final task. With this, our mission is now concluded. We have done our duty, and we can now both disappear into obscurity."

"May it be so," Tony said solemnly, letting the silence between them fill the air for a moment too long.

"Listen." The Russian accent now discernible on the overseas connection.

Tony clutched the receiver, his hands involuntarily moving it away from his face as if he could somehow separate himself from all the blood he'd spilled and the final witness he must still dispatch. He fought the urge to disconnect the line, to disconnect from who he had become, to disconnect from his own troubled memories.

*It's not really over, is it?*

"You and I share a bond," said the voice. "We both share a burden we will no doubt carry with us to our graves. There is no glory or pleasure in what we've had to do. We can at least take comfort in the knowledge that we served our countries, we served our fellow humans, we both paid a heavy price to accomplish what needed to be done. What is next for you?"

"I'm not sure," Tony said. "I will travel, put this behind me. There is one thing I am sure of though, my service to this cause is over. I am done. My new life begins today. All must now be forgotten."

"Listen, my friend," the man with the Russian accent insisted, "we are brothers in this; we are comrades. Please grant me one last request before you disappear. Let us break bread as brothers one time. Meet me in Barcelona. We will eat well, drink good wine and speak of what nobility may yet be rescued from this world. And after, we will depart as brothers. Do you have a family?"

"My family is lost to me now, I can never go back to them."

"I understand," said the voice on the other end of the phone line. "Perhaps you will find a woman here, one who speaks your native tongue, and maybe she can help renew your spirit. Either way, comrade, you must come to Barcelona."

*Enough! Never again will I allow myself to become a pawn in a game played by people who love power more than life itself. After this, I must erase who I became and find a way to start again.*

Tony agreed to the meeting. He gritted his teeth, his inner voice aching with regret.

*You've convinced yourself you are serving a higher cause, but if every time you are called to serve, you must relinquish a piece of your own humanity, you need to ask yourself: is humanity really worth saving if you are forced to sacrifice a part of your own in the process?*

# 2

# BLOOD BROTHERS

One can never judge a man solely by appearance, Tony mused, studying the jaunty man seated opposite him. Killers come in all shapes and sizes; where some exuded brute force, this one seemed to walk the world with a careless sense of ease and relaxed self-awareness. The Russians he encountered in Cuba were often crude, heavy-drinking, bombastic ideologues, their aggression worn like a badge of honor. But this man, Dimitri Ivanov, possessed a sophistication that belied his deadly nature.

Dimitri Ivanov, his affectatious Russian counterpart, spoke ebulliently of Barcelona, extolling a city alive with echoes of a storied past, its streets teeming with zest and vitality. Something about the boisterous atmosphere of the ancient city reflected the enchanting confluence of hope, struggle, joy, and passion that animated the Catalonian soul.

Tony found himself reflecting on the ancient ruins surrounding Barcelona, seeing in them vestiges of fallen empires, emblematic of history's ebb and flow. The weathered stones and crumbling façades of ancient structures, crafted by Romans, Celts, and Moors, served as a poignant reminder of the impermanence that humbled even the mightiest of civilizations.

A dark-haired Catalonian woman, flushing with warmth and mischief, delivered a plate loaded with ham, a variety of cheeses, and tomato-laced bread. The Russian held her dark eyes for a moment and examined the bottle on the tray. He reached for her hand and spoke to her in perfect Spanish: "*Se que eres hija de Catalonia, y un angel de luz y bellessa, pero temo que en este momento, me fallan las palabras en Catalán, asi que te pido con mucho cariño, en castellano, que nos hagas el favor de traernos una botella del Teso de la Monja 1956, creo que queda una o dos botellas en la cava del dueño.*"

("I know you are a daughter of Catalonia, and an angel of light and beauty, but I fear at this moment, the right words fail me in your native Catalan. So with great affection, using the mother tongue of Spain, I ask if you could do us the favor of bringing a bottle of Teso de la Monja 1956, I believe there are one or two stored in the owner's cellar.")

She smiled warmly and scurried off.

Tony ignored the Russian's charming banter, his hands clasped together on the table, biding his time, waiting for the right moment. He was not here to make new friends.

Dimitri continued, "You and I may share more in common than you think, my comrade. I love everything about this country. I've also been to your country many times—the country of your birth as well as your adopted country. Barcelona, Havana, New York, Miami—all wonderful cities in their own way, but Barcelona, ah *mi amigo*, this is an extraordinary place. In some ways you and I are like orphans, severed from the people we love most so that they may remain safe."

Tony winced at the thought of never seeing his family again, a bitter reminder of what the mission had cost him.

The young woman returned and poured him the requested vintage. She doted over the Russian and ignored Tony as if he were an unwelcome guest. Dimitri filled Tony's glass.

"Let us raise our glasses and make a toast to all those we love. May they never learn of the blood spilled in their name, and let us pray our actions will provide them with a reasonable chance at living joyfully in a less troubled world."

Tony wondered who atheists prayed to, or why God would concern himself with the prayers of men like him.

He touched glasses with his loquacious host, took a long sip, and lifted the smooth goblet to his nose, inhaling the fragrant bouquet. It elicited memories of a happier time, a time that seemed to belong to another life. An echo of his own waning past.

"*Es verdad*," he said to the Russian. "I was forced to abandon what I treasure most and I confess to you now earnestly, in the aftermath of too many bloody deeds, the price I paid to repair the damage others have inflicted on the world has been very high. I also wonder if I could ever justify the toll this has taken on the ones I love." Tony lifted his glass and peered into the blood-red wine. The residue of loss was still too fresh to voice, so he lapsed into silence.

"We are pawns in a larger game and the game is bloody and will no doubt go on without us," Dimitri said, his soliloquy picking up steam. "Take your Fidel, he began with a noble purpose, and like most revolutionaries, he succumbed to his own insecurities, his paranoia, and his vanity, blinded by his own idealism. Victim to the same malignancy that crippled Lenin, Stalin, and even Trotsky. All progenitors of change, but also the cause of so much senseless bloodshed. God forgive them."

Tony, all too familiar with senseless bloodshed, had no appetite for the topic. His thoughts wandered, aided by the soothing warmth of the wine and the azure sky. Fueled by the same wine and a compulsion to give meaning to madness, the Russian's pedantic verbosity persisted.

"I imagine you lost many worthy comrades in the ill-fated invasion fiasco. And I imagine many of those men believed themselves to be part of a noble contest, a battle for a worthy cause. I know some blamed Kennedy. He didn't fully grasp the brutal and ignoble shortcomings of the American security apparatus. Too much hubris, and wishful thinking. They failed him. But later, in the crisis with the missiles on Cuban soil, he didn't make the same mistake of trusting the CIA. Kennedy really showed some *cojones*. He had to stare down our Premier Khrushchev, and his own generals. Feckless people on both sides almost plunged the world into unfixable and catastrophic events. Kennedy and Khrushchev managed to avoid a war of annihilation during those twelve days. Nikita told me Castro was arguing for a preemptive nuclear strike. Can you imagine the mass destruction, had those missiles left their silos in Cuba? There would be nothing left. Nothing. Not a fucking thing.

"In the end, Khrushchev also did the right thing. For this, we all owe him a debt of gratitude. No one delivered bluster better than Nikita, but in the end, he took the deal, letting Kennedy frame this issue politically for his domestic audience, and permitting him to remove the missiles from Turkey without crowing about it. It's frightening to think how close the world came to total destruction."

Ivanov had to know some of his former associates were on The List, Russian operatives he eliminated. Tony had no desire to revisit any of it. Still the Russian persisted.

"You should know, Tony, I come to this business as an outsider. I would never speak so frankly in my own country, I've spent too many years outside Mother Russia to be deceived by all the propaganda. I fought here in Spain in '38 and when the International Brigade left, I continued fighting for the Republican cause. When Barcelona fell to Franco in '39 I remained in Spain, working under cover, doing what I could to support the resistance. Some things are worth fighting and dying for. I believe we are the same in this, my comrade. During the war, I spent five years operating against the Nazis throughout Europe and North Africa. Trust me, I have had my fill of bloodshed."

Tony refilled his wine glass. *I should just end this now.* His mood darkened, but he allowed the Russian to continue uninterrupted.

"Our esteemed Premier Khrushchev was not who he appeared to be on American television. He would've implemented more progressive reforms had this unfortunate event not happened. Khrushchev experienced Stalin's excesses firsthand; he oversaw the purges in Ukraine and witnessed enough carnage to last a lifetime. After the Cuban missile predicament it became clear to him how easily the world could be pushed into self-annihilation by zealots.

"Zealots exist in all political movements, Tony. The men who planned and executed the assassination wanted to force Khrushchev's hand, force a confrontation with the Americans. They wanted the rest of the world to choose sides. Unrestrained imperialistic capitalism, with all its cruelty and abuses, or the naïvely utopian Marxist vision of an egalitarian world, where the state provides for all according to their need. The Soviet zealots who organized the assassination of your president, like zealots everywhere, failed to fully understand the repercussions of their actions."

*Ah, now we come to it. He wants to make his case. It won't change anything. I have a mandate to fulfill and this Russian talks too much. Good, the longer he talks, the fewer the witnesses.*

"We knew who they were," Ivanov continued, his oratory filled with conviction. "All of them. Give them credit, these two men who were accustomed to being at the center of events, recognized they had to recede into history without anyone ever knowing what they did to ensure the world we lived in didn't perish in a cloud of reprisal."

Tony bided his time while his companion ordered another exquisite bottle of ten-year-old Rioja with a simple gesture to the waitress. She smiled at the Russian but continued to avoid eye contact with Tony.

He observed his host with a mixture of curiosity and wariness. They were about the same age, but the Russian exuded youthful vitality and a demeanor seemingly unburdened by his lethal interventions, traits that clearly captivated the young waitress. Yet, beneath the veneer of cavalier charm lay a hidden menace, a man capable of unspeakable things. Tony's hand instinctively brushed against the cold steel of his pistol, a stark reminder that this encounter was not merely social. Despite the wine, the candid conversation, the poetic overtones, the sea-laden air—visions of noble deeds juxtaposed with dark realities—the underlying imperative remained unchanged.

"Nikita Khrushchev had a soul, Tony, you can trust me when I say this. His conscience was part of his strength, but also a part of his weakness. I share this with you tonight because we are bound by a sense of sacrifice, honor, and duty. I share this because there are nuances in this story worth understanding. Our premier did not always trust his intelligence officers, and they did not always trust him."

"Why was that?" Tony asked, remembering his own dealings with men like Allen Dulles.

"Chaos, Tony. Chaos creates opportunities for men who could not otherwise hope to gain power. The cabal who hatched this godforsaken plan kept the group small. They planned to seize power in the chaos following a hostile confrontation with the United States. They were dangerous lunatics, obsessed with taking control. They flipped a few CIA operatives, which is why Johnson needed you, and an outsider like me, to help fix this mess. But you know all of this. You know the names of the unfortunate men who found themselves on The List. Believe me, Tony, Khrushchev had no knowledge of the plot to assassinate your president. I say this now to you to ease any lingering doubts you may still hold."

Tony scanned the immediate vicinity. The few diners left seemed to be finishing their meals. The street outside the café became quiet, no immediate threats present anywhere. This would not take long.

His host prattled on.

"The stakes were painfully clear," Ivanov intoned, his oration infused with melodrama. "Khrushchev relinquished power to salvage millions of lives. Your President Johnson, he too grasped the gravity of the situation. There were no easy choices. Your president will also step back when the time is right. He will become like us, fading into the shadows of history, his pivotal role concealed from the world. In the gauntlet of power and political exigency, some sacrifices must remain unaccounted for, buried beneath the burden of an unflinching commitment to humanity's survival."

Tony nodded in agreement. Noble words, he thought, well spoken and seductive. I still have one more task to complete. One more sacrifice to the cause.

"We too must recede into obscurity, Tony," the Russian continued, the wine seeming to inspire and elevate his prose. "We will receive no medals, they will sing no songs about us. Schoolchildren will never learn of what we risked, of what we sacrificed. They will never learn about the part of ourselves we relinquished never to be recovered. They will never understand that we did what we did for the greater good, so that the world might be saved from the calamitous actions of men whose desire for power exceeded their capacity for wisdom. You and I must live with the knowledge that we sentenced innocent men to die, erasing what they discovered, so others might live. This burden we carry to our graves. For this reason, you and I are brothers and always will be."

Cain and Abel were also brothers, Tony thought. No choice here but to complete the mission.

"I see the anguish in your face. We share the same torment," Dimitri insisted. "You look at me now and wonder if I don't feel the same way, because I drink wine and smile at the beautiful waitress and think of making love to her. It is true, Tony, wine dulls the vivid recollections of blood and death, and the warmth of a woman's body next to mine allows me, for a time, to connect with what is left of my soul. I cling to that memory, Tony. I embrace those things that allow me to keep this part of me alive. The alternative is a dark place where the distinction between good and evil is abandoned. A place where I lose any semblance of the man I once was. No, my friend, I will not yield to that dark abyss, not tonight, not while there is wine, not while there is a beautiful woman who finds comfort in what words and deeds my heart might design for her pleasure. Not while I still believe in noble causes and the possibility of redemption."

Tony's expression revealed nothing as he contemplated how to bring closure to the sordid business at hand. The killing had already hollowed out a part of him, and the Russian's words were beginning to resonate in ways he was not ready to acknowledge. Just words, he tried to convince himself. Just words.

"Now I imagine you carry a weapon with you. If not with you, then close by." Tony held Dimitri Ivanov's gaze and said nothing. He stroked the High Standard HDM concealed in his pocket, playing out the different ways this conversation might end. The waitress must be spared, he thought. Never again will I take another innocent life.

"No need to answer me. I know what you've been ordered to do. I received the same instructions. We are on The List. Yet here we are, still drawing breath, taking in the healing sea air of this ancient Spanish city, a city that has seen its share of death and senseless pain. The men who shot your president are dead, the men who set the plan in motion are dead, the men who aided them are dead, and the men who inadvertently discovered the truth are also dead. You know their names, you've seen their lifeless bodies. Those secrets died with them. Now there are just four of us: Johnson, Khrushchev, you, and me. We are the only ones left."

The café was empty now, only the dark-haired waitress remained. Setting down coffee in front of them, the waitress finally made eye contact. Tony shuddered under her penetrating gaze. For a brief moment, he imagined she could somehow see the ghosts of all the souls he had extinguished gathered around him, witnesses to the tragic undertakings etched into his conscience. Her smile was gone, her face somber and the fear in her eyes stirred something in Tony.

"I am not armed and I do not intend to take your life," the Russian said candidly. "Not tonight. Tonight, you will find me in my hotel room making love to our beautiful dark-eyed Catalonian waitress, Isabella. She will leave at first light and tomorrow at dusk you will find me here again enjoying exquisite food and wine and thinking about making love to Isabella again. If you want to kill me, you will have ample time to do so. Who knows, Tony, if you choose to end my life, you may very well be doing me a favor. This feeling of being alive, of being healed, of being human again that I experience when I lie next to a beautiful woman, it is a fleeting thing, as I cannot escape the memories of what I've had to do."

The Russian locked eyes with Tony, his grim stare sending tremors through Tony's frame—a visceral reaction to the disagreeable task at hand.

Dimitri pressed forward in unreserved disclosure. "These recollections, they come in waves, images, like a relentless tide flooding my awareness with a vivid montage. A story where I play the role of both hero and villain. Whatever sense of nobility I try to bring to the account will always be stained by memories of blood and pain. I say to you now, in all sincerity, as a brother in arms, I am not certain how my story will end. Maybe your bullet will save me from a never-ending confrontation with my own misgivings. However, it may also be possible that your own path to redemption begins with leaving the bullet meant for me in its chamber and simply walking away."

As the sun fell below the horizon, bursts of orange streaked through the deepening blue sky, illuminating the Mediterranean Sea in a breathtaking spectacle of light.

Tony shut his eyes, embracing the image and allowing the brisk salt-laden air to wash over him, while in the distance, the rhythmic ebb and flow of the sea provided a familiar refrain.

It had been a long while since the sea had afforded him such an immaculate, life-affirming moment.

He savored this one for a very long time.

# 3

# THE THINGS WE LEAVE BEHIND

The morning light crept through the Manhattan skyline casting a mosaic of shadows on the crisp white sheets tracing the contours of her form. A pillow lay nestled gently between her breasts, moving in tandem with each serene breath. Gabriel Hernandez lingered by the door, suspended between two worlds—the one he was leaving behind and the one he aspired to shape, grateful to have found a partner to share in this moment of transition.

He had endured losses—his parents, his sister, all gone—yet they were still a part of him, their memory a constant source of encouragement and inspiration. They'd be proud of what he had achieved—the praise of his peers, the book deals, the money, the awards—all of it a testament to their influence. But despite everything he'd accomplished, however fulfilling, the rewards always wound up feeling hollow. Until he met Rachel. She was the light in the darkness, the grace in the chaos, the person who brought out the best in him.

The future beckoned. He yearned for a life unrestricted by the relentless demands of professional achievement. Rachel inspired him to summon the courage to embrace uncertainty, to risk everything in search of a life lived fully, deeply, and without reservation.

His heart was full.

The machine whirred and sputtered. Steam filled the apartment with the rich aroma of freshly brewed coffee. He returned to his morning ritual, slowly pouring the liquid into a small white porcelain cup, knowing the fragrance would entice Rachel from her comfortable cocoon. As if on cue, she tottered sleepy-eyed out of the bedroom and into the kitchen, dressed in the *Greetings from Asbury Park* T-shirt given to her by a smitten singer-songwriter from New Jersey destined for great things. She wore an impish smile and ran her fingers through his hair while her body pressed up close, distracting him long enough to remove the cup from his hand.

"I didn't hear you snore last night," she said, sipping the hot coffee. "I guess all that growling took it out of you."

Gabriel smiled. "By all means, help yourself, I'll just make another cup," he said, kissing her and caressing her tenderly. "I don't recall making any growling noises, probably because I couldn't hear myself over your emphatic announcing to God that you were arriving any second." He paused to bask in the delicious memory.

Rachel's eyes grew wider. She pulled Gabriel closer and kissed him lustily on the lips.

"You taste like coffee," he said, feigning indifference. "And… you're going to make me late if we continue down this road to memory lane."

"I understand your concern, after all this is quite a momentous day for you," she said, and mimicked a newscaster's voice: "Today award-winning columnist and author Gabriel Hernandez will be taking an indefinite leave of absence from the prestigious *American Century* magazine, a publication he helped bring to national prominence. He leaves the magazine to pursue a contemplative life in the mountains of Vermont. Care to comment, Mr. Hernandez, on this surprise move away from the spotlight?" She held the coffee cup to his face pretending it was a microphone.

"Cute," Gabriel said sitting down at the granite kitchen counter and gazing out at the expansive view of Central Park afforded them by their penthouse apartment on the Upper West Side.

"But, seriously, it's not like you," she insisted.

"What's not like me?"

"The lack of pedantic pontification and visionary pronouncements about the future. Care to share what's churning through that magnificent brain of yours?"

The coffee machine hissed again and Rachel poured two more cups of coffee as she studied Gabriel's face for clues.

"Me? Share? You realize what a provocative question that is, given I'm about to down another cup of very strong espresso." Gabriel pretended to be distracted by the morning newspaper.

Rachel leaned forward on her elbows, patiently waiting for an answer. Looking up from his newspaper Gabe realized the love of his life was not inclined to change the subject.

"I think we've been over this enough. Money's not an issue, at least not for now, we can pretty much do whatever we want. I'm excited about leaving the city for a few years, forever if it feels right. I like the idea of not being tied to a deadline or an all-consuming investigative project. Am I going to miss the action, the thrill of the chase, the unlimited expense account? Sure I am. But the idea of leaving while I'm still at the top of my game appeals to me. Bernstein left the *Post* in '77, at the height of his influence, and he's doing fine."

Gabriel smiled and placed his hand on Rachel's midsection. There was a difference between success and fulfillment, and on some visceral level he felt certain they no longer needed to chase the trappings of success. It was different now, they had each other.

"I think it's the right time to step away, slow down and enjoy the fruits of what we've accomplished; create a home life together, make a family, away from the incessant clamor we've been living in." At thirty-two Rachel's biological clock was ticking and Gabriel, having lost his parents at an early age, welcomed the idea of starting a family.

On the surface, they inhabited different worlds. Rachel, an artist who dealt in abstract visceral connections, and Gabriel, a writer and journalist, who dedicated himself to the uncovering of inconvenient facts. They both shared a passion for their work, but they also shared a much deeper passion for their partnership. New York City had provided them with the propulsion they both needed to thrive in two different, yet highly competitive professions, but Manhattan was also a demanding mistress. The idea of creating a sanctuary away from the players and the noise, not to mention the enemies Gabe had made throughout his celebrated career, held sway.

"I think transitions are supposed to be a little uncomfortable. Isn't that the whole point? Change, moving out of our comfort zone. Besides, there's no shortage of corrupt politicians and aspiring felons in the world should I decide I can't live without writing about them. There'll always be another story to chase, here or somewhere else. I've had my share of the spotlight." He gave a self-deprecating smile. "I'm ready to try something else. You have a studio in the new house; you'll be able to work whenever you want. I can explore other writing projects, teach, and do different things. Our future is a blank canvas. Right?"

"I see what you just did there," she said, snickering at the metaphor. "Yes, a blank canvas, always a good way to begin something new."

"Listen, honey," Gabriel said, setting down the newspaper and fixing his eyes on Rachel, "speaking of things that are a little uncomfortable, I've been meaning to share something with you. I guess this is as good a time as any."

"This doesn't sound good," Rachel said.

"I know the relationship with your father is not your favorite subject. You've mentioned more than once that you haven't seen him in many years and that you've resigned yourself to the possibility that you may never see him again."

"Yeah, what about that?" Rachel said warily.

"Well, I've recently learned some things that I think you should be aware of. It sort of relates to our move."

"Go ahead, Gabe, let it out. What have you learned?"

"Your father, Antonio De Castro, also known as Tony De Castro, entered the country about three months ago from the Canadian border."

"How in the world did you manage to find that out?" Rachel demanded.

"The last time we talked about your father you said you had no idea if he was alive or dead. It sparked my curiosity. I mean, honey, when the woman I love says she doesn't know if her own father is alive or dead, what kind of investigative reporter would I be if I didn't try to find out?"

"Jesus, Gabriel, why didn't you tell me this before?" There was a mixture of anger and exasperation in her tone.

"I didn't want to disappoint you if I failed to learn anything. And I wasn't sure if he was even alive. At least now we know he's alive. He apparently has some health issues, he's been going back and forth from Montreal to the University of Vermont Medical Center in Burlington."

"How did you come by this information?" Rachel said, squirming at the thought of connecting with her father after so many years.

"A good reporter never divulges his sources," Gabriel said, attempting to inject a little levity into the conversation.

"I'm just not sure what to do with this, Gabe, and frankly, I'd rather not focus on it right now. It's beyond bizarre that my father might be living so close to where we're setting up our new home. But I refuse to think about it now. Nope, can't do it. Not going to get into it with you either. Too much on our plate. Can we please agree to just set this aside for now?"

"Of course," Gabe said wanting to defuse the tension. "I know it's a sensitive subject, understandably so, and I have no intention of forcing you into anything you're not comfortable with. This is just information. We can deal with it whenever you're ready."

"Thank you," Rachel said, relaxing. "I do appreciate your good intentions."

"You know, honey, one day we may want to start a family. One day soon maybe." Gabriel paused to gauge Rachel's reaction. "And when we do," he continued with a note of tenderness, "our kids will want to know about their grandfather. My family is gone, and in the end, family, the one we're born with and the one we make, is all we have to keep us tethered to the world."

"Oh, so you're waxing poetic now?"

"Go ahead and poke fun," Gabriel said, grateful for the release in tension, "but you asked how I'm feeling about our move and the changes ahead. This is what I'm feeling. This is what I consider important now. I'm more excited about the future we're creating than worried about the past we're leaving behind."

"I see," Rachel said, quietly picking up the discarded newspaper, allowing Gabriel's buoyant words to fill the space between them.

* * *

Rachel examined Gabriel's face as he busied himself preparing for the day ahead: deep brown eyes, dark complexion, prominent nose, and strong jaw, Gabriel bore little resemblance to the succession of Ken dolls she had taken as lovers in the past. Gabe was a thoughtful, self-possessed man who rarely took no for an answer— kind but not a pushover, someone accustomed to fighting for what he wanted. A man committed to righteous causes, propelled by a code of honor that defined his work.

She would follow him anywhere. But transitioning from the high-octane pace of Manhattan to a serene life in the mountains of Vermont would require significant adjustments. She knew there'd be new challenges, but she remained steadfast in the belief that the benefits outweighed the risks. She loved the kind of man he was, she loved his intensity, and she loved that behind all his intellectual firepower and bravado was a wounded and gentle soul that he revealed to her alone.

She tilted her head, noticing his laser focus as he arranged the documents in his briefcase. There was a heightened sense of anxiety about him these days. At first, she thought it might be the impending move causing consternation. Getting the new home ready required juggling schedules, deadlines, and priorities. They wanted to keep their plans secret until he was ready to announce his departure from *American Century*. The entire process was delicate and taxing. But something else seemed to be bothering him. He was often restless after breaking a high-profile story, particularly one that generated punishing repercussions for his subject, but this latest story was different, some lingering distraction, a weight he carried, a guarded apprehension. She often found him lost in his own thoughts, as if he was still trying to connect the threads to an enigma that remained just out of reach.

Perhaps the preoccupation was exactly what he said, the willingness to step out of their comfort zone. A leap of faith, away from the familiar and comfortable, into an unknown future they had yet to build.

*I too have to make peace with what I leave behind*, she thought. *To everything there is a season. Things will work out as they are meant to.* She had always been skilled at orchestrating her own reassuring thoughts. *It's going to be alright.* She repeated it to herself like a mantra, a habit formed from years of solitude.

One of her paintings had recently sold for an unprecedented sum of money, and she was meeting the buyer today. Money that helped facilitate the change of venue, the opportunity to look beyond the New York art scene and the endless courting of critics and collectors. She began to imagine herself with a child, she imagined how motherhood, family and nature might inform her work in new and unforeseen ways. She imagined how the move might bring freedom from the lingering demons of her past, a decisive step forward, an emancipation, a fresh perspective.

Rachel locked eyes with Gabriel who remained preoccupied with preparations for his final day at *American Century*. Catching her deep in her own ponderings, he seemed to read her thoughts. He smiled.

"Listen, baby," she said reaching for his hand and offering a comforting smile, "if you're planning on staying in that gorgeous suit, you better get moving or I will definitely make you late."

"I'm such a lucky man," he added, his eyes holding hers.

"Yes, you are. I'm lucky too. I guess," she offered with a little snicker as she kissed him goodbye.

Pausing on his way out the door Gabriel said, "Think about dropping by my little farewell soirée when you're done with your meeting. I have a thing I need to do at the office and then I'm meeting Michael for a drink before the final goodbye. Don't know how late I want to go. The celebration is likely to start early and end late whether I'm there or not. Oh, almost forgot, thinking we should hang in Boston for a day or two."

"Sounds nice. Lobster rolls on the beach?" Rachel asked.

"Oh yea, gotta get some lobstah while we're theyah!" he said in an exaggerated Boston accent. "I got roped into connecting with some old friends while I'm in Boston, couldn't say no, nothing major, I'll explain later."

"Okay, we'll figure it out. We're saying goodbye to hard deadlines. Right?" Rachel patted his butt and kissed him again on the lips. Gabriel offered a parting growl as he closed the door behind him.

No point in prying, she thought. They would have plenty of time to sort out whatever was bothering him. The man had a unique way of seeing the future, almost as if he could anticipate the next challenge before it happened.

*Whatever's eating him will blow over*, she reassured herself. *We're both putting a lot on the line with this move. I get why he might be getting the jitters. There is one thing he'll need to understand though, the idea of reconnecting with my father is a non-starter. There are some things that are just meant to stay in the past, and my father is one of them.*

# 4

## AFFLICTING THE COMFORTABLE

"So, are you going to miss me?" Gabriel pawed a handful of cashews and smirked at his childhood companion.

Brown leather chairs, muted lighting, and chestnut tones gave the Oak Room at the Plaza Hotel a distinctly masculine ambiance while twenty-foot ceilings, oak-covered walls, and enormous frescoes of Bavarian castles from a forgotten Flemish painter evoked a bygone era. The bar, a men only establishment before Prohibition, boasted a fabled history as a deal-making salon for many of New York's power brokers. Meticulously prepared martinis were delivered in chilled decanters by Jimmy the bartender who had been serving patrons at the Oak Room ever since his military discharge for, as he tells it, 'taking a bullet in the ass' at the Battle of Cherbourg in World War II.

It was three o'clock on a Wednesday afternoon. The piano player arrived early, ordered a drink and began noodling background music on a glossy black baby grand; a single white light illuminated his movements. Later, when the after-work crowd stumbled in, he would provide a soundtrack for their stories: classics, jazz standards, and tender melodies to accompany the evening's chronicles. On occasion he might invite an aspiring singer or an

28

established artist to join him at the piano and perform for the well-lubricated and appreciative patrons.

Engaging in weighty discussions over drinks at the Oak Room was one of the things Gabriel would miss most about New York. The lounge was known for discreetly accommodating high-profile patrons, a haven where private conversations remained private. Michael Rose, Gabriel's childhood friend and closest confidant, was no stranger to the Oak Room. He often relished the attention his office garnered him, but today was different. Today they were closing a significant chapter in their professional association, a partnership that earned them some measure of notoriety. Gabriel as a respected investigative reporter and Michael as the sometimes-feared chief of the Criminal Division for the Southern District of New York. Gabriel exposed maleficence and Michael prosecuted high-profile perpetrators, providing them free accommodation in the federal penitentiary system.

Despite being overachievers academically, they were considered interlopers at Riverdale Country School, their scholarship admissions branding them as perpetual outsiders to the elite social hierarchy. Both men attended Harvard, where they encountered similar social barriers. Growing up in Riverdale, an affluent enclave in the Bronx, provided a safe haven for the boys, yet the neighborhood's rough edges taught them the value of resilience. Michael, with his alpha-male persona and vigilant nature, often played the role of protector for Gabriel, who appeared more bookish and reserved. While Gabriel preferred to avoid physical altercations, his determination and defiance matched Michael's in intensity. Unlike Gabriel, who as a kid, preferred to talk his way out of physical confrontation, Michael didn't look for fights, but almost never avoided them.

Gabriel won early admission to Harvard the same year he lost his family in a car accident. That same year Michael's mother and father became Gabe's surrogate parents. He had carried a torch for Gabe's idealistic sister Laura, and her tragic death became a shared trauma of loss that helped forge a powerful bond between the two men.

The driver of the car was a reckless rich kid with a bad drug habit, a

Courtland, a family that held themselves above the law. The crash fueled an almost obsessive dedication to holding the self-appointed entitled class accountable. Gabe and Michael forged a formidable alliance bound together by mutuality and a predilection for righteous justice.

As adults, their partnership followed a familiar pattern. Gabe used words to expose adversaries considered untouchable, and Michael, a successful prosecutor, delighted in seeing guys in expensive tailored suits doing the perp walk. They shared a disdain for men of high net-worth and low moral IQ: entitled white-collar criminals born on third base convinced they had hit a triple; people who lived in a shrouded world of privilege who believed the law didn't apply to them. When it came to shedding light on the dark corridors of malfeasance, Gabriel Hernandez had no better partner than Michael Rose.

"Yeah, I'm going to miss you, but I still think you picked a good time to get out of Dodge," Michael said.

"I can't tell if you're being serious. I'm definitely going to miss doing what we do, but we're not moving to Australia, it's Vermont for chrissake."

Ever since they were kids Michael felt it was his role to protect Gabriel. Sometimes Gabriel thought he took it too far.

"I know, I know, but Vermont is far enough away from the heat we've generated to keep you from getting burned. At least it'll make it harder for anyone looking for payback."

"Like out of sight out of mind?" Gabriel asked.

"Listen to me. It would be better for everyone if you didn't do your usual victory lap. This is the perfect time to slip out of town. Stick with your plan, step away from the mess we created." Michael checked behind him, looking for potential eavesdroppers, then leaned in to emphasize his point. "Look, bud, we ruffled some feathers on this one. The people we went after don't play by our rules. Payback will no doubt be forthcoming. We might not know exactly how, where or when—but it's coming, and it could put you and the people you love in danger."

"Since when are we intimidated by anybody?" Gabriel pushed back.

"Don't be an ass, Gabe. Can you for once listen to what I'm telling you without litigating every word? Stay away from the arraignment tomorrow. Stay the fuck away from the press conference, and for God's sake no chest-thumping, no putting your dick on the table for everyone to admire."

"Why not? It's a nice one," Gabe said with a smirk.

Michael didn't crack a smile; his jaw clenched. The stern expression and harsh tenor caught Gabriel off guard. There was something unfamiliar in his tone; Michael Rose didn't rattle easily.

"I don't know how else to say this to you, man. We unleashed a shit storm with this thing. There is going to be blowback and the situation needs to be handled with a great deal of discretion—more discretion than usual, much more. Please, Gabe. I'm asking you to trust me on this."

"Yeah, okay I hear you, I too have concerns. But can you explain why this is causing you such distress?"

"There are people involved, forces at play, and a hornet's nest of unknowns that we don't want to antagonize any further. We had our reasons for taking it as far as we did. But we should be happy with what we accomplished and make sure we don't wade in too deep right now."

"We've been through similar things before," Gabe objected. "Anyone upending the system, anyone trying to hold powerful people accountable is going to make enemies. This is what we do." He raised his voice. "We expose assholes, we tell the truth, and consequences be damned. I'm asking you again, Michael, why is this one different? You wield considerable authority as Chief of the Criminal Division for the Southern District. Who in their right mind is going to fuck with you? And if they fuck with me they fuck with you. Right?"

As if on cue a smarmy-looking character dressed in a Members Only jacket and Jordache jeans approached the table making eye contact with Gabriel.

"Hey, aren't you the guy from the TV show, what's it called, *Chips*? Yeah, you're the guy who plays the motorcycle cop aren't you?"

Gabriel, believing the guy was on a day drinking binge, played along. "Yeah that's me, but sorry pal, not doing autographs today, havin' a meeting with my agent."

"Oh, no problem, wanted to say I was a fan."

"Thanks, man."

"Yeah, for a second I thought you mighta been that other douche bag, the writer dude, you know the one with his face pasted all over the newsstands because he's always meddling around in other people's shit tryin' to make a name for himself. Because if you were…"

Before the interloper could finish his sentence Michael shot up and confronted him. "Because what, asshole?" Michael was almost a head taller than the man who was trying to provoke Gabriel. He leaned in close, daring the guy to make some sort of move.

The provocateur took a step back and said, "Oh nothin', just a case of mistaken identity I guess." Within seconds Jimmy the bartender had swung around the bar and situated himself between Michael and the smarmy guy in the jacket. "Everything okay here, Mr. Hernandez?"

"Everything's fine, Jimmy," Gabe said, smiling as Michael sat back down. "Just a fan looking for an autograph. Why don't you take him to the bar and put his next drink on my tab. He seems like a nice fellow who could use a break."

"Sure thing, Mr. Hernandez, whatever you say." Jimmy put a beefy arm around the man and firmly escorted him to the bar area where he wisely refused the free drink and quickly found his way out.

Michael flashed through memories of their days as kids in Riverdale, recalling Gabriel's stubborn attempts to stand his ground against bigger and meaner kids who were about to knock the daylights out of him, convinced he could bullshit his way out of a beatdown, confident he had the situation under control as long as he just kept talking. At some level Gabe understood it was Michael's willingness, some would say eagerness, to resolve things violently that usually ended the discussion.

"What the hell was that about?" Gabe asked Michael, still smiling, ignoring the potential connection to the case for laying low Michael was attempting to communicate.

"Who knows? We can add him to the growing list of unknowns. Like why would the AG try to bury our investigation? I have to believe someone with a lot of juice was leaning on him to call off the dogs."

"Didn't work out the way he planned, did it?" Gabe said smiling, palming another handful of salted nuts.

"No, it sure didn't," Michael said, shaking his head. "But I think we underestimated some things, like how the Courtlands' contacts extend beyond my jurisdiction. This bullshit 'gentrification,' displacing lower-income families, and using public money for private gain, has global implications, and the support of people who don't hold back when they are threatened. Hell, LBJ declared war on poverty, these bastards have declared war on poor people. And if this is a war, it's pretty clear who's winning. We won a skirmish, Gabe, but this fight is far from over."

Gabriel scowled, peering through his cocktail, as if the answer to their questions could be found within the amber liquid swirling in his glass. While he didn't necessarily agree with Michael's sense of alarm, he did share his convictions. The relentless pursuit of power and wealth often bred corruption and exploitation, and in Ronald Reagan's America, their shared conviction seemed somewhat archaic.

The insatiable thirst for more—more money, more power, more influence— was like an addictive intoxicant that infected the soul. They witnessed how this voracious hunger distorted judgment and eroded the integrity of otherwise decent individuals. It enabled a world of unrestrained avarice where the strong preyed upon the weak, and their victims, often unwittingly, assisted in their own exploitation, fostering an environment where good men turned a blind eye while the corrupt openly rationalized their darkest impulses.

It was a game for some, and these self-appointed kingmakers and puppeteers played the game with relative impunity, manipulating the strings of power without allegiance to God or country or any discernible philosophy. For them, the pursuit of wealth, whether acquired legitimately or otherwise, was merely a means of keeping score.

Gabe and Michael leveraged their partnership intending to counterbalance the shadowy forces that wielded unchecked power to shape events. They were brash idealist who sought to, as Martin Luther King suggested, bend the arc of history toward justice, during a time when such things held little currency.

But some believed they crossed a line with their last collaboration and Michael was keenly aware of the peril in doing so.

"Look, Gabe," Michael said, with no shortage of bravado, "we took the gloves off on this one like the street brawlers we are, ignoring the warnings and pushing through the obstacles they put in front of us. We forced the AG's hand, and your work generated so much publicity it gave him a welcome boost with the law and order crowd, and now the money guys want him to make a run for the Governor's Mansion in Virginia. The AG is telling his boys that if I decide to play along, his people will back me for a run at the Senate when I'm ready. We got lucky, it turns out this could be a good thing for all concerned, a huge win. Let's declare victory and go about our lives."

Gabriel fixed a cutting gaze at Michael. "All's well that ends well, huh Michael? Are you asking me to lay low for my own good, or is this about you making a run for office?"

"No, you dumb shit! Things are changing. This game is bigger, wider, and deeper than we understood it to be. We inadvertently upended the order of things on a scale we're just beginning to understand. We're never going to put away every puppet master capable of pulling strings. There are large forces at play here, Gabe, and we are now in their crosshairs."

Gabriel watched as Michael's eyes glowed with conviction, his tone urgent and insistent. Until now they had always shared the attitude that each case, each story was part of a larger fight they were obligated be part of. They knew that any cause worth fighting for always carried the possibility of unforeseen reckoning.

"All I'm saying is you need to keep a low profile for your own good," Michael persisted. "Focus on the next chapter of your life. Skip the arraignment, skip the bail hearing, and skip the PR tour. You and Rachel have been planning your next move for your own reasons, I'm telling you you're making the right choice. Do what you set out to do, but be stealthy, make your move now. Do you get me, brother? Or do I have to beat this into you the hard way? Don't make me have to call your girlfriend."

The stress on Michael's face gave way to a devious smile, and he turned his head away trying to hold back a belly laugh. Gabe knew he meant every word, but he also knew Michael would allow him the space to sort out matters on his own.

"Holy shit, you're playing the girlfriend card? Are you kidding me?"

Gabriel punched Michael in the shoulder hard as he attempted to swallow his drink without choking. He was stubborn, but not reckless, he got the message. He just needed time to parse it all.

"Hey, can I ask you something?" Gabriel asked, changing the subject.

"Anything. What's on your mind?"

"Do you ever think about her? My sister and what she'd think of us now?"

Michael paused for a bit, and took a long pull on his drink.

"All the time. And I think she'd be really proud of us." He closed his eyes as if not wanting to yield to the painful echoes of loss he still carried.

Gabriel refrained from prying, he knew what Michael was holding back.

The driver of the vehicle that killed Gabriel's parents and sister got away with negligent homicide because he was a Courtland. A fatal drug overdose delivered his final and ultimate accountability. While his family's influence had shielded him from any formal charges, even they couldn't protect him from his own demons.

Gabriel and Michael ignored the advice of those who warned them not to take on the Courtland family. But now, as a result of their collaboration, there was a good chance the Courtlands would finally be held accountable, their illegal business practices were being exposed. The time had come to settle that score. This case was their retribution.

In a secluded corner of the Oak Room, Gabe took note of a curly-haired guy of unimpressive stature, dressed in a dark pinstripe suit and high-top sneakers, engrossed in lively banter with a stunning statuesque blond. He seemed animated and a little drunk; she radiated a classic California cover-girl glow. The guy with curly hair and high tops made eye contact with the piano player who nodded and signaled him to take a spot on the bench. He settled in at the piano and began to play while the exquisite blonde woman looked on adoringly. As he started to sing a hush fell over the room. His voice was immediately recognizable, but in keeping with the unwritten rule of the Oak Room, no one made much of a fuss as he serenaded his stunning companion…

*Some folks like to get away…*

"Hey, isn't that?" Michael asked.

Gabriel put his arm on Michael's shoulder as they prepared to walk out the door.

"Yeah that's him and his lady is a knockout. This is a good sign, buddy, it's going to be a great night, and I'm most definitely in a New York state of mind!"

# 5

# THE FIXER

The grand marble columns ascended majestically, their polished surfaces reflecting the dim glow of the golden arcade, an homage to old-world opulence. Its rich décor reminded Dimitri Ivanov of the Château de Chambord, the castle where the French Underground stashed priceless artworks to protect them from Nazi pillagers. Amidst this lavish backdrop, his host, Gregory Courtland, wove a narrative of wealth and influence, tracing the lineage of the edifice back to its progenitor, F.W. Woolworth, a titan of industry and an unlikely arbiter of taste.

Courtland painted a portrait of an era teetering on the precipice of transformation. The Woolworth building, the tallest building in the world between 1913 and 1930, stood not merely as a testament to architectural prowess, but as a symbol of shifting tides in the socio-economic landscape of New York City. As the vestiges of the old aristocracy waned, the nouveau riche ushered in an era no longer tethered to the conventions of old money, they reshaped the urban landscape and created lucrative opportunities for families like the Courtlands.

"Woolworth," Courtland intoned with admiration, "made his fortune by catering to the common wants of the working-class families, his five and dime emporiums quickly spread across America's cities, yet his aspirations rose far beyond the mundane." He pointed out how the structure, despite its rich history, bore the imprints of modernity, a monument that continued to evolve, incorporating new breakthroughs in technology and engineering.

"Impressive!" Dimitri said, admiring the view from Gregory Courtland's office.

"In due time, we'll move to buy out the old owners. We'll take full control of the property and register it as a historical landmark. Its status as a landmark will be leveraged to access low-interest government loans and other beneficial concessions. For now, we play the silent benefactors, keeping the current owners afloat. In the meantime, we plan to seize property in this neighborhood for pennies on the dollar and then use public funds to gentrify the area. Think of it as a test run before we undertake similar ventures on a global scale. But I imagine you're already well acquainted with our long-term plans."

"That I am. It's why I'm here. Our group wants to ensure you can weather the storms hitting your organization. We're worried about a certain overeager prosecutor over at SDNY throwing a wrench in your ambitious plans."

"I hear you loud and clear. We've dealt with aggressive prosecutors before. But this time, our usual methods aren't producing the desired results. Disheartening, sure, but we're not out of moves. Seems we have a zealot over at the Criminal Division in the Southern District that may require a different approach."

"Indeed," said Ivanov, studying the brash family scion. "Zealots are to be avoided in both war and business. I also hear Roy Cohn is not enjoying good health lately."

Gregory Courtland raised an eyebrow. He was beginning to understand the Russian gentleman sitting across from him would not be easily manipulated. The Russian knew things, and he seemed to carry a hint of menace underneath his polished façade.

"That's correct, it appears some of Mr. Cohn's past transgressions, legal and otherwise, have finally caught up with him." Courtland paused. "His political contacts are abandoning him. A powerful man who holds the secrets of other powerful men and has nothing to lose can become a bit prickly. Of course, we have our own political contacts, but I suspect we may have to explore alternate ways of addressing this problem."

"Cohn can be counted on to be loyal only to his own interests. He's always been a treacherous individual and his associates even more so," said Ivanov.

If there was any lingering apprehension within Gregory Courtland about the precarious state of his business realm under the scrutinizing gaze of an aggressive prosecutor, it remained concealed beneath a veneer of unflinching composure. Dimitri Ivanov, no stranger to the subtle theatrics of influential figures, recognized the practiced art of misdirection. Yet, despite the grandiose trappings that enveloped Courtland—the opulent golden cruciform lobby, the lofty barrel-vaulted ceiling, the expanse of marbled decadence, and sweeping panoramic vistas—his highly leveraged business empire teetered on unstable ground.

For Ivanov, well acquainted with the façade of invulnerability maintained by those raised in the lap of luxury, the ephemeral nature of power remained a reliable constant, a transient force, indifferent to pedigree or privilege. History offered ample reminders of the recurring folly of hubris. Allies must always be chosen carefully, and abandoned swiftly, should they become liabilities.

"My partners and I advise restraint in dealing with these matters. Perhaps if Mr. Cohn was at the peak of his powers he may have been more effective in avoiding the legal entanglements you currently find yourself in. His track record is impressive. Though he denies it, he is dying of AIDS. His shame and his vanity are a distraction. You will need to look elsewhere for the right solution. We want to ensure the damage here is properly contained."

"When you say restraint, what exactly do you mean?" Courtland bristled at the suggestion.

"Now's not the time for brute force solutions that could stir up more trouble than they solve. We're facing a scenario that demands strategic foresight and the cultivation of new alliances. It might mean finding someone within your ranks to shoulder the legal burden you're facing."

"You mean a patsy? Some sort of scapegoat? Are you suggesting I take the hit?" Despite his attempt at outward calm, beads of sweat betrayed Courtland's unease. "Let me make myself crystal clear. I won't spend a single day in a federal penitentiary. My family wouldn't stand for it. I'd sooner just disappear."

"Relax, Mr. Courtland. I'm not here to offer you up as a sacrificial lamb. I'm here to provide assistance, and part of that support involves helping you grasp the gravity of your situation, not just for you but for all involved. You still have options, but you need to step back. We have resources at our disposal that can work on your behalf. We're asking you to refrain from taking actions that could make matters worse."

"What kind of resources?" Courtland pressed.

Dimitri sidestepped the question. "We have vested interests here, and in this scenario, our interests align. I urge you to think ahead, to consider your partners, and let us lend a hand. When this storm blows over, you'll still be a wealthy man."

"This is all a bit cryptic, Mr. Ivanov." Courtland swabbed his brow, struggling to regain his composure.

"It's best for all parties to discuss these things without too much specificity, Mr. Courtland. You have one of Roy Cohn's former partners on your legal team, correct?"

"Yeah, Robert Mendelson. He's in-house counsel. What about him?"

"Mr. Cohn has been more than a mentor to Mr. Mendelson, he continues to offer protection and advice."

"And why is this a concern?" Courtland asked.

"Roy Cohn's passing will leave Mr. Mendelson exposed."

"Exposed? How so?"

"Mr. Cohn has been responsible for inflicting a great deal of pain and punishment throughout his career. Your organization had been shielded by his clout, in ways that may not have been entirely evident to you, just as the nature of your own partners, who they are and what they are capable of, may have eluded your comprehension. No need to go into the particulars, Mr. Courtland, suffice it to say that Mr. Cohn's clients and contacts include people who don't play by the rules. The loyalty forged in his sway won't easily transfer to Mr. Mendelson in his absence."

"I don't understand," Courtland said.

"I think you do, Mr. Courtland. You understand enough. The important thing here is to make sure your in-house counsel doesn't become a further liability. Keep him away from anything that may give the SDNY leverage."

"It may be a bit late for that. But anything he knows is protected by attorney-client privilege," Courtland insisted.

"Knowledge is power, Mr. Courtland. It can be used to help or hinder depending on who wields it. He who controls the narrative shapes history. We must control the narrative. This is an area where I have some experience. I am here to help, but you have to trust the process. It will neither be quick nor immediately obvious, but in the end, over time, you and your family will prosper by the approach I am advocating."

Dimitri Ivanov's eyes bored into Gregory Courtland from across the expanse of his ostentatious desk, his scrutiny piercing through a frightened man's cultivated veneer. The real estate mogul squirmed under Ivanov's penetrating gaze, exposed as a man accustomed to the shelter of family wealth and influence. Courtland's entire existence had been cocooned within the trappings of opulence, shielded from the repercussions of his reckless exploits. Business, to him, was a frivolous pursuit, a game played for amusement. Devoid of genuine hardship, he remained stunted by his inheritance, insulated from the crucible of life's trials and experiences that might have enriched his character and imparted lessons in resilience. Now, faced with unforeseen challenges, the façade of invincibility he had meticulously crafted was beginning to crack.

"Thank you for your time, Mr. Courtland. I will let myself out."

Courtland seemed relieved to be out from under the intimidating gaze of the Russian. "How do I reach you, Mr. Ivanov, should I need to follow up on what we discussed here?"

"Reaching me won't be necessary, Mr. Courtland. I will be in touch soon."

# 6

## THE COLLECTOR

Dressed in leather pants speckled with paint, Rachel cut through the urban chaos, a striking figure amidst the pedestrian tumult. Her high-top sneakers propelled her swiftly along the pavement, while a flowing white blouse hugged her form, and a charm bracelet, a gift from the inspired hands of a ten-year old admirer, adorned her wrist. She exuded an air of creative allure that commanded attention, a reality she had long grown accustomed to.

In the taxi, the driver's eyes dawdled too long on the rearview mirror, ignoring the snail-paced traffic ahead on Houston Street. Rachel dumped a twenty on the front seat, and hopped out of the cab to negotiate the remaining four blocks on foot. Once again she was running behind schedule. Fortunately, Amanda Taylor understood Rachel's ongoing battle with punctuality. As both agent and confidante, Amanda possessed an astute eye for talent and an inclination to overlook its quirks. Artists and watches don't mix well. However, Rachel preferred not to test Amanda's patience, especially on a day like today, when she was slated to meet one of her most influential buyers—a renowned Russian art collector.

Rachel knew him by name only; he was a patron of the arts with influential ties to gallery owners and museums throughout Europe and Asia. Over the past few years, this mysterious collector had become Rachel's most consistent buyer, the largest private collector of her work, each new piece acquired at a significantly higher price than the previous one.

Her entry into the European market afforded her flexibility, newfound wealth and permitted her a fluid identity as an artist. Rachel moved freely among the more successful New York-based artists like Jeff Koons, Robert Rauschenberg and Andy Warhol, but she kept a low profile. She grew out of the East Village scene but was not tied to any particular movement or trend, and she had long ago lost interest in the parties, drugs, and celebrity attention that many young artists found so seductive.

Courting the media and pressing flesh with buyers was part of the art game, but unlike many of her successful contemporaries, Rachel didn't embrace the process. She preferred to linger beneath the radar allowing her work to speak for itself. Providing descriptions, or excessive context, inhibited the intimate connection between art and observer. Process and motivation existed on one plane of communication, but Rachel believed a great work of art, by definition, had to transcend multiple levels of perception. The work either resonated or it didn't; explanations often intruded on the delicate intimacy the connection necessitated.

She slowed her frantic pace to pause briefly at the entrance of Amanda's SoHo gallery, taking a moment to catch her breath and steal a glance at her reflection in the window. *Showtime.* The gallery, ensconced within a three-story brick edifice, boasted two expansive windows and a doorway framed by intricately carved black borders, evoking the impression that the building itself was a masterpiece in its own right. Renowned for propelling New York's most iconic artists onto the stage of acclaim, the venue stood as a bastion of artistic emergence.

Stepping into the building, Rachel observed Amanda engaged in lively conversation with a distinguished gentleman, their exchange punctuated by the dramatic modulations of Russian consonants. Her attention was immediately drawn to the impeccably attired gentleman with tinted eyeglasses. Clad in a British-cut double-breasted suit, a crisply folded pocket square adorning his breast pocket, he exuded an aura of timeless elegance. A pristine white carnation nestled in his lapel—a nod to tradition that seemed plucked from the pages of a bygone era.

As she drew nearer she couldn't help a giddy thought: *he smells like money.*

He turned and greeted her with a warm smile and a hint of mischief in his eye. Before Amanda could make an introduction, he addressed her in formal English, tinged with a Russian accent.

"Ah madam, this genius requires no introduction. A pleasure to finally meet you, my dear. I have been following your work for years and I am most happy for this opportunity to make your acquaintance in person. Dimitri Ivanov, an honor to be in your presence."

Rachel, taken aback by the effusive greeting, placed her hand over her heart in a gesture of faux modesty and smiled.

He took her hand, kissed it, and bowed in exaggerated gallantry.

*Why does he seem so familiar to me?* she wondered to herself.

"The pleasure is mine, Mr. Ivanov. I can't recall the last time anyone referred to me as a genius, but I do feel it's been long overdue." A slight pause, and for a brief second Rachel regretted the cheeky retort, but the tension evaporated when the elder gentleman's smile gave way to a full-throated laugh.

"Then, my dear, it appears I have arrived at precisely the right moment." He placed his strong hands gently on her shoulders and gave her a kiss on each cheek.

"Please call me Dimitri." He held her a second too long in his piercing gaze and smiled affectionately. "Amanda has shared some of your history over the years; I understand you will be moving out of the city soon. Are you planning to move into permanent exile?"

"I wouldn't call leaving the city exile. We'll probably keep our apartment in Manhattan. How long we stay will depend on how well we adjust to our new surroundings."

"That seems prudent," he said approvingly. Rachel smiled; she could not shake the feeling, there was something familiar in the old gentleman. His dress, the smell of his cologne, the boutonniere; a character in a movie she had long forgotten.

"Tell me, Rachel—may I call you Rachel? Do you think living in this city has influenced you as an artist? There is more than a hint of darkness in what I consider to be your best work. Does this come from New York, or does your inspiration come from some other place?"

Rachel studied the Russian. She fell silent as she considered a proper answer. The old gentleman waited patiently for her reply. She had hoped to avoid any discussion of process, holding the belief that any analysis surrounding the darkness in her work would only diminish its power.

"A little of both perhaps," she said finally. "There is darkness in all of us, Mr. Ivanov, none of us escapes it."

"This is true, my dear." She held his penetrating gaze; his eyes seemed to be probing for clues.

"New York can be both beautiful and treacherous, and as with most artists, my work succeeds when the final result is personal, revelatory, and authentic; my environment is invariably a part of that experience. My work is my truth, my guide, my teacher, and my therapist," she continued. "I guess both the beautiful and the treacherous live within me, as do all my experiences, good and bad. Perhaps the need to navigate the tension between light and dark is what we all have in common with one another, Mr. Ivanov."

"Well said, my dear. Brava! You are as brilliant as you are beautiful. I promised Amanda I would not bore you with too many questions. And the truth is that your paintings and sculptures tell me all I need to know about you. You are a vessel, and that which flows through you speaks to me. This is the reason why I am drawn to your work and why I have become a devoted collector. Someday I would love to show you the places where I display your paintings. It might tell you something about me, about what we might have in common."

Rachel smiled. "Oh really, how so?"

"I own a dacha on Lake Turgoyak in the Ural Mountains. A place I visit to escape everything. I go there to sit with my thoughts, to reflect, to contemplate my own past. A magical place. In the long winter the ground is covered in snow as far as the eye can see. The land is rugged and stark; short days and long nights invite a stillness that inspires the contemplative inward journey. In the summer, the starkness of winter yields to a rebirth that fills the heart with hope again as the snow and ice recede. What was once a desolate and dying landscape is renewed with new life. You and your husband would be welcome guests. He is a writer, no? My retreat is a wonderful place to reflect on new endeavors."

"Sounds wonderful," Rachel replied, her tone polite yet guarded, her mind racing with questions about the enigmatic Russian gentleman's knowledge of her personal life. The mention of Gabe as her husband struck her as a bit intrusive and uncomfortably probing, a feeling she politely set aside.

"I would love to visit someday, Mr. Ivanov. I'm truly honored that my work resonates with you and that you've become such an avid collector. Parting with my creations can be difficult, but knowing they are appreciated by someone with your insight brings me great comfort."

"Dimitri, please, call me Dimitri," he responded, his tone warm yet subtly insistent. "I do appreciate you, my dear. Sometimes, it seems, a work of art chooses us rather than the other way around. I sense that you and I may be kindred spirits—moved by forces beyond our control yet blessed with the ability to perceive connections that elude others. For me, this awareness is both a burden and a blessing."

Rachel couldn't shake the feeling of familiarity that Dimitri's words evoked. 'Kindred spirits and the burden of knowing,' she mused silently, his enigmatic observations lingering.

"I am honored to be a caretaker of the part of you that lives in your art, such a pleasure to meet you and share this brief time together." He held her hand and pressed a paternal kiss on her cheek. "I had hoped to invite you and Amanda to join me for dinner, but she tells me you have a pressing engagement this evening. Perhaps the next time I am in New York, if time permits, we can share a meal together."

"It would be an honor to do so, Mr. Ivanov."

"Dimitri, please call me Dimitri. Can I offer you a ride anywhere? My car is waiting outside."

"Very kind of you, Dimitri, but I have a few errands to run," she demurred politely.

Back on Houston Street, Rachel found herself mulling her intriguing encounter with the mysterious collector. Was it a lapse of memory or a failure of courage that kept her from inquiring about Amanda's relationship to Dimitri Ivanov, or the motivation behind his unwavering support? His patronage had undoubtedly altered the trajectory of her career, his acquisitions always arriving at opportune moments with uncanny precision. While his demeanor exuded generosity, intuition, and charm, an indefinable disquiet lingered in his wake.

For reasons she couldn't explain, Dimitri Ivanov brought back memories of a time long ago, when she reveled in sharing her creations with someone who consistently saw the best in her and whose unwavering encouragement allowed her to imagine herself as a professional artist. For the second time today she found herself picking at an old emotional wound, long-buried memories of her father, the inscrutable and distant Tony De Castro.

Hailing a cab, Rachel resolved to abandon any disconcerting thoughts, and redirect her focus toward the horizon of possibilities that lay ahead, convinced that dwelling on old wounds would only hinder her progress.

# 7

# AUDACITY AND DISCRETION

Gabriel and Michael huddled in animated conversation while the famous and not-so-famous gathered to wish Gabriel a fond farewell. It was still early, many associated with the success of *American Century* would soon join in the celebration, those who helped create it, those who benefitted from it, and those who aspired to be part of it. *American Century* was picking up the tab and the drinks and the conversation flowed freely.

The guests, drawn from the cultural elite that formed the beating heart of New York City, engaged in the competitive revelry such occasions inspired. Advertising executives schmoozed with clients, clients schmoozed with personages of note, and writers swapped stories while editorial assistants did shots and flirted with each other; eventually, everyone would drink a little too much and some, if they were among the lucky few, would wake up in beds not their own.

Gabriel beamed, soaking in the adulation. He worked the crowded room like a veteran politician, kissing assistants, hugging co-workers and pressing flesh with the notable and notorious; his glass was always full, and food rarely touched his lips. Michael, playing the role of the cautious older brother, nursed his drink, and remained alert for any unusual activity. Like any older brother, his protective nature could be irritating at times, but it comforted Gabriel to know Michael always had his back.

At the far end of the bar, two men in ill-fitting suits fidgeted nervously, failing miserably to blend in at an event where everyone else craved attention. Gabriel acknowledged them with a nod, a flicker of recognition dancing across wandering thoughts—they bore the telltale signs of off-duty cops. With a variety of connections at the NYPD, Gabriel knew all too well the thin line between friend and foe within its ranks. Michael also took notice of the odd pair, and began to weave his way through the throng of revelers to investigate, but the men quickly vanished into the crowd before he could reach them. Ignoring the distraction, Gabriel returned to basking in the spotlight, savoring the attention of his peers.

As the room gradually transformed into a teeming mass of inebriated bodies, Mary St. John, vice president of accounting, made her approach, her sparkling blue eyes and non-accountant-like appearance belying her title. Jostled amidst thirsty partygoers clamoring for the bartender's attention, she waited for an opportune moment to extend her congratulations to Gabriel. Despite the constant interruptions, their mutual recognition spoke volumes—Gabriel's shrug and raised palms conveying a silent acknowledgment of the chaos around them. The unspoken chemistry between them, well known among their colleagues, remained a subtle allure that no longer held sway. With Gabriel's days of nocturnal escapades consigned to history, his relationship with Rachel remained bulletproof.

In between gratuitous hugs and generous pours Mary inadvertently pressed closer, her body's warmth mingling with Gabriel's amidst the bustling patrons. He felt a peculiar sensation surging within him. Dismissing it as the product of an alcohol-induced haze, he endeavored to refocus on the conversation at hand, though the distraction proved persistent. Engaging in a disjointed dialogue with an ad executive nurturing dormant literary aspirations, Gabriel wondered if the man sought guidance or absolution, either way, feigning attentiveness to the boozy ramblings proved taxing.

The mind-numbing exchange was incessantly punctuated by interruptions from well-wishers. A young reporter tasked with Gabriel's retrospective stopped by to offer his respects, fueled by a newfound appreciation of free libations. Meanwhile, an audacious copy editor, emboldened by the same indulgent appreciation, whisked him away mid-sentence by his tie, a sign that the party was kicking into high gear.

As the evening progressed, all conversation blended into a confluence of noise and festive voices. "We are going to miss you, Gabe," Mary said locking eyes with him, until someone else offered yet another fond fare thee well. Gabriel could not stop smiling. Soon he noticed the seductive sound of Mary's breathing began drowning out all the ambient noise. The warmth of her breath on his neck, the smell of her perfume or shampoo, or whatever it was, demanded his unwavering attention. Sweat began forming under his shirt. Each time someone reached over to order a drink, they nudged Mary a little closer. *What is this?* He fought off the urge to pull her next to him. Her full lips and flushed cheeks were suddenly irresistible. An alien voice inside his head demanded, *I want her.* He stared at her, she became a potent intoxicant infecting his thoughts. Primitive urges and impulses surged. Thirst. *Mouth feels dry.* Unquenched desire.

Breath quickened—something inside creating a potent mix of uncertain alchemy. *What the hell is happening?* Her heartbeat was a thunderous rhythm drowning out the clamor. Beads of sweat formed on his brow. Distraction. Elation. Tides of longing surged. As her hand brushed his, warm flesh ignited a flurry of sensations. Then suddenly a flash of light, its source impossible to discern.

He stood frozen, mouth agape, struck dumb by the sight before him. Awe enveloped him, a haze of endorphin-fueled disorientation shattered by a rift in his reality. Out of this enigmatic visual disturbance emerged an ethereal figure, a specter—a vision bathed in radiant light, transcending the mundane world of mortals. *Rachel! It had to be Rachel!* Drifting toward him like a dream, she moved in vivid hues breaching the monochrome throng. Beaming an effervescent smile, she glided among the shadows. Gabe languished, awash in unfamiliar impulses and deepening euphoria, rendered speechless by her presence. Before he could make any sense of it, she vanished, swallowed by Michael in a captivating embrace.

Then, darkness. Everything faded to black. Lights out.

* * *

Gabriel awoke to a world full of pain. Squinting, he lifted his head. Struggling with his tenuous hold on reality, he tried to swallow. His mouth was desiccated and metallic. *Where am I? Was I dreaming*? He couldn't remember getting home. The memory of being ushered out a side door by Michael and Rachel and of violently expelling the contents of his stomach behind the restaurant and then slipping in and out of consciousness was still distorted by the chemicals in his bloodstream.

*I must have been drugged.* He recognized the echo of a thought he had just before blacking out.

*Who did this to me?* Another echo, as he rubbed his aching head and attempted to steady himself on the bed. Muddled and bewildered ideation scrambled his fragmented recollection.

Rachel handed him a cup of coffee. "How ya doing?" Her face slowly came into focus.

"Peachy," Gabriel managed to say unconvincingly.

"Michael just left."

"Oh?"

"We got lucky, managed to get you out before anyone caught on to what was happening. Most people were too buzzed to notice. At first I thought you had outdone yourself and overindulged, drowning in a sea of booze and adulation. Michael thinks somebody slipped you something, trying to either discredit you or worse, some kind of retaliation. Said he should've seen it coming. We had a doctor come by to evaluate you while you were out. He gave you something to reverse the effects of the drug, said your vitals were stable and you'd snap out of it eventually. He told us to keep you hydrated, so finish your coffee and drink this." Gabriel gulped down the coffee and reached for the water.

"Thank you. You're an angel. Much better now."

"Take it easy and keep drinking the water. Michael said he's going to look into it, but he made a point of insisting we stick with our plan and skip the courtroom drama this afternoon."

"Wait, what plan?"

"To leave town."

"Oh, that. Of course. We're good, right?" Rachel caressed his forehead like a mother caring for a sick child.

"We're good except for one thing." Her expression became stern.

Gabriel braced himself.

"What is up with Mary St. John?" Her tone was tinged with suspicion.

"Huh? What?" Gabriel's ability to process information was hampered by something inside his head trying to beat its way out with a sledgehammer. He sat up, unsure of what came next, a punchline or all hell breaking loose.

"We'll stick to our plan and keep you out of trouble, but first let me tell you something about Mary."

"Mary?" Gabe's puzzled expression was almost comical.

"She's obviously harboring a thing for you. I don't think she understands how dangerous it is to mess with a hot-blooded Latin woman. I saw how she looked at you." Rachel cracked a sly smile but continued to feign outrage. "The lady's got a brass set, and I'm not talking about her huge breasts either. I'm not sure if she's brave, foolish or ridiculously naïve. She acted so polite, so disingenuously nice—like she had something to hide. I know that hand-in-the-cookie-jar look. What a fucking performance! But let me tell you, buddy, she's not fooling anyone. She's definitely not fooling me!"

"Wait, what?" Gabriel said, still unable to articulate a cogent response.

Rachel smiled. She leaned over provocatively and pulled Gabriel's head back. "Don't worry about it, stud. She's not the only girl with a brass set that's got a crush on you."

Gabriel eased up, catching the glimmer in Rachel's playful smile, a moment of levity in the swarming confusion of his meandering thoughts. His strength gradually returning, he drew her in, seeking comfort in the warmth of her attention.

The shadow of reprisal still loomed—a faceless menace, someone out there determined to do him harm. But here, now, in a fleeting reprieve from the chaos, he was still very much alive, and grateful to be wrapped in the arms of the woman he loved.

* * *

As expected, the courtroom teamed with voyeuristic spectators alongside an assortment of interested parties. Gabriel discreetly slipped into a vacant seat away from the curious onlookers, nodding politely to a well-dressed older gentleman tucked away in the shadows who greeted him with a curious smile. At a distance the man looked like he could be auditioning for a role in a Broadway revival of *Citizen Kane*, clutching an umbrella and sporting a suit adorned with a white boutonniere. Gabriel shook off the lingering brain fog from the previous night along with Michael's warning to stay away from today's proceedings.

Audrey Zornberg, senior counsel for the Southern District of New York, assumed first chair. Regarded as one of the nation's premier prosecutors, she exuded an aura of lethal competence. Today, there would be no courtroom pleasantries, no frivolous banter with the judge—this was a matter of grave significance, requiring steadfast resolve over theatricality. Seated beside her, Michael Rose maintained a posture of unwavering authority.

Michael's presence at the table conveyed a resolute message to all present: no one, not even the formidable Courtland family, was above the law.

Tension rippled through the courtroom, mirrored by the discomfort etched on the faces of the family members in the front row. Audrey Zornberg meticulously detailed Courtland's exploitation of debt in a lucrative urban revitalization scheme, unveiling a labyrinthine system of debt securitization that yielded staggering profits—profits confined to the exclusive realm of the Courtland Organization's investors. It was a pyramid constructed from hollow securities, designed to exploit government largesse and enrich only the privileged few.

The scheme was an elaborate and lucrative combination of forced urban renewal and securities fraud. Shady financial instruments were traded by high-profile investment firms who colluded with the Courtland Organization to defraud investors while also accessing Federal and State development incentives. Behind the shadowy paperwork affiliated offshore criminal enterprises seized the opportunity to launder obscene amounts of illicit cash.

The cash allowed the organization to erect grand hotels, casinos, and other developments without regard for the normal market dynamics. The grift required extraordinary political leverage and sophisticated accounting tools. Zornberg's voice, tinged with menace, noted that while the case today focused on the Courtland family, the probe into related crimes continued.

Sideways glances, nervous coughs and the stifled murmurs of interested parties rippled through the gallery.

Every major city in the country had declining areas where cash-strapped property owners were forced to sell at under-market value. The erosion of public services and infrastructure, sometimes by design, accelerated the decrease in values. Once those properties were acquired for a fraction of their worth, the government would then provide very favorable terms to rebuild, refurbish and gentrify. Teachers, cops, firemen, nurses, and clerks—the people who provided a city's essential services—were swept out of once-affordable neighborhoods, their homes replaced by high-priced developments and new public infrastructure.

Gabriel couldn't help but marvel at the audacity behind the scheme, and the overt brazenness provided riveting copy for his series. The Courtlands adeptly silenced detractors and circumvented regulatory barriers, crafting marketing ploys deftly designed to shield the politicians who lent their support. Phrases like "enterprise zones" and similar buzzwords became rallying cries on the political stage, veiling the machinations of power and profit.

Audrey glanced over at Michael. The steely determination etched on his face reflected his force of will, a fierceness unaffected by the power and influence of the Courtland family. Taking on powerful adversaries always carried unknown risks, but risks were part of the high-stakes game he now engaged in.

The gentleman with the boutonniere absentmindedly patted his lips with a beefy, well-manicured index finger, his head tilted slightly. The man's reflective demeanor hinted at a mind grappling with its own labyrinthine quandaries.

Elite defense lawyers shuffled papers and whispered muted counsel; failure was not an option. An advocate for the devil can never rest easy. Nervous asides and a waft of perspiration mingled with the scent of expensive perfume. The gallery was a potpourri of high net-worth individuals, a wealth manager's wet dream. There was blood in the water and the rich relish a spectacle.

Gabriel's attention kept shifting from the case Audrey was presenting to the well-dressed gentleman. He sensed this particular individual was not among those who came to witness a spectacle of schadenfreude. As he watched, he also pondered Michael's cautionary admonitions, insisting he put this saga behind him. He hinted at deeper perils, hidden adversaries, and unknown enforcers. But the idea that they had only scratched the surface of this story continued to arouse his investigative instincts.

Yet, some sensible part of him, the part that wanted to build a new life with Rachel away from all the madness, asserted itself. *Let it go. I've done my part. This is someone else's story now. What was that old saying about discretion being the better part of valor? Time to move on.*

This case wasn't just about Gregory Courtland, this case was about challenging the unquestioned preeminence of money and power. It was a high-stakes game, a challenge to the very fabric of power. And at its heart lay accountability. Gabriel's exposé had given the SDNY the ammunition it needed to take on the formidable Courtland family. And if there was going to be any reprisal, he'd be among the first to experience it.

Gabriel understood the risks. Every action generates a reaction. But what choice did he have? This was not a story he could walk away from. The drugging incident at his farewell party wasn't a random accident. It was a calculated message. But taking on the Courtlands was not random choice either, it was personal, something he owed to his family.

Television crews and reporters swarmed outside, an impending media storm preparing to generate outrage and, for some, unwanted attention. But Gabriel had other priorities now. Rachel. The move. A new life. He slipped out a side exit, determined to avoid the probing inquiries of his journalistic colleagues. No victory lap on this one.

Michael was right, he had done enough. Let it go. Declare victory. Leave the fight to someone else now. Make a new life, and never look back. Still, for Gabriel, unanswered questions had a way of creating an itch he had to scratch.

# 8

# HARD TO BE A SAINT IN THE CITY

*C*rap! *What are those guys doing here? We open in thirty minutes and the band is not even set up yet, no time for this shit right now.* Nick De Palma tried to dodge the two men in wrinkled suits making small talk with his bartender.

"Hey, Nicky, you holdin' anything?" one of the guys called out to Nick as he tried to dart by unnoticed.

"Hello, detective, nice to see you. Alana, bring these two gentlemen another round and put all this on my tab." Nick pointed to the empty beers still on the bar.

"Just inquiring for a friend, an eight-ball should be more than enough."

"Now, detective, I'm a legitimate business owner, I don't trade in illegal drugs."

"Good one!" The detective turned to share a chuckle with his partner. "Listen, Nicky, it's a favor, if you can't do it, you can't do it. Hey, how's your brotha holding up in Georgia?"

Nick flinched at the mention of his brother. He loved his little brother but the kid always seemed to be one or two steps out of sync with the rest of the world.

"He's struggling. The federal penitentiary in Atlanta is a powder keg, overflowing with Cuban Marielitos. Those hardened criminals Castro sent over to fuck with Carter are rough dudes."

"Yeah, we heard things aren't going well for him down there. Don't you hate it when the feds quote retail value of the weight they confiscate? They made it seem like Joey was running a major criminal operation. We know he's no kingpin. He just got mixed up with the wrong people that's all."

"Yeah. The kid's got a good heart, but he's a bad judge of character."

The detectives shared another chuckle. "I'll say. Driving a truckload of weed across state lines with an undercover DEA agent would definitely fall into that category. Rumor has it you're on the line to some Russian businessmen, such as they are, for the money used to finance his little operation. Shit, the vig on that must be crushing, and those guys make the local goombas look like debutantes."

"I don't concern myself with rumors, detective. I've got a legitimate business to run."

"This place is hot, Nick, you're doing well here. Best club in Newark by far, imagine what you could do on the other side of the river. Shame if one bad decision by your little brother causes you to abandon your plans to go big time. Or worse."

Nick winced again. "It would be a shame. Let me see if one of my guys can help you with that eight-ball. You gotta be careful with cocaine, detective, it's a dangerous drug."

"Don't lecture me, Nicky, think of it as a favor for a friend."

"Okay. If you say so."

"Hey, if you guys are done with your little personal chat, we got serious business to discuss," the cop with bad skin and shiny loafers said, interjecting a little hostility into the conversation.

The friendly cop spoke up again. "Nick, you still hangin' out with your East Village faggot friends?"

"What do you mean?" Nick asked, looking puzzled.

"You're banging some artsy-fartsy chick who lives in the Village aren't you?"

"I have a girlfriend in the city if that's what you mean."

"Yeah, that's what I mean," the friendly cop confirmed.

"What's my girlfriend have to do with anything?"

"We need something handled, Nick. Need a guy who can blend in with a certain type of crowd."

"Pretty sure I'm not interested in doing anything that's going to jeopardize my standing in the community," Nick answered, completely unaware of the irony.

Both detectives laughed out loud. "Give us a break, jerkoff. This isn't coming from us, we're just delivering an assignment." The hostile cop was starting to get on Nick's nerves.

He understood the shakedown, but still the good cop, bad cop routine grated on him. They knew about the money he owed the Russians, so he knew he really wasn't going to have much room to negotiate.

"Look, Nicky," said the one playing the good cop. "This is important, you can blend in with a certain type of crowd better than most, you know what I'm sayin', and the assignment comes with incentives."

"Oh really?"

"Yeah," said the cop with the bad attitude. "It's an important assignment involving important people. Do I need to spell it out for you?"

"I'm listening, detective. I believe you said something about incentives?"

"How would you like to see your brother moved to a nice cushy minimum-security federal facility like Allenwood, maybe even get out on work release?"

"If your people have that kind of juice with the feds, you definitely have my attention."

"And the vig you owe the Russian shysters on the confiscated weed goes away. You'd still be on the line for the principal of course, but now you'll get twelve months to pay it back interest-free." The good cop added the cherry on top.

Nick didn't bother trying to understand how these cops could access the kind of connections to move his brother or make his debt to Russian loan sharks more manageable. It was Newark, everyone here knew somebody who knew somebody.

"Sounding better by the minute, detective. What do you need?"

"It's not a heavy lift, but it needs to be handled very carefully. We need to send a message to some high-profile types. You deliver a clear message, no one gets hurt, but we take it right to the edge. You understand what I mean?"

"Yeah, I think so. But you guys know plenty of people who specialize in this kind of shit, why me?"

"We're going to put you on a long-term retainer," the detective with bad skin interjected.

"What does that mean?" The sound of the hostile cop grated on Nick's nerves.

"It means we retain you to do whatever we need done whenever the fuck we need it done, that's what a retainer is."

Having played his part, the bad cop turned around and resumed his small talk with the bartender. Watching Alana pretend to give a shit was a thing of beauty. I ought to give her a raise, Nick thought to himself.

"Like we said, Nick, this needs to be handled with a light touch, a sophisticated approach by someone such as yourself, no heavy muscle. We need someone who can blend in with the artsy crowd, someone who knows the city and can mingle without standing out. The message has got to be delivered clearly and firmly, but with a certain amount of finesse. If you run into trouble, we're going to give you a get-out-of-jail-free card."

"What kind of trouble?" Nick didn't want any more trouble. He already had his hands full.

"If you do it right, there's no trouble. But if something goes sideways, there are contingencies and such. You make a call; everything gets worked out."

"What about Joey?"

"The transfer could be in the works in a matter of days."

"Okay, what are the details?"

"Let's take a walk."

Nick didn't really have a choice. These guys were just messengers, and if whoever sent them could transfer Joey out of the Atlanta Federal Penitentiary, and could negotiate with the Russian money guys, no telling what they could do to him if he refused. He didn't want to know the details. He knew enough about how things worked to understand that knowing too much about who does what can get you killed.

# 9

## HOME

The sun streamed in through the east-facing windows, flooding the expansive living room with light. The interplay of shadows and illumination formed an ethereal glow surrounding her countenance. Each window in their new residence framed stunning vistas of Mount Mansfield, revealing a tapestry of green and brown, balsam firs and heart-leaved paper birch, a living canvas set against rock and stone.

Vaulted ceilings, exposed wood beams, and an open layout offered a refreshing departure from the cramped confines of city living. Rachel appreciated the opportunity to have some alone time in the new house while Gabriel stayed behind in Boston to catch up with some old college buddies. As she roamed through the spacious rooms, tracing her fingers along the smooth surfaces of the polished wood furnishings, she found herself drawn to Gabriel's softly illuminated study. In her mind's eye, she pictured him immersed in his work, his gaze occasionally drifting toward the quaint bungalow that housed her art studio. She recalled Dimitri Ivanov's questions about how the change in scenery might impact her creativity. Relishing the idea, she imagined herself drawing inspiration from the adjacent natural splendor. The thought of raising a child in this idyllic setting stirred maternal longings.

She envisioned weekends spent with friends, skiing or hiking and sharing intimate conversations by a crackling fireplace. As she walked through the master suite the scent of cedar wafted through the air, she smiled as her eye caught the sight of Gabriel's attire neatly arranged in the expansive walk-in closet. *He's always thinking ahead, such a reliable type-A.* Yet, mingling with her sense of anticipation, swirled the unease stirred by Gabriel's desire to connect with her estranged father. Visions of a hopeful future collided with painful memories of loss and abandonment.

She was only a child when her father vanished from their lives, leaving behind a void that time couldn't fill. Despite the years that had fallen away submerged feelings resurfaced, bringing with them raw and brittle remembrances.

Yet, amidst the ache, she clung to some of the happy memories of their fleeting moments together. Sometimes, upon his return from his mysterious absences, he would retreat into himself, lost in a world of his own. While others found his imposing presence intimidating, the instances when he revealed his softer side, offering gentle words of encouragement, remained palpable. He was a paradox—both wise and troubled, oscillating between profound silences and impassioned lectures fueled by his relentless intellect. As a child she noticed in her mother a wariness, a reluctance to do anything that might trigger his darker tendencies, a hesitancy that kept her mother at arm's length. But in their shared moments of reading or play, her father's burdens seemed to evaporate, replaced by a warmth that animated their connection.

These recollections dwelled in shades of complexity and contradiction. Her father nurtured her curiosity for art and literature, instilling in her a quest for deeper understanding, urging her to peel back the mysteries of the universe and explore the hidden truths beneath. From a young age, he treated her not as a helpless child, but as an equal in intellect and potential.

Pausing before the mirror, she was transported back to their shared past.

In times of sickness, his attentiveness and gift for devising the right remedy enveloped her in a cocoon of love and devotion. Yet, as she stared at her reflection, his presence seemed to materialize within her, evoking a torrent of conflicting emotions. Love mingled with fear, anger danced with feelings of abandonment and resentment, all swirling in a tempest of reminiscence.

As always, she found solace from unsettling emotions by accessing her intuitive creative vision. Reflexively she retreated to her desk, where the blank pages of a sketchbook awaited. With each stroke of her pencil, she sought to capture the essence of her inner tumult, channeling the paradoxes inherent in her relationship with her father onto the waiting page.

Art had always been her refuge, a vehicle to navigate the vicissitudes of life and unearth hidden truths. Like Gabriel, she desired to build the home that eluded them in their tumultuous pasts. Her father's disappearance and her mother's sudden death had left her grappling with a profound emptiness from a young age. Similarly, Gabriel's childhood was marred by the loss of his parents in a fatal accident, leaving him adrift in a sea of grief.

They shared a devotion to their work. Turning pain into purpose forged a deep bond between them, anchoring them to a common vision of home. With each stroke of her pencil she found herself drifting further away from the abyss of despair, drawing strength from her creative gifts and the hopeful future she shared with Gabriel.

As they embarked on this new chapter in their lives, she resolved again and again not to let the ghosts of the past haunt their future. Any reconciliation with her father would have to wait; her focus now centered on making this house a home, a home filled with love and belonging.

Deep in the flow of hope and remembrance, her hands worked unconsciously, tapping into the source material that revealed itself through her art. Setting aside her pad, she barely took note of the sketch taking shape: Gabriel and a small child, a little girl dressed in white holding his hand, their faces radiant and otherworldly.

Gabe would be home soon, and the vast expanse of the house felt strangely cold. She gathered a handful of logs from the pile on the porch and carried them inside, the shifting wood echoing in the open spaces. She arranged the logs in the hearth, forming a perfect triangle, and nestled crumpled newspapers beneath them.

The art of kindling a fire—a skill she inherited from her father—was another faded memory made vivid again. Memories that cast a long shadow over her conception of home—the home she yearned for and the one she struggled to forget.

# 10

## THE UNRAVELING

Glassy-eyed and aching, Helen strained to recall the last time she slept in a comfortable bed. She barely recognized herself in the mirror.

*Have I been wearing the same clothes all week? Silly to give it a moment's thought considering what Tony has been going through.*

The sight of his frail body connected to the instruments monitoring his vital signs sent shivers through her tired body. Until this devastating sickness, the sixteen-year difference between fifty-four and seventy seemed insignificant. This was no longer true. Tony was fighting an existential battle, and he appeared to be losing.

Helen pulled her hair into a ponytail, buttoned her blouse, and lifted her head defiantly. *This will not break me*, she said to herself. She stepped out of the private hospital room and gently closed the door behind her. In the hallway, she greeted his attending physician.

The doctor's bedside manner was direct. "His prognosis is not good. We removed the head of the pancreas, parts of the small intestine, the gallbladder, and the bile duct. It's a procedure we call a Whipple. We cleaned out as much tissue as we can in an effort to impede the spread of the disease. However, tests show the cancer is still spreading. I believe his situation calls for more aggressive therapy, a combination of radiation and chemo. It's risky, but our options are limited."

Helen paused, taking care not to betray the piercing emotions she was containing. She pulled back a strand of greying hair and steadied herself. "You doctors know best. If you think there is something more you can do to extend his life then you must do it."

The doctor placed his hand on Helen's shoulder. "I promise you we will do everything in our power to help your husband."

Helen looked away, determined not to lose her composure. *We've been through too much together, I'll be damned if I choose this moment to come apart.* Regaining her poise, she turned to face the young physician. "Doctor, Tony appears increasingly disoriented, often unaware of where he is. The drugs seem to…" Her voice trailed off.

"Yes, the symptoms are a common side effect of the treatment. Our hope is he will regain full control of his faculties as the effects subside. The drugs can sometimes bring about a temporary state of disorientation, a sort of delirium that can mimic dementia in elderly patients. A body can only tolerate so much intervention before the mind rebels. Our goal is to force the cancer into remission while maintaining some quality of life for Tony, but the therapy itself can be toxic. Sometimes the way the human psyche protects itself from trauma is to develop an alternate sense of reality. I expect Tony will continue to slip in and out of lucidity while we pursue this aggressive treatment."

"I appreciate all you are doing for him, doctor."

"Would you like me to review his prognosis with him now?" the doctor asked.

"No, doctor, I would rather tell him myself," Helen said. "I think it's better if he hears it from me."

* * *

She sat by his bedside, reflecting on their unlikely meeting and the life they had built together.

Tony had become a steadfast ally, a beacon of stability amid a sea of uncertainty and sorrow. She met him following the death of her first husband Aaron, and when he offered to help continue their work with displaced Palestinian families, she was grateful for his support.

Her affection for him matured over time, his presence a subduing influence on her querulous and, at times, explosive sentiments. There were moments in their work together when her righteous indignation erupted into a blaze of wrath, ignited by the egregious insults inflicted upon the Palestinians by her own people. The lingering memory of her late husband's uncompromising fealty to the Israeli establishment often clashed with her burgeoning awareness of the systemic injustices endured by the innocent souls and marginalized families caught in an irrational geo-political chess game.

Yet, in Tony's calming presence, she found a way to stay focused, to channel her rage into the pursuit of justice, to become a more effective advocate for those in need. She recognized that his support allowed her to find within herself the strength and perseverance to make a difference in the lives of those who were forced to live in a desolate landscape of suffering.

"Helen!" His voice stabbed through the tranquil hospital room.

"Helen," he called out again, a plea carrying an urgency that belied his weakened state.

"Tony, I've spoken to the doctor," she replied, her voice tinged with concern.

With a sudden surge of strength Tony seized her arm, his eyes ablaze with determination. "It's done!" His raspy voice rang with single-minded tenacity. "Batista is departing, tomorrow we march toward Havana!"

* * *

*Havana, Cuba – New Year's Day, 1959*

A viscous humidity clung to the night air, enveloping the mountainous terrain as a weary moon cast feeble light through a veil of clouds, signaling the imminent arrival of dawn. Tony's messenger arrived with urgent news: Fulgencio Batista, the embattled president of Cuba, was poised to flee the country aboard a military plane, laden with ill-gotten gains and accompanied by an entourage of enablers. In Santa Clara, the 26th of July Movement had dealt a decisive blow to Batista's regime, destroying his army and scattering his loyalists.

Contemplating his next move, Tony considered the option of seizing the airfield to intercept Batista and expose his corruption. Yet, the suitcases carried by the departing dictator held only a fraction of the wealth he plundered. Allowing Batista to escape might be the swifter route to rid Cuba of his oppressive grip. With the revolutionary forces poised to storm Havana, the absence of its tyrannical ruler would leave his followers in disarray, unable to mount any significant resistance.

After sending word to Fidel, Tony sought solace in the familiar ritual of lighting a cigar, improvising a shelter against the impending rain with an old tarp. While the pattering of raindrops accentuated the earthy scent of Cuban soil, memories of what he left behind flooded his thoughts. "I am weary of blood and politics, I miss my family," he murmured, the lament carried away on the night breeze.

When Fidel's response arrived, it echoed Tony's sentiments; victory was close enough to taste. "Prepare to advance on Havana. Cuba is ours!"

Tony arrived at "The Movement" later than most, but he took immense pride in their accomplishments. His Partido Ortodoxo had a hand in crafting the Sierra Maestra Manifesto, a blueprint for a democratic government to follow Batista's ousting. He revered his friends Raúl Chibás and Felipe Pazos, instrumental figures in uniting opposition forces behind Fidel Castro. Together, they envisioned a new, liberated Cuba, free from the grip of colonialism.

As the rain continued to pound relentlessly, Tony wrapped his Thompson submachine gun in burlap, and reflected on the circuitous path that led him to this moment. Once an entrepreneur with a thriving coffee business and his own aircraft, he now found himself entrenched in the final days of a grueling guerrilla war. Unlike Che Guevara, who supported global revolution, Tony's motivations were grounded in pragmatism. He sought change for his family and country, but he had no interest in spreading communism across Latin America.

His thoughts drifted to his wife and young daughter as the rain extinguished his cigar and any hope of sleep. Despite the fatigue weighing heavy on his bones and the gnawing hunger in his belly, Tony remained resolute in his commitment. He would march on Havana, but soon after, his family would become his first and most important priority. He rested as best he could, believing he sat at the threshold between the old world and the new.

Emerging out of the Sierra Mountains, Tony and his comrades were greeted by jubilant supporters offering cigars, rum, and meager sustenance. The celebrating *campesinos* and their families stirred memories of a past life. Tony, unrecognizable in his long beard and dirty fatigues, smiled in gratitude for the hospitality they offered. He wondered what would become of these simple folk in the chaos of transition, and what would become of his own family in the uncertain days ahead when the rhetoric of revolution must give way to the practicality of wielding power.

*I've been away too long. It's time to get home.*

* * *

Things moved quickly after those first few days and the world took notice. Fidel and Che Guevara emerged as mythical figures to revolutionaries throughout Latin America, larger-than-life heroes to those who had long suffered under the yoke of American colonialism. Tony warned Fidel and the other leaders of The Movement that while Batista had been defeated, potent forces would surely gather against them. They were disrupters of the old order, and the old order would not give up control easily. Che agreed; he was well aware of the brutal nature of American intervention when they believed their interests were threatened.

Che, however, welcomed his notoriety. He predicted that Allen Dulles, the director of the CIA, would soon put a price on his head.

"Let them come," Che told Tony. "They will make me famous and generate great support for our cause throughout all of Latin America." Che's vision for the Revolution went far beyond Cuba. Fidel was more concerned with consolidating power. Tony, physically drained and weary of politics, longed to be back with his family.

Fidel's progressive initiatives like agrarian reform, free education and healthcare for all Cubans, equal rights for women and Afro-Cubans, inspired his followers and were embraced by a majority of his countrymen. However, shortly after taking power Castro set up offices in the penthouse of the Havana Hilton Hotel, availing himself of the hotel's well-stocked wine cellar and pantry while holding court for journalists and foreign visitors.

Tony and other members of The Movement began to witness a transformation in Fidel, a shift toward a perception of himself as an indispensable force in the new Cuban regime. This transformation unsettled many who had fought alongside him against Batista. Some disillusioned fighters retreated to the mountains once more, only to be hunted down ruthlessly by Fidel's forces.

In Havana, Tony reunited with his old comrades Chibás and Pazos, key figures in the creation of the Sierra Maestra Manifesto. While they shared Tony's vision of a democratic Cuba, they grew wary of Fidel's consolidation of power and the authoritarian measures imposed on the populace. Tony had already rebuffed an offer to lead an intelligence unit tasked with rooting out dissenters.

During a private dinner, Tony and his allies voiced their concerns. "He claims not to be a communist, and pledges to uphold democracy, yet he stifles opposition and suppresses dissent," Pazos lamented, his expression one of disbelief.

"He has sidelined transitional Prime Minister José Miró and is dictating policy with little regard for democratic processes," Tony added in agreement. "Violence is sometimes necessary to bring about change, but loses its moral justification once victory is achieved. We risk becoming oppressors, purveyors of fresh injustices if we continue down this path." He lowered his voice to a whisper. "It's one thing to kill a man in order to liberate a country from oppression, it's quite another thing to kill a man because you are offended by something he wrote."

Chibás interjected, his words laced with trepidation, "The closure of the National Lottery, casinos, and brothels has left thousands without livelihoods, without means to support their families."

Pazos leaned in, as if to avoid prying ears. "Prime Minister Miró's resignation is imminent, and I may follow suit. I have contacts in Miami. Your family farm, Tony, may not survive the agrarian reforms. If you're fortunate, they'll only seize your land."

"Why do you say that?" Tony asked, pushing aside his food and reaching for the wine.

"I am not without resources and trust me, old friend, my days here are numbered," Pazos said. "And if you think clearly about what is about to happen, you will consider getting your family out while you still can. Give this serious thought. If you decide to leave, I can help arrange it."

"Raúl, what do you say? Are you leaving too?" Tony turned to his other companion.

"I can't say for certain, but I don't think Felipe is wrong. You have a young family to consider. Land is replaceable, but other things are not. If he can get all of you out safely, go."

* * *

*University of Vermont Medical Center – November 1986*

Helen caressed Tony's head. As he thrashed and mumbled in his drug-induced daze, clumps of hair came loose in her hands. Tony was losing his hair, she feared he may also be losing his mind.

"What are these tubes? Was I wounded?" Tony blinked repeatedly, trying to focus. "*Mira.* Castro is becoming dangerous," he whispered. "I fear Cuba is no longer safe for us. I have a way out, for all of us, you, me, and Raquel. We can make a new life in Miami; we are no longer safe here."

Helen lifted a hand, signaling to the waiting nurse not to respond to his ramblings. She held Tony's hand patiently. "Yes, my dear, we will do as you say, but let us keep our plans secret for now. First, we must get your strength back."

Tony pressed his fingers to his forehead, struggling to gain his bearings, moving through time, fighting off old demons in a fever dream of troubling recollections.

"I couldn't say no. They blindfolded me. Who knows what they would have done to my family if I said no," he said, choking on his words.

"Who blindfolded you?" Helen inquired, her tone resigned yet tethered to his struggles against the drug-induced delirium brought on by his chemotherapy. Despite her growing familiarity with these episodes, she often found herself ensnared in the turbulence of his fevered disclosures.

"We don't have much time," Tony murmured.

"I know," she said, holding back tears.

# 11

## THE INDISPENSABLE MAN

MIAMI - FEBRUARY 1961

"I think you should agree to meet him."

"Hey, how's your son doing?" Tony interjected, changing the subject. "Is he going to continue his acting career? What was it like rubbing shoulders with Spencer Tracy?"

Felipe Pazos, looking professorial in his wire-framed glasses and well-tailored suit, had transitioned to the world of economics, earning acclaim as an advisor in Latin American affairs. He maintained a hand in politics, as a consultant to governments and business entities around the world. Felipe had provided Tony a lifeline out of Cuba and continued to be of great help to him, but Tony couldn't resist needling his stodgy benefactor. His son, a child actor, had a role opposite Spencer Tracy in the big-screen adaptation of Ernest Hemingway's novel about an old Cuban fisherman, *The Old Man and the Sea*.

"I see my son about as often as you see your daughter Raquel, which is to say, not that often. But don't change the subject. The Director is interested in meeting you. He's read some of your work and I've suggested you could be helpful to the cause."

"Is it true they call you guys the Nine Wise Men?" Tony continued the ribbing with a chuckle.

"So-called," Felipe answered, unamused. "The proper name of the organization will be the Alliance for Progress. Listen to me, there are forces coalescing around the idea of removing Fidel, and given all you've done to encourage them, you should seriously consider stepping into a leadership role. There is a place for you in all of this. It's our best hope of building the Cuba we all envisioned."

"Che told me about Dulles a long time ago, about the women, about how he likes to mix it up with his operatives in the field. He also told me about illegal assassinations and other unsavory things. This man has been involved with some nasty shit. What do you have to say about that? About working with a man who has so much blood on his hands?"

"I say this. Who got your family safely out of Cuba? Who helped you get the loans you needed to start your transportation business here in Miami? Who do you think is bringing you wealthy clients? And who *doesn't* have blood on his hands?"

Felipe pulled his glasses off and pointed them at Tony. "How do you think I am able to access all these resources on your behalf?"

"I had my suspicions that you and Miró were involved with those people. But why look a gift horse in the mouth? I have a family to feed. Seriously though, do we really want to be in bed with the CIA?"

"It's just a meeting. Besides, you don't think that we will get rid of Castro by writing more manifestos, do you? Miró is establishing a government in exile. What are *you* going to do? Fidel came to power because men like us were willing to fight and die for what we believed in."

Felipe's response hit home. Tony knew as well as anyone that words alone do not change history, not unless they can inspire men to act.

"Okay, Felipe, I will do this for you."

"For me? You do this for Cuba, or don't do it at all."

"You're right, old friend, I stand corrected. I'll do this for Cuba, *and* for you. By the way, I need to buy a new plane." Tony was adapting to the way things were in America. He wasn't above leveraging his position for personal gain.

"Take the meeting and I'll see what I can do about getting you a loan for a new plane."

\* \* \*

"I beg your pardon, Tony, but would you mind putting the blindfold on?" The driver, another Cuban expat trying to build a new life in Miami, handed him a blindfold from the front seat of the car.

"Is this necessary?"

"If you ask me, no it's not, but el Jefe likes the cloak and dagger stuff. I'm just a driver, what do I know?"

"Manuel, no? Isn't that your name? I've seen you around."

"Yes, that's my name. And I also know who you are, you were one of Fidel's commanders. I fought in a guerilla division under Che. Like you I've made a home in Miami, but I still want to help bring about a Cuba *libre*, but this time a Cuba free of all dictators, including communist ones. We exchanged one authoritarian leader for another. That's not what I bled for."

"And you think Dulles can help liberate Cuba?"

"I do. But like I said, I'm only a driver."

"Yeah, only a driver," he said, sarcastically.

"I'll tell you this about el Jefe. He doesn't mind getting his hands dirty. He trusts nobody until they prove themselves and he will test you to see what you're made of."

"You learned all those things just by driving?"

"I hear a lot of things, but I keep my mouth shut. I think that's why he likes me."

"I understand," Tony said, nodding his head.

"I think you'll like him, he's going to do a lot for the Cuban people."

"Thanks for the insight." Tony could hear the tires pulling onto a gravel road and the sound of aircraft taking off. The ride only lasted about a half-hour. He surmised he was at an airfield not far from the city.

Manuel stepped out of the car and, without a word, opened the passenger door.

"You can take the blindfold off now," he said. His folksy demeanor was now replaced by a professional formality. They were next to a large airplane hangar. Manuel led him into a sparse office inside the hangar, lit by a single bright light dangling from the ceiling. "The Director will be with you shortly."

*I guess the el Jefe thing was just between us Cubans*, Tony mused. Inside the office, two large men in dark suits and thin black ties patted him down and pointed to a metal chair, then left without another word.

After he had sat alone for over an hour, a tall grey-haired man entered the room. He possessed a carefully groomed white mustache and was dressed in a well-tailored double-breasted tweed suit. The old spymaster held an unlit pipe in one hand and a lighter in the other. Allen Dulles smiled knowingly but said nothing. He leaned on an old metal desk and examined Tony as if he were about to make a purchase. He lit his pipe and let out a plume of smoke.

"You got rid of the beard. That's good. We don't like attracting too much attention to ourselves in this line of work. We've heard good things about you, Tony. I like to take the measure of a man before I take him into my confidence. Your reputation precedes you, the work you did in Cuba and your influence with the resistance here in Miami is notable. I've been keeping an eye on you, reading the articles you've been circulating, and taking note of your impressive network of contacts."

Tony listened politely. It was clear Director Dulles wanted to establish his own bona fides.

"We have plans in place that I believe align with your ideas and my guess is you are probably familiar with some of them. I'm here with you today because I want you to understand I am someone you can trust to get things done. When our interests align, you will find no better ally. I also want you to understand some fundamental things about how I operate. I have what might be considered a simplistic view of things. I operate under a simple premise. You are either with us or against us, and when I say us I mean the United States of America and our interests around the world. Do you understand, Tony?"

"I believe I do, sir."

"Good. Because Jacobo Guzman, the president of Guatemala, didn't understand this simple premise, and as you know, he is no longer president of Guatemala. Mohammad Mossadegh, the prime minister of Iran, didn't understand our vision of partnership, and he is no longer the prime minister of Iran. And Fidel Castro, a man with whom you have some history, does not appear to fully comprehend his situation. Do you see where this is headed?"

"It's pretty clear, sir," Tony replied, locking eyes with Dulles.

"The problem with the Cuban resistance right now is that you have a variety of actors with strong opinions. Very challenging to organize and coordinate such a movement. Intellectuals and idealists butting heads with businessmen who did well under Batista. All of them ready to squeeze out Castro, along with Conrad Hilton and Meyer Lansky, but for entirely different reasons. Do you consider that an accurate assessment?" The Director paused to gauge Tony's reaction.

Tony bristled at the suggestion. "The Mafia has no place in Cuba," he said forcefully. "I have no problem with Hilton building hotels in Cuba as long as he's paying his taxes and hiring Cubans to do the work. I will not ask Cubans to spill blood so that the Mafia can set up shop again in Cuba. The mob alliance with Batista was a symptom of everything wrong with that diseased regime. We will not allow it!" Tony could feel his muscles tensing. He stood up and began walking toward the door.

"I don't disagree with you Tony. I don't believe the Mafia belongs in Cuba. Please have a seat and indulge me a little longer. Those people will never again have significant influence in Cuba. However, they have certain skills that can be useful to us."

He turned and looked the Director in the eye. "We don't need their skills, we have all the skills we need. We Cubans can clean up our own house."

The Director smiled and held open his arms, his pipe still in one hand, the lighter in the other. "This is exactly what I wanted to hear you say. I do think it's time we gave the Democratic Revolutionary Front and its affiliate networks some teeth. You've heard about Brigade 2506?"

"I have, but only bits and pieces."

"Right now, that's all there is, bits and pieces, but soon it will be much more. You will soon have all the information you need, all the resources you need, and the full backing of the United States government. I need someone to be my eyes and ears on the ground, and my hammer should something need hammering. This operation will be for Cubans by Cubans, with help from our organization, of course. However, it is of paramount importance our involvement remain covert. You've had experience with this kind of action in Cuba, no?"

"Yes." He looked at Dulles with a mixture of admiration and skepticism.

"And you have a reputation for getting things done. In our business, a man with the ability to do what has to be done is irreplaceable. Someone who knows how to adapt to circumstances on the ground. I can teach a man the art of clandestine operations. Hell, there are hundreds of ways to kill a man and I can teach you all of them. What I can't give you is the will and determination to do what has to be done. Such qualities make a man indispensable. Do you understand me, Tony?"

"I believe I do."

"If you are who I think you are, you will become my indispensable man. We are in a global battle against the evils of communism. The communists want to take over the world, one country at a time. They push this worker propaganda, but it's all a ruse, a false narrative to get the common man to rise up and put them in power. Once they are in power, they become dictators, despots that nationalize businesses, like the one you left behind in Cuba. They murder anyone who objects to their practices. Cuba is only one battleground, we cannot let them succeed here or anywhere else. You are either with us or against us. Do you understand, Tony?"

"I do understand." Tony found the man arrogant and condescending, but also quite persuasive. He created the convincing illusion that he operated from a deep sense of conviction, a warrior for a righteous cause. His rhetoric reminded Tony of Fidel Castro. Allen Dulles lacked Castro's charisma, but his ability to access the virtually limitless resources of the United States government more than made up for it.

"Can I count on you to do what has to be done to rescue the Cuban people from communist enslavement?" Dulles sounded more like an American evangelist than a spymaster. He shuddered to think what atrocities a zealot like this might be capable of unleashing. Dulles was recruiting him for what in his mind was a sacred crusade. Tony concluded it would be decidedly unwise to say no.

"Yes, Director, you can count on me." Tony's stomach churned, as if his body was rejecting the words that seemed to involuntarily come out of his mouth.

"Good. My people will be in touch, they'll fill you in on the details. There are some things we need to clean up here in Miami. We need to get everyone rowing in the same direction. We can't win this thing with dissenters in the ranks. Do you understand what's required here?"

"I believe so." He could guess what Dulles was alluding to. It was not a task he relished undertaking, but he knew change could not happen with words alone, a unified front was imperative to any movement.

"Good. We're going to have you spend a little time at The Farm. You'll receive excellent training there. All the resources you'll need will follow. Things are moving quickly, you'll be able to choose your own team and they will lack for nothing. They'll be under my protection. And by the way, how's your family doing? Are they adjusting well?"

The question was like a knife piercing Tony's façade of safety.

"They are doing well, thank you."

"Your daughter is, what, seven years old now? Kids are most resilient, they adapt quickly."

"She's seven, turns eight in December and yes, she is a resilient child."

"And your wife?"

"She's fine, sir."

"Happy to know this. A man needs a good woman by his side, someone who is supportive but doesn't ask too many questions."

"My wife is good, sir," Tony insisted.

"That's good. Very good indeed. Look, I have my hands full in Washington right now; the new president is not particularly experienced at this sort of thing, and he's not the sharpest tool in the shed despite his Ivy League education. He asks a lot of questions. I'm going to be assuring him that this thing is as buttoned up as it can be and you are going to help me make sure that it is. I'm not sure we'll be meeting again before this thing gets underway. Just know you have my unwavering support. We'll use intermediaries to communicate, but you'll always be able to reach me if you need to. I like to keep a hand in things when I can. Sound good to you?"

"Yes, of course." Again, the words came out of his mouth as if it were someone else speaking. *What did I just agree to?* he thought to himself. *It doesn't matter. I have to do what's best for my family.*

"Almost forgot, follow me," Dulles said. "I want to show you something before I leave." Director Dulles lit his pipe and strolled out of the office in a puff of smoke. They entered an adjacent airplane hangar.

"You fly an old Cessna 170 right?"

"Correct."

"And business is good?"

"Yes, occasional light freight and executive transportation." Tony was certain the Director knew *exactly* how his business was doing.

The Director walked toward a gleaming new plane in the private hangar and tapped his pipe on the pilot door. "This is a modified Cessna 172, a new prototype of the plane we use to train our pilots. Hidden compartments, radar jamming, and a bunch of other new gadgets our boys cooked up. Do you like it?"

"It's a beautiful plane," Tony said.

"It's yours now. My people may call on you from time to time to transport sensitive items or personnel, but only on occasion, it won't interfere with your normal business. Go ahead, get in, try it on for size. I'll have our guys give you the full rundown on it."

When Tony emerged from the plane, Dulles was gone and Manuel was standing there waiting to drive him home. The large men in dark suits were also gone.

"Pretty spooky guy, isn't he, el Jefe?"

"Yeah, I guess so."

"Where am I taking you?" Manuel opened the door of the black sedan. When he settled into the back seat, Manuel reached back and handed him a black sack. He mistook it for another blindfold. It wasn't. There was something solid inside. The bag contained a handgun and a silencer. Holding the bag, he came to the realization that he had crossed into a very different world than the one he had grown used to.

Manuel turned to face Tony and smiled. "Well, it looks like I'm *your* driver now, Jefe."

Tony considered his interaction with Dulles in pensive silence. For some, this battle would be less about fighting communism and more about a way to regain hotels, casinos, and real estate. There was lots of money to be made in Cuba for entrepreneurs and self-appointed freedom fighters alike. He still believed in a free Cuba, though deep inside, some part of him knew it didn't matter what he believed. He was committed now. He had to do what was best for his family. There was no turning back.

# 12

## SEEDS OF DISCONTENT

Events on the ground were spiraling out of control.

"Can we get an update, for God's sake? I can't see a damn thing from here!" Tony's voice reverberated over the churning sea as he barked at the radio operator. "I should be out there with those men. Shouldn't have listened to Dulles. We could be making a difference right now, instead we're stuck here, helpless, and I can't even make out what's happening!"

The boat pitched and rolled with the waves, while the green CIA rookies attempted to retch out their disgust portside, but the wind and the sea returned their pitiful regurgitations. Tony scowled, sensing trouble on the horizon. *Our planes were supposed to take out Castro's air force.*

The radio crackled with an update.

"Two bombers down. No escorts. They're taking heavy fire, something about a mix-up with the time zones between Nicaragua and Florida. The escorts missed their mark."

"That can't be right," Tony snapped.

"And there's more. The president is grounding the remaining sorties," the radioman stammered, clearly shaken by the news.

Javier, a fiery Cuban also recruited by the CIA, stormed over to the radio operator. "Get Langley on the line now, or there'll be hell to pay. How are our men supposed to hold the beach without air cover? They're being slaughtered by Castro's planes. What the hell is going on?"

"I'm just the radioman. I don't give the orders."

"THEN DO YOUR DAMN JOB AND GET LANGLEY ON THE LINE!" Javier exploded with fury, his face flushed red. "Tony, what's the plan? Guys are getting slaughtered. They promised us support, but all we got were bombers with no protection. Are you fuckin' kidding me?"

Tony shook with rage, but he knew he had to contain his own revulsion. The mission was unraveling, but he could not allow himself to overreact. Tensions on the boat were running high. Volatile conditions. Many of the men had close friends and family on that beach. A shit show to end all shit shows. How could the mighty U.S. military mess up something as basic as coordinating time zones?

"Javier, stand down!" Tony shouted. "He's just doing his job. This isn't the time to lose your shit. Stand the fuck down, *pendejo*."

As the chaos unfolded around him, Tony darted back and forth, scanning the horizon, straining to make out the scene on the beach. One of the boats was ablaze, and the acrid smell of burning flesh wafted over the waves. Tony's stomach churned. Castro's planes continued their merciless assault on the shoreline. It was a bloodbath, and there was nothing he could do to stop it. The chaos became virulent, contagious, infecting every witness, every operative—senseless, avoidable, and self-perpetuating.

Even the seasoned CIA operatives from Langley found themselves swept up in the mounting fury and frustration of the Cuban operatives.

Manuel, Tony's right-hand man, moved closer, his eyes brimming with tears, and struggled to put on a brave face, but could not hide his anger from Tony. "This is going south, boss, a tragedy for the ages. How did we let this happen? Our people on that beach are as good as dead or captured."

"Too many things went wrong, too many promises broken," Tony said, looking away and trying to abate the bitterness smoldering inside.

*A leader must never give way to his emotions*, he thought. *Anger must be contained, tempered with logic. War is unpredictable, a warrior must adapt. This is not the time and place to hold those responsible accountable.*

"We should've landed in Trinidad as we originally planned, where the terrain was more favorable. The men could've found cover in the mountains if things went wrong," he said to Manuel.

"Do you think Dulles betrayed us, Jefe?"

"I think Dulles overestimated his influence with the president. Eisenhower trusted Dulles in a way Kennedy doesn't. More hubris than intentional betrayal. Dulles strikes me as a man who does not fully calculate the cost of his actions. He is driven by his hatred of communists and anyone else who might oppose the order he would impose upon the world. This is a new president, young, idealistic, and inexperienced in covert operations. A politician, with a different agenda, someone far more sensitive to public opinion than Dulles."

"But our people are being slaughtered," Manuel bellowed.

"Hubris and incompetence form a deadly combination, Manuel. Also, fuck them! This is going to come back to haunt all of them. I'm done with these arrogant assholes." Tony was seething as he too wrestled with his own self-control.

Javier continued to fuel the escalating tensions on the boat. He wanted someone to blame, a confrontation, a release of pent-up rage. Sensing a potential explosive confrontation, some of the men had un-holstered their weapons

Tony pushed Manuel aside and shouted to the mob of festering operatives. "Everybody STAND DOWN! Castro is not on this boat. No one here missed the rendezvous point. No one here is derelict in their duty. I know every man here is ready to fight. I am with you. But we can't fix this disaster. Not today. There *will* be an accounting of what happened here, but not today. Today we stand down. Today we focus on what happens next, on how we take care of our own. We have families, and the men on that beach also have families. They are counting on us to fix this. To take care of their families as if they were our own. The CIA regulars among us are frustrated too. They have worked side by side with us and they don't deserve to be the target of your wrath." He looked directly at Javier as he spoke.

Javier looked around, and he saw how the anger in the men's faces gave way to Tony's sensible exhortations. The men pulled back and huddled in groups. Javier returned the sidearm to its holster.

Javier leaned into Tony's ear and hissed. "Someone's going to pay for this."

"No doubt someone will. But that payment will have to wait."

The craft began making its way to the tiny island of Culebra off Puerto Rico where a plane waited to take them back to Miami. Tony sought solace in the sound of the craft making its way across a darkening sea, ever mindful of the poisoning bloodlust consuming Javier. Waves of repercussions cascading into the future.

* * *

*Sensitive Compartmented Information Facility (SCIF) – December 30, 1962*

"Gentlemen, Operation Zapata was a tragic failure. We lost over a hundred brave souls, and hundreds more are now prisoners of war. President Kennedy, misled by faulty intelligence and conflicting counsel, made a fatal misjudgment. In addition, there was failure of covert protocols, too many information leaks, and when the press got wind of it, the political winds shifted against us. When plausible deniability was no longer an option for the president, our cause was lost." Tony De Castro, dressed formally in a suit and tie, was addressing a gathering of Cuban counter-revolutionaries and intelligence operatives. He was in no mood to mince words.

"For those of you looking to hold someone accountable, there's plenty of blame to go around—bad logistics, miscalculations of every sort, including stronger local resistance than anticipated. Some of you may be eager to heap all blame on the president's shoulders. But such simplistic and reductive conclusions can be litigated in some other forum—I have no interest in entertaining them here. What I do know is the president's brother Bobby is doing everything possible to back-channel the release of our captured fighters, and for that, we owe him our continued gratitude. Many of you were at the ceremony just yesterday in Miami, where our brigade's flag was handed over to President Kennedy, and promises were made that it would one day fly again over a liberated Havana. Whether those promises will be honored, only time will tell. History, not us, will be the final arbiter of who is to blame for what happened at the Bay of Pigs."

Tony's voice hardened. "I declare to all gathered here today, I am severing my ties with any efforts to overthrow Fidel Castro. While I remain committed to the cause of a free and sovereign Cuba, I refuse to engage in alliances with the American Mafia and individuals like Sam Giancana. Such associations will only pave the way for unaccountable violence and unforeseeable ends, undermining the very principles we strive to uphold.

"I am turning the page on this regrettable chapter of our history, and I urge you to do the same." Tony surveyed the faces before him, noting the lingering resentment and anger that had taken root following the Bay of Pigs. The sense of betrayal hung heavy in the air, a poison infecting the souls of those who once fought for what they believed to be a just cause. He could see it coursing through some of them, a venomous fervor threatening to consume them.

Some would find a way to move past it, but for others, the bitter injury remained, festering and malignant. Convinced of their betrayal by President Kennedy, they nurtured grievances and contemplated schemes of collaboration with the very enemy they once opposed.

For those men, their destinies became intertwined with Tony's. It was only in the reliving of that moment that he realized, his face would be the last face they would ever see.

# 13

## THE LAST MISSION

"*Hola, Raquelita. ¿Cómo estás?*" Manuel greeted the precocious nine-year-old with a warm smile, glancing around the room. "I think your father is expecting me."

"Happy Thanksgiving, Manuel! Do you want some pumpkin pie?" Rachel offered cheerfully.

"It's okay, little one," Tony intervened, stepping into the room with a small American Tourister suitcase in hand. "Manuel doesn't have time for pumpkin pie. He has to take me to work now." Setting down the suitcase, Tony scooped up his daughter.

Always inquisitive, his daughter bombarded him with questions. "Why do you need your suitcase? Where are you going? When will you be back?"

"I have to go on a business trip for a few days, maybe longer. Your mother will explain. Do you know what I need now?" Tony responded gently.

"What, Papa?"

"I need you to take care of your mother while I'm away and pay attention to what she says."

"I will, Papa."

"I also want you to promise me you'll continue your studies and you'll continue developing all the gifts God has given you. Especially your artwork."

"Yes, Papa. I will."

"Right now, I need you to pick out two of your best drawings for me so I can take with me more evidence of your brilliant talent. Will you do that for me?"

"Yes, Papa," his little girl nodded eagerly, immediately rummaging through her box of drawings. "But why do you say these things if you are only going for a couple of days? I don't want you to go."

"I know, Raquel. I'll be back as soon as I'm able."

She lovingly chose two of her best drawings and handed them to her father. One depicted two old men engrossed in a game of chess in the park, while the other was a portrait, portraying a little girl, much like herself, her head angled in a thoughtful pose.

Tony felt something slice through him as he examined the drawings. He swallowed hard, managing a smile. "These are beautiful, Raquelita. Your drawings get better and better every day."

"I love you, Papa."

"I love you very much, Raquelita." Tony's eyes glistened with emotion.

"We have to go, Jefe," Manuel broke in.

"I know," Tony replied, embracing his daughter tightly.

Milagros, Tony's wife, stood nearby, her composure faltering as she held back tears. She had endured so much, silently supporting Tony through his absences and uncertainties. It wasn't fair, Tony thought. *She intuits more than she says. I wish I could tell her where I was going. But doing so would only put her at risk. She's been a good wife and mother. She deserves better. I wish I had told her more often how much I love her.*

But his inner reflections remained buried, silenced by the cold tyranny of secrecy and duty.

"*Adiós*, Milagros. Take care of our little girl."

\* \* \*

In the back seat of Manuel's car, Tony allowed his thoughts to drift, imagining the divergent paths his life might have taken. A serene existence, immersed in the art of building his coffee empire, maybe even dabbling in the intricacies of rum distillation, crafting Cuban spirits with painstaking precision. He could envision an airfreight enterprise rooted in Cuba, fostering trade connections throughout the Caribbean. It was a dream of a tranquil life tantalizingly within reach before it was disrupted by the unpredictable vicissitudes of fate.

"They sent a private jet for you, Jefe. Don't know where you're going, but you are definitely going in style," Manuel remarked as he pulled into a private parking hangar at Miami-Opa Locka Executive Airport.

"Keep an eye on my family while I'm away, won't you, Manuel?"

"Of course. I won't let anything happen to them," Manuel reassured him.

"You're a good man. Take care of yourself and your beautiful family. Always remember, family comes first."

"*Sí, claro.* Family first," Manuel echoed, touched by Tony's gesture as the two men shared a rare moment of camaraderie. Their bond transcended politics, forged in the crucible of revolution and the enduring aftermath of war. Tony knew he could trust Manuel to safeguard his family in his absence.

As he boarded the impressive aircraft, Tony marveled at the luxury of the JetStar. It was a far cry from the clandestine operations he had grown accustomed to. Suppressing the gnawing apprehension about the mission ahead, he mentally reviewed the instructions provided by Allen Dulles.

The circumstances seemed surreal. The assassination of the president of the United States had been followed swiftly by a summons to meet the new president, Lyndon Johnson. Sworn in on Air Force One amidst national turmoil, Johnson's urgency underscored the gravity of the situation. Allen Dulles, dismissed by JFK after the Bay of Pigs debacle, orchestrated the meeting invoking duty and the urgent call of national security.

"I couldn't say no," Tony mused to no one in particular. "How could I refuse the leader of the free world during a time of crisis?"

* * *

Heavy curtains shrouded the bay windows of the Georgetown townhouse, the inner ambiance somber and diffuse. Secret Service agents, stoic figures in dark suits, prowled the premises. As Tony stepped inside, he noted the strategically positioned men on nearby rooftops and the assorted Secret Service vehicles that dotted the street. This was no ordinary residence. It was a fortress, concealing the man who had ascended to the presidency just five days prior, a troubled leader conducting the nation's affairs from the shadows.

Out of deference to the fallen president, his widow and children remained ensconced in the White House, shielded from the public eye until arrangements could be made for their safe transition to private life. Suspicions of a broader conspiracy persisted, leaving Johnson, the new occupant of the Oval Office, a prime target for any would-be assassin. His own family remained secure at One Observatory Circle, the vice-presidential residence nestled within the D.C. Naval Observatory.

Tony was escorted into a spacious study, where Lyndon Johnson, sleeves rolled up and clutching a glass of Scotch and soda in one hand while brandishing a copy of the *Washington Post* in the other, awaited his arrival. The scene struck Tony as improbable as any he could imagine: a Cuban immigrant, the son of a farmer, thrust into the epicenter of American power.

"Don't just stand there. Come on in," Johnson beckoned, his Texan drawl resonating through the room. "I was just reading what those hacks at the *Washington Post* had to say about my speech last night. Went better than expected. We're hell-bent on seeing President Kennedy's legislative agenda through, no compromises. But not everyone's on board, especially with our next push for Civil Rights legislation. The South's rattled, and they may jump ship if we plow ahead too aggressively. But I say, if we truly want to honor Kennedy's legacy, we've got to act decisively, even if we have to ruffle some feathers. I said come in, son, we have a lot of ground to cover and not much time. Want a drink? Something to eat?"

"No thank you, sir," Tony replied deferentially, taking a few hesitant steps forward.

"Have a drink, it will take the edge off. Dulles tells me you were one of his top men in the field during the whole Bay of Pigs thing. He insisted the stink of pig shit stirred up by that godforsaken fiasco should not lessen my confidence in you."

"That's generous, sir."

"Generous or not, he says you're a man who I can trust to get important things done discreetly. Which is exactly what we need now. I need men I can trust. I need a man who can operate off the grid. I need your help. Your country, your adopted country, needs you. These are extremely dangerous times and I cannot bear this burden alone. Can I count on you, son?"

"You can, Mr. President. But forgive me for asking, sir, you have tremendous resources at your disposal. How can a simple man like me be of service to a great man such as yourself?"

"Good question, it shows humility. Humility is a good thing, but it should never get in the way of believing you can accomplish great things. I know plenty about simple men. Like you, I was also born in humble surroundings. Grew up poor in a small farmhouse outside Stonewall, Texas. Lived and worked among simple people who struggled each day to feed their families. My daddy was a simple man, but he always encouraged me to dream big and try to make a difference in the lives of others. How do you like your Scotch?"

"Ice and soda water."

"That's how I like it." Johnson poured Tony his drink and leaned against the desk next to him. Tony remained standing, still in awe of his present circumstances.

"I want you to know I hold genuine admiration for your people." Johnson stretched out a long arm and put it on Tony's shoulder.

"Thank you, sir."

"I'm not just blowing smoke, you understand. I lived a good chunk of my formative years working closely with many who proudly trace their roots back to Latin America. The sound of the Spanish tongue and the customs of your rich cultural heritage were among my earliest and most enduring impressions. I've got nothing but respect for our hard-working Latin American brothers and sisters. And mark my words, you'll see firsthand my dedication to the Alliance for Progress, a legacy left by President Kennedy himself. I plan to support programs to benefit the poor of all races in our country. I ain't doing this just to pay lip service to Kennedy's memory, although that's part of it. No, I'm doing it because it's the right thing to do."

"Thank you, Mr. President."

"Listen, we've had our fair share of missteps down in Latin America. I've had dealings with Allen Dulles and his brother John Foster back when he was secretary of state. Those fellas stuck their noses into places they had no business sticking 'em. And I'm well aware that sometimes they couldn't tell where their own interests ended and the country's began. They were tough, self-righteous bastards who never once questioned their own motives. Some might argue they did more harm than good. And let's not forget about the United Fruit Company, pulling strings to kick poor farmers off their own land. They had the American government wrapped around their little fingers, all to keep the locals slaving away for pennies. Well, we're gonna set things right. We need to win over our Latin American neighbors, 'cause they're right next door, and that's the best way to keep the commies out of our backyard. You can't win hearts and minds if you're always swinging a sledgehammer to squash a fly. But that's not why I called you here, son."

"I'm at your service, Mr. President." Tony wasn't sure what else to say. Whatever Johnson wanted, he was pretty sure he was not going to have much of a choice in the matter.

Johnson straightened his towering frame, clasping both hands firmly on Tony's shoulders, locking eyes with him in a way that demanded attention.

"Now I want you to listen to me carefully, what I'm about to tell you is of vital importance. The fate of our nation hinges on the success of this mission. Do you grasp the gravity of the situation? We are in crisis here."

"I understand, Mr. President. I know I wouldn't be here otherwise."

"Exactly." Johnson's hands remained firm on Tony's shoulders, his gaze unwavering. Tony stood his ground and locked eyes with Johnson believing this president respected strength.

"Dulles may be a sonofabitch, but sometimes you need one to get things done. I have a task for him. I'm appointing him to a special commission to certify that Oswald acted alone, and that the plot to kill Kennedy was solely his doing. This is vital, we cannot afford any doubts about the legitimacy of our government. Take a seat, son."

Tony sat, bracing himself for what came next.

"I have something else in mind for you, something even more crucial than what I need Dulles to handle. It'll take some time to explain and maybe even longer for you to wrap your head around it, but first, are you hungry? I'll order us some sandwiches. Sound good to you?"

"Of course, sir."

"Six days ago, the president was assassinated right in my home state of Texas, in broad daylight. Our initial fear was that this was part of a larger plot by right-wing Southern extremists opposed to Kennedy's civil rights policies or some such thing."

Johnson paused to make the sandwich order, then drew his chair closer to Tony's.

"Did you know that when Lincoln was assassinated, the plan was to simultaneously kill Vice President Andrew Johnson and Secretary of State William Seward?"

"No, Mr. President."

"It's a fact. They didn't just want to eliminate the president; they aimed to strike a mortal blow to the entire government. Seward was injured but survived, while Johnson's would-be assassin lost his nerve.

"In the aftermath of JFK's assassination, we couldn't rule out a wider conspiracy. We feared the worst. That's why I insisted on taking the Oath of Office promptly. We needed to reassure the public that the government was still functioning, while signaling to our enemies that our chain of command was steady and unbroken. We need to be prepared for anything, including more assassinations. Some accused me of acting hastily out of personal ambition. They misunderstood my motives. I acted to protect the nation. You understand, don't you son?"

"I understand, Mr. President," Tony replied.

"President Kennedy made his fair share of enemies, and God bless his brother Bobby, that man takes stubborn pleasure in picking fights. Bobby's got smarts for sure, but politics requires a different kind of smarts. Now, don't misunderstand me, anyone in politics is bound to make enemies, but the Kennedys had a knack for painting targets on their own backs. Their old man raised those boys believing it was their destiny to shake up the world. But those who aim to disrupt the status quo often find themselves facing off against those who are hell-bent on maintaining it. And they paid a heavy toll for daring to envision a better world. God knows that family has seen more than its fair share of tragedy."

"They certainly have, sir." Tony couldn't help but recall how President Kennedy's failure to send ground troops to aid the counterrevolutionaries at the Bay of Pigs invasion stoked resentment among many, including CIA operatives.

"It's no secret Bobby and I don't see eye to eye, he didn't want me as vice president, but despite our differences, I have a deep respect for that family. My heart goes out to Rose Kennedy, she's known more sorrow than any mother should bear. Rose knows politics. Her father, Honey Fitz, was Boston's mayor. The saga of that family, the rise of the Irish in Boston from underclass to highest office in just three generations, is a classic American success story. But Rose never forgot her roots. She instilled in those boys the notion that with great privilege comes great responsibility. She groomed them for public service, while their father taught them the art of wielding power."

Johnson paused, as if considering how much more to disclose.

"Joe, the old man, might have had dealings with shady people, not sure. What I do know is he used his wealth and influence, he pulled strings and called in favors to secure votes. Frank Sinatra crooning his campaign jingles—

how does anyone compete with that? I reckon that Joe made promises he might not have shared with his boys right off, maybe waiting for the favor to be called, as it were. Meanwhile Jack and Bobby had no qualms about rattling the cages of the old guard in this town, the men behind the scenes who pull the strings."

Tony sat up, attentive to Johnson's eye-opening revelations.

"Regardless of how he won the election, Kennedy had grand visions for the future," Johnson continued. "Like FDR, he aimed to create opportunities for all Americans, to quell the specter of nuclear war, and to lift impoverished nations out of despair. They say the times make the man, and make no mistake, Jack Kennedy embraced the challenges of his time. He grew into the job, fueled by a grand vision, influenced in no small part by his mother Rose. But his boldness in tackling monumental issues with innovative ideas earned him plenty of adversaries. The Kennedys underestimated the pushback that comes with challenging the established order—much of it coming from good ole boys from my part of the country. But it turns out my worries about Southern right-wing treachery were wrong. Though I fear the truth may be far darker."

"How so?" Tony asked, mesmerized by Johnson's analysis.

"I brought you here because the stakes are sky-high." His voice, laden with gravity. "I need someone who's not afraid to roll up their sleeves and get their hands dirty. I need someone who can help me clean up this godforsaken mess, because the truth of this matter is so volatile that if it ever sees the light of day, it will almost surely start a war— a war that could extinguish millions of innocent lives. Hell, that war might just be the last one we ever fight."

"How can I assist you, Mr. President?" Tony interjected, his breathing laborious, the constriction in his chest intensifying with each second of Johnson's protracted preamble.

*For pity's sake*, Tony thought, his heart caught in his throat, *just tell me what you need me to do.*

Johnson rose from his chair, his imposing frame casting a long shadow across the room, his commanding presence and innate sense of authority compelling compliance. He clutched a sealed binder, handling it with a reverence befitting an article of profound consequence. Abandoning his folksy demeanor, his visage grew grave and foreboding, and he locked eyes with Tony. "I know who assassinated Jack Kennedy, and there are only three souls on this earth privy to the information I'm about to entrust you with. You're about to become the fourth."

The images from television broadcasts hadn't done justice to Lyndon Johnson's aura. He projected a force of will, the intimidating presence of a man comfortable wielding devastating power. Tony sensed he was on the brink of undertaking a mission unlike any other he had confronted before. He felt a vise grip tighten around his throat, his body instinctively coiled tight as he braced himself for what was to come.

Whenever leaders begin preaching about the necessity to take firm action to avert war, it is a predictable indicator that blood will be spilled.

# 14

## LOOSE ENDS

"So, this target, you knew him?" Aaron probed, his voice cutting through the steady drumming of rain against the van's windshield. Tony's eyes remained focused on the raindrops, their hypnotic rhythms capturing his wandering thoughts. A neglected half-eaten sandwich lay forgotten on his lap, a doleful reminder of how even the wet-work at hand, urgent and fatal, can become drudgery. It had been nearly a year since his rendezvous with Johnson, a year spent methodically erasing anyone tied to the Kennedy assassination, each task inching him closer to the end of his grim assignment. Aaron's probing grated on his nerves. Annoyed by the aimless chatter, he reminded himself the waiting was getting to both of them.

"He was an acquaintance," Tony replied, his voice distant. "He was once a zealous revolutionary, passionate in his convictions, then he turned on Castro. He convinced himself that anyone associated with enabling Castro was an enemy."

"And you?" Aaron pressed. "You were a part of the Cuban Revolution, weren't you?"

"I was ready to fight and die for The Movement's ideals," Tony affirmed.

"But I became disenchanted when the reality fell short of its promise. Javier shared my disappointment, but his passions worked against him after the failed attempt to take back the island. He saw Kennedy's withdrawal of support as a betrayal, and passion conjoined with bitterness can drive a man crazy."

"Do you blame him?" Aaron queried.

"I empathize," Tony conceded. "I've walked a similar path. Believing the enemy of my enemy is my friend can produce strange bedfellows. I backed Castro until he became another tyrant, and later I cooperated with the CIA until their promises crumbled into dust and they bedded down with mobsters."

"Then why are we here?" Aaron's question hung heavy in the air, his weariness palpable after twenty-four hours of surveillance.

Tony shot him a pointed glance. "We execute the mission, Aaron. We don't question the targets. We do what's necessary, regardless of personal qualms. I chose you for this task because you understand the cost of inaction."

Rain began hammering down in torrents, and the truck, posing as a service vehicle for Max Gomez Plumbing, was transformed into a small prison, noisy and claustrophobic. Tony, ensconced within this metal shell, felt the deluge pressing down, harassing him with its ceaseless pounding. His gaze drifted to the deadly accoutrements concealed within his toolbox, each item a silent witness to the grim tasks forced upon him. In the dim light of the van's interior, their presence was a chilling reminder of the obligations that awaited him beyond the confines of his makeshift sanctuary.

"I understand," Aaron murmured, his voice tinged with resignation. "But confronting enemies will test one's fortitude. I do recognize there's always a price to pay, a burden to bear. My family paid dearly for my escape, sacrificing themselves so I might live. I'm determined to honor their sacrifice."

"I imagine you've been asked to do things in your career that you had second thoughts about. No? Evil doesn't always wear a swastika." Tony wondered if his companion grappled with the same moral ambivalence that plagued him.

"We Israelis tend to view everything through the prism of survival. It makes it easier that way," Aaron explained.

"How so?" Tony asked.

"We don't permit ourselves to forget how our people suffered. We will never again allow our enemies to perceive us as weak. This is at the core of our training, part of our commitment to God and country. In Israel military service is compulsory. As a soldier, or covert operative, we don't have the luxury of pondering abstract morality. When we receive orders, we don't ask why, we execute them knowing that our actions are in the best interests of our people. Whatever the mission, someone in a position of authority must have determined it was essential for our survival. We don't afford ourselves the luxury of doubt or second-guessing. If someone or something is deemed a threat, they become a threat to Israel, a threat to our survival, and they are dealt with accordingly—efficiently and without mercy."

Tony listened in silence, the rain providing a melancholy backdrop to Aaron's chilling introspection.

"I'm blessed to have a good partner in life," Aaron remarked. "My wife understands that I must sometimes do things that are best left unexamined. She too is driven by a strong sense of duty, but in her, it finds a different expression. She believes that respecting the rights of all people is the ultimate expression of our faith, and essential for our survival. While some might consider her activism to be in conflict with the work I do, and at times it may be, in reality she embodies values that are very much a part of our Jewish heritage. We don't agree on everything, but our long-term goals are the same—a stable Israel, one that can thrive in peaceful coexistence with its neighbors. She's a good woman, we counterbalance each other. Her advocacy for displaced Palestinian communities serves our shared objectives."

"You are fortunate to have someone like that by your side," Tony acknowledged. "Sharing the load lightens it somehow. Things might have been different for Javier if he'd been blessed with such a partner. But he let the bitterness consume him. He believed Kennedy bore full blame for the failure of the invasion. The resentment he harbored made him a mark for the wrong people."

"The Russians?" Aaron's question ventured deeper into the nature of their mission.

"Yes, they got to him. The enemy of my enemy is my friend—it's a dangerous way to look at things. Javier's disillusionment was like an incurable cancer that poisoned his mind."

Tony hesitated, realizing he divulged more than intended. But it was too late. Aaron's fate had been sealed by the agreed-upon protocols. He, too, was on The List.

A shadow moved out of the rain and both men snapped into readiness, adrenaline pushing aside the weariness.

"There he is!" Aaron said.

"Time to act," Tony declared, his hand instinctively reaching for his toolbox. "Remember, we're here to inspect a leak. Buzz me in once you confirm he's alone."

"And if he's not?" Aaron queried.

"Buzz twice, they both go," Tony replied curtly. "Let's get this done."

In the rain-soaked street, Tony's resolution hardened. No room for second-guessing.

The newspapers would report that a veteran of the Bay of Pigs invasion was found dead of a drug overdose in his Miami apartment, alongside the former soldier, an unnamed companion, also deceased.

As they drove away from Javier's apartment, the road ahead besieged by the downpour, buried thoughts clawed at Tony, scratching out unwelcome discernments under the cover of darkness.

*Of course, my name will also be on The List. And if they are with me, my wife Milagros and my little girl will most certainly become two more casualties of this ill-fated undertaking. There has got to be another way.*

# 15

## THE SOUNDS OF SILENCE

---

### HAVEN PSYCHIATRIC CENTER, NEW YORK - FEBRUARY 1985

---

"I have a voice."

"There it is," the doctor said, her voice resonating with appreciation for the long-awaited breakthrough. "So beautiful to hear your voice after so many years of silence. When you're ready, please tell me what you remember about the last time you used it."

The young woman sat upright, and her eyes seemed to fix on some distant setting.

She spoke in trancelike tones. "I was ten years old. Thrilled to be allowed to attend the parade with my mother. As expected, the president's motorcade made its approach toward Dealey Plaza. People jostled one another to get a better glimpse of the president and Jacqueline Kennedy. Every part of me tingled with anticipation, even at that age I felt I knew them, I knew we were all joining in something special. Jackie was radiant, almost otherworldly.

"Many were excited to have the president visit, but some, a small vocal group resisted his incursion into the South. There were wanted posters with his image on them posted around the city. A provocative full-page advertisement appeared in the *Dallas Morning News*, framed in a black border, you know, the print style used in funeral announcements, it accused the president of committing crimes against Americans.

"An intermingling of unease and anticipation rippled through the gathering. Something on the periphery was shifting, moving into focus. As a child I had no point of reference, I didn't know it then, but the experience was the beginning of a transformation in me."

"Interesting." The doctor leaned forward thoughtfully, navigating the conversation, but careful not to interrupt her hypnotic articulation.

The young woman continued in a distinctive monotone. "The thrill of being immersed in the moment, caught up in the irresistible pull of history, was abruptly fractured by the sudden sound of gunfire." She paused, adjusted herself in the chair, and looking up, allowed the recollection to transport her. "Waves of fear and horror washed over me. Shots seemed to ring out from every conceivable direction."

She paused again, her eyes reaching beyond the confines of the office, then resumed in her mesmeric intonations. "It was a long time ago, yesterday, or moments ago. Time is fluid. For me the effect of these events remains ever-present. I imagine this may sound odd to you, but this is what I need to say. Words so often fail to convey the fullness of experience. They can become useless, get in the way of a deeper comprehension."

"I understand. Please continue," the doctor said, her expression calm yet probing.

"The imagery seared itself into my awareness. I can see his face right now, handsome and confident. His smile, warm and familiar. My parents, like many at the time, believed he was someone who arrives once in a generation, an agent of change who emerges at unique crossroads in history. They spoke of him in reverential tones. A consequential figure. The keeper of the flame. The torchbearer for a new generation. They spoke of him fondly, as if he were a family member, a missing loved one arriving home after a long absence.

"Your depictions are captivating, please go on."

"I witnessed everything through the lens of an 8mm movie camera I had just received as a birthday present. The president and Jackie centered in the frame, my eye glued to the viewfinder. After the first shot everything began to slow down. Time shifted. I saw a bullet pierce his neck. I saw it in slow motion, frame by frame. An aberration I couldn't explain, still can't. A visual imprint impossible to ignore.

"Another bullet entered and exited his head with explosive savagery. Gruesome for anyone to witness—inconceivable horror for a child. Still, I couldn't look away. Irretrievable parts of the president came to rest on the First Lady's beautiful pink coat. Red on pink. A stain that can never be removed. I couldn't look away. In the front seat, Governor Connally was also wounded, but my lens remained glued to the president. The First Lady, like me, was now caught in the undercurrent of unaccountable events. She attempted to exit the moving vehicle, to escape the ensnaring grasp of fate—the motorcade, the weight of her destiny, the fate of her children. She couldn't—none of us could. She was pushed back in by a Secret Service agent. Violence birthing new realities.

"Some might suggest I imagined all of this because of the other film, the Zapruder film. But I have my own my recording. Some secrets are meant to remain hidden, some are meant to be revealed at the appointed hour.

"I bore witness as the tremors of history rippled through time. It shattered something within me—severing the innocence of childhood and tethering me to a new awakening."

"What exactly does this mean to you? How did it change you?" The doctor rubbed the back of her neck, evaluating the young woman's unfolding narrative.

"I became intertwined in a surge that reshaped everything in its wake. A heinous act altered the ordained path. At the time, I did not have the means to articulate the experience, yet I desperately yearned to comprehend it, so I looked inward."

"Say more about this. Did you feel yourself becoming untethered?"

"It wasn't only *my* awareness that shifted. History itself recalibrated, altering the trajectory of the future. The global psyche bore witness to a trauma it couldn't wholly fathom. The child within me retreated into a cocoon of silence, a shield against the incomprehensible. With time, my perspective morphed. I came to view it as a gift, an opening. An opportunity to understand the mysterious connective tissue that binds us to the shared human ordeal."

The young woman stared intrepidly into the expanse of recollection. "As I withdrew from the lens, chaos reigned. Screams pierced the air, souls scattered in disarray. My mother, a pillar of strength, attempted to contain her anguish behind a trembling hand. I stood amidst the tumult, feeling as though I teetered on the brink of an abyss, pulled by an unseen force into its depths. The urge to cry out, to offer solace to my mother, welled within me, yet remained stifled by an inexplicable calm that settled over me, an oasis amid the storm."

"So you're suggesting that your subsequent silence wasn't a symptom of trauma but a conscious decision?"

"Both."

"Please explain."

"As I grew older, I grappled with the mystery. I endeavored to dissect every iota of those pivotal seconds, hoping that by unraveling each strand, I might glean insight into their profound impact on my psyche. I searched for a way to decipher the enigmatic sequence of events, to unravel the tangled threads of fate.

"I studied the forensics. I learned how a high-speed military projectile can penetrate and 'punch out' a conical section of a skull, a phenomenon known as the cratering effect. The projectile impacts the head and penetrates the soft part of the skull. It perforates a hole in the outer membrane. The hole begins forming at approximately the same diameter as that of the entrance area, but then the bullet collides with hard cortical bone, shattering it. It passes through into the inner, more pliable trabecular layer and as this happens, the area expands, roughly in the shape of a cone, until it finally breaks out a wider hole taking with it cerebral matter.

"I learned what happens in the interaction between the two bodies, the bullet and the bone, during collision. According to Newton's Second and Third Laws of Dynamics, both bodies are deformed and 'stick' together immediately after breakage."

She repeated this reflectively, allowing the words, never before uttered, to rush over her. "Both bodies are deformed and stick together immediately after breakage."

"Is this a metaphor?" the doctor asked.

"Perhaps. But something fractured within me. I wasn't alone in my brokenness. From that fracture emerged a new iteration of myself. Perhaps, in a deliberate counterpoint to the malevolence unleashed that day, my own faculties were brought into sharper relief. Yet, lacking the tools to articulate such phenomena, I remained cloaked in silence."

"And now, after so many years, do you believe you possess the requisite tools? Is this why you've chosen to break your silence?" the doctor inquired.

"I've gained a deeper understanding, new avenues and new tools to articulate my experiences. I share this with you now because it's time for me to forge ahead. Therapy is no longer necessary. I grasp my purpose more fully. I've made a conscious decision.

"I am not unique in what I experienced. It was particularly traumatic for me because I was so young, and because I didn't have a relevant point of reference. But I found the insight I needed in other places."

"What sort of places? Can you give me an example?" the doctor asked, pausing to make a notation in her journal.

"Tibetan Buddhists embrace the practice of Sahaja, meaning spontaneous enlightenment, a recognition of the unifying elements of spirit, matter, subject and object. Also, there is the Japanese art of Kintsugi, where breakage and repair are considered vital parts of the history of an object, something to be honored, not hidden. The philosophy of Mushin embraces non-attachment, the acceptance of change, and the embracing of the forces shaping the arc of human existence.

"While I didn't choose this role, I've come to realize the necessity of embracing all that it has brought me. The events of that day transformed the destinies of millions. Mine is just one thread in the vast tapestry of related narratives. There's solace and depth in silence."

The young woman continued in reflective expression. "The spoken word is but one way of communicating. And I no longer need words to tell my story. Let these suffice, and allow us to bring closure to our meetings.

"I have something far more useful to me than simple speech—I have a purpose. I am an artist. Please, call me Dallas."

# 16

## UNREQUITED

Michael stared at the red droplets floating in the soapy water. He plopped his razor into the mixture and lifted a towel to his face, pausing to study the bloody nick in the mirror.

The wound offered a temporary distraction from the looming apprehension. It was a familiar shadow of an old demon he never fully exorcised, a sickness he never fully recovered from. Succumbing to the symptoms meant descending into an abyss of regret—a danger he couldn't afford.

Rachel had returned to New York on a business errand after nearly a year of self-imposed exile, and invited him to accompany her to an art event. A steady stream of ruminations invaded Michael's thoughts.

*Why didn't I just make an excuse? I should have said I had a prior engagement, pressing business; something, anything. But how could I say no to Gabriel when he asked me to look after her? I couldn't say no.*

*Have to keep pretending. It's been a year since I've had to pretend. Pretend I don't love her, pretend I don't want to hold her and never let her go. Pretend I can ignore the scorching desire consuming me when I am near her.*

*Gabriel is like a brother, and Rachel belongs to Gabriel,* he rationalized, though he knew deep down that Rachel belonged to no one.

It was all a lie and he knew it.

He took a hard pull from the Scotch resting on the bathroom sink.

Nothing to be gained by dwelling on regrets, but this one haunted him. He regretted not telling Rachel about the blinding light that struck him the very first time he saw her. He regretted never sending her the letter inspired by their first earth-shattering encounter. The letter, kept hidden, a pointless indulgence marking his effort to give voice to the inexplicable force that left such an indelible mark on him. He never sent it. He hesitated until it no longer mattered. Too late now. Gabriel got the girl they both loved. Michael kept the note.

* * *

"Hey, bud, thanks for accepting the invite. So good to see you." Rachel stood radiant, beguiling in a tight-fitting black satin suit, stiletto heels, and a form-fitting white blouse, open at the collar. French cuffs, pearls, and a white pocket square completed her breathtaking look.

As he returned her smile, a pang of longing swept through him, a reminder of his unspoken desires concealed beneath the guise of friendship. "*I am the pretender*," he silently confessed to himself, a solitary admission buried beneath the surface of his composed exterior.

She hugged Michael. He kissed her casually on the cheek.

"Amanda is sending a car but we have a little time to catch up before the madness begins. Want a drink?"

"Boy, you sure do clean up good," Michael said, taking in her scent, each intoxicating breath pulling him deeper into what might have been. He beamed. "Yes, a drink would be good. Bet you don't have a chance to wear that outfit in Vermont too often."

"Quite true," Rachel snickered. "You have a gift for understatement. I know this isn't exactly your scene, but I so appreciate you agreeing to join us anyway."

"Are you kidding? I love hanging out with brilliant artists and the glitterati that follow them." The warm liquid soothed, forming a mélange of tension and euphoria. *I can do this. I am the pretender.*

"You are such a liar, Michael, but tonight I welcome the posturing."

Michael held her gaze for just a second too long. *If she only knew.* "I only lie when it's absolutely necessary and this is definitely not one of those occasions. I consider it an honor to be invited, I honestly do." He offered his best disarming smile.

There was purpose in his role as guardian, a position he embraced with quiet determination. The unsettling episode at Gabriel's farewell gathering served as a stark reminder of the lingering dangers surrounding the Courtland affair. Though the media frenzy had subsided, the specter of revenge loomed ever-present. *Smart move to keep a low profile in Vermont*, he mused, mindful of persistent grudges and lurking threats.

As the Courtland family pursued an appeal against the verdict, Michael remained resolute in his commitment to hold them accountable for their crimes. The notion that the ordeal had reached its conclusion felt premature, a sentiment underscored by the ongoing tensions that simmered beneath the surface. Rationalizing his presence in Gabriel's absence, Michael sought reassurance in the conviction that his vigilance was both warranted and necessary.

"Tell me, who is this new artist? Must be something special if you're leaving your sanctuary in the woods of Vermont?"

"She's a multi-media performance artist named Dallas. There is quite a buzz around her, I'm told her work defies description. Amanda is hosting a private reception for a few guests after the event."

"I remember Amanda, a sharp businesswoman and a tough cookie in five-inch heels if memory serves correctly. Who else will be there?"

"A few of Amanda's friends and clients. A small group. There is an older Russian gentleman I want you to meet. An interesting character. Someone who has been collecting my work for years, his name is Dimitri Ivanov. The guest of honor will also make an appearance. I've read that Dallas doesn't speak, or chooses not to speak, possibly the result of a traumatic childhood experience. No pressure to make awkward small talk I guess. Oh Christ, did that sound insensitive?"

Michael belted out a hearty laugh. "No, not insensitive. Okay, maybe a little, but it's good background. I might have thought she was just ignoring my boring chatter. Looking forward to seeing her work. Who else?"

"I believe Mr. Ivanov is bringing a few guests, other art collectors I presume, and Amanda may have invited a few others. Not sure, but it's supposed to be a small group in a private area away from the hubbub. The main after-party will be the usual mix of what did you call them? Glitterati. And of course, the usual group of art investors that attend these sorts of things. Honestly, as much as they drive up the value of my art, I find some of them can be a bit mercenary. It's all about money and status for them, less about the work itself. Amanda says I'd be amazed at how often she is paid with a briefcase full of cash."

"Do tell," Michael said, raising an eyebrow.

"Whoops! Guess I shouldn't be telling you that, you being in the business of prosecuting criminals and all of that kind of activity." Rachel's eyes twinkled.

Michael pretended to ignore the bait.

"Anyway, I don't think Mr. Ivanov is like that. Although I didn't spend a lot of time with him, and to be honest, I don't know much about him. But something about him felt familiar. The man seems to have an intuitive appreciation of my work, as if he understands me on some deeper level. Hard to explain. But it does feel validating when someone feels connected to me through the work I create. I'm looking forward to seeing him again, I think you'll like him."

Michael felt it again, Rachel's innocent words triggering a searing urge; a yearning for her to fully grasp the intuitive connection that bound him to her, but as always, he clamped down on those feelings and buried them deep where they could do no harm. Or so he thought.

# 17

## THE DALLAS EFFECT

The theater buzzed with anticipation, and a palpable energy pulsated through the sold-out crowd, each individual hovering on the brink of an immersive encounter. Dallas, rumored to possess a transcendent gift born from the crucible of suffering, awaited her moment ensconced in shadows. Rachel, attuned to the alchemy of creative transmutation, how pain gives birth to art, tingled with the promise of catharsis. In the waning light, she reached for Michael's hand, their connection a tether to the ineffable.

As the lights dimmed and the audience fell quiet, a numinous aura rippled through the theater. Intermittent flickers of light danced on a white screen, until an old 8mm film crackled to life, projecting grainy scenes of Dealey Plaza and the fateful motorcade. The whir of the projector punctuated the hushed anticipation, each frame rousing collective memory and unspoken dread.

Dallas emerges, a spectral presence in the dim glow, her cello a vessel for elegiac strains that pierce the silence. The mournful refrains are juxtaposed incongruously with a smiling JFK, foreshadowing a future just seconds away. But the fateful moment is delayed. The audience, spellbound, bear witness to a visual elegy, a silent symphony of grief and foreboding.

The camera zooms in on the president and his wife, then cuts to the face of a young girl filming the motorcade. There is no sound. A silent movie set to solemnly prescient music. The little girl's face is beaming with excitement. The next moment she recoils in shock. Flash cut to her mother, her face reflecting dismay, fear and horror building to a crescendo of anguish. Dallas illuminated in red, her instrument now weeping a lament almost too sad to bear.

With each repetition, the montage expands, each frame triggering a fragment of collective memory buried in the chronicles of time. The tragic images repeat on an expanding loop, stretching time. A second cellist joins Dallas in the mournful refrain, a violin now enters the mix and the montage careens forward.

Jacqueline Kennedy appears in her blood-splattered pink coat witnessing the swearing-in of Lyndon Baines Johnson on Air Force One. Cut to John Kennedy Jr. offering a poignant salute before his father's funeral carriage. The carriage led by a riderless horse, boots reversed in the stirrups, exemplifying the traditional symbol of a fallen warrior looking back at his troops one last time. Behind the president's son stands a stoic Mrs. Kennedy dressed in black. Images and music coalesce in a symphony of sorrow and resilience, a testament to the enduring resonance of loss.

Dallas is bathed in a halo of ethereal light, a luminous beacon of possibility, her figure swathed in the diaphanous folds of a flowing white gown. With each deft movement of her fingers upon the fretboard, she summons forth the raw essence of heartbreak and sorrow, weaving a haunting melody that reverberates through the cavernous space.

Rachel, enraptured by the mesmerizing spectacle unfolding before her, feels the tendrils of catharsis ensnaring her, inexorably drawing her into a maelstrom of emotion. In that transcendent moment, the barriers of individuality dissolve, and she finds herself intricately woven into the collective tapestry of sorrow and longing that envelops the room.

Bound by the common thread of shared grief, each member of the audience becomes a vessel for the unspoken anguish that permeates the air, their hearts beating in unison to the melancholic rhythm of Dallas's solo. Sharing in a transitory moment of communion, they are no longer disparate beings, but interconnected souls united in their quest for absolution amidst the unfathomable depths of unspeakable things. In the theater's asylum, time stretches and folds, swelling waves of memory and emotion are punctuated by shimmering lights and transmutant sounds. And as Dallas's bow dances across the strings, her music a requiem for what was lost and what endures, the audience is held in a timeless trance, bound together by the weight of history and the promise of redemption.

The music ebbs and flows while the quivering voice of Bobby Kennedy eulogizing his fallen brother reverberates from all sides.

*"When he shall die, take him and cut him out in little stars, and he will make the face of heaven so fine, that all the world will be in love with night and pay no worship to the garish sun."*

The visual narrative pulls the audience back and forth through time. Helicopters with shirtless soldiers, boys with guns, smiling, smoking, drinking and bleeding through fresh gunshot wounds. Vietnamese huts burning in violent reprisal.

Two violins, positioned on either side of Dallas, suffused in a narrow crimson glow, penetrate the darkness like beacons of hope. Dallas, animated, vibrant, radiates dominion over the transfixed.

Behind her, images flicker on the screen, depicting the ravages of war as napalm engulfs Southeast Asian jungles in flames. The juxtaposition of sound and imagery creates a visceral experience that resonates with the audience on a primal level.

One of the violins, caught in the throes of the music's intensity, takes on a life of its own, with blazing notes, distorted and electrified, growling over a backdrop of blues and gospel progressions ascending from a church organ. Musicians and instruments emerge in and out of shadows and light. Power chords explode from an electric guitar.

Footage of the slain body of Martin Luther King on the deck of a Memphis

Hotel. His affirmation, *I have a dream*, reverberates over and over through the hall, urgent and persistent.

Bobby Kennedy lies dying on the floor of the Ambassador Hotel in Los Angeles. Ted Kennedy choking back tears, quoting his fallen brother. His voice, broken and faltering, echoes throughout.

*"Some men see things as they are, and ask why. I dream of things that never were, and ask why not?"*

The attendees continue to be drawn into a fluid and irresistible current of shared concurrence. They travel the shifting currents of time, while enthralling portrayals of life-altering events continue to flood the screen. The music sends waves of elevated awareness rippling through the transported assembly.

Dallas, radiant at the center of it all, seamlessly transitions between instruments—keyboards, violin, cello—her movements an expression of creation and catharsis. The music she conjures spans continents and cultures, weaving together disparate threads of gospel hymns, Irish laments, and the primal rhythms of African drums.

Time oscillates forward and backward. Buzz Aldrin lands on the Moon; bodies litter the killing fields of Cambodia; napalm burns human flesh and jungle landscapes. Ecstatic hippies dance at Woodstock, juxtaposed against the image of a dead student lying face down and bleeding at Kent State University.

The *Enola Gay* takes off from the Northern Marianas. Little Boy and Fat Man generate mushroom clouds over Hiroshima and Nagasaki. Richard Nixon flashes the peace sign as he boards a helicopter. Toyotas roll off production lines by the thousands. Police clash with protesters in Chicago and Birmingham. The army clashes with protesters in Prague. Israeli tanks roll across the Sinai Peninsula. Steve Biko's battered body is released by his captors in South Africa. Attack dogs are unleashed on civil rights marchers on the Edmund Pettus Bridge in Selma. George Wallace blocks the entrance to the University of Alabama. The Beatles play on the Ed Sullivan Show. Bob Dylan uses an electric guitar at the Newport Folk

Festival. A Buddhist monk sets himself on fire, Jimi Hendrix sets his guitar on fire. Pete Townshend demolishes his equipment at Monterey. The Clash destroy the stage at CBGBs. The Sex Pistols bleed on their rabid followers.

Potent visuals continue in relentless insistence. Ronald Regan and John Hinckley, Jack Ruby and Lee Harvey Oswald. A West German helicopter bursting into flames. Israeli bulldozers obliterating Palestinian homes. John Lennon's eyeglasses shattered on a Manhattan sidewalk.

Each strand of connected thread pulsates with the rhythms of Dallas's impassioned performance. She traverses the array of instruments with grace and fluidity, her virtuosity intertwining with the ensemble to create a gut-wrenching soundtrack for the surging revelations unfolding on the screen.

Behind a gossamer curtain, a choir materializes, their ethereal voices soaring in harmonious union, apotheosizing spirituals and ancient hymns. Their presence adds spiritual depth to the auditory onslaught, elevating the collective experience to a state of transcendence.

At the nexus of this shared consciousness, each participant discovers a link to the other in a timeless dance of revelation and understanding. Through a sublime exchange of music and imagery, they encounter the redemptive realization that they are not alone, but rather part of something far greater than themselves.

Rachel clings to Michael's arm, her tears flowing freely as darkness descends on them like a comforting shroud. In the absence of light, their surroundings envelop them in an eerie stillness, punctuated only by the soft rustle of fabric and the faint murmur of collective emotion.

Then, as if summoned by some unseen force, a canopy of celestial light pierces the darkness as on stage a single beam of light extends up, reaching for some indefinable source. It is as though they have been visited by a divine presence, a messenger from unknown origins.

As the light expands, casting an ethereal radiance over the theater, the stunned attendees find themselves bathed in a luminous embrace. Rachel and Michael, along with the others, move in reverential silence, guided by the gentle glow that binds them.

They make their way out of the building in serene quiet, their hearts radiant, elevated by a sense of connectedness. Some wipe tears from their eyes, while others simply cling to their loved ones, embracing the communion of profound revelation.

* * *

Michael, dazed by the breathtakingly beautiful performance, proceeded toward the lobby, nestled against Rachel. For a while, words of any kind seemed superfluous. They paused by the exit, basking in an intimate aura of shared bliss. Amanda and her guests followed close behind. She smiled and gingerly broke the stillness.

"Cars are out front to take you to the after-party. I'll be heading over in a short while. My guess is you can all use a drink right now. I know I can. Meet you at the club." She turned around swiftly and walked back into the venue.

Following her was an older well-dressed gentleman accompanied by two younger men.

"Mr. Ivanov, so good to see you again. This is my friend Michael Rose." Rachel extended her arm to shake his hand. The old man lifted her hand and gently kissed it.

"It is such a pleasure to once again be in your presence, my dear. What I witnessed tonight has opened a hole in my heart and I am eager to find solace in your company. Mr. Rose, it is an honor to meet you, sir. We have a car waiting as well. Permit me to collect my companions, I look forward to continuing our conversation at the reception."

Michael shook Dimitri's hand. "Nice to meet you, Mr. Ivanov. Rachel speaks fondly of you. I too look forward to sharing a drink later."

"And so it shall be, and please call me Dimitri."

As Rachel entered the private car, Michael's pulse quickened. They rode the short distance in silence, soaking in the moment, basking in the comforting refuge they each provided the other.

# 18

## ENCOUNTERS IN THE DARK

Buoyed by a lingering attentiveness, Michael observed the Manhattan throng racing past the windows of the sleek black sedan. People swept along by the relentless tide of everyday life, moving with tenacious energy toward unknown ends, hidden ties binding their fates, ties obscured by the tyranny of the urgent, and the mundane obligations required to make ends meet. The genius of Dallas's transformative artistry had succeeded in laying bare these invisible bonds, inviting fresh perspectives on the unseen connective threads that animated their interconnected lives.

Beside him, Rachel, bathed in contemplative afterglow, welcomed a quiet moment of reflection.

At the Limelight, a fashionable nightclub housed within a storied edifice, Michael found himself immersed in a place of both allure and history. Pausing in the foyer of the newly renovated venue, he cast a discerning eye over the plaque that chronicled the colorful history of the impressive building—a grand cathedral constructed in 1852. The lofty ceilings, adorned with intricate arches, and the luminous stained-glass windows bore witness to its ecclesiastical origins. Once the revered Church of the Holy Communion, it had played host to illustrious congregants including Theodore Roosevelt and Edith Wharton.

As he awaited entrance into the private gathering, Michael found himself amused by the irony of the location.

"Something funny?" Rachel asked.

"Nothing really. This building was once a house of worship, you know, a place where people presumably gathered to pray and seek redemption. Tonight, people are gathering to worship at the altar of fame, and maybe hope to find release of a more carnal nature. It's interesting to me how each generation has to invent their own way of connecting with like-minded disciples."

"You are full of surprises, Michael. It appears the evening is bringing out the philosopher in you."

"It's possible the philosopher was always there and just needed a little encouragement." Michael met her eyes and held her elbow as she stepped into the elevator.

Amanda's guests gathered in a private section off the second-floor balcony, cloistered into a space where a choir might have assembled during the celebration of Mass. The area allowed everyone to mingle without having to yell over the music or rub elbows with the uninvited.

"I recognize your face from somewhere, Michael. You are in politics perhaps? I am certain I have seen your face in the newspaper." Dimitri Ivanov smiled at his new acquaintance.

"It's possible. I am chief of the Criminal Division for the Southern District of New York. Speaking to the media about certain high-profile cases comes with the territory. I've grown used to it, but it's not my favorite part of the job."

"I suppose it is a good thing for a democracy that when the government exercises its coercive authority, it does so out in the open under the scrutiny of a free press. This is not the case in my home country, although there are some who are calling for more transparency in such things."

Michael observed the Russian gentleman, noting the subtle grace that belied his imposing stature. His companions, equally reserved, remained at his side, their silence echoing the unspoken authority of his presence. Michael acknowledged them with a casual nod, recognizing their deference and vigilance. Dimitri made introductions, and following a polite exchange, they smoothly transitioned to a vantage point in the far corner of the bar, where they could survey the reception with watchful eyes.

"Tell me, Mr. Ivanov, what do you do for work? Do you still live in Russia?"

"I am a Russian citizen but have lived away from my home country for the better part of my life. I have been privileged to do many things throughout my career. I am an art historian by education. After World War Two, I served as a consultant to various Western governments who were attempting to track down historical artifacts stolen by the Nazis. The Russians, French, and Germans all lost priceless artworks and they sought my help in recovering them. I did not fight on the Russian front during the war, but I did do my part to undermine the Nazi scourge while living in Spain, Italy, and North Africa. I am proud to say, many of the masterpieces I helped recover now hang in the Louvre, the Hermitage, the Metropolitan, and even the Smithsonian."

*Interesting*, Michael thought. *A Russian who does business openly in the free world, a connoisseur of art and history. Not your typical communist ideologue.*

"Fascinating. And now you're also a private collector? Does the current regime in Russia permit such things?" Michael tilted his head and focused on the older man's features.

"That, my friend, is a complicated question. Because of my years of service to the Russian government, I am permitted dual citizenship. I live my life outside the normal constraints of the Soviet apparatchik. In order to recover priceless Soviet treasures plundered by the Nazis, I required the ability to collaborate with many different government agencies throughout Europe and America. And yes, this comes with certain privileges. For example, I operate a private business, earn a good living, and collect inspiring art. Also, when time permits, I teach art history at the University of Madrid. Life has been good to me. Now, how about you, Michael Rose? What brings you to this gathering? Where is Rachel's husband? Does he not attend these events?"

Michael studied the Russian; it was obvious he had left out important details from his impressive resume.

"Under normal circumstances, Gabriel would have been here. However, Gabe and Rachel are in the middle of a construction project on their home. Not sure if you've ever had a large project go sideways with your contractor, but managing these things can often get complicated. It would have been impractical for him to leave home at the moment."

*A half-truth, but close enough*, Michael thought.

"So as a result, I have the honor of escorting the talented Rachel Rivers to this event tonight. I am not particularly well informed about art, but, as the saying goes, I know what I like. Tonight's performance was something completely unexpected. I don't think I exaggerate when I say it shifted my perception of how we are invariably connected to the past. I'm still reflecting on it."

"Well said, I agree with your observation Michael." Ivanov smiled approvingly. "Great art can change the way we experience the world around us. I think our love affair with art does not have to be based on anything other than what speaks to our hearts. True art, in whatever form it takes, is designed to communicate ideas and feelings which cannot be communicated in any other way. I understand Gabriel is a writer, a good one I'm told. He uses words to uncover truths others would keep hidden, no?"

*Curious why he keeps coming back to Gabriel.*

"Yes, his is a different form of artistry, but one that can also touch the lives of many people." Michael held Dimitri's eyes, both men taking the measure of the other, parsing the hidden meaning behind their words. "Gabriel and I have been friends since childhood. And while I do think he is an artist in his own right, I think he would describe himself differently."

"Oh? How so?"

"I think he sees himself more like a warrior. A crusader for truth and justice. Kind of like Superman in the comic books."

Both men laughed at the analogy. *He's probing for something and concealing his motivation for doing so. Still, an interesting guy*, Michael thought.

"Gabriel and I, we're cut from the same cloth," Michael offered. "I wield the law, and the courtroom is my forum, he wields the written word and public opinion is his forum. On occasion, we collaborate and use our respective platforms to shed light in dark places, exposing malfeasance that violates the law and offends our sense of justice."

As the rhetorical dance gained momentum Michael's trained eye focused on subtle cues. The hint of a condescending smirk, and cheeks flushed with signs of an excited pulse. The mention of Gabriel's absence and questions about public appearances tweaked Michael's defensive instincts.

*Could this be about the Courtland case? Or perhaps just idle chatter? Sometimes it's hard to switch off the circumspection that comes with the job,* Michael mused to himself.

"You teach art history at the University of Madrid. Why Madrid?"

"Ah, Michael, you think like a prosecutor." Ivanov chuckled, a glint of amusement in his eye. "You look for details that don't fit the narrative. Very good. I like the way your mind works. I am a romantic and an idealist and there is no better haven for romantics and idealists than Spain."

"Why is that?" Michael inquired.

"Because Spain is where idealists go to die and where romantics are reborn. I fought against the Fascists in the Spanish Civil War. When our side lost and my countrymen went home, I stayed. I fell in love. I taught art and had my heart broken. Then the Nazis invaded. I fought the Nazis in North Africa. I fell in love again, had my heart broken, and again I returned to Spain. I helped recover precious art, I helped save lives, and I taught others how to appreciate the beauty and vital knowledge embedded in the masterpieces of the past. Back in Spain, I fell in love once more. This time, I fell in love with an idea; the idea that a man can restore himself in the arms of a woman, that a man can be reborn in the presence of something beautiful. I fell in love with the idea that art and beauty and love and passion can transmute darkness into light; that these things can open a door to a place where transformation and redemption are possible, even for a man like me. Even for a man who has witnessed so much ugliness, so much pain and destruction that he could be forgiven for losing faith in all humanity. Spain provides a fertile ground for rebirth. The only other place that comes close is Cuba."

"You paint a compelling picture, Mr. Ivanov, and it makes me want to visit Spain. But tell me more about Cuba. Were you there on official government business?"

"Ah, Michael, it's clear why you rose to the top of your class. I worked there during the early days of Castro's regime as a private citizen. I became an informal liaison between Castro's government and his Russian benefactors. There were huge cultural barriers to overcome, but my years in Spain, my fluency in Spanish, and my affinity for the arts allowed me to help build bridges and foster positive communication between disparate parties."

"Interesting," Michael said.

"Yes it was, but it didn't last. I lost faith," Dimitri continued. "I lost faith in Castro's revolution when he started jailing and killing writers, painters and musicians, and when members of his party indulged in the very excesses they criticized in the previous regime."

"Were you there during the Cuban Missile Crisis?"

Dimitri paused and looked away. "Let's find an accommodating bartender. Looks like Rachel and Amanda might be lacking a cocktail as well. Perhaps we should inquire about additional refreshments."

Michael stood up slowly, pondering the abrupt shift in the conversation. His mind flooded with questions. Had he let his training as a prosecutor overcome his good manners? Dimitri Ivanov had lived an adventurous life—a World War II operative in Europe, a Russian with dual citizenship, and a fighter in the Spanish Civil War. Enough adventures to fill several lifetimes. Rachel was right, he was an interesting character, yet something about him was hard to pin down.

*The Soviet Union didn't grant its citizens free rein to travel the world and acquire wealth unless they were somehow useful to the government*, Michael thought. *A Russian agent? Maybe, but he didn't come across like a communist zealot. And why is he so interested in Rachel and Gabriel?*

*Try to relax and enjoy the evening*, he admonished himself. *Lots of expats fought in the Spanish Civil War. Hell, Hemingway lived in Spain, fought in the Spanish Civil War, and saw combat in World War Two, he also lived in Cuba, and he wasn't a Russian spy.*

Dimitri Ivanov made his way toward Rachel and Amanda while Michael looked over the crowd below and the few guests gathered in the VIP area. Dimitri's companions huddled in quiet conversation. Rachel and Amanda seemed to be entertaining themselves by pointing out some of the more outrageous outfits among the revelers. Wall Street types in padded-shouldered Armani were mixing it up with yuppies, artists, and undernourished trust fund babies in revealing dresses. Cocaine, Stolichnaya, and Dom Pérignon were making the night a wonderful thing.

Dallas, the guest of honor, stood apart, smiling, silently taking in her surroundings. Dimitri approached the young artist and kissed her on each cheek while holding her hands. He lifted Dallas's right hand and put it over his heart and whispered something in her ear. She glanced quickly at him and then looked away, her body becoming rigid. She looked troubled by the exchange. Dimitri let go of her hand, smiled, and turned toward Amanda and Rachel. As Dimitri walked away, Dallas gradually regained her Zen-like appearance.

After speaking briefly with Amanda and Rachel, Dimitri returned to where Michael was waiting. His two companions nearby nodded and resumed their positions at the corner of the bar.

"Tell me, Michael, are you a Scotch or bourbon man? In Spain, I drink mostly wine, but here I will enjoy a good Scotch from time to time. The ladies are drinking Cabernet, what can we get you?"

"I'll never say no to a good glass of Scotch," Michael replied, wondering what it was he said to Dallas that caused her to react the way she did.

"Excellent! I never trust a man who has not a single redeeming vice."

Michael met the Russian's gaze and chuckled at the Churchillian remark.

"The bartender says he can open a nice bottle of Glenfiddich for us. Let us send the ladies their wine and continue our conversation. I am interested in learning more about your work. You have been involved in some high-profile prosecutions and if I am not mistaken, you have a reputation for taking on the type of white-collar cases your predecessor often chose to ignore. I am not too familiar with New York politics, but I know enough to understand you don't seem beholden to the established order of things."

"How so?" Michael always preferred to ask a question than answer one and the Russian now appeared to dispense with any pretense surrounding his lack of familiarity with Michael's work.

"Well, I imagine in some ways New York is not much different from Madrid or Paris or Moscow. Most large cities organize around power, money, and commerce. There is a well-established hierarchy, sometimes transparent, but often opaque. Men with money and connections are accustomed to operating a certain way within that hierarchy. They are used to bending the rules and creating ordinances and laws to suit their purposes. Some of those laws are unwritten, but no less binding than what has been codified. In America, the Carnegies, Rockefellers, Mellons, Fords, and the Kennedys—all built wealth by creating their own rules. Now today, you may have new players in the arena, but the game is the same. You, my friend, seem to be willing to hold certain people accountable to the law in ways they are likely to resist. I have to say this takes, pardon my Spanish, *cojones*."

Dimitri laughed as he touched his glass to Michael's.

Michael smiled and pondered the motivation behind the question. "Yes, I suppose it does. But I believe healthy societies require a reliable legal framework. Without laws that are fair and evenly enforced, we risk sliding into either anarchy or fascism. I don't set out to make headlines or make a name for myself. I take on the hard cases because I believe this is the responsibility I've been entrusted with. It's my job."

Michael allowed the Scotch to warm the atmosphere around him, enjoying the thrust and parry of the conversation.

"Teddy Roosevelt is one of my heroes," Michael continued. "He wasn't exactly a bleeding-heart liberal. He came from the patrician class but he recognized the corrupting power of unchecked business interests. Roosevelt understood the need for the government to rein in the power and influence of the industrial oligarchs of the Gilded Age. He believed our democracy required a counterbalance to unchecked power. I think every generation faces similar challenges. So, do I have balls? Yeah, I think you need to in my line of work. But what drives me is faith, faith in our system of justice, faith in the promise of America."

"Well said, Michael." Dimitri released a genial laugh. "It appears I am not the only idealist drinking thirty-year-old single malt at this bar. And my guess is I am not the only romantic here who's had his heart broken." He glanced over toward Rachel.

Michael flinched as if Dimitri's prescient observation had poked an exposed wound.

"I think you should consider visiting Spain, the Mediterranean has healing powers for men like you and me. Michael, do you sometimes feel like you are swimming against the tide?"

"How so?"

"No matter how hard you try, no matter how often you succeed in putting away a corrupt official or a dirty businessman, another one moves in to take his place."

"That sounds more cynical than idealistic, Mr. Ivanov," Michael said with a smile.

"Call me Dimitri, please. And a cynic, my friend, is nothing more than an idealist with a broken heart."

"Are we speaking about love or politics, Dimitri?"

"It's all the same, Michael. Love of country, the love of a woman, the love of an idea, the faith we put in our fellow man; when we learn, as we all eventually do, that our faith has been betrayed, our hearts break. When we realize those who ask us to sacrifice everything for a higher purpose were themselves only serving a small and self-serving agenda—our hearts pay the price. When we learn that our most noble aspirations can easily be used against us, we inevitably have our hearts broken. This is how cynics are born."

Michael followed Ivanov's gaze again to Rachel, radiant and glowing, enjoying the unfolding spectacle below her. He noticed two men he had not seen before, approach the area where the women were gathered. As they addressed them Rachel's body language shifted into a protective posture, and she frowned. Amanda turned away, avoiding them entirely.

Dimitri turned to order another Scotch as Rachel made nervous eye contact. Sensing something was off, he rushed over to investigate.

"Hi, I'm Michael," he said fixing on the intruders.

"Well hello, Michael," one of the men replied, his voice tinged with sarcasm. "I'm Nicky." The man, outfitted entirely in black—black leather pants, a black leather blazer, a black shirt, and a skinny black tie—radiated sleaze. Michael wasn't sure if the unwelcome individual was trying to look like the caricature of a gangster or a rock star—either way, he took an immediate dislike to the man.

"Hey, Joey, say hi to Michael. I don't think he's from Jersey," he said laughing. "That's my brother Joey over there." He pointed to the other man who was also dressed like a wannabe gangster.

"Hi, Michael," Joey said, waving with mock enthusiasm.

"I was just reminiscing with Rachel. I'm sure we met before, but she doesn't remember me. We were at a party, I think it was Lou Reed's apartment."

"I don't think so. I'm pretty sure I would have remembered you," Rachel said with thinly disguised scorn.

"So, you've never been to a party at Lou Reed's place?"

"I have, but I'm sure I've never met you there."

"Oh come on, try to remember. You were pretty wasted. We were doing lines in the bathroom when to my pleasant surprise you offered to give me a blow job."

Michael felt a rush of adrenaline, his entire body coiling in preparation for confrontation. He became hyperaware of his surroundings, everything slowed down.

*Don't overreact. Just enough to shoo this guy away. Don't let this get out of hand*, a warning he had given himself many times before in his youth. A warning he rarely heeded.

"Okay, I think we're done here, you have to go now, leather boy. I'm asking you politely to leave now, but in a few seconds I won't be so polite, and I promise you this evening won't end well for you."

The man in the leather suit glanced at his brother and nodded.

"Leave? Rachel and I were just getting reacquainted. But okay, I can take a hint. Let me just say goodbye."

Michael turned to Dimitri to see if he was witnessing the tense exchange. His two guests, now flanking him, were also watching.

The man in the leather suit seized Rachel's hand, drawing her close in an unwelcome embrace. Before she could protest, his lips met hers in an unwanted kiss, his grip grinding her against his body. With a visible expression of revulsion, Rachel pushed away.

Michael hesitated for a fraction of a second, his disdain palpable as the man in the leather suit smirked and taunted, "Brings back memories, doesn't it?"

In a flash of fury, Michael yanked back the man's hair and delivered a swift blow to his collar bone, causing him to gasp and clutch at his neck in agony. As the confrontation escalated, Michael's rage triggered a trance of adrenaline-fueled violence. Bones cracked beneath his fists as he resisted leather boy's retaliation, the visceral sound mingling with his own searing pain, before a blow to the back of his head drove him sideways, causing his knees to buckle.

In the discordant chaos, Dimitri Ivanov's swift intervention blurred into the fray. One of his associates, brandishing a weapon, swiftly landed a blow on Michael's blind-side assailant and sent him reeling backward, crashing into a table laden with drinks. In a matter of seconds the incident was over—two assailant provocateurs lay on the floor neutralized, Rachel remained unharmed, while the other guests at the Limelight barely registered the altercation.

As the commotion subsided, Michael struggled to remain upright, his legs betraying him as dizziness threatened. He became dimly aware of someone steadying him, and the authoritative voice of Dimitri Ivanov penetrating the mental fog as he issued commands.

"Amanda, please get them all out of here NOW! Carlos will help Michael out. Use the private exit, speak to no one. We'll stay here and handle this. Michael was not here and this did not happen. Do you understand?"

"I do. Let's move." Amanda's voice cut through the tension, urgency propelling them toward the exit. Dallas moved in stunned passivity. Rachel looked over her shoulder at Michael and muttered, "What the fuck just happened?" Her expression was a frenzied oscillation of shock, dismay, and guilt. Michael, grappling with disorientation, stumbled forward with Carlos's support, his consciousness wavering.

A barrage of questions swirled inside Michael's battered brain, but the specific queries remained elusive, slipping away like ghosts in the night.

# 19

## DROWNING... IN A SEA OF LOVE

"Michael, I'm Dr. Rosenberg. I can confirm that you've experienced a concussion. I'd categorize it as moderate or stage two. Can you tell me where you are?"

Michael looked around. "I am at Gabriel and Rachel's New York apartment."

"Correct. Can you tell me what day it is?"

"It's Friday night or early Saturday morning."

"Correct. It's past midnight on Friday night. Michael, I believe the blow to your head will not result in any long-term damage, however, I would advise you to consult with your personal physician once you're feeling up to it. For now, look out for intense nausea, dizziness, headaches, or mental confusion. If any of these symptoms arise or persist, don't hesitate to head to the emergency room. Your doctor will want to rule out cerebral hemorrhaging. It would be unusual in this case but potentially dangerous if it occurs. I recommend icing the contusion, and please, listen closely, this is crucial, I need you to stay awake for the next five hours. It may sound counterintuitive, but we want your cognitive functions restored before you sleep. You can rest lying down, but avoid REM sleep for about five hours. Do you think you can manage that?"

"Yes I can, doctor, and thank you."

Michael unconsciously rubbed the swelling, while Rachel brought him a fresh bag of ice and gently placed it on his head.

"Gabriel wanted to drive down tonight, I told him it was unnecessary and that you would give him a call tomorrow."

"Good call," Michael agreed.

"Michael, I'm so sorry to have put you through this. I'm so embarrassed."

Michael held the bag against his throbbing head.

"Who were those assholes?"

"I don't have a clue. I've never seen either one of them before. They were so creepy, I would've remembered them."

"So, I'm guessing no oral sex in Lou Reed's bathroom?" Michael chuckled.

"Really, Michael?"

"I'm sorry, just trying to find humor amidst the insanity of it all. But you're right, it hurts when I laugh."

"Poor baby." Rachel removed her jacket, her curves no longer camouflaged by the silk blazer.

"I set you up in the master bedroom because the TV is in there. Maybe it'll help you stay awake."

Michael was still trying to piece everything together. *What were those guys doing there? Why did I leave the scene of an altercation?* He vaguely recalled administering several blows to a predatory stranger in a public place. The performance, the intriguing conversation with Dimitri Ivanov, were all a jumble of images in his foggy brain.

"It's okay, Rachel, I'm fine. I can stay awake for five hours on my own. I should head home."

"Absolutely not! You're not leaving here and you're going to do as I ask. This is non-negotiable. I'm partly responsible for that bump on your head and I am not going to be responsible for you slipping into a coma because I let you go home. What? Are you afraid I'm going to attack you in your sleep or something?"

"No," he said.

*If she only knew how desperately I want her to attack me.*

"No? Is that all you have to say? No, you're not afraid I'm going to attack you? Or no, you're not going to leave, or no, you're not going to stay? I need to know you're going to cooperate, Michael." Rachel sounded wound up and exhausted. Michael sat on the couch looking at her magnificent face. Once again, words failed him.

"Rachel," was all he could muster. But when he spoke her name, he gave away much more than he intended. Her name sounded like a prayer, a plea, a yearning to be unshackled from the prison he had built for himself. A sound so invested with everything he had buried deep inside, it shook him.

"You protected me, Michael." She leaned over gently, her fingers caressing the swollen bump on the back of his head. In that moment of shared trauma and sympathy, she found herself enveloped in his arms, their mutual comfort providing a brief respite from the turmoil around them. But then his lips found hers. It was unclear who surrendered to who. Tears rolled down her cheeks as they both succumbed to the magnetic force pulling at them, a force beyond the power of either to control. He was alive in a way he had never been alive before. She held him close. He kissed her, hesitating at first, but the fierce desire he had held back for so long would not be contained. He took his time, deliriously kissing every part of her face.

She stopped him and stood up with a look of steely determination.

*Is it over? I crossed a line. I should pull back, retreat, maintain composure, forget it ever happened; a moment of indiscretion driven by extraordinary circumstances.*

His heart raced while his mind and body attempted to resist irrepressible reactions. He remained silent, trying to think of something to say.

"Michael," she whispered, "you're a beautiful man. You think too much, and you feel too much. You and I are so alike, we experience things deeply, so deeply it hurts. It frightens us sometimes."

"Yes," he confessed, hours ago the admission unimaginable, now urgent and undeniable.

"I know you, Michael, I see you. There's a part of you, a deep yearning that you keep hidden from the world, but you can't hide it from me. It's okay, I've always known it."

Before he could form a cogent thought, before he could provide the right affirmation, she pulled away and slipped out of her black satin slacks.

Crouched upon him now, kissing him on the face and lips, she held his head in her hands as they both released years of unquenched desire and denial. No words were required, their movement was a resplendent symphony of yearning and release. She shuddered. Ecstasy comingled with grace, channeling a healing power, abundant and overflowing.

Part of him felt reborn, a new man. And yet, some haunted part of him recognized that the surreal moment of graceful bliss could not last.

*Be present!* he pleaded with himself. *Savor this. Just a little while longer.*

# 20

## TIES THAT BIND

"We wanted to make sure Michael is okay. How's he doing?" Dimitri Ivanov and Amanda Taylor stood inside the front door of Rachel's apartment. Michael greeted the visitors from the couch fully dressed again in his evening attire.

"I'm a little sore, but I'll survive," Michael said. "Thank you for your concern."

Ivanov nodded. "Listen, my friends, there's a place not far from here famous for their excellent Cuban coffee, and the owner is an old friend who will make us a breakfast fit for kings. Who is up for a short ride? I have a car waiting, we can all go."

"It's a lovely offer, Dimitri, but I need to shower and get a change of clothes before I even think about breakfast." He looked at Rachel and Amanda, the tension and magical encounter of the previous night still palpable in the atmosphere.

Amanda broke the awkward silence. "If you gentlemen don't mind, why don't you go ahead and grab some coffee and let me and Rachel regroup. We've all had a pretty challenging evening, and I, for one, need to catch my breath."

"Okay, I can take a hint." Michael turned to Rachel and she gave him a subtle nod. He fought off the distracting undercurrent of shared exhilaration coursing through him and struggled to form the cogent thoughts required for polite conversation. Dimitri's glance seemed to penetrate his unconscious thoughts.

"I'm not sure I'm ready for a full breakfast right now, Dimitri, but I would appreciate a ride home. I have questions about last night. I got knocked on the head pretty hard and the details are still a bit foggy."

"I am happy to drive you anywhere you want to go, Michael. I can answer your questions on the way."

* * *

Michael surveyed the landscape rushing by the window of the town car—mothers strolling babies, dogs ambling joyfully with their owners, and Saturday morning joggers dodging meandering pedestrians. His head ached. In one incredible night his entire world had been upended.

"It's unfortunate our evening ended so abruptly, Michael," Dimitri said, breaking the silence. "I enjoyed our conversation."

"As did I. Would you mind if we got our coffees to go? We can talk at my place if you have time. I'd welcome continuing our chat, but I really do need to get cleaned up."

"As you wish, Michael. I am at your disposal."

Michael lived in a spacious Upper West Side apartment close to Dimitri's breakfast spot. His well-appointed home included a study with floor-to-ceiling shelves overflowing with books and artifacts from his travels. The walls were cluttered with framed artwork. In a corner of his elegant living quarters, sitting apart on a black marble stand, was a stunning statue of a naked woman holding up a glass orb.

"You have excellent taste, Michael. It appears you have understated your appreciation of art."

"I didn't say I didn't appreciate art, I said it wasn't my area of expertise."

"I recognize some of Rachel's work."

"Gifts over the years." Michael looked in the fridge to see if there was anything to offer his guest. He found nothing but beer and a chilled bottle of champagne.

"And this beautiful sculpture?" Dimitri asked.

"Not Rachel's. I bought it in Paris. It reminded me of the Statue of Liberty, but without clothes." Michael smirked.

"Again, you are being modest. The work is based on a painting currently hanging in the Musée d'Orsay in Paris. The painter is Jules Lefebvre and the painting is entitled *La Vérité*, French for *The Truth*. But my guess is you already knew about Lefebvre. The resemblance to the Statue of Liberty is not coincidental. Mr. Lefebvre and Frédéric Bartholdi, the man who designed the statute in New York harbor, were contemporaries and collaborators. The woman assumes a classical pose often associated with the illuminating ideals of the Enlightenment. I believe our yearning for truth is embedded in our higher consciousness, Michael, only most men do not have the courage to seek it, nor the wisdom to recognize it when they've found it."

"Once again, sir, I can't tell if your words reflect the cynic or the romantic in you. But the statue is among my favorites. Will you allow me a moment to shower and we can take up where we left off." The old Russian perused Michael's impressive library while he showered and gathered his thoughts.

*I need to get my bearings here. My head hurts, my heart aches and my new friend has a way about him that's setting off flashing red lights.*

* * *

Michael joined Dimitri in the study holding a towel around his neck and pressing a bag of ice to his head.

"I have to ask you to help me fill in the parts of last night I'm having trouble recalling."

*I wonder what happened to the asshole I clobbered. Why didn't someone report it to the police? Why did Dimitri insist they leave the scene? And why did his companion brandish a gun? Can't make this sound like an interrogation,* Michael thought.

"I am happy to help put your mind at ease, but in this matter you need not have concerns."

*Why shouldn't my mind be at ease? I should have filed an assault report. I still have time to file one. Need more time, more info, got to figure out how these things are connected. Something doesn't add up here.*

As the mental fog gradually lifted, Michael considered how involvement in a public altercation, then subsequently leaving the scene, could adversely affect his public persona, and therefore his career. His job was to enforce the law, not to take it upon himself to administer punishment. Then there was Rachel, and the unknown aftereffects of the surreal entanglement following the confrontation. His inexplicable actions over the last day had the potential to undermine everything, everything that mattered to him, and everyone he cared about.

*So, yes, please,* Michael thought, *go ahead, try to put my mind at ease. It's possible what I did at the party might have been justifiable. But God knows I am guilty of something.* His head was throbbing and his once reliable moral compass was doing pirouettes. Putting his mind at ease was going to be a long-term undertaking. *Fuck! I need a drink.*

"Please. I'm interested in getting your perspective," Michael said.

"First let me say, Michael—and I have given this considerable thought—I believe the incident last night was not a random act. To my eyes, the confrontation was a deliberate provocation intended to embarrass you, and perhaps send a message."

*Sounds about right,* Michael thought to himself. "Interesting. Walk me through your analysis. Let's begin with what happened to the guy I hit."

"Okay, Michael, I am happy to tell you what you want to know. But I'm sure you are familiar with the concept of plausible deniability. If there is a larger play being made against you, there may be things here best left unexplored."

"I'm listening." *This guy definitely sounds more like an intelligence operative than a professor of art history.*

"I noticed the look on Rachel's face when those men approached her. She did not recognize them and appeared uncomfortable around them. We were in a private part of the venue, invited guests only, and those characters stood out as uninvited guests. Given the private nature of our gathering, I would have expected the two men to back off once the situation caught your attention. It was as if they were intentionally trying to provoke a confrontation. Also, all the focus was on Rachel. The other women present, Amanda and Dallas, were not approached. Rachel was singled out. Did it appear that way to you, Michael?"

"Yes, one of them pretended to know Rachel, while the other guy stood by."

"You said something to him, didn't you? Something indicating the gathering was a private one?"

"Yes, he made an offensive remark about Rachel, I asked him to leave. I may have implied an unfortunate end to his evening if he didn't comply."

"Did you threaten him?"

"No," he snapped. "Okay, I suppose my exact words could have been interpreted as a threat, although I believe I reacted with restraint. That asshole was way out of line. I distinctly remember trying to refrain from escalating the situation."

"Right after that, two things occurred simultaneously from my vantage point," Dimitri said. "The other man put down his beer and then walked behind the couch area and circled back, situating himself behind you. He then pulled something out of his pocket. What followed happened fast. Before any of us had a chance to react, the man you were talking to grabbed Rachel. You hesitated, then administered a blow to his throat that appeared to incapacitate him. You followed it with another to his jaw." Dimitri smiled. "Very impressive by the way. My guess is you've been in altercations before. But I digress. Before you could do any additional damage, you sustained a blow to the head and fell to your knees. Carlos, who is licensed to carry, pulled his weapon and took out the assailant. Don't worry, Michael, he didn't shoot him, he knocked him out with the butt of his gun using only the force required to neutralize him."

*There is it again*, thought Michael. *Who uses the word neutralize? Not common usage for an academic.*

Dimitri went on. "My other guest confirmed the man you hit was down and then checked to see how badly you were hurt. You are a tough individual, Michael, you attempted to stand up several times but your legs buckled. It is remarkable you maintained consciousness after the blow you suffered. You appeared dazed and disoriented."

Michael rubbed the large bump on the back of his head and studied the Russian's face and body language. His years as a prosecutor led him to another observation. *This man appears well acquainted with violent scenarios.*

"Out of concern for Rachel, Amanda, and Dallas, I wanted to ensure this was not part of a larger attack. As I said, things escalated fast. Dallas appeared to be in a state of shock, the other women were also stunned. The attack triggered my protective instincts. I instructed Carlos to escort all of you off the premises right away and I stayed behind to manage the situation." Dimitri Ivanov paused as if trying to determine how much more he should say.

"Now here, Michael, is where I am going to edit my narrative for your protection. Let me put your mind at ease, we did not use excessive force in dealing with the men in the altercation, but we did remove them from the scene. I informed the manager that our party had been disrupted by two individuals that had breached their security. He apologized profusely and suggested the incident should be handled discreetly by all parties. His desire to avoid negative publicity for his venue worked to our advantage. He didn't recognize you, though he knew Rachel and Amanda."

Michael's skull throbbed, and a confluence of images raced through his mind's eye: flashes of the performance, Rachel's naked body, a strange man in a black gangster suit falling backward in slow motion, the sharp blow to the head; the sequence jumbled in his awareness. *How did I let this happen?*

"So, what happened to the assailants?" Michael asked.

"We removed the two men from the premises and… well, we had a conversation with them. The one you hit looked like he might require medical attention. We offered to help of course, but we insisted they answer a few questions first. Their stories did not hold up. The one you injured said he and Rachel were old friends, the other man, the one who hit you, claimed self-defense. They had a lot of cash on them and within a short while they were asking me to make a phone call to their lawyer. Men like this don't typically have a lawyer's name at the ready, so out of curiosity I allowed it.

"I made the call and talked to their representative myself. Without admitting to a crime, the person on the other end implied these boys were hired labor, they botched whatever job they were sent to do and would have to answer to their employer for their sloppy work. We arrived at an acceptable understanding in this regard, no need to go into details here. I was assured this was a closed matter and that these men would never again be a threat to you or Rachel. The man with the broken jaw was given something for the pain and Carlos dropped them both off in Newark, New Jersey at an agreed-upon location. I phoned Amanda at about two a.m. and we said we'd check on you and Rachel in the morning. That's the extent of it, Michael. I imagine you are inclined to want more details concerning my conversation with the lawyer, but I think it's best we not go down that road. Last night you were assaulted in a club by two unknown individuals who were escorted off the premises while you were being attended to. Period, end of story."

"That's quite a story." Ivanov's assessment of events seemed plausible. There was a long list of people who would benefit from discrediting him and intimidating Gabriel, and he suspected Dimitri had a good idea who sent those men. *Message delivered and understood*, Michael thought. The altercation lined up with what happened to Gabriel the night of his going away party. Someone was keeping tabs and trying to discredit both men. The question was who? Either the Courtlands or people associated with them. His next move was unclear. Filing a police report would only create more questions. Questions that would speak to his judgment, his composure under fire, and his self-control. His thoughts remained scrambled. He decided he wouldn't press his guest further, at least not until he regained his bearings.

"Dimitri, I owe you a debt of gratitude. I'm grateful you stepped in to make sure no harm came to Rachel."

"I have protective instincts, Michael, just like you. I've grown to appreciate Rachel through her work and through our brief interactions. She is special and, just like you, I will not allow harm to come to her if it is in my power to prevent it. I believe you would have done the same in my position. It's unfortunate we were confronted with these unfortunate events, but perhaps, if one is looking for something positive to come out of all of this, the incident has brought us closer." Dimitri Ivanov studied Michael's face for a reaction. "We are getting to know each other better and one thing is clear to me, Michael, there is more to you than meets the eye."

"I was thinking the same about you, sir," Michael said. He placed his hand on Dimitri Ivanov's shoulder, and despite apprehensions, he found himself inexplicably drawn to the old Russian's charm.

* * *

"How's everyone doing today?" Gabriel asked. "Is Michael okay?"

Rachel paced the floor of their apartment, biting her fingernails and pulling on the phone cord as if she could somehow detach herself from her present reality.

"Truthfully, we're all a little shaken, Gabe. Michael took a pretty hard knock to the head but he's okay. The doctor who looked at him last night said he sustained a mild concussion. He recommended he stay awake for several hours to make sure the injury wasn't more serious than it appeared. He wanted to go home, but I insisted he stay here so I could make sure he followed the doctor's instructions."

"You did the right thing. Is he still there? Can I talk to him?"

"No, he went home. Amanda and a friend came over this morning, her friend gave him a ride. Try calling his apartment, although I wouldn't be surprised if he's sleeping. He didn't get much sleep last night. He looked like shit this morning."

Rachel tried to not think about why Michael didn't get much sleep. Not the time to dwell on it. Last night's events arrived like a cyclone shattering the foundations of her world. Still trying to gather the broken pieces, she didn't have the wherewithal to face Gabriel's questions right now; fortunately, she wouldn't have to.

"Okay, I'll try reaching him. I want to make sure he's okay. We've had some strange encounters since the Courtland story broke, wonder if he thinks these incidents are related?"

"He didn't mention anything."

"He wouldn't have, he wouldn't want to alarm you. I shouldn't have even brought it up. Listen, honey, something happened yesterday I need to talk to you about. I didn't want to bother you with it yesterday before your event and now, given the circumstances, I realize it's not the ideal time to have this conversation with you, but it can't wait."

"C'mon, Gabe, this is all very cryptic, please just spit it out." The irony of Gabriel struggling to be forthcoming only amplified her own guilt and it manifested as irritation.

"You remember I reached out to your dad about six months ago?"

"How would I not remember?" Rachel snipped. "I also remember I told you not to expect a response, yet you insisted."

Gabriel paused, her irritation evident. Rachel tried to modulate the tension in her voice, realizing the stress she was feeling had little to do with what Gabe was trying to say.

"Well, what I didn't tell you was that I had reached out to him multiple times. I didn't want you to be hurt by his lack of response, which is why I never mentioned it."

"Okay." Rachel fell silent.

"Are you angry with me for reaching out again?"

"Not angry, Gabriel, as I've said before, I believe your heart is in the right place. But when it comes to my father, I'm used to disappointment. We've barely spoken, only once or twice since college."

"I know, I know. But I just felt it was worth the extra effort, given he's the only family we have left."

"Okay, so I'm guessing something's up and it's urgent."

"Yes. He called, or rather, his wife called. He's dealing with some serious health issues. Part of the reason he didn't respond is because he didn't want to be a burden."

"Or so he says." Rachel didn't try to hide the bitterness in her voice. As Gabriel ventured into a delicate minefield, she noted his attempt to do so cautiously, but with his typical determination.

"He has lymphoma and has been receiving treatment at UVM. His wife said he has been asking about you. She said he's exhibiting symptoms of dementia. The doctors say his fragile mental state is most likely a side effect of the drugs he is receiving."

"Okay, not really sure what to do with that right now." Her voice crackled with emotion; she found herself woefully unprepared to confront the possibility of her father's death, an unwelcome proposition on any day, unfathomable in her present state of mind.

"Helen, his wife, explained how the drugs cause your dad to ramble on about many things, chemically induced delusions mixed in with familiar things. She said he keeps talking about you and your mother and why he had to leave you behind. She wants to take care of him at home but the hospital is hesitant to release him. They think they will need professional assistance if his dementia progresses. She asked if I would come see him. Rachel, I want to go see your dad, I think it's the right thing to do. She wants me to go today."

Silence. Rachel leaned against the wall, clutching the receiver with both hands away from her face. The emotional roller coaster she was on could careen out of control at any moment.

"Rachel, are you there?"

"I'm here. Are you asking my permission or telling me that you're going?"

"Not sure, more the latter I think. Unless you feel strongly I shouldn't go."

"I love you, Gabriel, but I have so many mixed emotions around my father, I'm not sure I can make a clear-headed decision, not right now. If you think it's the right thing to do, then go. But I'm planning on staying in New York for a few more days, maybe longer. Is this something you can handle on your own?"

"Yes, absolutely," he insisted.

It had been nearly a year since they'd relocated to Vermont, and parts of her still missed the fast-paced life of Manhattan. Beyond the longing for the city and the lingering effects of the assault, there were other pressing reasons to extend her stay. Business matters demanded her attention, and she needed time to process the tumultuous events involving Michael. Muddled reasoning turned her thoughts to sludge, she felt trapped in a dark place, and lacked the strength to confront the disconcerting emotions surrounding her father. If Gabe intended to tackle this situation, he would have to do so alone.

"I want to handle this," he insisted. "Your dad needs help, and it might offer a chance to reconnect, to mend fences between you and him. I understand why you can't join me. I'll keep you updated, and we can decide together what's best for all of us later."

"Okay, Gabe. That sounds like a reasonable plan. I love you."

"I love you too, baby. I'll check on Michael at home now and head to the hospital in about an hour."

Rachel ended the call and stared at the couch where she and Michael had surrendered to the pent-up longing that seized them just hours earlier. The echoes of their encounter lingered in a disorienting pall.

The connective tissue holding her world together seemed to be torn asunder. Michael's magnetic pull and the resurfacing of unsettled issues produced a volatile concoction of desire, shame, and disappointment that threatened to shatter her carefully constructed life.

*This needs to be contained. But how?*

# 21

## IN THE NAME OF THE FATHER

---

### UNIVERSITY OF VERMONT MEDICAL CENTER - OCTOBER 1987

---

"Who are you?" Tony snapped, his irritation evident as he fidgeted uncomfortably on the sticky patent leather hospital chair, grappling with the wires and tubes connecting him to machines monitoring his vital signs.

"I'm Gabriel Hernandez," came the hesitant reply. "I'm Rachel's… husband, meaning boyfriend." *Shit*, he thought. *Not a good start.*

"Boyfriend? Husband? Which is it?" Tony said, not bothering to hide his impatience.

Gabriel leaned in, lowering his voice in an attempt to clarify his initial response. "Rachel and I aren't officially married, but I told the nurse I was your son-in-law. It was the only way they'd let me in after visiting hours."

"Okay, Gabriel, 'boy husband.' What brings you here?"

"Helen suggested we check in. We've been trying to connect with you for months. We didn't know you were ill."

"Where's my daughter?"

Gabriel attempted to maintain composure. Even in his weakened state, battling cancer, Tony De Castro exuded an air of intimidating authority that demanded respect.

"Rachel is attending to urgent business in New York. She thought it would be helpful for me to check in, introduce myself and find out if there was anything we could do."

Gabriel could feel Tony's dark eyes penetrating his polite façade, sizing him up, determining his worth. With his Spanish accent, thick-rimmed glasses and thinning white hair, he remained a formidable presence. After what seemed like a very long time, Tony broke the silence. His expression softened, and the lines on his forehead smoothed out a little.

"Okay, nice to meet you, Gabriel." He extended his hand and gave Gabriel a firm handshake. "I didn't know Rachel was in a serious relationship, but in truth, there is much about my daughter I am unaware of. Nobody's fault but mine I suppose. Let me ask you, son, tell me again your last name. Where are your people from?"

"My last name is Hernandez, Mom and Dad were born in Puerto Rico; they came to New York when they were very young. I was born in Riverdale, in New York City."

"So, you are Boricua?"

"Yes, that's my ancestry."

"Ancestry? And Riverdale, that's the Bronx isn't it?"

"Yes, it is. But I consider myself a mix of experiences and influences not defined solely by my ethnicity or where I grew up. I try to avoid labels and tribal stereotypes." Accustomed to people making assumptions about him because of his looks or his heritage or the neighborhood he grew up in, Gabriel defaulted to his standard defensive response when someone inquired about his background. Rachel's father didn't seem impressed.

"My parents, like many Puerto Ricans, were a blend of diverse cultural influences, European, American, and Latin American. Puerto Rican yes, but also New Yorkers in every sense of the word. They came to New York long before I came into the world and they adapted and thrived in New York long before people from Puerto Rico did so in large numbers. I lost both my parents in a car accident at a young age. So, I am most certainly Puerto Rican, but where my people are from doesn't actually tell you much about me."

"I see," Tony said, his voice tinged with condescension.

Tony stared at him as if he were an errant student who failed to complete an important assignment. "That's an interesting little speech. I understand how it might be useful in some situations. However, allow me to suggest some things to you about your heritage. How old are you?"

"Thirty-seven," Gabriel answered.

*Nothing wrong with his cognitive ability as far as I can tell. Heck, the ornery old Cuban seems sharp as hell.*

"I'm sorry you lost your parents at a young age, my condolences," Tony said. "But I have to tell you, and maybe this is something you would have understood by now if they were still alive—this thing about your background, your particular Latin heritage, this is more than a geographic or a tribal stereotype as you called it."

"Yes, I agree," Gabriel said.

"Listen, son. Our heritage—and I say 'our' because I'm Cuban, and while I have called many places home in my long years, we share an inescapable history. We are bound by our cultural DNA. Within us is the blood of conquerors and slaves; *conquistadores* and a people who, against all odds, would not allow themselves to be exterminated. Our ancestors did more than survive, they thrived, and managed to influence the politics and cultures of the greatest colonial powers on earth. You and I share this, it flows in our veins, it is an essential part of our cultural, spiritual, and intellectual grounding. It informs how we think, and how we feel. It is an inexorable part of who we are."

"I do understand," Gabriel said, attempting to interject a thought.

"You can blend in all you want, and no doubt assimilation is in part how you survive, thrive, and conquer; but your core, your Latin blood, your Puerto Rican DNA will express itself in ways that define the most important parts of you, whether you're aware of it or not. It's ancestral and inevitable. Your love of music, literature, food, dance and sex; all of it is part of your inheritance. Your intellect—and if you are with my daughter, I must assume you have demonstrated above average intellectual capacity—your instincts and intuition, the things that bring you success and joy, the things that make your heart sing, they are embedded in your blood. I've just met you and I bet I understand more about what makes you tick than most of your Anglo friends."

Tony grinned, the satisfied, patronizing smile of a professor who just achieved an important breakthrough with a stubborn student. In less than fifteen minutes Tony was breaking Gabriel down and forcing him to reflect on his own identity. Her father was behaving like a man unwilling to waste precious time with niceties. Gabriel wondered if he was about to launch into another long lecture or if he'd be able to get a word in edgewise. He remembered how Rachel complained about her father's pedantic nature. Despite the pushback, or perhaps because of it, Gabriel found himself enjoying Tony's company.

With a newfound connection established, they engaged in small talk as nurses came in and out of the hospital room checking Tony's vitals and administering medication. Gabriel told him about his work as an investigative reporter and the desire to build a new life in Vermont. Tony shared intriguing details about Rachel's childhood in Miami, and her early life in Cuba.

Sitting side by side in the sticky blue patent leather hospital chairs, the pungent aroma of antiseptic cleaner filling the air, Rachel, while not physically present in the room, remained present all the same. She was the thread that connected the two men as an unspoken yet undeniable certainty began to coalesce between them. A bond formed from an implicit understanding that either man would, without hesitation, sacrifice everything to protect her.

Suddenly, Tony fell silent. He closed his eyes and began to speak in barely perceptible tones.

"I couldn't say no," he murmured, barely audible. "Too much at stake. The only way to ensure their safety was to leave."

Gabriel's eyes fixed on Tony as he shifted in his chair, restless and agitated.

Having surreptitiously entered the room during their conversation, Helen now quietly interrupted and signaled for Gabriel to follow her to the corridor outside. Her emerald green eyes shone like beacons against her olive skin, her weathered face radiating wisdom and compassion. She was small in stature but moved and spoke with intense confidence and determination.

"I'm so grateful you came, Gabriel. I know Rachel and her father have been estranged and I appreciate your desire to repair what's been broken. Family history can be a difficult thing for outsiders like us to navigate. He's a decent man with a complicated past." Helen's Israeli intonations lent her words a unique cadence, a blend of South African and Australian influences.

"I agree family history can be complicated," Gabe said. "It's difficult for me to fully grasp the nature of the issues between them because Rachel doesn't like talking about her father. Can you explain what just happened in there? He seemed so sharp at first, we had a good conversation. But then he seemed to slip away, speaking in hushed tones, as if he were in the middle of an important conversation. I assume the shift is due to the medication and intermittent dementia you told me about?"

"Yes. He slips in and out of time consciousness. Lucidly in the present in one moment, and then he shifts to some other point in time. The doctors say he could be reliving an old trauma or creating a subliminal fantasy. The treatments take a toll on him, but he is a tough old man. I believe he will recover, at least that's what I tell myself. I also think there may be something else causing him to disappear into delirium, regrets that relentlessly push to the forefront of his awareness as he confronts his own mortality."

"You said on the phone he'd been asking for Rachel?"

"Oh Gabriel, losing contact with his daughter has been the biggest regret of his life; it's like a tormenting wound he's been unable to heal. Like you, I'm not privy to the full story of their estrangement. I do know it was a profound loss, a loss he believes he is helpless to correct." Helen's voice was tinged with sympathy.

"And these rantings, do you believe they're history or fantasy?"

"I'm not sure. He's lived an interesting life. I met Tony in Israel. I lost my first husband while he was on a mission with Tony. He was a retired IDF officer who did contract work, private security, things of that nature. Tony and Aaron worked on an assignment together in Paris. I was told my husband fell protecting a high-profile client. The details remain classified and Tony doesn't like speaking about the particulars. I learned not to ask Aaron questions, I knew there were details he couldn't share with me. I understood the need for secrecy. I have some inkling of how the business they were in works. Aaron was an honorable man. Tony was devastated by his death. I see it in his face every time I mention Aaron's name. A painful memory for both of us. There are events from that time I too prefer to keep buried. Too painful. Some things you never quite recover from. I will not say more about this."

As Helen spoke her shoulders bent forward as if the memories she referred to added to the burden she was already carrying.

"Tony came to Israel to deliver the news of Aaron's loss in person. He sat Shiva with us, and when he learned of the work my husband and I did assisting Palestinian families, he offered to help. He returned to Israel often, and eventually made it his home. He helped us find homes and jobs for displaced Palestinian families; he helped us lobby the Israeli government for aid. Tony protected us from the settlers and the zealots who resented the work we did.

"Some considered it blasphemy that we, as Jews, would dedicate ourselves to helping Palestinians. We did what we did out of a commitment to justice. We believed, given our history, Israelis have an obligation to stand for justice for all people. We didn't succumb to the idea that because Jews suffered atrocities, we were justified in victimizing the Palestinian families occupying land we believe is ours by birthright. On the contrary, Aaron understood firsthand the malignancy of unanswered injustice.

"Tony worked hard to fill the void left by Aaron's death. Shared grief, kindness and compassion gave way to a deeper connection between us."

"Are you saying when he slips in and out of time, he believes he is back in Israel or some other time and place?"

"Yes. But as I've said, I never pushed him to share details about his past. I understand the burden of such things, the burden of keeping secrets and of dwelling too long in regret."

"How do you manage it? Do you go along with whatever time and place he is visiting or do you try to bring him back to the present?"

"It depends. Sometimes he gets so anxious. At times very sad. Sometimes his recollections awaken in him a fire that seems to reanimate him. So, I let him go on. You'll understand better if you decide to spend more time with him. His mind is still sharp. You should know his memories surrounding Rachel are painful. Tony believed he had to leave Rachel and her mother in order to protect them. A high price for any father to have to pay, it hurts him to speak of it."

A cloud seemed to pass over Helen's features, the light in her green eyes dimmed. The sadness and determination in her face triggered memories of Gabriel's own mother, of her fiery will and empathetic heart.

He still believed Rachel needed to find a way to repair her relationship with her father, convinced, now more than ever, it was the only way for her to free herself from her toxic past.

He had just met Tony and Helen, yet something about their story, intriguing and irresistible, lured him into their orbit.

# 22

## UNPACKING THE BAGGAGE

NEW YORK CITY - OCTOBER 1987

"Wait, let me try to wrap my head around this, because I don't think I heard you correctly. I haven't spoken to my father in over a decade and you're telling me you've invited him to live with us?"

*This can't be happening. Not now.*

Gabriel seemed to be insisting on continuing his efforts to repair a relationship with a father she had given up on long ago. Rachel's knees weakened and she sank into a nearby chair, trying to steady herself as she wrestled with the surreal scenario Gabe was attempting to put forward.

"I can't imagine this was his idea," she said, her fingers anxiously twisting the receiver's cord.

"It's not his idea. He doesn't even know we're considering the invitation."

"Then why are we considering it? Why, Gabriel?"

"Rachel, please, I know this is a lot to process. Just take a deep breath and hear me out. I promise however we move forward, we move forward together. Okay?"

"I'm listening," she said, a sharp pang of guilt gnawing at her insides.

"Your dad has cancer and the prognosis isn't good. The doctors believe they can stabilize him for now, but if he doesn't respond to this next round of chemo, any further treatment is likely to do more damage than the disease. He's also suffering from a form of dementia, which might be temporary. It's intermittent, probably brought on by the drugs."

"Don't think I'm unsympathetic, Gabriel, but I let go of my father years ago and even under normal circumstances this would be enormously intrusive, for all of us."

"I agree, honey, it's a challenging proposition. But consider this. I believe we can stabilize him and arrange for either home care or placement in a facility that can tend to him in what may be his final months. There's a brief window where we can assist in this transition, provide help, and while he's still coherent, maybe fix what is broken between you two. Helen mentioned he's filled with regret when he drifts into the past, particularly regarding how he treated you and your mother. I think there are some powerful unresolved issues he needs to confront before it's too late." He sighed. "I don't know, Rachel. We have this opportunity to do something worthy, something that might provide you both with a chance to repair, to find forgiveness and closure. But the window to act on this is very narrow. We don't have the luxury of time."

Gabriel fell silent allowing Rachel a moment to catch her breath and deal with her instinctive resistance to anything that had to do with her father. Some part of her, a part buried underneath years of animosity, was still capable of feeling compassion for a dying man.

"Couldn't we offer to help without taking them into our home?"

"We could, and frankly it might be our only option. Your dad's a proud man. But if he's willing, I think he'd make an interesting houseguest for a short while. We have the space, and once he is stabilized, we can help transition him back home or to the right facility. I think there's a lot more to your dad than we know. He's lived a fascinating life. I'm curious about him, I'd like to get to know him better myself."

"Okay. I have serious concerns but I'm going to trust your judgment here. I do have two conditions though." The irony of Gabriel trying to convince her to allow her father to move into their home had not escaped Rachel.

"Okay, shoot."

"We don't house them in the studio," Rachel insisted.

"No problem, the second-floor guest suite will work fine. What's the other condition?"

"I need to stay in New York for a few more days, maybe longer."

"Okay. What's going on?"

"Honestly, Gabe, I need more time to process all of this. I realize there's baggage associated with it that I need to unpack and come to terms with. Part of me thinks you're right and it may be time to address these things, but I need more time to wrap my head around it. I also have unfinished business with Amanda and this client of hers that has been so supportive. I think it would be wise to leave things on a better note than we did after the performance. This client is facilitating a lot of the success we're having."

"Okay, I understand, makes sense, no problem. Take your time with this, except now I have a condition I'd like you to consider."

"Okay, what might that be?"

"I think we should get married. Will you marry me, Rachel?"

"What the fuck, Gabriel?"

"'What the fuck, Gabriel?' That's your answer?" Gabriel replied, his tone a mix of hurt and incredulity.

"Sorry, I didn't mean it that way. But what the fuck! We are about to cross an emotional minefield, and *this* is when you want to talk about a wedding? Now, on the phone?"

"I'm sorry, it just came to me. I feel an urgency I can't really explain. I love you and I want to be married to you and I want to do it while your dad is still alive. Meeting him, being alone in this house, being apart from you, all of it has helped me see and feel things clearly. I want to be connected to you for the rest of my life. I never thought we needed the trappings of a traditional marriage, but I'm thinking differently now. I love you, and I want you to be my wife and I want to be your husband, and I want to do it as soon as possible."

Gabriel's proposal hovered, a baring of the soul, vulnerable and urgent, in search of a validating response. She sensed the entire impulse to pose the question caught him off guard as much as it did her.

Her mind raced, her thoughts a mélange of conflicted feelings.

*How can I agree to marry Gabriel so soon after what happened with Michael? How would Michael react? Am I ready to spend the rest of my life with this man?*

As she grappled with myriad scenarios, an epiphany manifested, something unequivocal and transformative. The debate became irrelevant; she recognized the inextricable bond between them. That question had been settled long ago. Whatever transient alchemy took hold with Michael the night of the assault had to be compartmentalized and set aside. She had been seeking clarity and Gabriel's proposal provided it. Every thread of her destiny now converged into alignment. She would become Gabriel's wife.

"I love you, Gabriel, and of course, I will marry you, whenever and however you choose." Her voice cracked, her eyes welled up and the tears flowed freely.

"I am so grateful to have you in my life, Rachel. I think part of why I seem so obsessed with your dad is because he brought you into this world. I'm part of you and you're part of me. We'll figure out the rest as we move through this together. Do what you have to do in New York and I'll keep you posted on things as they develop here. I love you, Rachel."

"I love you too, Gabriel," she said warmly.

The intoxicating rush of emotion did not last as a new tidal wave of disruption seemed to loom over her, a force she could either ride or succumb to. But one truth, one she had been slow to embrace, emerged with unmistakable certainty: the era of burying the past had come to an end.

It was time to move forward, and wherever that path may lead, she would never again be traveling it alone.

# 23

## STARTING OVER

"Where's Helen?"

"She needed a break. I asked her if we could hang out alone for a little while."

"So, we're hanging out?" Tony asked. Wide grin and eyes twinkling. "Then let's get the hell out of here, *hombre.*"

"I don't think your doctors would appreciate my moving you at the moment. Anyway, I'm pretty sure I couldn't untangle you from all the machinery you're plugged into without killing you. Mind if we just hang out here?"

"Sure, what choice do I have?" Tony sank back into his chair, shoulders drooping slightly.

"Listen, Tony, I have to ask you a serious question."

"Okay, *dale.*"

"I know you haven't seen Rachel in many years and you share a complicated history. But I think... I feel it's important to... What I'm trying to say is..." Once again, Gabriel found himself fumbling for words in Tony's presence.

"What *are* you trying to say? I thought we were going to hang out. Do you have any dominoes?"

"Dominoes? Like pizza?"

"Not pizza, *pendejo*. Actual dominoes, like the game. Didn't your father teach you how to play dominoes?"

"Oh dominoes, yeah he taught me. Yeah, I can get some. But wait, let me… Tony, I want to ask you for permission to marry your daughter."

"My permission?" Tony asked, pausing to consider the nature of the question.

"Yes, ask your permission for your daughter's hand in marriage," Gabriel repeated.

"Well, you are living together aren't you?" Tony said, adopting a paternal tone.

"Yes, we are."

"You have the means to support her, don't you?"

"Yes, I do."

"Then you don't really need my permission now do you?"

Tony held Gabriel's gaze, and seemed to want to weigh his next words carefully. Gabriel opened and closed his mouth silently, allowing Tony the space to gather his thoughts.

"I do appreciate the gesture," Tony said. "You've come to me like a man who honors our culture and traditions. This is what an honorable man does. A man who understands the meaning of respect. A man who wishes to be worthy of marrying the person I treasure most in this world. I do not take this lightly."

In the quiet moment that followed, Gabriel felt the earnestness of Tony's words settle around them like an invisible mantle. It wasn't just about permission; it was a validation of shared values and the profound responsibility that came with loving and caring for those we treasure. Tony's blessing wasn't just a formality; it was the recognition of a continuum that began with his ancestors, threading through him and binding future generations to all those who came before.

"Of course you may have what blessings are mine to give, son. I grant you my permission by whatever claim I may have to such authority. And I trust you to do everything within your power to love and protect her, with your life if necessary, for the rest of your days.

"I promise you, sir, I will always care for her. I will do everything in my power to care for and protect your daughter, and would willingly exchange my life for hers should I be called to do so."

"I believe you, son, and I'm grateful you took the time to ask me. Now let's play some dominoes. I think Helen has a set somewhere in here." Tony pointed to a stack of books and personal things at the other end of the hospital room.

Neither man acknowledged the tears descending down the careworn face of a father who had sacrificed everything for the daughter he treasured.

* * *

*Offices of the United States District Attorney,*
*Southern District of New York – October 1987*

Rachel stepped into Michael's office clad in a charcoal-gray suit, its belted jacket and slightly oversized slacks infused with an air of professional reserve. Despite the conservative attire, no one would ever confuse Rachel with a typical assistant United States attorney. She exuded an innate allure that defied any attempt to blend into the background. Michael, highly attuned to her sublime presence, detected an unmistakable shift in their dynamic as she entered.

"Thank you for making the time, Michael," she began, her voice a little too formal. "I know this is sudden, but I had to talk to you. How are you feeling?"

Michael offered a faint smile. "My head feels fine, the rest of me, well that remains to be seen."

"I know exactly what you mean. Can we talk openly here?"

"Yes, of course." Michael motioned to the worn leather couch across from his desk. Their brief exchange triggered an old memory, one that brought back a deep sense of foreboding. It was the same feeling he had when two police officers approached Gabriel's house on the day of the accident. He and Gabriel were chatting about what it might be like if they were to live on the same college campus. They had just come inside seeking shelter from the scorching summer heat, but as the police officers approached the front door, a gust of cold air seemed to rush through the house. He never forgot how that chill wind had shaken him to his core.

As they settled into their seats, Rachel's demeanor softened. "Can we be candid with each other?"

A shiver seized him. "Absolutely." His clipped reply masked a wave of trepidation.

Without preamble, Rachel delved into the heart of the matter. "We shared something special the other night, Michael. I won't trivialize it as a moment of weakness or some other clichéd excuse, but you know, neither of us can ignore what's at stake here." As she spoke she fidgeted with a charm bracelet on her wrist, a multi-colored glass thing that looked as if it had been made by a child.

Something inside him resented her businesslike tone. His stomach tightened.

"Here's the thing." Rachel stopped fidgeting. "You and I are at a crossroads. We can acknowledge the experience for what it was, we can appreciate it as the expression of something powerful between us. But at the same time, we have to recognize the damage we might do if we allow what happened, however beautiful, to shatter our relationship with Gabriel."

She hesitated, her face flushed, but determined. Michael felt his heartbeat accelerating, his body coiled up and tense. He scrutinized her in guarded silence.

"If you and I were to attempt to build a future together by destroying such a vital part of our past, we'd risk losing who we are. We'd risk losing everything. We'd be venturing into uncharted territory detached from our sense of true north. Gabriel is my true north, and I know he's yours too."

The weight of Rachel's cold logic compounded the pressure in his chest, each word a blow to the gut, stealing the air from his lungs. Her words exposed the void that surrounded him, obliterating the delusion that hope could triumph over reality. Her affirmation exiled him to a future without her, where each breath would be tainted by her absence. In that moment he made himself a solemn promise—he would never again allow a woman to hold such power over him.

"I love you, Michael, and I want you in my life, but surrendering to the idea we could somehow… It would break us. I'm sure of it."

The lips that once captivated him were moving, but he no longer focused on the words coming out of them. Her stiff bearing suggested determination, but her eyes, yes he could see it, still there, pain, vulnerability. Doubt.

"We have to find a way to reconcile the love we share for each other with the love we share for Gabriel."

*Gabriel. He doesn't deserve this. What have I done?* Avoiding her eyes he fastened his gaze upon the wall clock behind her. The second hand was chronicling his slow descent, mocking the hours wasted reaching for something beyond his grasp, while something seemed to take hold in his chest.

"We have to find a way to channel this without destroying the bond between the three of us." She said, nervously tugging at the elastic charm bracelet on her wrist.

*Her eyes are welling up. It's not all business is it? I'm not just another fanboy that can be easily dismissed.*

Michael wanted to fight for her. But fight who? Gabriel? His own conscience? He struggled to remain calm, trying to summon the strength to do the right thing. But he also wanted to tell her she was wrong, explain, forcefully if need be, that some part of him knew with absolute certainty they belonged together. Bottled-up words lodged in his throat, not unlike the undelivered letter she had inspired him to write when they first met.

But still he said nothing.

"Am I crazy, Michael? Why are you looking at me like that? I feel like you think I'm crazy, not making sense. Am I making sense, Michael? For God's sake say something!"

A forced smile stretched across his face, and he ached to contrive a mitigating argument, to produce some combination of words that might make a difference.

"There's not much for me to say. Is there? You make perfect sense. But love is a form of madness isn't it? How can we manage to be so clinical when we are in the grip of madness?"

Tears rolled down Rachel's face as she shook her head helplessly.

"I don't like this, Rachel! I don't like what I'm feeling. It's cold," he blurted out suddenly. Then paused to recalibrate his thoughts. "But," he said, grinding out the syllables, "I don't disagree with you. Beginning a life together by betraying someone we care about…" Michael took a deep breath and looked away. "I just don't see how…" His voice faltered, while the thing in his chest, dense and unyielding, hardened its grip.

"So I'm not crazy?"

"No you're not crazy, Rachel. Any more than any of us is. We can't undo what we've done. We can't not feel what we feel. It's not crazy to recognize the price of building a future on destruction and betrayal, but it still sucks. I get it, we have to find a way through this, and however reluctant I may be to accept it, I do see why we have to keep this private between you and me."

Rachel wiped at the tears and struggled to regain her composure. "You're a beautiful man, Michael, we're lucky to have you in our lives. I'm blessed to have you in my life."

"I just want you to be happy, Rachel. Safe and happy." The utterance seemed to come from some other person, someone far more in control of his emotions than Michael felt at that moment. But the words rang true, and there was something liberating in saying them out loud. The ultimate test of his fidelity, fidelity to love and friendship, had to be the willingness to let go of the woman he loved, so that she might live a happy life—however painful that sacrifice might be.

"There is one more thing you should know, and I feel I need to be the one to tell you."

"One more thing?" he asked incredulously. "Can't this wait, Rachel? Jesus, can't we just take a minute to…"

"I'm sorry, Michael, it can't wait. Gabe will tell you himself soon enough, but I think it should come from me, considering all we've been through. Gabe wants us to tie the knot, soon. We all knew this day would come, but he's adamant about doing this while my father is still alive, and we have no idea how much time he has left."

Strange, but this time Rachel's reveal didn't feel like another blow to the gut. A numbness settled over him, a realization that he wasn't in control, he never had been. The die had been cast, it was out of his hands. Seared by the flame he carried for Rachel, he could burn no more. Maybe the ache he felt in her presence would fade in time, maybe not, but he doubled down on his promise to himself. No woman would ever again hold such power over him. He would burn no more.

"Congratulations," he said, swallowing hard. "Gabriel is a good man." He spoke calmly, choking down the tumult within. "We share something special you and I, we both love a good and decent man. Please know, no matter what, I will always treasure the friendship we share."

They sat for what seemed like a very long time, both drained and unwilling to pick at the raw, pernicious wounds they had opened. Rachel put away her tissues and began counting the charms on her bracelet as if they were prayer beads. Michael watched in silence as the clock's second hand ticked off a countdown to their inevitable parting.

Suddenly his intercom buzzed, slicing through the awkward silence. It was his assistant, Andrea. "Sorry to interrupt, Michael, but Audrey says she has something to show you, says it's urgent. Do you have a minute for her?" Andrea Gold was much more than an executive gatekeeper, she was his guardian and protector. Michael knew she wouldn't have interrupted him unless she believed the matter warranted immediate attention.

"Give me a minute, I'm just wrapping up here."

Rachel examined her puffy eyes in a compact mirror and reached for her oversized sunglasses. "It's okay, Michael," she said, reverting to an overly formal tone, "I've already taken up too much of your time. Are we good?"

"Yes, we're good, or will be soon enough. We'll all soldier on."

"Yes we will. By the way, Amanda says hello, she feels terrible about how the evening ended. She's trying to organize a dinner before I head back to

Vermont, asked me to extend an invitation. I can check in with you once we figure out the details."

Michael stood up as Rachel gathered herself to leave.

"Rachel," he said gently as he began reaching for her hand. She locked eyes with him, but he hesitated, then withdrew his hand. "Please don't take this the wrong way, but I won't be attending any dinners for a while."

She offered a plaintive smile as the door closed behind her.

Michael knew eventually he'd have to find a way to put this behind him, and perhaps someday he'd be able to look back and savor the fleeting moment of exquisite perfection they shared. However, today was not that day.

He sat at his desk, staring at the clock counting the seconds since her departure, pondering his shifting fate, wondering how this unforeseen dalliance would affect his relationship with his closest friend and confidant. *I've never hidden anything from Gabel, not sure I can start now.*

But before he could fully process having to face the unsettling choice between confession and concealment, the door to his office flew open.

# 24

## SINS OF THE FATHER

The sun was peeking through the curtains as a tired Helen, dark shadows under her eyes, greeted Gabriel. "Nice to see you again, Gabriel," She smiled, fingers combing through her hair in a futile attempt to conceal her weary state. "To what do we owe this visit?"

"Well," Gabriel said cheerily, "I have a surprise for you."

"Oh?"

"I'm here to relieve you for the next two days. I hold in my hand the key to a lovely suite at the Hilton Hotel just a few blocks from here where you can sleep, take a bubble bath, order room service, visit the spa—or do whatever makes you happy, courtesy of Rachel and me. Tony and I are going to play dominoes, eat pizza, argue about Hemingway and politics, and maybe even sneak in a glass of Scotch if you and his doctors will allow it."

"Oh Gabriel, that's very nice of you, but…"

Gabriel interrupted before Helen could register a polite objection. "Helen, I'm sorry, but I'm going to have to insist," he said with a smile. "This man is about to become my father-in-law and we need more time to bond." Gabriel knew the gift would be more palatable if he emphasized his own self-interest.

"Also, I think you can use a break and I checked, the doctors say the pause in Tony's treatments will continue for at least a few more days. So, taking some time to replenish your own strength will be good for everybody. Right, Tony?"

Tony, looking more animated than usual since the respite in his chemo, smiled at the two of them. "Whatever you two decide is fine with me. But did I hear something about a glass of Scotch?"

"Gabriel, this is an unexpected kindness," she said, her voice wavering slightly. "I would be lying if I didn't admit a long bath and something other than hospital food would be a godsend right now. How can I refuse such a generous offer? But let's keep the Scotch business between us, small amounts, and only if he agrees to eat."

"Agreed!" Gabriel said, handing her the room key and smiling.

Overcome with gratitude, Helen's outward demeanor remained stoic, as if keeping her tears contained was by sheer force of will.

\* \* \*

"She's a good woman, Gabriel, she's been through a lot. Your kindness is much appreciated. Now that she's on her way, did you bring the drinks?"

"I sure did. It's right here in my overnight bag. I brought proper rocks glasses too. Let me pour you some. What do you want on your pizza?"

"I'll take the Scotch neat, you choose the pizza."

Gabriel ordered the pizza and poured two glasses of Scotch.

They allowed the Scotch to warm the space between them and fuel their mutual curiosity.

"So, what are you going to write about now that you left your job at the magazine?" Tony inquired.

"Not sure," Gabriel said. "I'm beginning to think telling your story would be an interesting project."

Tony's gaze pierced through Gabriel, as if trying to weigh his intent. "I would not recommend it," he said, his tone suddenly abrupt. "My story is best left to the forgotten past."

"Why?" Gabriel asked, instinctively pushing back on the resistance to his suggestion. "From what I can glean, you've had a very interesting saga—Cuban expat, successful entrepreneur, community leader, counterrevolutionary. I know I've mentioned this before, but sometimes, after your treatments, you seem to go back in time to relive past adventures. Maybe it would be helpful to write some of them down."

"I don't think so," Tony snapped. "There are some things I'd rather not revisit, and besides, it's nobody's business."

"Of course," Gabriel said, restraining his investigative impulses. "I don't mean to pry. But I'm interested in family lore, in learning more about what Rachel was like in her formative years. Was she always precocious? Smart? A daddy's girl? Tony, my family is gone, I'm eager to start a family with Rachel."

"Now that is something I want to encourage wholeheartedly. *¡Si, hombre!* I would love to live long enough to be a grandfather. I missed too much of Rachel's childhood."

"I imagine that must have been hard."

Tony winced. "Yes, it's a hard truth I am doomed to carry with me always."

"I want to be able to tell our children stories about their *abuelo*, what Mommy was like when she was little. Things that will connect them to our shared history."

"Rachel, we called her Raquelita, after my mother," Tony said, his tone softening. "She Americanized her name in college, and yes, she was a most curious child. Precocious, insightful, an old soul with an uncanny interest in all things at an early age. Not just drawing, but a genuine curiosity about all forms of expression—art, music, literature, poetry."

"That makes sense, given the career path she chose," Gabriel said.

"Please understand something, Gabriel, if I seem reluctant to delve into my past it's because I've done things I am not proud of. The work I did…" Tony hesitated, taking a moment to reflect, to measure his words. "When Rachel was very young I participated in political activities, first in Cuba and then later in Miami. As you probably know, any political movement has to contend with zealots and extremists. Some of the political people I connected with in Miami could be reckless, some would say dangerous. And at some point, as a result of my activities, it became clear to me that the best way, the only way, to protect Rachel and Milagros was to disappear."

"Can you say more about that?" Gabriel said, encouraged by the candid disclosure.

Tony emptied his glass while he pondered Gabriel's question. "Once I crossed a certain line, invisible to me at the time…" Tony paused. "I had no choice, Gabriel," he whispered. "I couldn't say no." His eyebrows gathered in a pained expression, his gaze seemed fixed upon a distant recollection.

Gabriel remembered Tony using the phrase before. He poured him another drink and waited until Tony was ready to expound. Sometimes the best way to encourage someone to open up is to remain silent and wait until they're ready.

"There were many Cuban expats in Miami who believed Castro would not last. Many in that community who wanted to hasten his demise. Many Americans too, the CIA and others, who shared that goal. The CIA convinced us they could help the Cuban exiles take our country back from Castro. They promised to provide everything we needed for a successful counterrevolution: arms, training and most importantly, air cover. They would take out Castro's air force, take out the batteries protecting the beaches. They trained and financed a Cuban invasion force, *Brigada Assalto 2506*, Brigade 2506, to lead an uprising against Castro. Upon establishing a beachhead, the self-proclaimed provisional government would request American aid and the U.S. would send troops in to secure the island. It was all bullshit. Sloppy from the get-go. The plan was conceived under President Eisenhower and sold to Kennedy as a quick, easy way to dispose of Castro. *Hombre*, were they wrong! When the thing started falling apart Kennedy realized his intelligence people had made a terrible miscalculation. Alarmed by the cascading fuck-ups, and fearing the political fallout, he pulled the plug in the middle of the operation, abandoning the Brigade to slaughter by Castro's forces. He made a lot of enemies that day."

"I remember learning about it in college. A huge blow to the young president's credibility," Gabriel said. "So you were living in Miami then, with Rachel and her mother?"

"Yes. I was still living at home," Tony said. "After the failure of that operation, I tried to distance myself from the CIA and the people who were committed to getting rid of Castro. They started working with some unsavory characters, big-time gangsters who wanted their casinos back. Some of the Cubans involved with the Bay of Pigs had axes to grind. They held grudges that poisoned their judgment. I wanted no part of it."

"So you were working with the CIA and then quit after the Bay of Pigs failure?"

"It wasn't so easy," Tony explained. "I owed them. The CIA helped build my transportation business. From time to time they would ask a favor, the kind you can't say no to. Take this person here, move this cargo there. It wasn't often, but it was a 'no questions asked' proposition. It's how they work. I realized too late, I had made a deal with the devil."

"Did you feel threatened by them?" Gabe asked.

"The threats were never explicit. It was manageable. Allen Dulles was out of the picture and the 'favors' I did for them were infrequent. I didn't think my family was in danger at the time. But that all changed after the assassination." Tony took a long pull on his drink.

"You worked with Allen Dulles?" Gabriel said, wide-eyed, attempting to process Tony's stunning narrative.

"Look, son, some things… Some things…" Tony's voice trailed off and he paused, taking in the weight of the moment. "I'm not well, and it may be best if these secrets die with me. But you are family now. You should know why I abandoned the woman you love, and her mother. And, while I don't think the threat to me or my family is of concern any longer, we, as men, should always be aware of *anything* that might ever threaten our families, even if the threat is not an immediate one." Tony's voice grew stronger now, commanding, infused with urgency.

Gabriel scrutinized Tony's face; he seemed more lucid than at any time since they first met. While some of his previous delirious ramblings hinted at covert activities, he now seemed clear-eyed and energetic. Gabe wondered if this burst of vigor stemmed from the hiatus in the drugs used to treat his cancer or from a deliberate and urgent need to unburden himself before he ran out of time.

"Yes, I knew Allen Dulles. He recruited me to be his point person with the Cuban expats. He was fired in November of '61 after the failure of Operation Zapata as he called it. While the CIA remained engaged with the Cubans in Miami, I didn't have much contact with Dulles until after the assassination."

"The Kennedy assassination?" Gabriel asked.

"Yes."

Tony's admissions landed with a jolt. A sudden chill seized him, as Gabriel stood up in stunned awareness. Whatever latent theories and conjectures he may have harbored about Rachel's father were on the threshold of being corroborated.

# 25

## CROSSROADS

Audrey Zornberg bolted into Michael's office clutching two brown manila envelopes. She paced relentlessly, stalking the length of his office while she gathered her thoughts.

"Two important things, need to get your input before we get tangled in the weeds with this one," she began.

"Okay, I'm all yours," Michael said. Still reeling from the gut punch he had just endured, he smiled and feigned unwavering focus.

"It's about the Courtland lawyer we opened a file on."

"Mendelson, the Roy Cohn shill?"

"The very same. He's vulnerable. We have him on mail fraud and tax evasion, but his real value is what he can deliver on the Courtlands themselves. I think we can flip him. He was asking all the right kinds of questions. I've made no commitments, but I think he understands how vulnerable he is. Not sure if he's more afraid of us or the people he's working for. So the question is, do we pursue this, given all the sensitivity around

171

the initial charges we brought against the Courtlands?"

"Hell yes! It's what we do best. Good work, Audrey, keep me posted. What's the other thing?"

"Take a look at this." She dropped the first envelope on his desk while continuing her stalking movements, like a hunter about to corner her prey. The envelope contained several eight-by-ten crime scene photographs featuring two men with bullet holes in the back of their heads.

"These two were found in a car in Newark. Looks like a mob execution. One bullet each to the back of the head. Ballistics show they were shot at close range. It's likely the shooter was known to the victims."

Michael studied the photographs, and for the second time that day, got the air knocked out of him. He recognized the bodies. They were the men from the party, the men who had assaulted him.

"Hey, wasn't that Rachel Rivers, Gabriel Hernandez's girlfriend that I just saw going into the elevator? You guys are all pretty close, right? I thought they moved to Vermont. Weird coincidence to see her in here today."

Michael swallowed hard. Audrey Zornberg had just dropped a bombshell, delivering information that could completely upend his career. He was ill-prepared to process a new onslaught of unwelcome information. Lost in a maze of improbable occurrences, he fell into stunned silence.

*This isn't good. Need time to figure out my next move.*

Pushing aside the photographs, he feigned interest in other paperwork on his desk, hoping Audrey wouldn't notice how hard his heart was pounding.

"Yeah, that was Rachel. They moved to Vermont about a year ago. She's in New York to take care of some business, stopped by to say hi."

Michael handed the photos back to Audrey and attempted to quiet his thumping heart. He worried that Audrey, trained at spotting deception, sensed something was not right.

"How did these wind up on your desk?" he asked, while his mind raced through innumerable scenarios. "A murder in New Jersey, how does this become our problem? Shouldn't this be handled locally? And what's the coincidence?" He peppered the fiery prosecutor with questions, seeking time to consider his next move.

"The primary jurisdiction is local, but they notified the FBI because of what they found at the scene," Audrey explained.

"Which was?"

"This is where it gets weird. In this type of scenario, a pro would torch the car, and scrub the scene. But they didn't bother."

"Low-level enforcers maybe?" Michael gave no indication through his line of inquiry that he knew something Audrey didn't. He didn't want to tip his hand, not yet. He needed to hear how she was connecting the dots.

"I'm not so sure," Audrey said. "It's almost as if they wanted someone to find this."

She produced a plastic baggie containing a VIP invitation to a reception at the Limelight. Scribbled on the back was the name Rachel Rivers. The invitation linked him directly to the victims of the murder. The situation was rapidly escalating, threatening to engulf his professional reputation in flames.

Maintaining plausible deniability when Audrey showed him the photographs of the men at the party was one thing, but now the stakes had soared to dangerous heights. Every move he made from this point forward was fraught with peril. Time was running out, and the repercussions of his next step could be dire.

"I understand why you'd want to bring this to my attention. Rachel and I were together at an event at the Limelight several nights ago." *That's good, always lead with the truth.* Michael's survival reflexes kicked into overdrive, he could almost hear the play clock ticking down as he evaluated his options.

"Gabriel asked me to keep an eye on Rachel and escort her to this event. His involvement in the Courtland prosecution is widely known. And you know we definitely stirred the pot with that case."

"Well aware. I was doing a fair amount of pot-stirring from lead chair, remember?" Audrey smiled.

"Of course, not the kind of thing I'm likely to forget. You were brilliant."

*Ego stroke from her boss? Come on, you need to do better than that to get her to shift focus. Need to buy more time.*

"Do you think this is related somehow?" Audrey probed, considering the potential connection.

"I can't say."

Michael's mind spun through a whirlwind of potential options, each one branching into a maze of unpredictable consequences. Audrey's insistence on probing into the Newark murders added another layer of complexity. He chastised himself for not immediately reporting the altercation with the assailants at the party; his delay only fueled suspicions. Though his secret wasn't murder, Audrey wasn't interested in his moral lapses, but carrying the weight of remorse clouded his judgment. With each passing moment, his silence cast a darker shadow over his involvement. Tick tock.

He wanted to find out how Dimitri Ivanov connected to these events, but at the moment he urgently needed to deflect Audrey's scrutiny. She was relentless, her tenacity was what made her such a good prosecutor. A part of him longed to come clean, to tell Audrey everything, free himself from the lie of omission, knowing she'd keep digging until she found the truth. Besides failing to report the incident, he had committed no crime.

Part of him, the part that wrestled with a pervasive feeling of guilt, wanted to delay anything that would lock in a course of action. *Need to buy more time. Tick tock.*

Audrey pitched her plan. "Look, we don't know how or if this is related to the Courtland case. It's also possible this is something Mendelson might be able to shed light on if we flip him. You said Gabriel's keeping a low profile and chose not to attend the event, it stands to reason that *he* must have cause to be concerned. I'm assuming you also share that concern?"

*She won't let this go until she figures out who might be doing what to whom.*

He wanted to figure out the same thing, but do it first.

"Gabe is concerned. The crimes he exposed and the people we are prosecuting have deep contacts within our own government. I advised him to be cautious precisely because I had concerns over potential payback."

"Okay," said Audrey, pointing to the envelope, "then I don't think I'm out of line suggesting we take some precautionary measures here."

"What do you have in mind?

"A security detail on you and Rachel Rivers for starters."

*This is not where I want this to go.*

"Worth considering. However, knowing Rachel, she will resist the idea," Michael said.

Once Audrey got hold of a case, she attacked it like a pit bull, and now her protective instincts were also being triggered. *Have to find a way to shift her focus, evaluate the next move from a different angle.*

"A request for extra security will raise flags within the department and I'm not entirely convinced it's warranted yet." He was stalling, flailing at a solution, departmental politics not his best play.

"How so? And forgive me for saying so, since when do you give two shits about how things look internally when you think it's the right thing to do?"

"Here's the thing," said Michael, "we took on the Courtland case against the advice of the AG, and we did so with cover from Gabriel's investigative reporting."

"Okay, I'm following you. But…"

"I see one of two scenarios playing out here," Michael interjected, keeping Audrey engaged in examining alternative tactics. "The AG was right, we did stir up the wrong hornet's nest at the wrong time, and we are now looking at the prospect of using dwindling resources to protect our flank, doing so at a time when we're facing budget cutbacks. We risk getting our wings clipped in the pushback. Not the best timing, given we're going to need resources to move on the Mendelson thing. Inviting scrutiny will cost us."

*Budget concerns were not going to cut it with Audrey, need a stronger argument, need to buy more time.*

"Okay, but we are talking about protecting our own here," Audrey countered, bolstering her case.

"True, which by the way, if it plays out this way, the first person who will get extra security will be you."

"Me?" Audrey's response was laced with surprise, her puzzled expression reflecting the unexpected turn in conversation.

*Bingo!*

"Yes, you. You were first chair on this. *You* were the masterful prosecutor who brought down the hammer." *Ego stroke.* "You were brilliant and you received more than your fair share of media attention for it. We are far from knowing for certain if this incident is the result of the Courtland case, but if it is, and we are requisitioning unbudgeted resources, we are going to have '*I told you so*' shoved so far up our asses it's going to get really uncomfortable making any move without unwanted interference from Washington. But, either way, you were the face of this prosecution and as you insist, and I agree, we need to protect our own."

"What's the other scenario?" Audrey asked.

"What?"

"You said there were two possible scenarios, two ways this could play out."

In truth there were many ways this might play out, but for the moment he wanted Audrey focused on just two of them. He had to guide her to the right play.

"The other scenario might be the hit has nothing to do with the Courtland case. The connection to me and Rachel is incidental and opportunistic, deliberately set in motion to distract local law enforcement from chasing the most likely perpetrators."

"New Jersey wise guys looking to move the spotlight out of their backyard?" Audrey suggested.

"Exactly."

"So how do we play this with local law enforcement?" Audrey asked.

"We tell them we are considering a possible connection to the Courtland case but encourage them to follow whatever local leads they might have because we haven't confirmed an actual connection to our office. Their turf, their local expertise is the better option; that should appeal to their parochial instincts."

"But we'll also open a formal investigation, right?" Audrey countered, back in pit bull mode.

"Yes of course, but let's keep an eye on what they come up with, and let's keep our investigation under the radar for the moment. I do want you to consider having a security detail with you until we figure out what's what."

"Absolutely NOT! I can handle myself and I don't want my privacy compromised."

*Got her!*

Michael knew Audrey would react negatively to having a security detail, providing him the temporary deflection he needed. Her taste for attractive young women was considered an open secret. A security detail would bring unwanted attention to her lifestyle and she knew the optics would not be good for her career.

"Look, I trust your judgment on this," Michael said, relieved he had succeeded in shifting her focus, at least for the moment. "I'm going to check with Rachel and find out how much longer she's going to be in town. I'll discuss security options with her and Gabriel. We can revisit the entire case when we hear more from the locals in New Jersey."

*Only a matter of time before Audrey, or somebody else, connects me to the two dead bodies in the photographs.* He grappled with vexing conundrums, uncertainty and paralyzing delay.

*The game is shifting. I'm being played. Who though? Who's pulling the strings? Are the Courtlands moving on me, or is it the people who will be exposed if we continue following where this investigation leads? Are they trying to send a message or are they looking to inflict permanent damage?*

If he could identify who was pulling the strings, the people responsible for setting up the altercation, and then tie them to the drugging attempt at Gabriel's party, he could develop a rationale for not coming forward sooner. He was protecting a source. He didn't want to tip his hand, luring in the perpetrator. He thought it best to reveal all relevant details once all the dots were connected. Audrey might object to not being included, but her concerns could be managed.

The longer he hesitated, the narrower his options. Tick tock.

# 26

## FORGIVE US OUR TRESPASSES

Tony paced the confines of the hospital room. His voice was animated and burning with the cadence of a man running out of time, running out of the acuity required to unravel a history he spent almost a quarter century burying. He continued his startling confession, while Gabriel sat glued to his seat awestruck and attentive.

"Dulles reemerged from the shadows of exile to become part of the Warren Commission. The only member of the commission with experience in covert operations. Johnson embedded him to ensure the Commission arrived at the right conclusions."

"How did you guess Johnson's motive?'

"No guessing. I knew, because Johnson himself told me." Tony looked out the hospital window, as if it were a portal to the past.

"Lyndon Johnson confided in you?" Gabe said incredulously.

"Yes. He was obsessively driven to legitimize his presidency. Johnson believed the nation's stability hinged on moving beyond the assassination and dispelling lingering fears of a broader conspiracy. A prolonged investigation could unearth secrets that needed to remain secret. In that

178

respect, Dulles was a like-minded ally. Dulles didn't want congress delving into his own past—his covert activities, his collusion with his brother John Foster, the former secretary of state, and his ties to the oppressive United Fruit Company. He had no desire to have his own skeletons surface in a thorough investigation into the assassination of an American president. His role on the Commission ensured what needed to remain secret, remained secret."

"How did you come to meet President Johnson?" Gabriel asked.

"Allen Dulles facilitated the introduction. Johnson needed an operative he could trust, someone that would report directly to him, someone who understood how to navigate through and around the CIA, and someone who never appeared on a government payroll."

"Tony, this is a fascinating story. Unbelievably so," Gabriel said, unintentionally betraying his skepticism.

"Listen carefully, son," Tony insisted, his voice tinged with gravity. "The fact that my story seems incredible to you is a good thing. It's why I believe what I know is no longer a threat to my family. But remember this, truth is more dangerous than fiction. I'm entrusting you with this because, in my estimation, if you are the one left to safeguard our family, your knowing is less dangerous than your ignorance."

"I understand, and I will endeavor to be worthy of that trust. Please continue," Gabe said.

"Johnson already knew who killed Kennedy."

"How did he know?" Gabe interrupted in astonished excitement. The idea that this man, his soon-to-be father-in-law, held the key to one of the great mysteries of his time felt surreal. It was almost as if he were observing the exchange from a distance, his own involvement in the unfolding narrative too staggering to absorb.

"He learned Kennedy was killed by a rogue KGB plot. He learned the explosive truth from Nikita Khrushchev himself the day Air Force One touched down on the tarmac with Kennedy's body inside. The Soviet premier gave Johnson a choice: go public with the discovery and almost certainly trigger a war between the world's largest nuclear powers, or choose an unsavory solution that would maintain peace."

"An unsavory solution?"

"Yes." Tony visibly recoiled at the remembrance. "Once I understood the stakes, I couldn't refuse."

"What was being asked of you? Why couldn't you say no?" Gabriel prodded.

Tony hesitated, then resumed his pacing. "Johnson and Khrushchev needed someone to eliminate anyone connected with the plot, as well as anyone who inadvertently learned of what transpired. There was a list, anyone who could unveil the truth had to be dealt with. Any Russian, any American, any mobster, any Cuban—innocent or not, they all had to be eliminated. Anyone who stumbled on the truth found themselves on The List. The president and the premier sealed the pact by agreeing to relinquish power, fade into history."

"They're both dead now," Gabriel observed.

"Yes. When they are commemorated, it won't be for the decisive action they took during this pivotal moment in history. They were confronted with a harrowing dilemma. Fearing the truth would lead to bloodlust and eventually nuclear war, they chose to bury the truth at all costs."

"How do you know…" Gabriel's voice trailed off in stunned recognition.

Tony seemed lighter in his unburdening. He grew quiet, negotiating the room with pent-up energy, as if trying to capture something essential that had eluded him for too long.

"You see, Gabriel, if I said no then I would no doubt have become a name on The List. A mysterious casualty of some unfortunate accident. And there was no guarantee that Rachel and her mother would not have also become collateral damage. I never returned home again after my meeting with Johnson. I sent word to Milagros. She moved to a new house. I arranged for her financial support and for people to look after them. Then I went to work assembling the resources I needed to execute this unsavory assignment."

"You…" again Gabriel's voice trailed off, unable to complete the thought.

"Yes, Gabriel. My Russian counterpart and I. We erased a part of history others deemed too volatile. Too dangerous to be entrusted to the institutions designed to protect us from the very thing they now sought to conceal. I left Rachel and her mother behind because any association with these events would have endangered their lives."

Gabriel sat motionless, unable to utter his thoughts, unable to fathom all the implications of knowing. The answers to his probing questions carried an unforeseeable gravity—the weight of Tony's unburdening was now his to bear.

Tony continued, his voice lowered to a whisper. "Every action carries a cost, Gabriel. Every decision propels you and those closest to you toward uncertain destinations. You may never fully comprehend the repercussions of the choices you make, but you will inevitably pay the cost. None of us can ever escape our fate."

With the gruesome truth of his confessions finally exposed, the old man sank into his chair, closed his eyes, and surrendered to weariness. In the stillness of the hospital room, Tony's dark secret descended on Gabriel, embedding itself in his consciousness as the grave implications of its concealment bore down on him. Relentlessly.

# 27

## PLAUSIBLE DENIABILITY

The teachings of Michael's Harvard mentor, the polarizing and brilliant Samuel Huntington, echoed through the uproar of his persistent deliberations. Huntington posited that all global conflicts were like dramatic allegories, follies fueled by the unchecked hubris of narrow-minded men. This hubris, he argued, inevitably led to miscalculations, and in the realm of geopolitical power struggles, miscalculations almost always proved fatal— to someone, somewhere. Huntington's insights felt particularly relevant in Michael's current predicament. No room for hubris or miscalculations.

The confrontation and subsequent blow to Michael's head provided Dimitri Ivanov with the opportunity to take control of a volatile situation. His violent reaction to the provocation was a serious miscalculation that provided an opening to adversaries in a larger game. The Russian's actions, presumably on his behalf, thrust Michael into a deepening quandary: admit to leaving the scene of an assault, or become an unwitting accomplice to the cover-up of a much larger crime. Both options were infused with peril, leaving no desirable alternative.

The Courtland case drew him into a deadly game of chess against a stealthy opponent. Backward induction, the Siberian Trap, and the Englund Gambit were all useful tactics on the chessboard, but when bodies start showing up, things get real. A wrong move could prove disastrous.

* * *

Ivanov's New York apartment overlooked Central Park, its French Colonial décor and faint, lingering scents suggesting infrequent use. Situated in the Dakota, renowned for its esteemed residents like Lauren Bacall and the tragic legacy of John Lennon's assassination six years prior, a setting that exuded faded old-world grandeur.

Stepping into the opulent study adorned with portraits of celebrities, Michael couldn't help but notice the prominence of Rudolf Nureyev among them. The legendary Russian ballet dancer, known for his bold defection from the Soviet Union in 1961 due to KGB harassment over his open homosexuality, raised intriguing questions. What connection did Ivanov have to Nureyev? Was he somehow involved in the dancer's high-profile escape? The photos offered an unabashed exhibition of Ivanov's wide range of social contacts.

But there was no time for Ivanov's curious anecdotes now. The unearthing of details surrounding events at the Limelight demanded an acceptable explanation from the man. More than answers, he required a strategy to counter the slippery descent into ethical compromise. Options were narrowing by the minute.

"Rest assured, Michael, I had nothing to do with the death of those two idiots. But the news does not come as a complete surprise. They failed to accomplish their assignment and were probably held accountable by their handlers—nothing to do with us. I wanted to ensure those men would never again attempt to intimidate you or Rachel. Like you, I acted to protect someone I care about."

"Well, I'm not sure it worked, because I can say with a high degree of confidence that the evidence connecting them to the event, and by extension me, were planted on those corpses deliberately. It's not unreasonable to conclude that someone is trying to send me a message."

"A message? Tell me your theory. What do you think they're after?" Dimitri said with a sense of authority at odds with his previous fatherly demeanor.

*This was a man unaccustomed to being questioned*, Michael thought.

"What they are after is what I'm here to talk to you about. I'm not here to accuse you of anything, sir." Michael softened his tone. "I'm here to ask for your help in unraveling the unusual circumstances that surround this whole affair. Your perspective and advice would be appreciated. The assault, and the events that followed, happened fast. I should have tempered my reaction, used greater restraint."

"You regret punching the guy in the throat and cracking his jaw?" Dimitri said.

"Yes, in hindsight. I overreacted to what I perceived as an immediate physical threat. The blow to my head further clouded my judgment. I should have stayed behind and called in the authorities, regardless of how it might appear to the press."

Michael hoped a softer approach might elicit Ivanov's cooperation. Men like Dimitri Ivanov do not intimidate easily.

"A criminal prosecutor is going to make enemies, assuming he is doing his job properly. It's well known Gabriel Hernandez and I have worked in tandem, often pursuing high-profile adversaries, bringing their abuses to light, and ultimately to justice."

"Noble aspirations indeed," the Russian mused, wandering to the window to take in the expansive view of Central Park.

"It's also well known the case my department brought against the Courtland family had serious ramifications for people not used to being held accountable. I'm pretty sure I'm not telling you anything you don't already know."

"Go on, Mikhail, you have my attention."

Michael paused, noticing Dimitri used the Russian version of his name.

*That's new. Wonder if this is his way of trying to gain my confidence.*

"It's also clear to me," Michael continued, "that while we have not known each other for a long time, you have, your experience has…" he hesitated, choosing his words carefully.

"Yes?" Dimitri Ivanov turned from the window and glared at Michael.

"Your background, based on your own telling, places you in some intriguing circles," Michael remarked, pausing to survey the opulent setting and adornments of Dimitri's apartment.

"I don't know many art professors who travel with security or who can arrange for such luxurious surroundings when visiting New York," Michael continued. "My suspicion is your involvement with the individuals who attacked me may have inadvertently put them in jeopardy."

Michael was treading carefully in an effort to elicit Ivanov's cooperation. "Not that you've necessarily done anything wrong, Mr. Ivanov, but I'm keen to understand your perspective on this matter, especially in light of these unusual events."

The older man raised an eyebrow and looked at Michael as if he had just passed gas in church. "I'm Mr. Ivanov now? That's not a good sign, Mikhail."

"Allow me to clarify some things for you," the older man offered, his voice tinged with authority. "But first, let me ask you, are you here as the head of the Criminal Division for the Southern District of New York, or are you here as a friend asking for help?"

"I am who I am, Mr. Ivanov." Michael didn't like the question, but he resisted the impulse to deliver a more pointed response. "But today I come as a friend, someone concerned for the safety of his friends who may be in danger."

"Fair enough. Then I have to ask we go back to first names here so I'm not feeling as if I'm being interrogated."

"Of course, you're right, Dimitri. This isn't an interrogation, and I recognize it's sometimes difficult for me to separate my official role from a personal one. They are intertwined, but I'm not here in any official capacity. Gabriel and Rachel are family to me. I know you care about Rachel and have been supportive of her career."

"Okay, Michael, in the spirit of friendship, let me begin by addressing some of your concerns. It is true I teach a course in art history at the University of Madrid from time to time. I also disclosed that I am a businessman with a spectrum of interests and contacts. Many of the people I work with around the world are well known, established businessmen of integrity; influential men who run successful enterprises and contribute to their communities. However, not all of them are. I believe this would be true for just about anyone who has been successful in business. I don't believe this comes as news to you. I come across, and on occasion do business with, people and organizations that sometimes cut corners, leverage influence, and at times engage in practices that, let us say, put them in legal jeopardy."

"Yes, point taken, please continue."

"When we last discussed the matter we agreed the men who assaulted you were likely hired by someone to intimidate and harass, maybe more. Interestingly, these men believed they had protection from the police, indicating they were working with well-connected people. Had we called the police, they likely would have been released within hours and the story would read very differently than it does now. They would have had the opportunity to, how do you say it, spin the narrative. It's possible the goal was to create a controversy, to embarrass you publicly and weaken your moral authority. We were not the police and therefore not so easy to manipulate. In my discussion with the person who claimed to be their attorney, I made it clear they failed at whatever job they were sent to do, and as a result, they now had put their employer in jeopardy."

Dimitri Ivanov took a seat next to Michael and leaned in for emphasis.

"Now it is possible you might have handled the situation differently had you been there, but you were *not* there. You were injured. I did what I believed the situation required."

He held Michael's gaze.

"I offered a solution acceptable to their representative. Fix this, leave these people alone and I in turn would agree to leave their employer out of it. I let him know my name and certain business affiliations. I made it known his employer would not be happy knowing of my involvement. I believe he understood why. Deeming it an appropriate resolution, the representative agreed to the conditions of my cooperation. He requested we drop the two men in New Jersey, a reasonable request in light of our exchange, and a prudent precaution considering the morons we were dealing with. I obliged. Carlos dropped them off at the prescribed location."

*Business affiliations?* Michael evaluated the plausibility of Dimitri's explanation and the inferences of the details he didn't disclose.

"It has always been my practice to use the least amount of force required to achieve the desired result. As you say, a man in your position makes enemies, you have as much insight into who may have sent those men and what they might do as anyone. I defused the threat through fortuitous and decisive action. I believe the matter is now settled and Rachel will never again be approached in this manner. If they met with an unfortunate end, it is no concern of mine. Nor will I shed any tears for them."

Michael rubbed the creases on his forehead as if he could erase what was inside. Dimitri's story lined up with the events as he understood them. The confrontation could have been dismissed as another strange night in New York, overshadowed by the more disconcerting entanglement with Rachel. When dead bodies connecting him to the Limelight fiasco showed up, everything changed.

Trusting this man required ignoring his gut instincts, which didn't sit well. Was Dimitri Ivanov a fortuitous ally, or an adversary surreptitiously moving pieces on the board, hiding in plain sight? Time would tell—but the game clock was still counting down and Michael needed to protect his flank. Mostly, he needed to buy time.

He decided to cut right to the chase. "Dimitri, do you know who's behind all of this?"

"My guess is, with a little digging, you could ascertain this as well as I. But you are asking the wrong question, my friend."

"How so?"

"I don't want to discourage you from pursuing whatever course of action you deem appropriate, but my advice for you is that you proceed with great caution and try to think several moves ahead."

"This is precisely what I'm attempting to do," Michael said.

"An autopsy will reveal one of the men had a broken jaw and other injuries. One option might be for you to report all you know to the appropriate authorities right away. However, coming forward now will put you at the center of the conflict; though it will also allow you to tell your version of the story before an investigation reveals you conspired to conceal relevant facts surrounding this case. This as a course of action aligns best with what your laws prescribe, but it also amplifies the events and your subsequent decision-making."

"There are benefits and liabilities to any course of action I take," Michael muttered, saying the quiet part out loud.

"Indeed," Dimitri agreed. "Your liabilities here remind me of Ted Kennedy's Chappaquiddick dilemma in 1969. An inopportune controversy centering on his failure to immediately report his accident. You did not commit murder, but you may have inadvertently invited the perception that you are withholding information to protect yourself. This could have detrimental long-term implications for you. To be blunt, these events have the potential to haunt you for the rest of your career. In Ted's case, it cost him a chance at the presidency in 1980. Jimmy Carter used Chappaquiddick as a bat to beat Ted into submission. In the end, the unintended consequence of those actions led to Ronald Reagan, a failed movie actor, becoming president of the United States."

Michael noted Dimitri Ivanov presented his observations in the cold calculated manner of a seasoned strategist. *Clearly not his first rodeo.*

"Events ripple in time in ways we cannot always predict," Ivanov said, inviting Michael to consider how the past and future become interwoven.

Michael paced distractedly around the apartment, his gaze fixed on the serene vista of Central Park framed by the Dakota's windows. Despite the tranquil scene outside, he couldn't shake the sense of impending danger lurking in the city below, masked by the natural beauty before him.

His thoughts turned to Ted's tragic missteps, particularly his fatal delay in reporting Mary Jo Kopechne's drowning. The burden of his family legacy, compounded by personal demons, had led Ted down a path of flawed judgment and troublesome developments. Michael, seeing the parallels between Ted's plight and his own, vowed to not succumb to a similar fate.

Ted's story served as a cautionary tale, a reminder of the irreversible repercussions of indecision and inaction. As he contemplated the fallout from the events at the Limelight, Michael resolved to take decisive action, determined not to let this one moment permanently alter the trajectory of his life.

"Mikhail," the Russian interjected, drawing Michael's attention back to the current conversation with the Russian pronunciation of his name—accentuating a level of intimacy between them that did not yet exist. "What if they apprehended the individual responsible for dispatching those men? What if it became clear that the motive behind the slaying had no connection to you, Rachel, or Gabriel? Suppose it transpired that some minor underworld figures harbored grievances against the assailants and strategically planted the party invitations to divert suspicion from the obvious perpetrators? You're a prominent prosecutor, frequently seen on television. Surely, there are numerous criminals who recognize you. Is this not accurate?"

"It is," Michael replied.

"What if the whole thing was just another incident of disruptive behavior by two criminals who had a history of getting into trouble?"

"Certainly a plausible scenario," Michael conceded, mulling over the implications. "But apprehending whoever eliminated these individuals and ensuring their story aligns with the facts as you've described them presents a significant challenge."

Dimitri simply nodded, leaving his statement to linger in the air, laden with unspoken implications.

*Is Dimitri implying he can remove this onerous albatross from around my neck? But at what cost? I couldn't possibly allow myself to incur such a perilous debt.*

As he felt the pressure mounting, the way forward became ever more complicated by his own vacillations. He wanted to do the right thing. But what exactly was that? A sense of urgency gripped him, compounding the opaque machinations closing in on him. He needed to reach out to the one person he trusted above all others, his closest advisor—before the clock ran out.

Tick tock.

# 28

## IN TOO DEEP

The engine snarled in response to Michael's aggressive footwork prodding his vehicle past the more prudent drivers heading north on Interstate 91 toward Stowe. His mind churned relentlessly, replaying the warnings he brazenly disregarded while pursuing the Courtland case. He reflected on his counsel to Gabriel, insisting he maintain a low profile. They upended things, ignored the unwritten rules and provoked the ire of people whose ambitions extended far beyond mere avarice. History teemed with the corpses of well-meaning idealists who disrupted entrenched power arrangements. In a rush to hold the Courtlands accountable for old debts, they forgot they were not immune to someone else's determination to settle scores.

He needed to identify all the players, decipher their strategies, and devise his own defensive maneuvers. However, if he were honest with himself he'd acknowledge his ability to read the board had been hampered by his own moral failings, conflicting priorities, and emotional entanglements. The dictates of the law clashed with powerful instincts of self-preservation. Hindered by his own muddled thinking, he knew Gabriel could help him find his footing. But, for the first time in his life, there were truths he dared not divulge to his closest confidant.

⋆ ⋆ ⋆

Arriving in Gabriel's Vermont home Michael attempted to maintain a casual tone but his compulsive pacing betrayed an unsettled state of mind.

"So, Rachel's dad is living with you now?"

"It's only temporary until he completes his chemotherapy."

"I see," Michael said. He was distracted; they both knew he didn't make the trip from New York intending to chat about Gabriel's new house guest.

"He's resting now. I do want you to meet him if you have time, he's a fascinating character. How ya doing, buddy? What's eating you?" Gabriel said, looking concerned.

"Not sure where to start." Michael launched into a detailed summary of all that transpired since the incident at the reception, leaving out the part about his tryst with Rachel.

"So, this Dimitri Ivanov, this is the same guy who has been buying Rachel's work over the past few years?"

"Correct."

"Does Rachel know you suspect he might be more than an innocuous art lover?"

"I haven't discussed my conversations with Dimitri. She knows some of his history. He's quite the talker, not shy about discussing his exploits. Russian operative in Europe during the war, worked in Cuba during the Castro revolution."

"Cuba?" Gabriel raised an eyebrow.

"Yes, why?"

"It's not important, I'll tell you later. So, do you think he had anything to do with the bodies? Do you think his security people might have done this?"

"He says no, and I'm inclined to believe him."

"Possibly an accident? Ivanov's security used a little too much force and it went south on them. They staged it to look like a hit to deflect attention."

"I can't rule it out. But I think it's unlikely they would have been so sloppy. I'm inclined to believe Ivanov is sincere in his desire to protect Rachel. There is a genuine connection there, some combination of paternal affection and arts patron."

"What about witnesses at the party? Anybody not part of your group see you deliver a punch or receive a blow to the head?"

"Unlikely. It was dark, it happened very quickly. We were in a secluded private area."

"Okay, well if you want to get this out in the open, what about Audrey? How do you think she'll react given she's already been kept out of the loop? How's this communicated to the investigators in Jersey? What do you think the fallout will be from the delay in communication?" Gabriel peppered Michael with questions in order to evaluate the implications of each course of action.

"I don't know. I'm not too worried about Audrey, although I would have to explain why I didn't immediately identify the perpetrators as soon as she showed me the pictures. Not sure about the lead investigator in Jersey. We have local and federal looking at this now and at best it doesn't reflect well on my decision-making. I break someone's jaw, leave the scene of an assault, and the two guys involved turn up dead in the front seat of a car twenty-four hours later. Not something easily swept under the rug."

"I agree, on the surface, it's an incriminating scenario. Even if you come forward right now, any defensive explanation you offer will be met with skepticism and come with a certain amount of liability."

Michael staggered like a fighter who had absorbed one too many punches. Gabriel looked concerned—it was a strange role reversal between the two old friends.

"Okay, Michael, let's think this through. Dimitri Ivanov, is he a bad dude?"

"No, I don't think so. Maybe. I think he knows people. I think he travels in circles where he meets high-level players in all types of businesses. Hell, he's friends with Rudolf Nureyev."

"The ballet dancer?"

"Yeah, I think so. There were a bunch of pictures of Nureyev with a number of prominent people, Henry Kissinger, Gerald Ford, Pierre Trudeau. Some of them included Ivanov."

"Interesting," Gabriel said. "This guy gets around."

"He has friends in high places, and probably low places too, but I don't think that alone makes him an outright criminal. Knowing criminals and being a criminal are two different things."

"Yeah, maybe. Did you run background on him?" Gabriel asked.

"Yes, nothing too deep. On paper, he's exactly who he says he is. A dual citizen of Spain and the Soviet Union, academic background, previous government work, investments throughout Europe and America. No real red flags other than the anomaly of a citizen of a communist country having significant private capital invested around the world."

"Yeah, I'd say that's an anomaly. Do you think he's currently operating for the Russian government?

"He fits the profile. However, spies don't usually list their occupation on their résumés, and I didn't think it would be prudent to access CIA intel on him right now. There could be tripwires on his file, I didn't want to risk the extra attention. Anyway, my take is that he mostly operates in the private sector now, leveraging contacts for the highest bidder."

"Understood." Gabriel rubbed his chin as he began assembling the pieces to the narrative.

"Ivanov's worldview is more romantic than ideological," Michael added, "detached from the usual dichotomy of capitalism versus communism. Whatever game he's playing it doesn't appear tied to any political ideology."

"If true, that would make him a particularly dangerous adversary," Gabriel said, pointing out the obvious.

"I'm not entirely convinced he's an adversary."

"Do you think he can help you fix this?"

"Yes, I do, but asking for his help might compromise me in unforeseeable ways."

"How so?"

"He described a scenario where evidence emerges indicating the hit was part of some kind of gang activity, a turf war, unpaid debts, something consistent with low-level organized crime. A perp would confess to planting the invitation as part of an ill-conceived scam. They plead down in exchange for cooperation."

"That would certainly get you off the hook."

"Yes, it would. Off one hook and possibly onto a bigger one."

"How did you leave it with him?"

"I thanked him for his advice and told him I had to think about my next move. I didn't ask for help and he didn't really offer to take any specific action."

"Better that way, he's providing plausible deniability."

"What do you think I should do, Gabe?"

Gabriel stood up and began to pace the room. After pondering Michael's circumstances for a long while he answered, "You do nothing."

"Nothing?" Michael rubbed the back of his neck.

"Yes, do nothing. First, you're not guilty of murder. You were attacked, and you experienced a concussion. You were, have been, and likely still are, *impaired*. We could find ten doctors to testify to your state of mind in court without breaking a sweat. You're not yourself. When you examined the crime scene photographs you couldn't ID the assailants because of your disoriented cognition. This lines up with the provable facts. You experienced a head injury that impaired your judgment. I know you, brother. You're off your game. It's obvious."

Michael wanted to tell Gabriel everything, everything that happened, everything that confirmed his impaired judgment, his lapse of reason, his broken moral compass. But he restrained the impulse; he had to keep his head in the game, and right now his head was throbbing either from the blow he received two weeks ago, or from the impossible situation he was wrestling with.

"This investigation will proceed alongside a hundred other cases. You were a victim of an assault, you were not the perpetrator of anything. You're the chief of crime for the Southern District of New York. You're not the bad guy,

Michael, you put bad guys in prison. The way you deal with this is to go on with your life and do nothing about it. Let it play out. This does not have to be your Chappaquiddick."

"What about Dimitri Ivanov?"

"What about him? What about *do nothing* didn't you understand? He's an international businessman who has been a collector of Rachel's work and has befriended both of you. That's it."

"Should I ask him…?" Gabe didn't even let him finish.

"Nothing! You ask him nothing. If he makes a call on your behalf, that's on him. You ask for nothing, do nothing, and let the thing play out. Any move you make to intervene or to influence the investigation will expose you to legal jeopardy. Let the chips fall where they may. When and if the time comes and you're forced to make a move, you'll have a better idea of who is moving against you. In the meantime, do what you do best: introduce bad guys to accommodations within the federal penitentiary system."

Michael smiled, and for the first time in days, the tension in his neck and shoulders eased up a little. Gabriel's advice made sense: focus on the presumption of innocence, and don't force the play. Doing nothing ran counter to how each man had approached their respective callings, yet now, as the stakes were being raised, Gabriel, the more impulsive of the two, counseled restraint.

Despite finding comfort in Gabriel's advice, a gnawing unease haunted him. The lingering desire to come clean and confess everything to Gabriel, every detail of what transpired the night of the performance, including what happened with Rachel, tugged at his conscience, yet he continued to suppress the urge to confess, attempting to keep it tightly under wraps.

"Tell me more about Rachel's dad. What's he like?"

* * *

The Scotch warmed his insides and soothed frazzled nerves. Michael settled into a comfortable chair surrounded by familiar photographs and paintings. The two men sat across from each other, the light of the fireplace illuminating their careworn faces. A fragrant balm of burning wood filled the room, and the occasional crackle of embers punctuated their quiet reflection. Having dealt with Michael's immediate dilemma, they allowed themselves a moment to relax and enjoy a respite in their portentous deliberations.

Gabriel offered a sympathetic nod to Michael. "You look like shit, buddy. You're spending the night and getting a good night's sleep, maybe take a day or two before you jump back on your white horse and charge back into the fray. I want you to meet Rachel's dad, but I have to share some things with you first."

"Sounds ominous," said Michael, welcoming a change of subject.

"Tony has pancreatic cancer, a serious diagnosis under any circumstances, very low survival rate. The treatment consists of exposing him to just enough toxic chemicals to kill off cancer cells while not killing off the patient. It takes a huge toll on his mind and body, he's out of it for a day or two after. In addition to the chemo, they give him sedatives to make him more comfortable, and more cooperative. While in recovery he goes into a sort of drug-induced delirium, in and out of lucidity."

"Delirium?"

"Yes, it's strange, you have to experience it firsthand to fully appreciate it. It's like he's moving in and out of time."

"What do you mean?"

"His wife says he can slip into a delirious state, behaving like a man possessed by his memories. Lucid in one moment, then suddenly transported to another place altogether. He speaks to you as if you are part of the history he's reliving. I've seen it on multiple occasions. It's a little unnerving. Once he tried recruiting me for a rescue operation after the Bay of Pigs invasion."

"Bay of Pigs?" Michael flashed a questioning look, then disregarded the sudden visceral twinge.

"Yeah. One minute we're having a lucid conversation about what it meant to have Hispanic heritage and the next he's passionately arguing for a rescue mission to extract stranded fighters in Cuba."

"Interesting. So do you think it's just a fever dream?"

"It's not. He was reliving, not inventing, burning anger and fear rising to the surface intermittently. Also, I did check out parts of his story. Certain things, like Kennedy's people changing the original invasion site for the Bay of Pigs, happened exactly as he described, it's a detail that's not part of the official record. However, a retired CIA operative corroborated the story for me. He wouldn't say much more. Not the first time a spook has clammed up around anything to do with JFK."

"No surprise there. Lots of official obfuscation around that period of history. Too many secrets, too many agendas, too much power in the hands of the wrong people," Michael agreed.

"Yes, but there's more. Lot's more." Gabriel's voice flared with excitement.

"Can't wait to meet this guy."

"Wait." Gabriel poured another round and listened for activity in the guest suite. "I want to be discreet here. I feel like my involvement with Tony is crossing some invisible line, but honestly, the lure of this story has been impossible to resist."

"It's who you are, Gabe, don't fight it," Michael laughed, sympathizing with how easily the personal and professional can get entangled.

"Tony has opened up to me, he considers me family now. I think his need to be so forthcoming stems from the realization that he's a man running out of time."

"It's not uncommon for someone at the end stage of life to want to unburden themselves," Michael said.

"None of us know how much time we have, but most of us haven't lived the kind of life Tony De Castro has. He's traveled quite a bit, spent time in Israel, married an Israeli who worked with displaced Palestinians."

"Is she an Arab?" Michael asked, with a hint of incredulity.

"No, she's an Israeli Jew."

"Interesting," Michael commented. "Not particularly popular with her peers I imagine."

"Not popular, but definitely courageous. Her first husband was ex-IDF, did contract work for Mossad. Lost his life while working with Tony."

"How?" Michael's prosecutorial instincts began kicking in.

"Unclear. Tony hired him. The details of the operation are sketchy. Helen thinks the assignment involved security for senior-level government officials. She's unsure of the specifics. Wives of operatives learn not to ask a lot of questions, and the events surrounding her husband's death are clearly a painful subject. I didn't have the heart to press her for details. I doubt she knows more."

"Understandable. Although, it's a little hard to parse out how Tony would have been involved with both Cuba and the Israeli government."

"I need your take on all of this, Michael. Since Rachel's been away, Tony and I have had hours and hours of mind-bending conversation."

"Sounds like you two have hit it off."

"We have. But I have to confess, getting to know her old man has helped me cope with Rachel's absence. It's the longest stretch we've been apart since we've been together. Feels like she's dodging coming back home. I get it, though. Having him living with us is not easy for her. To say she's not exactly thrilled about reconnecting with her dad is putting it lightly. She's dealing with a lot. Work's really taking off for her."

Gabriel's words penetrated Michael, twisting at his insides, stirring up again the urge to unburden himself of the guilt.

"She's the main breadwinner now," Gabriel added. "The partnership with Amanda is paying off big-time. I think she believes her work has suffered since leaving New York."

"Maybe she just needs more time to adjust." Michael looked away.

"I really miss her, Michael, more than I thought I would. She's coming home soon. I'm going to marry her."

"That's fantastic news!" Michael surprised himself; his tone reflected warmth, but inside, a hot storm raged. *Confess! Tell him everything*, his inner voice screamed, *let him know, it's now or never. You owe it to him. You owe it to yourself.* Despite the inner clamor, something held him back from delivering the explosive confession. "I figured it was only a matter of time before you made it official. She's an exceptional woman, and she brings out the best in you. Congratulations! I'm genuinely happy for you both." Michael raised his glass, locked eyes and touched his glass to Gabriel's. He had become so skilled at compartmentalizing his own feelings that he could utter those words as if somehow he was not surrendering a part of himself in the process.

"She'd be good for anybody. I just got lucky," Gabriel offered in an uncharacteristic note of humility.

"Yes, you did."

"I want the best for her, Michael, and I think repairing the relationship with her dad will help her heal a painful part of her past. She's carried this wound for most of her life and I feel like I have this unique opportunity to be a peacemaker between them, to help them both find closure. I think he's opening up to me in part because he desperately wants to reconnect with Rachel before the clock runs out."

"Tread carefully, my friend," Michael warned. "Your heart is in the right place, but family issues can be complicated."

"I know, I know, but I'm committed now. I think Rachel will come around. And I have yet to tell you the most mind-blowing part of his story."

Gabriel pulled on his ear, staring into space. As he contemplated his next disclosure, the fire in his eyes grew brighter.

"Okay, I'm listening, buddy. You have my full attention, although my glass is empty." Michael stood up and poured himself a drink. The Scotch helped eased his conscience. Watching Gabriel burn with curiosity and insight brought back memories of their work together, and helped take his mind off his own entanglement.

"I now understand why Tony abandoned Rachel and her mother all those years ago," Gabriel affirmed.

"Why did he leave?" Michael asked eagerly.

"Michael, what I'm about to share with you, I share with you not as a professional collaborator, but rather as the only family I have left. I'm emphasizing this to you now because I am about to reveal a narrative that may be hard for you to process. Tony confided in me because he believes my knowing certain things will better equip me to keep my family safe. You're family, Rachel is family. Tony will soon be family. So I don't think I'm violating his confidence by disclosing what I've learned. Should anything ever happen to me, it will be up to you to protect the family. Just as I would do for you."

"I know you would, brother," Michael insisted. "And while I wish you'd get to the fucking point already, I'm compelled to assure you that your faith is not misplaced. We're brothers, I'd take a bullet for you and I know you'd do the same for me."

Whatever Michael needed to repress in order to compartmentalize his feelings toward Rachel had to be so. Rachel's counsel was prescient. The wisdom of letting go what passed between them became abundantly clear following Gabriel's affirmation. Rendering asunder familial bonds would most certainly be ruinous for all of them. Gabriel was family.

"Rachel's father had connections to the CIA, going way back to his days as a member of the politically active Cuban exiles in Miami. As a sharp, savvy businessman who got caught in the crosshairs of the Castro Revolution, he stood out among his fellow exiles and caught the eye of the CIA brass in the early sixties. But when Tony's covert gigs started putting his family in jeopardy, he was forced to make an impossible call. Circumstances dictated he create some distance between his activities and his family, eventually separating from them entirely for their own safety. That decision has been eating away at him, haunting him all these years. Helen says it's a recurring theme of his drug-induced delirium. He has confessed as much to me in a state of full lucidity."

"So, you think the fevered ravings of an old Cuban who is being pumped full of drugs to within an inch of his life, proves he worked as an operative for the Agency?" The prosecutor in Michael shifted into skeptic mode. He wanted Gabriel to back his disclosures with evidence.

"Look, bud, I understand what you're getting at, but I'm not preparing this story for publication or the courtroom, at least not at the moment. I'm confident there is a high probability everything Tony's told me is based on his own experiences rather than some drug-induced fantasy."

"So Tony worked for the CIA?" Michael repeated skeptically.

"Yes, he was an off-the-books operative for the CIA. But there's more, much more, and I need you to stay with me on this. If you don't buy the first premise, then the next part of his story may be too much for you to handle."

"The next part?"

"I was hesitant to share this with you but based on what I said earlier, I believe it's the right thing to do."

"I understand, buddy," Michael affirmed. "Revealing something shared in confidence requires no small amount of trust. Please continue."

After pouring himself another generous measure of Scotch, Gabriel took a long pull before resuming.

"Tony is communicating things outside the purview of the average person, or even the typical CIA agent."

"How do you mean?"

"Not only does he know undisclosed details about historical events like the Bay of Pigs invasion, but he was also engaged with individuals at the center of these events."

"Like who?"

"Like Allen Dulles."

"The former head of the CIA?"

"Yes."

"Pretty high up in the chain of command," Michael remarked.

"Yes. Dulles enjoyed the spy game, kept teams of operatives all over the world reporting directly to him."

"Wow. Teams of covert operatives accountable to no one," Michael said.

"Yeah, not the kind of thing that you want scrutinized by the press or anyone else for that matter," Gabriel said, the gravity in his tone unmistakable.

He continued, "So Tony leaves Cuba after the Castro revolution and becomes a U.S. citizen in 1960. He works as a government contractor, a 'community liaison,' eventually working with the CIA in '61, he becomes a lead operative in Operation Zapata, the ill-fated Bay of Pigs invasion. A covert CIA asset with access to money and resources. Then in December of 1963 he falls off the map. Rachel remembers seeing her father for the last time on Thanksgiving Day, November 28, 1963. Shortly before her tenth birthday."

Gabriel paused to gather his thoughts and gauge Michael's reaction.

"Okay, so he falls off the map in late 1963. What next?" Michel asked.

"Nothing. Four years later he establishes residency in Israel in 1967, and from there he stays off the radar."

"So what are you getting at? Where's the lynchpin in the case you're forming?" Michael prompted.

"Okay, you know what happened in November of 1963. Who does Tony meet with in November of 1963 causing him to abandon his family and fall off the radar?" Gabriel locked eyes with Michael.

"Yes, that would be the question, presuming the timeline is correct," Michael said.

Gabriel rose from his seat, the tension coursing through him palpable. Turning away from Michael, he seemed to pause to gather his thoughts before proceeding with his startling narrative. He retrieved two ice cubes and plopped them into Michael's glass, the clink of the cubes against the glass punctuating the charged atmosphere.

"The timeline *is* accurate. On November 28, Thanksgiving Day 1963, Tony De Castro is whisked away by private plane to a secure townhouse in Georgetown where he meets with Lyndon Baines Johnson. Johnson ascended to the presidency just six days earlier, which means it's six days following the assassination of John F. Kennedy."

"This is getting interesting. Though it's a big leap from Allen Dulles to LBJ."

"Not really. It was Dulles who recommended him," Gabriel answered.

"For God's sake, Gabriel, please get to your theory."

"It's not a theory, Michael, it's history."

"It's a theory until the evidence determines it's a fact, and right now I'm inclined to cite Occam's razor. The simplest explanation is the most probable one. It's a fever dream."

"Fuck Occam's razor, Michael!" Gabriel said, raising his voice. "Are you paying attention?"

The burning tension hardening on Gabriel's face caught Michael off guard. The enigma surrounding Rachel's father had ensnared Gabriel and there were very few people in the world who could match his skill at unearthing buried secrets.

Gabriel continued. "Lyndon Baines Johnson, the thirty-sixth president of the United States, acting on the counsel of former CIA director Allen Dulles, recruits Tony for a classified mission."

"Johnson himself taps Tony?" Michael asked.

"Yes."

"Why?"

"This is the part that requires you to dial back your skepticism a little and understand how Tony's story lines up with actual events."

"Gabriel, you might not have enough Scotch in the house if you continue circling around your central theory. Please get to it!"

"I have another bottle," Gabriel said, attempting to defuse the building tension.

"Please, Gabriel, don't make me have to kill you in your own home."

"Okay. Johnson speaks to Russian premier Nikita Khrushchev on the secured hotline they installed after the Cuban Missile Crisis. Khrushchev drops a bomb on the new president, metaphorically speaking. He tells Johnson that a rogue KGB operation was responsible for orchestrating the assassination of John F. Kennedy."

"Okay, we are getting into a highly questionable area here, my friend. This sounds like another conspiracy theory from someone with delusions of grandeur."

"Yeah, I get that, Michael, and I'm going to give you a chance to establish the witness's credibility, but please stay with me as I connect the dots for you."

"Okay, then please move on."

"Johnson received the explosive news with great skepticism but he's laser-focused on the volatility of the moment. After the assassination, his own legitimacy is in question. He's not sure if he should trust Khrushchev's version of events, but he couldn't game out how Khrushchev would benefit perpetrating this elaborate fabrication. Here's the kicker, Khrushchev tells Johnson he'll resign his office to prove he's committed to avoiding war. He promises Johnson that anyone who participated in or had any knowledge of the rogue assassination plot would be dead before he left office."

"Wow!" Michael found himself, uncharacteristically, at a loss for words.

"Khrushchev, the man who had brought the world so close to nuclear war a year earlier, agrees to relinquish power. As you know, Khrushchev resigned in October 1964."

"He was forced to resign," Michael said.

"That's the official story, but his actions were the result of a promise he made to Johnson. He spent five months out of Moscow directing the cover-up operation. He could have resisted the party's push to remove him from power, but he allowed it to happen; by promising to give up the premiership he convinced Johnson he was sincere. He offered a voluntary regime change as recompense for the regime change forced by the assassination."

Michael remained speechless. He took another sip of Scotch, his skepticism colliding with compelling historical facts and his respect for Gabriel's ability to get to the truth of things.

Gabriel continued, methodically laying out his case. "Johnson agreed with Khrushchev, the truth had to be concealed from the American people and the rest of the world in order to avoid a catastrophic world war. He knew the hawks in his cabinet would demand a war of merciless retaliation. Kennedy advisors like 'Bombs Away LeMay', chief of staff of the air force, were itching for a fight ever since the Cuban Missile Crisis."

"The news of a Russian-orchestrated assassination would've definitely triggered American bloodlust," Michael said, catching on.

"Undoubtedly."

"And the Russians would have had no choice but to respond in kind."

"Exactly."

"Leading to the end of civilization as we know it."

"Correct. So, given the potentially devastating outcome, everything's on the table, and no measure undertaken to avoid that kind of cataclysm would be considered too extreme."

"Okay, I follow you. How did they keep it a secret?"

"Great question! This brings us back to why Tony De Castro was summoned to do the unthinkable. In the name of preserving civilization, he was ordered to take lives, some innocent, some not so much. Commit murder, or in CIA parlance, terminate his targets with extreme prejudice."

"Yeah, I can see how that would be a compelling pitch given the circumstances," Michael agreed.

"They concealed the truth about the JFK plot by killing anyone who had anything to do with it, Americans and Russians. Johnson needed someone outside the traditional intelligence community because some of those people were targets, either because they were involved or because they got too close to the truth."

"That's a lot to process, my friend."

"Tell me about it. But it adds up. Two men assigned to eliminate a list of targets. Anyone privy to the truth found themselves on The List. Khrushchev and Johnson handpicked a team of two trusted operatives to do the dirty work. Tony was one of them. Apparently, he met his Russian counterpart but he's been tight-lipped about details."

"I understand why he'd be hesitant to name such a man," Michael mused.

"Definitely," Gabriel agreed. "And then we have the alleged lone gunman, groomed by the KGB, shot dead on national television within twenty-four hours of being captured. Unlike virtually every other political assassin, who insists on claiming their place in history, Oswald, for the short time he remained alive, claimed to be a patsy. He never laid claim to any philosophical justification. His recruitment, likely coerced, and the assistance he received on the ground, along with his subsequent elimination, were all part of the original KGB plan."

"I see how the pieces of this story might fit. So Oswald's recruiters, the people who aided and abetted, and anyone who learned about the plot stateside, were on The List?"

"Correct."

"Was Jack Ruby an operative?"

"Drug-addled, mentally unstable, deeply in debt, and easily groomed for the task, he was part of the original KGB conspiracy. His handlers were compromised CIA operatives who worked through the mob. They too were silenced by Tony."

"If this is true, doesn't this mean that you and I are now on The List?" Michael asked, a hint of concern in his tone.

"If the operation was ongoing I would imagine so. But I don't think it is."

"You don't *think* it is? Isn't that something you want to be sure of?" Michael asked, his eyes cutting through Gabriel.

"I'm as sure as one can be with these types of things. Tony shared this information reluctantly. He knows he doesn't have long to live. On the outside chance that someone, somewhere is still engaged in this godforsaken cover-up, he thought it prudent to unearth long-buried secrets. And now, for exactly the same reasons, I'm reading you in," Gabriel said, a grim twist forming on his mouth.

"And this is your houseguest?" Michael asked incredulously. "Rachel's father is the man who altered our understanding of history by silencing anyone with knowledge of the Kennedy assassination?"

Gabriel drained his Scotch, poured another one pensively, and left the question hanging in the air.

"Tell me again why President Johnson enlisted Tony De Castro for the most sensitive cover-up in human history."

"I know it sounds crazy, but it all comes back to Allen Dulles. Dulles was the director of the CIA during the Eisenhower administration, a man with unprecedented leeway to meddle in the affairs of duly elected governments around the world. The blunders perpetrated by the Dulles brothers continue to reverberate even today—remember it was also Dulles who helped put the Shah in power in Iran, which led to Khomeini's revolution, which led to the hostage crisis. Eisenhower favored those types of operations at the start of the Cold War because he believed them preferable to armed conflict. But I digress. Over the years, Dulles built a vast network of covert operatives funded through secret black ops budgets. Are you still with me on this?"

"Yes, absolutely, I'm following you, but it's still not clear how Tony got tied up with all of this."

Michael observed the spark of Gabriel's investigative instincts lighting up his synapses. Still, he attempted to remain impartial.

"Just stay with me. So Allen Dulles fails spectacularly with the Bay of Pigs invasion. He embarrasses the new administration and gets himself fired. Two years later Kennedy is assassinated. In the confusion following the assassination Johnson has two immediate priorities. First, he must reassure the country his presidency is legitimate. Second, he must eliminate anyone who has knowledge of Russia's involvement with the assassination. In this, his closest ally is the premier of the Soviet Union. Both men had just seen the world come dangerously close to nuclear war during the Cuban Missile Crisis. That kind of thing can provide a certain clarity of thought, even to the fiercest nationalist."

"One can only hope," said Michael.

"So Johnson turns to Allen Dulles," Gabriel explained, his whispered voiced laced with intrigue. "He requests direct access to an intelligence operative, someone capable of functioning outside the normal channels. Dulles introduces Johnson to Tony De Castro, an asset who had proved himself trustworthy following the Cuban fiasco. Johnson had a reputation for cultivating his own sources, so the request for a direct report didn't seem all that unusual.

"He rewards Dulles with an appointment to the Warren Commission. He's the only member of the Warren Commission with experience in intelligence operations. He made sure the Commission arrived at the appropriate conclusion in a timely manner, over the objections of the Kennedy family. Theories about a broader conspiracy were never thoroughly investigated."

"Why would Dulles agree to such a thing?" Michael asked.

"Dulles's interests aligned with Johnson's. Several covert operations under his watch violated U.S. law and international norms—assassinations, the removal of democratically elected leaders, the pursuit of his own corporate interests over democratic ones, and so on."

"Okay, makes sense from a tactical perspective. So Tony now reports to President Johnson?"

"Well, kind of. They only meet once. Johnson hands him a list of names and explains the mission. The names on The List, originally twenty-six, twenty Russians, and six Americans, were targeted for elimination. The List grew, and anyone who learned the truth about the operation had to be added to it, no exceptions. Johnson tells Tony he will have a single Russian counterpart with the same mission. They are only to communicate when the job is completed. Tony would be given a covert identity within the CIA providing him continued access to resources, money and intel. His true objective was a secret held by only four people; anyone who happened to discover his actual mission was added to The List.

"They would never meet again. The implications of what Johnson imparted didn't require parsing. Should Tony turn down the assignment, his name would be added to The List. If anyone else, including his family, learned of the mission, they too get added. Rachel and her mother would become casualties of his new assignment. Tony never went home again. Rachel was just a child."

Michael took a long sip of his drink, pausing to reflect on the incendiary narrative Gabriel unveiled. "Gabriel, my friend, this is a powerful piece of storytelling. But surely there's no way to corroborate all of the details Tony shared?"

"There's more. Helen's first husband was ex-IDF and regularly worked for Mossad. Apparently, Tony connected with her former husband through Israeli Intelligence contacts."

"Is Tony's wife aware of your theory?" Michael asked.

"No, most of my conversations with Tony have been in private. She encouraged me to talk to him, help him get stuff off his chest about his past, but she hasn't pressed me for details about what transpired between us."

"Okay, so Helen, his own wife, is in the dark about all this?" Michel rubbed his chin as he evaluated Gabriel's unfolding narrative.

"I don't think she's entirely in the dark. I suspect she's harboring her own theories. Keeping them to herself, a survival instinct honed from her previous marriage. She knows enough about Tony to recognize he did things he regrets, ugly things in service of a cause, not unlike her ex-husband. I think that's enough for her. To her credit, she realizes that as Tony approaches his final chapter, the need to unburden himself is strong, and she may not be the best person to hear his confessions."

"I can see why," Michael agreed.

"There are still things I haven't wrapped my head around," Gabriel continued. "Tony partners with Helen's ex-husband, Aaron, they meet in Israel around January of 1963. Then one day, Aaron leaves and never comes back. Tony returns to Israel to break the news to Helen. All he can tell her is that Aaron has died in the line of duty. Shortly after, Tony moves to Israel and takes an active role in the outreach work Helen and her husband were doing in Israel. He ends up marrying her. He only moves back to the United States because of health issues."

"What do you think happened to Aaron?"

"My guess is Aaron found himself on The List."

"Gabriel, let's assume for a moment that what you've so artfully pieced together is not part of the drug-induced ramblings of an old man with a vivid imagination. The evidence tying Tony to the cover-up remains mostly circumstantial."

"I've corroborated what I can, but as I said, we're not in a court of law here, Michael. I'm coming to you with this because… I don't even know what to do with it." Gabriel acknowledged a sudden cloud of unease darkening his mood.

The mission to mend the fractured relationship between Rachel and her father was careening toward a collision with the explosive revelations Gabriel unearthed. Gabe's investigative instincts were poised to clash head-on with an overpowering desire to shield the person he cherished most in the world. The tough decisions Gabriel grappled with resonated with Michael, as he too had to grapple with his own Faustian choices.

"I suppose one could make the case that an elderly man nearing the end of his life, burdened by a guilty conscience, concocted an elaborate tale to justify abandoning his family and seek forgiveness," Gabriel mused.

"Maybe," Michael replied, withholding judgment as Gabriel oscillated between two troubling scenarios: exposing Rachel's father, an old man dying of cancer, as a fabricator of spectacular deceits; or, conversely, a cold-blooded killer behind one of history's most intractable unsolved mysteries. Truth can be a burden too heavy for one man to carry, and it seemed to Michael that his friend was now inadvertently assuming a part of that burden. Going public with the story would be devastating to someone he loved and possibly open wounds that might never heal.

"We have to consider what's best for the people we care about, Michael," Gabriel muttered and said no more.

Amidst the swelling uncertainty, Michael couldn't ignore the nagging concern that his friend might not have fully considered all the potential ramifications of his discoveries. If Gabriel's conclusions were indeed accurate, how should justice be served? Murder, after all, is a capital crime. Did the pursuit of truth justify the collateral damage exposing it would bring? Tony's impending demise infused such deliberations with an elevated sense of urgency. In this case, bringing the truth to light held the potential to destroy the very thing Gabriel had set out to repair.

Michael pondered Gabriel's conundrum. Gabriel's loyalty to family demanded he consider the potential damage to Rachel's fragile connection to her father. His intention had been to foster reconciliation, not to unearth buried truths that could inflict fresh psychological wounds. However, concealing the truth felt like a betrayal of the principles at the heart of their life's work.

The leap from disbelief to astonished recognition was forcing both men to weigh exposing what they knew against the solemn commitment to protect family.

Meanwhile, in addition to his desire to protect Gabriel, Michael found himself embroiled in his own ethical quandary. He strained to balance deeply ingrained principles while staying true to who he was and preserving a bond forged over a lifetime.

Loyalty clashed with self-preservation, as desire gradually chipped away at noble aspirations.

As the substance of their deliberations bore down upon them, draining them physically and mentally, the numbing effect of alcohol quieted ominous thoughts. Aching for the solace of sleep, he bid Gabriel goodnight and stumbled toward an awaiting bed.

# 29

## RIPPLES

Alone in his study, warmed by the remaining embers of a dying fire, finding no refuge in sleep, Gabriel's thoughts drifted. His sister's voice, once the guiding animator of his conscience, fell silent, leaving him to navigate a labyrinth of disconcerting thoughts alone.

Tony's incendiary disclosures cast a looming shadow over the person he most wanted to protect. They unraveled an alternate version of history, meticulously crafted by two leaders facing cataclysmic choices. While they may have averted immediate catastrophe following Kennedy's assassination, the carefully constructed façade was being undone by the burden of concealed truths— the toll of harboring a contrived reality rippling through time, threatening to levy unimaginable costs.

Piercing that veil of deception would introduce a new set of difficult choices. Wield the sword of justice, expose the bloody cover-up, and embrace the inevitable notoriety. He would be celebrated as having solved one of history's greatest enigmas. But aside from personal acclaim, what would be gained? Perhaps preventing a nuclear conflict once warranted deception, but that no longer applied. It was a different fallout he would be unleashing with his revelations. And who would bear the brunt of that fallout?

Ensnared in a web of unanswered questions, Gabriel grappled with the cryptic puzzle. How did the rogue faction of Russian operatives execute their plan? Who possessed the precise marksmanship to strike a moving target multiple times from eighty-one meters under adverse conditions? And who erased the crucial forensic evidence, concealing the threads of a broader conspiracy? Were all the American and Russian collaborators systematically purged from existence, or did some elusive few evade the reckoning? Did the Warren Commission, charged with untangling the net of deception, deliberately obscure the truth to safeguard global stability, or were darker motives at play?

Further lingering uncertainties gnawed at Gabriel's conscience. Could The List still be active, its ominous specter looming over them all? Was his answer to Michael's question, uttered in the fog of the moment, dangerously cavalier? The allure of diving deeper into the mysteries proved almost irresistibly tantalizing. Yet, he continued to weigh the agonizing choice: to leave the unanswered details where Tony buried them, or do as he'd always done, expose the truth. In the dimming light Gabriel recognized a clear and immutable force that bound him to Tony. It was a bond forged in the crucible of shared conviction, a bond so potent that they were prepared to sacrifice everything without a moment's hesitation, even if it meant laying down their lives.

Rachel.

The cover-up had already exacted a price, designating Tony's family as expendable casualties. A once-united family was now fractured, its patriarch vanished, its matriarch surrendering to heartbreak, and its daughter haunted by the specter of abandonment. Reuniting Rachel with her ailing father before his inevitable departure offered an opportunity for closure and renewal, a chance to liberate her from the clutches of a toxic past.

It was a noble objective. Still, the cost of his complicit silence, was not easily dismissed.

Exposing Tony's role in the concealment of history would undoubtedly unleash new, unpredictable collateral damage. If safeguarding Rachel from that fallout demanded he rethink his priorities, so be it. The choice to shield Rachel was his, so he committed to opening the door to forgiveness and allowing secrets buried long ago to stay that way.

As the fire's exhausted embers faded, Gabriel sat in darkness, his fate now inextricably bound to Tony De Castro. He knew what had to be done. Time was a luxury neither man possessed. One question lingered, gnawing at Gabriel in the dark: could Michael, driven by his own peculiar sense of duty, be trusted to leave the past undisturbed?

* * *

*I'm dying. The doctors say it's cancer but I know better. I've carried the burden of secrets for too long, they consume me from the inside. I don't fear death, that old companion circles like a vulture. The souls that haunted my dreams now approach in waking hours. I'm tired. I've lost the will to resist them.*

The need to unburden himself became irresistible, still he feared the unintended cost of doing so. Once unleashed, the specters hidden by uncontainable secrets would be impossible to restrain. Even in this unsettled state of mind, he understood some of what he knew must remain hidden, only he struggled to discern which of the many buried parts of his past must never see the light of day.

His thoughts wandered, relentlessly traversing dark corridors, connecting faces and places, blood and regret, shattered hopes and lofty illusions, broken friendship and betrayal. Moving through time and events that he did not wish to visit ever again.

*I can end this, all of it. I can do it right now.*

Somewhere among his possessions lurked a Beretta 92 semi-automatic pistol. A reliable weapon, a trusted tool used in the interest of saving lives, now offering a solution to his torment.

*"I can fix this for you. One last time. It would be messy, but it would be over... once and for all."*

*Not a very honorable way to go out, and I would never allow it in my daughter's home. Maybe, maybe when I get back to my own home.*

"Yes, that'll work, I'll be here, you can reach for me anytime. But why wait?"

*No! Not yet. I must see Rachel again. I must make certain she is safe.*

"Safe? From what?"

*You know. You were there.*

"That's all in the past. Erased. We can erase this too. I can help."

Amidst the longing for deliverance, inside the hollow vacuum within his heart where Rachel belonged, lay the unbearable weight of untold undertakings. The encumbrance of regret, heavy and unrelenting, laid siege, while aggressive white cells multiplied and consumed. There a glimmer of hope remained, a light in the encroaching shadows. It sustained him.

*Just a little more time. I have to tell her what it cost me. I never intended for events to turn out the way they did. I only wanted to make a better world for them.*

*Please! If I could only speak with her and explain how impossible choices were forced upon me all those years ago. In the end, I disappeared so they could remain safe. She needs to know how much I love her, how much it cost me to leave her and her mother behind, she needs to know how terribly I missed her all those years. I pray it's not too late.*

\* \* \*

Alone in the kitchen, Helen stifled the sensations swelling in her chest. *Not now. I refuse to show weakness. I am resilient. I will not fracture.* With deft hands she wielded the sturdy kitchen knife, slicing through the vegetables arrayed on the cutting board. *Should tears surface, I'll blame the onions, it's nothing more. I will not break!*

*I miss my home, Israel. I miss sitting and kibitzing among my friends. My heart returns to them, those strong people, the brave ones who refuse to surrender to impossible circumstances and lost causes. Palestinians and Israelis who insisted on living peacefully, raising their children with respect for each other. Shunned by their own, yet undeterred, clinging on to hope even if hope meant exile until they could return home safely. How many times did*

*Tony assist them in escaping to a better life? More than I can count.*

*I'm strong but unprepared for this new trial. I feel I'm being tested, entangled in the anguish of illness, regret, and looming death. Tony's a fighter, but this is a fight he's not going to win. It's only a matter of time. His is a lost cause. Even so, my place is at his side. Isn't it? I couldn't be with Aaron in his final hours, perhaps this is how I find closure, in the easing of Tony's passing when the time comes.*

*Death is no stranger; I've witnessed more than my share. Yet, Tony's disturbing laments, his bouts of anger, fear, and remorse, his need to voice unspeakable thoughts during delirious rants, have been difficult to hear. I must dismiss his unhinged outbursts, prevent the words from taking root. Listen patiently until the darkness dissipates.*

*I'm grateful for Gabriel's help. Grateful to have a break during the hours he stays with Tony. So much loss between the three of us, we've learned to move past it, but still, revisiting the past always stirs something unfathomable in me. Tony's demons are somehow tangled up with my own.*

The scent of freshly cut onions filled the kitchen and the tears, contained no longer, flowed freely. Tears for the loss of her husband so many years ago. Tears for the loss of so many broken lives caught in an endless conflict between Israel and Palestine. Tears for the families destroyed by violence. Tears for the ones that she will never see again. Tears for Tony slowly giving way to the cancer devouring him. And somewhere behind the tears, behind the sympathy for all who suffer—rage. Rage for the injustices perpetrated against innocent men, women and children. Rage toward those who in the name of security commit atrocities. Rage at the lies and misdirection. Too much pain buried in the past to stomach the unearthing of such remembrances without awakening seething, long-repressed rage.

Arron always loved her cooking. The fragrant aroma of a simmering Shakshuka filled the kitchen with enticing memories of a happier time and place. She called upon those memories now to strengthen her in this hour of unanticipated trials.

# 30

# REVELATIONS AT THE GATES OF DELIRIUM

Shards of sunlight pierced the delicate window coverings and sliced into Michael's throbbing head. *Too much Scotch, too many unanswered questions, too little time to sift through it all in a single night. Can't decide what inflicted more damage, the Scotch or the strained rationalizations and relentless ruminations. Need more coffee!*

Chipper despite the booze and sleepless night, Gabriel bounced into the guest room and greeted Michael with a fresh cup of coffee in hand. "Ready to meet Tony? He's up, alert, and eager for company. Helen's whipping up a nice homemade meal to help with the hangover."

"It smells great," Michael said wearily.

The suite Tony occupied functioned as a comfortable in-law apartment. A large bedroom abutted a small living area outfitted with a couch, a reclining chair, and a bookcase with a built-in TV. In a corner of the living area stood a small table and chairs where an unfinished game of dominoes sat waiting.

Meanwhile, Tony's wife bustled about the kitchen, filling the house with tantalizing aromas.

"Tony, allow me to introduce you to a good friend of ours. This is Michael Rose, he's the chief of the Criminal Division for the Southern District of New York and an occasional collaborator in my work. Michael's like a brother to me."

"Chief of the Criminal Division sounds like an important job. Am I under investigation?" Tony smiled and offered a firm handshake. His hands were bruised from too many IV punctures, but his eyes glimmered, alert and penetrating. "Nice to meet you, Michael. You must forgive me if I don't stand up, they have been pumping me full of chemicals that are supposed to kill the cancer in my body. I am not sure what will kill me first, cancer or the damn cure. To think I've survived all that I've survived and it will be some medical technician in a white lab coat that will finally finish me off."

"It's a pleasure to meet you, Mr. De Castro. From what Gabriel tells me you're more than a worthy match for anyone in a white lab coat. He tells me you have repeatedly cleaned his clock at dominoes, which I applaud, as I believe any lessons in humility gained through a game of dominoes will serve him well."

"Yes, this is true. Gabriel and I are getting to know each other through the time-honored tradition of matching wits over a game of dominoes. He is a good man, but from what I can tell, it will take much more than beating him at the game to keep him humble."

The three men shared a hearty laugh.

"You see what I mean, Michael? Sharp as a tack, watch yourself," Gabriel chuckled.

"What business brings you to Vermont, Michael? What news do you have of my daughter in New York City? I am hoping to see her soon. It's been many years and I'm not sure how many more sunsets I have left."

The old Cuban's vulnerability and charm impressed Michael. He detected a slight accent, and a hint of sadness in his voice, but not enough to encumber his eloquence.

"I had some business to attend to in Boston and decided to take a short break to visit an old buddy," Michael explained, concealing his true motive. "As for Rachel, she's holding up alright in New York. Dealing with that classic artist's dilemma, you know? The more success she gets, the more the business side of things starts to get in the way of producing art. I imagine she's eager to get home to family and to do what she loves best. And you, sir? How're you feeling?"

"Me? Well, if I were a cat with nine lives I'd say I'm on my ninth one." The old man's gaze drifted into the distance as if lost in some far-off recollection. "When did you say Rachel was coming back?"

"He's strong as an ox, Michael, don't let him fool you," Helen said interrupting the banter, a plate of olives, cheese, fig spread, warm pita, and serrano ham in hand. "I brought you boys something to snack on while you chat, brunch is going to be a little while longer. I never ate ham until I met Tony. When we traveled through Spain, I think it's all we ate. It pleased me very much to find a butcher who carries Jamon Iberico here in Stowe. Try some."

Michael admired Helen's poise under pressure, graceful in her attempt to redirect Tony from dwelling too much on painful memories.

"It's true," said Tony. "The French and Italians know how to cure ham, but there is nothing like Jamon Iberico, *hombre*. Michael, where are your people from?"

"My people? I grew up in Riverdale, in the Bronx."

"No, son, I didn't ask where you grew up, I asked you where your people are from."

"I'm Jewish, although I'm not religious."

"So, you are a Jew that doesn't believe in the God of Abraham?" Tony glanced at Helen.

"I embrace my cultural heritage and the wisdom of the Torah, but I don't necessarily buy into all the mythical stories about the Promised Land and God speaking from burning bushes."

Helen shook her head and interrupted the exchange.

"Tony, let the man enjoy a nosh without provoking a debate about Jewish identity. You just met him, he seems like a nice man. You heard Gabriel say he is like family to him and Rachel, that's all you need to know. Please forgive Tony, Michael. He enjoys a good argument and there is nothing better than religion or politics to get him going."

"It's perfectly alright, Helen, I too enjoy a good argument. There's an innate tension between faith in the ancient texts of my people and the need for factual evidence in the work I do."

"Our people." Helen smiled. "You are not alone in this."

"Our people." Michael nodded his head in acknowledgment. "I confess I embrace a cultural inheritance based on stories handed down over thousands of years with some hesitation. I believe mythical narratives of some sort underpin every society. It's how our forefathers made sense of the world and handed down foundational values to future generations. Do we really believe George Washington never told a lie?"

"I warned you, Michael," said Gabriel. "You're a career prosecutor and Tony's already elicited a confession from you before you've had your first bite." The tension in the room evaporated in a fit of laughter once again.

Taking advantage of a disarming moment, Michael shifted topics. "Tony, Gabriel and I share a passion for history, and I understand you met Lyndon Johnson. What was he like?"

"Yes, Johnson, I met him once. Introduced to him by a man named Allen Dulles, a brilliant man with a monstrously huge ego, and a myopic worldview. He also possessed a well-deserved reputation as an epic philanderer. If someone were trying to make a case that power is the ultimate aphrodisiac, then Allen Dulles and Lyndon Johnson would be exhibits A and B, two homely-looking men who got more tail than Frank Sinatra."

Michael and Gabriel exchanged awkward glances. Helen left the room, pretending to not hear Tony's racy comments.

"Dulles and I worked together in an attempt to remove Fidel Castro from power. We failed. I was young and disenchanted with the broken promises of the Cuban Revolution. Dulles obsessed over anyone he considered an adversary, hell-bent on preventing any communist regime to take hold in this hemisphere." Tony offered his analysis with unusual vigor.

"I considered him a mentor of sorts, even though his methods were, shall we say, disagreeable at times. In those days I believed the United States of America represented the best hope for a stable and peaceful world. Dulles saw himself, somewhat deludedly, as a warrior for freedom and democracy. For a while, I too embraced the American myth." Tony's tone held an air of nostalgia. "But so much of what the United States did in Latin America was plagued by hubris and willful ignorance. Only later in life did I come to fully understand that American foreign policy was more about economic imperialism than a quest for a world grounded in justice and democracy. There are murderous regimes currently in power simply because they were led by useful idiots happily bought off by American interests. God help us all."

Tony made the sign of the cross for dramatic emphasis. He seemed to be enjoying the attention.

"Still, a man must pick a side and as a young man with limited knowledge of the larger world, I fell for the propaganda, seduced by the idea that promoting 'progress' across the developing world would make the world safer for future generations, even if at times it meant using a little too much force. In those days I wanted to be counted among the generation of idealists who helped shape the New Frontier."

"So you worked with Allen Dulles and LBJ?" Michael asked, attempting to redirect Tony toward his original line of inquiry.

"What do you think of the ham, Michael?" Tony said, evading the question. "Have you had Jamon Iberico before? The cheese is Manchego, Spanish, aged from goat's milk."

"It's delicious, thank you. You've lived a fascinating life, Mr. De Castro."

"Do you think so? Fascinating is not the word I would use."

"You have seen much. I understand why Gabriel speaks highly of his honored guest."

"Yes, Helen and I are grateful for the generous hospitality Gabriel has shown us."

Tony nodded at Gabriel and offered a warm smile.

"Johnson was an ambitious and hardworking hillbilly who understood the fundamental essence of human nature. He understood the primal motivators behind public men: power, money, sex, and love. He used his keen intuitive insight to reduce all political matters to their most elemental forms, and through that understanding, he developed the ability to get almost anyone to do his bidding. His persuasive skills were legendary, unmatched in any arena."

"Did he get you to do his bidding?" Michael continued to probe. It was clear why Gabriel found Tony so interesting. Like Gabriel, he was drawn to Tony's keen insight and raw honesty. Tony projected credibility, the kind of witness that could turn a jury.

"I'm no different than anyone else, once Johnson had you in his grasp he did not let go until he got what he wanted. I will say this about him, he had a noble heart. It's a shame he got caught up in events outside his control."

"Meaning Vietnam?"

"No, not Vietnam." Tony's hands began trembling, his eyes watered and the color left his face.

"Michael, you're leading the witness and I believe the witness needs a break," Gabe interjected.

"Yes, let us pause for now." Tony suddenly appeared distracted. "I'm sorry, gentlemen, but I have a plane to catch. I will call on you when I return. You are good men and I promise you, you will be rewarded for your service." Tony looked away, eyes focused on an invisible horizon.

Gabe and Michael exchanged glances, uncertain how to respond. Tony's focus began slipping away as if he were being transported to another place in time. Right on cue, Helen interrupted, offering refreshments. "It won't be much longer, boys. I made some fresh lemonade, Tony's favorite unless you two want something stronger."

"Thank you, Helen, lemonade is perfect. I'm going to give Michael a tour of Rachel's studio," Gabriel added. "We'll let Tony rest and come back for lunch in a bit."

Gabriel locked eyes with Helen.

"Okay then, boys, enough banter for a little while," Helen said, with a concerned eye on Tony.

"I have a plane to catch," Tony insisted, his hands still trembling.

"We have a little time, my dear, we still have a little time." Helen held Tony's hand as the men exited the suite.

On the way out the door Michael was shaken by the brief exchange he overheard.

"Helen?" Tony muttered.

"Yes, Tony. What is it?"

"Bring me my gun."

# 31

## SYMPATHY FOR THE DEVIL

Dimitri Ivanov set aside the menu and wine list and, speaking perfect French, delivered his instructions to the waiter. The server's haughty façade crumbled under the weight of Ivanov's directives while Rachel stared into space, inattentive and distracted. A fawning sommelier followed soon after to offer ingratiating words in both French and English, complimenting Dimitri's most excellent (and extravagant) wine selections.

"In an unusual display of candor, a distinguished French diplomat, who will remain unnamed, once confessed to me, 'there are three things in which the French unequivocally excel: food, wine and insolence.'" Dimitri smiled and looked at his guest with some concern but continued to offer lighthearted repartee.

Rachel endeavored to maintain focus as Ivanov, resplendent in his impeccably tailored suit, tinted glasses and signature carnation, attempted to capture her attention. She nodded politely as he held forth on a range of subjects that delighted him.

"Even the Italians, renowned for their cuisine and the exceptional wines they produce, acknowledge that the French create the finest wines in the world," Ivanov declared with a confident smile. "In Bordeaux, Burgundy, Alsace, the Loire Valley, and the Rhône, you'll find vineyards that have thrived for over two millennia. Their ancient roots penetrate deep into the earth, imparting a minerality and depth of flavor unmatched anywhere else in the world. While Bordeaux seeds may sprout in California or Chile, they'll never yield a wine that rivals the complexity and character of those nurtured by the ancient French soil. Tonight, we commence with a wine from Alsace, a region shaped by both French passion and German precision. Over the centuries, control of this area has oscillated between France and Germany, resulting in wines that some would argue embody the best of both worlds."

Amanda, perched between Dimitri and Rachel in a luxurious red velvet booth, laughed and teased the Russian, endeavoring to involve Rachel in the banter. "You see, Rachel, this is what happens when you dine with a history professor, one gets a lecture with every uncorked bottle of wine."

"Fortunately for all of us," Dimitri replied, "I am most capable of lecturing for as long as we require the wine to flow."

Amanda let out a hardy laugh. "Rachel, I assure you this is no idle boast." The ladies laughed and rewarded their host with smiles and gracious applause. Rachel appreciated the banter, but still, her ruminations persisted. *It will soon be time for me to go home, to face Gabriel and a father I haven't seen in over twenty-three years. So much has happened since I left Vermont.*

The prospect of seeing her father stirred long-dormant emotions, and the thought of seeing Gabriel again after her night with Michael filled her with unease. While she was determined not to allow what transpired with Michael to alter her connection to Gabriel, she feared that concealed truths inadvertently rise to the surface. She loved Gabriel, but memories of that evening pulled at some part of her that she had yet to fully come to terms with.

"Tells us of your plans, Rachel. I understand you are preparing to return home soon. How has your Gabriel fared on his own?"

"Gabriel is doing very well thank you."

The old Russian was charming and the connection they had established a year ago grew warmer after a glass of wine, no point in hiding the conflicting feelings she was wrestling with.

"Gabriel is fine. However, here among friends, I have to admit I am dealing with some anxiety about going home."

"Why is that?" Dimitri glanced at Amanda as if looking for clues as to how to proceed. Amanda smiled and nodded.

"I have been estranged from my father for most of my life," Rachel began, her voice tinged with a mix of sadness and resignation. "I was only nine years old the last time I saw him, and we've only had one or two conversations since. When my mother passed, I was at a crossroads, just accepted to both Vassar and the Pratt Institute. I was alone and unsure of what to do next. I needed guidance, but all he could offer was money. He assured me that all my expenses would be taken care of regardless of what school I chose. He gave me the number of an accounting firm that would handle all the payments. He apologized for not being at my mother's funeral and said that someday he would explain why. That was fifteen years ago and I haven't heard from him since."

"I see," Dimitri said, studying Rachel's face. "And now?"

"And now my father is facing terminal pancreatic cancer, and Gabriel, with my reluctant approval, has invited him to stay in our home while he undergoes treatment."

"Your father is terminally ill?" A shadow seemed to pass across Dimitri's face.

"Yes, I'm afraid so."

"I see. Does your reluctance to see him have anything to do with why you extended your stay in New York?"

"Truthfully, yes. Gabriel reached out to my father in an act of compassion and I didn't have the heart to stop him, yet part of me is very uncomfortable with the whole situation. I feel guilty that I don't share Gabriel's same sense of compassion, although I understand his motivation. He's a good man who believes in always doing the right thing. I just need time to process the whole situation."

"Your father is dying and you don't even know who he is. You feel guilty because you cannot grieve for him, your heart cannot grieve for a father you don't really know."

"Yes, that's it!" Rachel's eyes widened as Dimitri gave voice to her conflicted feelings.

"And now he is staying in your home and it feels like an invasion. A ghost from your past has now taken form in your sanctuary, and you are being asked to reconcile the years of absence and feelings of abandonment with his own fragile presence and uncertain future."

"Yes, Dimitri, that's exactly how I feel. I'm all mixed up and I fear my confusion could come between me and Gabriel. It's hard to explain."

"It's not hard to understand, my dear. Gabriel is acting from a strong sense of compassion, which is admirable, yet there is much in your past you have yet to unravel. You need time to catch up."

"Yes, thank you. You are wise, Dimitri Ivanov. You have captured my angst perfectly."

Amanda interjected, shifting the focus of the conversation. "Perhaps we should order some food. What do you recommend, Dimitri?"

"I hope you don't mind. I took the liberty of ordering for all of us ahead of time. The chef here at Grenouille is the only chef in all of New York that has earned three Michelin stars in both the U.S. and France. I promise you, you will not be disappointed."

As if on cue the waiter placed a tower of raw oysters at the center of the table. "Now pay attention, as the wine will take on a completely different character on your palate once you've tried the oysters," Dimitri suggested.

"Oh yes, remarkable how that works," Rachel said, momentarily distracted from the weight of her reflections, the wine soothing her doubts and warming her spirit.

"The brininess of the oyster brings out the ancient minerality of the wine, but the best is yet to come," Dimitri assured them, then attempted a shift in topic. "But first, if you will permit me, I have some important information to share with you, Rachel. I wanted to find the right time and place to communicate this and unfortunately, I have not been able to find the right occasion until this moment. I fear I may have waited too long."

Rachel, taken aback by the cryptic shift in tone, looked to Amanda for some indication of Dimitri's meaning. She imagined it might have something to do with her and Michael the night of the performance. Did Dimitri know something about their liaison? Her heart raced.

"Rachel." Dimitri's tone was infused with fatherly concern. "I have had the good fortune and privilege of doing many different things in my life. Throughout all my undertakings I have always attempted to let my heart and conscience guide my actions. As I've told Amanda and others, many years ago, I worked closely with various government agencies recovering art treasures stolen by the Nazis during World War Two. The work allowed me to travel freely throughout the world, engaging with people in all walks of life. That period in my life opened many doors for me, I made many contacts and those connections allowed me to pursue a wide variety of ventures."

"Yes," Amanda interjected, "you've had a very colorful past."

"Yes, colorful indeed." Dimitri Ivanov peered over his tinted glasses at Amanda, who smiled and lifted her glass.

"Now you've just shared with me that you know very little about your father and this lack of insight causes you to feel apprehension as you contemplate a reunion with him."

"Yes, this is true," Rachel agreed.

"I think I may be able to help you."

"How so?"

"As I've said, I've not found the right opportunity to share this with you until now."

"Share what?" said Rachel, growing impatient.

"I know your father. More precisely, I knew your father many years ago. Our paths crossed when we were both doing work for our respective governments."

"My father worked for the government?"

"Yes. He worked as a consultant to the U.S. government on Cuban issues. Consultant is the term given by the American intelligence apparatus to operatives who take on projects outside traditional channels intended to remain highly confidential. I too was a consultant, for the Russian government."

Rachel stared at Dimitri, dumbfounded.

"Your father was an operative for the CIA. His contacts in Cuba and Latin America, his facility with languages and his considerable intellect, made him an ideal asset for the CIA. I don't know too much about his assignments, but our paths did cross when we were each doing covert work for our respective government sponsors. We had similar skills. Even though many years have passed, I still cannot reveal to you the exact details of our assignments. I can tell you we were engaged in important and, at times, dangerous work. Your father was an idealist with a brilliant mind and extraordinary tactical skills. Your government held him in high regard."

Rachel felt a rush of conflicting emotions. Overwhelmed, she could not find the words to articulate all the questions coming to the surface.

"So, my father..." she said hesitantly. "My father... you knew my father? Why didn't you tell me? Why didn't you tell me that the first day we met? You know my father? Do you speak to him?"

"I haven't spoken to your father in over twenty years."

"How well did you know him? Did he ever mention me?"

"We were not very close, but we understood each other. The last time I saw him was long ago, we shared a glass of wine in Barcelona. But please listen to me, I do know this—like me, he was committed to his work, important work that called on him to make sacrifices. He made sacrifices for the cause he believed in. Do you understand what I'm trying to tell you?"

"No. I don't."

"He believed that America, despite all her flaws, represented the best hope for a peaceful and prosperous future for all people. As a Cuban refugee, he believed his young family would be safe in America. At that time you were probably just five or six years old. I can tell you he sacrificed much for the cause. I did the same for my country and my desire to help shape a better world. Only now, after meeting you, do I fully understand how much your father sacrificed, and this saddens me very much."

"Is this why you have been buying my work? Out of pity? Amanda, did you know?" Rachel looked confused and hurt.

"Amanda is learning of this for the first time, just as you are. Please, Rachel, do not confuse my appreciation for your work with my connection to your father. You, my dear, are a great artist and no one can ever take that away from you," Dimitri insisted.

"Rachel, I didn't know any of this, I promise you," Amanda blurted, appearing just as blindsided as she was.

Rachel wiped tears from her eyes. Dimitri turned away an approaching waiter with a gesture as Amanda slid over to Rachel's side of the booth and held her hand.

Dimitri Ivanov placed both hands on the table. "Rachel, I had no idea who you were when I purchased my first painting. You don't use your father's last name. When I decided to invest in Rachel Rivers's work I wanted to learn more about your background, who you were. I wanted to learn what motivated you to create such compelling paintings and sculptures. When I learned your true name, Raquel De Castro, it was only then that I made the connection. It has been five years since I discovered this about you and since then many others have come forward to validate the remarkable work you do. And as you know, I have only just recently been presented with the opportunity to meet you. This knowledge of your family's history was not something I felt I should blurt out at our first brief encounter a year ago. The incident at the party cut short our next meeting and now I am learning how much pain the events of long ago have caused you. My intent here is to provide some measure of context for your return home. Some perspective for the moment when you are face to face with your father again. Some opportunity to repair the damage done by the events of the past."

"Context? How?" Rachel attempted to block out thoughts about the money from Ivanov's purchases and how that money contributed to the very comfortable lifestyle she and Gabriel now enjoyed.

"Your father's work made him a target."

"A target?"

"Yes. Men who engage in covert political activities are targets, their families are targets, and their acquaintances are targets; innocent people who can be used to control or punish an operative. Your father's opposition to Castro made him a target. His work for the American government made him a target. I remember how I lived all those years ago, moving from place to place, and what I would have given to have been able to have a family. I can't imagine what it must have been like to have a daughter like you and fear for her safety. I can't imagine what I would have done if I had a daughter like you and had not been able to see her. The sense of loss would have been unbearable."

Floodgates opened and long-suppressed memories spilled into her comfortable surroundings. She remembered how his whiskers would scratch her face when he kissed her in the morning, the smell of his aftershave, his polished black wing-tip shoes. She remembered the lectures about locking the door, about not trusting strangers. She remembered how he seemed to take everything too seriously; how he treated her mother sternly. She remembered his insistence that she sit upright at the table, that she apply herself to her academic and creative work, that she not use slang or develop "vulgar" manners unsuitable for a well-educated young lady.

She thought about her mom who never really seemed happy but always tried to put on a happy face. She remembered how her mom would always defend her father. "He really loves this family," she would say, "he just wants us to be safe." Rachel just wanted to know why. Why weren't they safe? Why did they have to move around so much? Why couldn't she have friends over like the other girls? When other girls were having sleepovers, her entertainment consisted of playing dominoes with her father, baking cookies with her mother and watching episodes of Ed Sullivan or *The Twilight Zone*, her father's two favorite shows. But even watching TV could provoke a long monologue about some injustice being perpetrated somewhere in the world. On too many solitary nights Rachel remembered having to fall asleep to the sound of loud interminable lectures.

He would be home for a while then he would disappear for months at a time. "Daddy's away on business," her mother would say. "Where?" she would ask. The answer, always the same, "He's away, but he'll be back soon." Then, suddenly one morning, he left and never came back.

"Rachel," Dimitri said, watching tears course down her cheeks. "Rachel, your father's a good man."

Rachel reflected on her mother's unwavering façade of strength, how she always insisted her father's return was imminent, urging Rachel to be grateful for their blessings. Then one day her mother's heart just gave out, the doctors said that a blood clot she had probably lived with for years had finally burst. Rachel, eighteen years old, harbored no doubts about the truth: her mother had died of a broken heart.

"Rachel." Dimitri's voice gently called her back to the present. "Rachel, your father's a good man," he repeated, his words offering a new way to understand her own history. "He did what he had to do to protect you and your mother. Please, hear me out. I am as certain of this as I am of anything—I implore you to trust me, Rachel. Your father loved you, deeply, more than you know."

"Amanda, how could you not have known?" Rachel's voice quivered with a mix of disbelief and frustration. "All this time, my biggest patron knew my estranged father?" Rachel's face turned red as her eyes bored holes in Amanda.

"I told you, I'm hearing this for the first time," Amanda answered, her tone tinged with sympathy.

"I heard what you said, but you'll excuse me if it strains credulity," Rachel retorted, anger coloring her tone. "This… this news casts a shadow over everything." Her hands trembled with emotion. "A shadow over my work, my legitimacy as an artist. How can this be happening?"

"Oh my God, Rachel, I know how this may seem to you and I know how complicated your relationship is with your father."

"Complicated? Complicated?" Rachel's voice rose in anger. "You have no idea! I'm learning now that my father was some kind of spy. I… I… I have no words." Rachel's anger gave way to more tears.

Amanda leaned in, wrapping her arm around Rachel's trembling shoulders.

"Please believe me, I would never do anything to intentionally hurt you," she pleaded. "You are exactly what you were before you heard this news. An accomplished artist that creates moving and profound work. Dimitri Ivanov may be your patron, but he's not the only one who believes in you. Others have validated your work by opening their checkbooks. Your work is on display in museums and prominent galleries. No one can ever take that away from you."

Rachel didn't physically recoil from Amanda's touch, but her body remained tense. She inhaled deeply, allowing Amanda's words to seep in, but unsettling questions continued to swirl.

She sensed a seismic upheaval within, her convictions about her father shaken to their core. It was too overwhelming, too immense a shift to process all at once, a tidal surge of emotions drawing her deeper into a sea of uncertainty. Amidst the troubling internal chaos, a survival instinct kicked in. It was time to return to the one person that could guarantee her sanctuary. Gabriel.

# 32

## THE ART OF FORGIVENESS

The gravel groaned under the weight of the Land Rover making its way around the horseshoe driveway. The leaves had almost completely fallen off the trees, patches of red, yellow, and gold carpeted the grounds around her home. The chilly air hinted at snow and crackled with possibility. Gabriel, wearing a flannel shirt and a parka vest, sprung out the front door and toward the vehicle, beaming like a child whose gift-laden parents have just returned from a long vacation.

As she opened the door, hesitation gripped her, and a chilling rush of doubt threatened to dislodge her homecoming. Trembling, she stumbled forward into his awaiting embrace. In that moment, her old life shattered into fragments, and the future stretched out before her like an unformed canvas, ripe with the promise of renewal. They held each other tightly, time suspended, all reservation melting away.

In Gabriel's arms, she found relief from all lingering doubt, a tether anchoring her to the cherished world she almost lost. If her old life had been swept away by the inexorable currents of fate, then here, in this embrace, lay the crucible where she would reconstruct her new life.

The façade of strength she labored so assiduously to project gave way. She wept like a child. She wept for her old life. She wept for the little girl who had been abandoned by her father. She wept for the guilt of sharing herself with another man. She wept for the inescapable thread comingling pain with love. She wept for the misplaced compassion for a dying father, for the tenuous brevity of life and the cruel uncertainty of providence.

Here there was refuge. Here, in the echoes of her sobs, she found release from the shackles of her unsettled past. Here the mending of all that remained broken would begin. She was home.

"I missed you so much. I don't ever want to be away from you for this long again," Gabriel said as he kissed the tears from her face.

"I don't either. The attack at the club, my father's illness, his presence in our home after all these years… I lost my bearings."

"Well, you've found them again. We'll get through this together, nothing's going to hold us back. Do you believe that, my love?"

"Yes, I do. I do believe." For a brief moment, Rachel thought of Michael and wondered how he would fit into this new way forward. She put aside the thought and wrapped her arms around Gabriel. "If you're with me, I'm ready for whatever comes next."

"Good." Gabriel smiled.

"Is he here now?"

"Yes, but he may be sleeping. Let's go check."

Rachel held onto Gabriel's arm and steeled herself for her next encounter.

* * *

They found Tony asleep in the leather recliner, Hemingway's *The Old Man and the Sea* open on his lap. Gabriel sat in the chair next to him while Rachel stood.

"Tony, I have someone here who wants to see you."

Tony squinted and reached for his thick dark-rimmed glasses. "You can't be serious, *hombre*. I am too tired to answer any more of his questions. He speaks like a man who is about to empanel a grand jury."

"No, it's not Michael, he left two days ago. Tony, it's Rachel, your daughter. She's here."

"Raquel?" Tony fumbled with his glasses and tried to straighten his shirt, squinting his eyes as if trying to focus on an apparition. "Is that you? Gabriel, please, help me stand up."

Rachel gazed down at the frail figure before her, a mere shadow of the once formidable man she remembered from childhood. He appeared weathered and worn, an ancient relic of a distant past, his once-commanding presence now diminished by disease and the passage of time. As he made a feeble attempt to rise, struggling to summon the vestiges of dignity that had long ago abandoned him, Rachel felt the stirring of compassion within her soul.

Amidst the receding tide of resentment, she found a sense of concern and empathy, a desire to rediscover the father she once adored. She realized the demons of her past, once foreboding, were beginning to lose their grip in the burgeoning light of forgiveness.

"It's alright, Papa. You needn't strain yourself," she reassured him gently. "Yes, it's me. How are you feeling?" Her father, fragile and vulnerable, bore little resemblance to the heartless tyrant she had conjured in her imagination. Recalling Dimitri's surprising disclosure, she began to understand that this man had sacrificed more than she could fathom for reasons she had yet to fully grasp. Now, he stood before her not as a man running from his own past, but as a father, yearning for one last chance to embrace the daughter he had left behind so many years ago.

"You are much more beautiful than your photographs. I have missed so much of your life and I am sorry for that, *hijita*. I am sorry. But my God, you are so beautiful and now all words fail me. Please forgive me if I cannot yet find the words to express what is in my heart; but just know this, it is full, very full. I am so grateful to have survived long enough to be here with you," he murmured softly.

Tony's hand shook and his knees seemed barely able to sustain him. Gabriel instinctively wrapped his arm around the old man's waist to steady him.

Rachel leaned in to plant a kiss on her father's cheek. His scent carried the sharp tang of rubbing alcohol, and his unshaven face prickled against her skin. "We'll have plenty of time to find the right words, Papa," she murmured. "I'm grateful that you and Gabriel had the chance to bond. He mentioned you've been sharing your secret domino strategies with him."

"Yes, yes, he is a fine man. *Un hombre bueno*. But I have not taught him everything I know, he still has much to learn about dominoes and about other things too." Tony smiled and seemed to drink in her visage like a man who had been lost in the desert for too long.

"Sit, Papa, sit. You do look strong, but there's no need to stand for me. Let me sit with you for a while before I get settled in."

"As you wish, Raquelita. I am so happy you are home. I am happy you have found a good man to share your life with and I am happy that I will live long enough to attend your wedding."

"Attend?" Gabriel interjected. "The father of the bride does more than just attend. My parents are gone. You, sir, are the patriarch of this family, and you will take your place of honor among the guests joining us for our celebration."

Gabriel sparkled with a fresh sense of fulfillment. It was clear to Rachel that Gabe attained something uniquely rewarding in his connection with her father and felt a sense of accomplishment in orchestrating the long-anticipated reunion. Memories flooded her mind of the conversations they shared, mapping out their journey into this new phase of life—discussions about continuity, roots, and the importance of honoring our ancestors.

Though the length of Tony's remaining time was uncertain, Rachel finally felt the presence of a father in her life again. The trio sat together, relief washing over them as the reconnection unfolded with warmth and familiarity. The fruit of Gabriel's efforts toward reconciliation had lightened their respective burdens.

As the weight lifted, tears flowed. The rediscovery of a lost father, and the shift toward healing, granted access to something new, something that felt like grace. Something inside her seemed to avow… *just in the nick of time.*

# 33

## CHANGE OF FORTUNE

The library in Gregory Courtland's estate bathed in the dim glow of a late afternoon sun. The room boasted all the lavish accoutrements of accumulated wealth: dark mahogany panels lined the walls, while the faint aroma of leather and aged paper hung in the air. The embattled New York real estate scion sat behind a large oak desk, his fingers toying with a silver paperweight featuring Napoleon in battle regalia. Across from him, Dimitri Ivanov, cold and businesslike, settled into an elegant leather chair, an inscrutable expression stretched across his face.

"I'm delighted to see you, Mr. Ivanov. I was afraid you'd forgotten about us." Gregory Courtland forced a polite smile.

"Oh, we haven't forgotten about you, Mr. Courtland. It was necessary to allow your situation to play out. As I mentioned when we last met, we prefer to take the long view when it comes to strategic alliances."

"Well, my situation didn't play out the way I would have preferred, Mr. Ivanov," Courtland intoned, barely concealing his scorn. "Fortunately, my legal team has been working around the clock to leverage all the resources we'll require to put this entire ordeal behind us. They tell me we should fare better on the appellate level."

"I don't think that's going to happen, Mr. Courtland." Ivanov shot Courtland a steely gaze. "Your tactics have proven ineffective, it's time for a new approach."

"Why would you say that? I'm told we have a solid case. Do you know something we don't?"

"I know a great many things you don't know, Mr. Courtland. But as for the matter at hand, you won't be pursuing that appeal. You'll be making a deal with the AUSA," Ivanov said, assuming a tone of finality.

"Have you lost your mind, sir? What makes you think I'm going to cut a deal with the AUSA? A guilty plea will likely mean I won't be able to do business again in New York." Courtland's visage, wide-eyed and confused.

"Exactly. The good news for you is that you will probably not serve any jail time. If you do it will likely be for no more than a year, and you'll be in very comfortable surroundings. A place like Allenwood Federal Penitentiary, very nice facility I'm told." Ivanov leaned forward, eyes glinting with cold confidence.

"You *have* lost your mind!"

"I assure you, Mr. Courtland, I am quite sane. Are you familiar with opposition research?" Ivanov responded, calm and unwavering.

"What opposition research?" Courtland said, looking dazed.

"When a political candidate runs for major office, if they have the proper funding and support, they hire a firm to undertake a thorough investigation of their opponent. They do research to ascertain vulnerabilities. The goal is to uncover anything in their background that can be used as leverage. Political careers are made and unmade by things that never see the light of day. Information is power, Mr. Courtland." Dimitri Ivanov's soft-spoken reply resonated with subtle menace.

"What does that have to do with me?"

"I work with the best opposition researchers in the world, unmatched in their ability to access information. Former intelligence operatives from Britain, the U.S., and, of course, Israel—the best of the best." Ivanov's calm demeanor belied the devastating implications behind his words.

"I ask you again, sir, what does this have to do with me or my pending appeal?" Courtland asked, shifting in his seat, his voice cracking.

"It has everything to do with your appeal. I have a file on you and your family that is as comprehensive as it is damning. In truth, I was disappointed to learn how easy it was to acquire the lurid details surrounding you and your siblings. Procuring this sort of information is not inexpensive."

Unsettled, eyes darting, Gregory Courtland's forehead began to bead with perspiration.

"You see, Mr. Courtland, Roy Cohn is dead and unfortunately for you, his secrets did not die with him. Take you, for instance. Among the things your file reveals is that on two separate occasions, your predilection for rough sex resulted in the unfortunate demise of two young women."

"That's not possible!" Courtland stammered, his face paling.

"One single woman found dead of asphyxiation could potentially be pled down to an accident, involuntary manslaughter—the inopportune result of an over-exuberant sexual encounter. But two? Now that's an entirely different matter."

Courtland, his mouth agape, managed to summon an unconvincing bit of bravado. "You're bluffing, there's absolutely nothing to tie me to any such incident."

Dimitri Ivanov leaned forward and fastened his eyes on the stammering real estate baron, intoning softly, "I never bluff, Mr. Courtland. You see, Roy Cohn, the person you called after both incidents, did exactly as you asked. He made the problem go away. The bodies were disposed of and any evidence of your involvement was carefully removed from the scene."

As the Russian spoke, the moisture building up on Courtland's face required wiping, while his eyes seemed to want to leap from their sockets. Ivanov handed him his pristine handkerchief and continued.

"Cohn was a treacherous ally, Mr. Courtland; he always hedged his bets. He always insisted on maintaining leverage on anyone he ever had dealings with. It was the wellspring of much of his influence. Prior to disposing of all the aforementioned evidence, he documented it—photographs, fingerprints, and personal items that would conclusively tie you to the violent murder of two young women."

"That's not possible." Courtland's insistence rang weak and unconvincing.

"You keep saying that, Mr. Courtland, but I think you know where this is going."

Courtland wiped his face with the handkerchief, his hands trembling. "I don't know anything."

Ivanov leaned back, almost amused, his voice dripping with condescension. "That, sir, may be the closest you've come to uttering the truth since I arrived here."

Courtland's eyes darted around the room, as if looking for a way to escape. "I don't…"

Ivanov cut him off with a wave of his hand. "Let me tell you how this plays out. You will withdraw your appeal and negotiate a settlement with the Southern District of New York, the details of which will be provided to you. In the settlement, you will agree to divest your controlling interest in all Courtland family holdings. Courtland real estate assets will be absorbed by a holding company, a consortium of business people I represent. The Courtland family will retain some interest in the consortium but nothing resembling control. Yours will still be a wealthy family, but all significant business decisions will be handled by the consortium. Some accommodations will be made for your private residences. Furthermore, I can assure you that your time at Allenwood will be short and not unpleasant."

Gregory Courtland felt a sense of defeat washing over him. "What about my children?" he said, his voice breaking. "My brother's children?"

Dimitri Ivanov responded matter-of-factly, as if discussing the weather. "They will never have to work a day in their lives, neither will their children. You are giving up control, Mr. Courtland. Your family's wealth will diminish, but certainly not in a way that will affect your lifestyle."

Gregory Courtland shot back, a desperate last stand reply, his voice hoarse. "What if I don't agree to your terms, Mr. Ivanov?"

Dimitri Ivanov responded, his voice icy, decisive, a chilling smile on his lips. "If you foolishly choose to ignore these generous terms, you will likely spend the rest of your life in jail, along with losing control of all your real estate holdings. As for the fate of your family, well, who can say? Is that clear enough for you, Mr. Courtland?"

Gregory Courtland released a guttural noise, a sound not unlike the agonized wail of a wounded animal.

"Look at it this way, Mr. Courtland, you have suffered a grave self-inflicted wound today, but you still draw breath. And it is possible, though not likely, that your image may be rehabilitated and you may still have a role to play in our affairs. Time will tell."

The weight of Ivanov's words settled like a dark cloud over the ornate office. Courtland's face turned ashen, betraying the raw shock of a man blindsided by fate, a fate he could have never imagined and was ill-equipped to navigate.

# 34

## FALLEN ANGELS

At Gabriel's behest, Michael made his way to Stowe two days prior to the official wedding ceremony. Sequestered within the confines of Gabriel's study, the pair reveled in their fraternal bond. No bachelor party antics, just two men celebrating a connection forged from shared sorrows and fortified by collective triumphs. Outside, the snow-crowned mountains provided a majestic backdrop as men outside labored to erect a tent for the impending festivities.

Gabriel and Rachel extended invitations to a few close friends, encouraging them to partake in the tranquility of Stowe's surroundings. The sprawling mountains and stunning landscapes, crisp air, and ancient woods offered the promise of respite—renewal for mind, body and soul.

With a celebratory glass of whiskey in hand, they immersed themselves in meandering recollections, weaving tales of childhood escapades, reminiscing about departed loved ones, and recounting the battles they had waged and won together.

"You've done well for yourself, old friend," Michael said, raising his glass.

"Thank you. I do feel blessed. And having you here means the world to me, you're the only family I have left." Gabriel smiled as their glasses met.

"I wouldn't miss this for the world. How's Tony doing?" Michael inquired. "He's family now too."

"He's okay. He had his last radiation treatment a couple of days ago, and as per usual, the meds are wearing him down. Doctors say they've bought him a little time, but they can't say how much. Even under the best of circumstances, he won't be with us long. We thought about putting off the ceremony until he fully recovered from the treatment, but there's no guarantee he'll ever fully recover."

"And Rachel? It seems she's found her way to a place where she can embrace the old man in his final days."

"Yes, it's the best thing to come out of all of this. Her compassion has overridden her resentment, which has been good for both of them. You can see how it's lifted her spirits."

"You did the right thing here, Gabe. I'm proud of you."

"Thank you. It means a lot to me to hear you say it."

"The part that still baffles me," Michael said, raising an eye over his glass, "is how Dimitri Ivanov wound up entangled in all of this."

"I hear you. The sudden disclosure of his connection with her father landed like a bomb on Rachel. It troubled her, but she's made her peace with it. Something good did come out of it, the new insight helped her reclaim a part of her past."

"It's true, I've noticed it myself. Letting go of all that resentment has been good for her. That Dimitri knew Tony all those years ago and then turns up as a generous patron of Rachel's work is a remarkable coincidence. Don't you think, Gabe? Call me cynical, but it seems a little odd."

"Yeah, it's… complicated," Gabriel muttered, the creases in his forehead deepening as he pondered Michael's suggestion. "Gotta say though, I'm inclined to focus on the positive. Ivanov provided crucial context to her relationship with Tony, it opened a door in her heart, allowing her to understand, forgive, and reconnect with her father. Can't discount the good he's done." Gabriel stared past Michael, rubbing his unshaven jaw.

"Fair point. But can we really attribute all of this to mere coincidence?" Michael prodded, his skepticism lingering.

Gabriel began pacing. "I don't know, Michael. Look, I agree there's a lot to unravel and that all these events can be subject to multiple interpretations, however…" His voice trailed off, an idea dispersed and left unsaid.

"Occam's razor?" Michael said with a smile.

"Yes, Occam's razor. Sometimes the simplest explanation is the right one. You and I are skeptics by nature, trained to find perpetrators, trained to look for corroborating evidence. Maybe the right way forward is the one that lets us carry on with our lives. Dimitri Ivanov is an art professor who has a history of supporting emerging artists. He and Tony share a connection that predates us all. Maybe he saw an opportunity to help the family of an old colleague. A straightforward and benign explanation," Gabriel reasoned.

"And a plausible one. But you know it's never been our practice to give the benefit of the doubt without confirming the validity of the evidence," Michael said. "But I'll allow that Ivanov has yet to give any indication that he intends to do harm with the information he has. On the contrary, he seems to have a genuine affection for Rachel and appears to want to be helpful to all of us. Yet the fact remains, I was involved in an altercation and the people involved were murdered. That truth persists regardless of the angle we choose to view it from." Michael paused but seemed to stop himself from expounding further.

"Believe me, Michael, I understand your concerns." Somewhere at the edges of his awareness, Gabriel harbored an unease, a hint of peril gnawed at the unanswered questions. The List. He unconsciously rubbed the back of his neck as he paced the length of the room.

Michael appeared lost in unspoken deliberations as he scrutinized the melting ice cubes in his beverage. He hesitated, as if second-guessing himself, and then pressed on.

"I agree not everything needs to be viewed in a nefarious context, and I recognize the potential ramifications are profound and unpredictable. All I'm suggesting is we proceed carefully, remain attentive. If these men were connected as we suspect they were, then we're now, unwittingly or not, involved in whatever deception they were part of."

"I do understand," Gabriel insisted. "But you should also understand I'm not approaching this as an investigative reporter. I can't do that. This concerns more than just me. Digging further and exposing what I find could crush the only family I have left, including you. I don't intend to unleash a maelstrom of collateral devastation. My family is now my first and only concern."

Resisting the instinctive urge to expose secrets lurking in dark places was no easy task. Some mysteries were best left unexplored. He recognized Michael's need to learn more about how the enigmatic Ivanov fit into the unfolding events, especially as it related to the Russian's connection to the unfortunate altercation at the party. But Michael had reasons of his own to allow some details to remain shrouded. If there was a larger truth at play here, Michael would have to chart his own course of action. For Gabriel, the issue was settled the moment Rachel reconciled with her father.

Michael kept silent for a very long time. "Okay, Gabriel, I understand. I'm with you. You and Rachel are family. We'll sort it all out in due course. I'm clear on what's important here."

Gabriel touched his glass to Michael's. He let out a huge breath of relief and sank into a comfortable seat across from Michael.

"Hey, does your future father-in-law know Dimitri will be a guest at the ceremony?" Michael asked. "The old Russian seemed very pleased to have been invited."

"You've spoken to him recently?"

"Yes, we've been in touch. The man can be quite charming."

"Like the devil?" Gabriel asked, his tone provocative.

"Maybe." Michael twitched, the question struck a nerve.

"Rachel and Amanda felt he should be included, and now that his connection to Tony is out in the open, it seemed like the right thing to do."

Gabriel emptied the remaining Scotch into Michael's glass. Michael lifted it to his face and peered through the translucent liquid.

"So, Tony knows Dimitri Ivanov will be a guest at your wedding ceremony?"

"Yes, I told him, but not sure if it registered in his present state of mind."

"How do you think it will go down when they meet?"

"Not sure. The Russian knows of Tony's condition and by all accounts he's looking forward to reconnecting. As for Tony, it's hard to tell how he'll receive the news. He can be condescending and mercurial, but also gentle and wise; not sure which Tony we'll get when they meet. Frankly, Michael, I'd prefer them to meet on some other occasion. There is so much we don't know about these men, how things might have ended with them, the reunion has the potential to be volatile. I don't want it to spoil our day."

"I hear you. I understand Dimitri is scheduled to arrive tomorrow," Michael said.

"So I've been told. I have mixed feelings about this."

"About the meeting?" Michael asked.

"About all if it. It's almost as if I'm being pulled into some larger movement of events," Gabriel mused, his voice weighted with the burden of realization. "Like something, I don't know, a thread from the past weaving its way into present circumstances. Ever since the Courtland thing broke, it's like you, me, and even Rachel, we're riding this momentous wave, caught in a forward surge. It seems all we can do is try to keep our heads above water and follow where it takes us."

"Well put. I sense it too. A strange feeling I can't quite explain." Michael paused. "Hey, I just had a thought. Why don't we arrange for Dimitri and Tony to meet tomorrow instead of the day of the wedding ceremony? A meeting will give them a chance to get past any potential awkwardness before your celebration; clear the air early."

"I think that's a great idea, buddy. Can you help arrange it?"

"Of course."

"They can meet privately right here in the study," Gabriel offered.

"Done. I'll bring Dimitri over tomorrow after he gets settled."

"I'll talk to Rachel and Helen, I'm sure they'll be happy to set it up with Tony."

\* \* \*

Michael's head ached, specifically, the area where he sustained a blow; it throbbed with an insistent foreboding. Still the injury paled in comparison to the damage he had inadvertently inflicted upon himself. His questionable judgment began when he left the scene of an altercation, then compounded later that night when he made love to his best friend's fiancée, setting him on a wayward path, drawing him deeper into discordant circumstances. For the first time in his life, he couldn't be completely honest with Gabriel. For reasons not even clear to himself, he didn't tell Gabriel that someone confessed to the murder of the two assailants from the party, an improbable alignment of exonerating circumstances foretold by Dimitri Ivanov with eerie prescience. The fallout of all that transpired since that evening continued to cloud his faculties and amplify the flawed decisions that had brought him to this precipice.

He was not alone in traversing the grey area of conflicting choices. Gabriel's uncharacteristic reluctance to probe deeper into Tony's narrative also flirted with the evasion of inconvenient truths. Unspoken contrivances prevailed, their divergent paths inadvertently taking them further into the murky recesses of compromise and concealment.

# 35

## THE LION SLEEPS TONIGHT

Michael wandered the expansive grounds surrounding the Trapp Family Lodge, his mind a jumble of fragmented conjectures and unanswered questions. Audrey Zornberg's unexpected disclosure churned in his thoughts, her report marking the conclusion of AUSA's investigation into the deaths of the assailants who had targeted him.

As he pondered the improbable series of events she outlined, Michael sought a unifying theme to the tangled web of unlikely events that had transpired in the preceding weeks. With each step through the manicured gardens and along the winding paths, he grappled with the bewildering details of his current dilemma, determined to unearth the concealed correlations that seemed to loom just beyond his grasp.

Each word of the improbable scenario Audrey described echoed like a persistent refrain. The resolution of his crisis ought to have ushered in a wave of relief, yet an unsettling feeling lingered, stubbornly refusing to release him. The reprieve felt transitory, as if the storm still prowled the horizon, biding its time before unleashing its fury once more.

Two days ago Audrey entered his office bearing the resolution that would free him from the risk of unwarranted, but nevertheless damning, accusations.

* * *

"Alright, chief, it seems the situation in New Jersey unfolded just as you anticipated. The connection to our office was indeed an attempt at misdirection," the senior counsel reported, clutching a file tightly but refraining from handing it over to Michael.

"Wait, back up. Are we talking about the two bodies that showed up a couple of weeks ago?" Of course, Michael knew exactly what she was talking about.

"Yes. It looks like local law enforcement caught the guy based on a tip from a snitch. They found the murder weapon. The guy basically shit himself, gave up the whole scam."

"He confessed?" Michael asked, his tone incredulous.

"Pretty much. The evidence they obtained painted a pretty clear picture, he didn't have much choice," Audrey confirmed.

"Mirandized?" Michael asked.

"Yeah, clean confession. His lawyer encouraged him to cooperate in exchange for leniency."

"What's his story?" Michael inquired. A chilling sensation accompanied his pounding heart.

"The guy claims he was just trying to collect on a debt and the thing went sideways. The two victims were dealers looking to move up in the world by freelancing on somebody else's turf. They owed money on a dope deal that went south, then failed to meet the terms of the loan. The conversation got aggressive, the perp panicked. He claims he was just trying to scare them into paying up, but they pushed back a little too aggressively, so he shot them."

"What about the invite?" Michael continued probing. The resolution was almost too tidy to hold up to scrutiny.

"The shooter tried getting creative. He stumbled upon a discarded invite for the Limelight event, and apparently he reads the newspapers. He knew that Rachel Rivers and Gabriel Hernandez were partners. A clumsy attempt to leave breadcrumbs at the scene that might steer the investigation away from New Jersey, knowing the famous investigative reporter had plenty of high-profile enemies in the big city."

"Didn't work out for him," Michael said.

"Nope, a little too clever for his own good. Should've just torched the car," Audrey quipped.

"So, he's turned state's evidence?"

"Yeah, he's prepared to give us some mid-level distribution guys. We'll see how that works out. Either way though, it's out of our jurisdiction."

"Well, the good news is we don't have to requisition extra security while the penny-pinchers are looking to cut budgets," Michael said in a casual tone, attempting to disguise mixed feelings of relief and apprehension.

"Yup. That is good news." Audrey held Michael's eyes for a few seconds as if unsure of whether she should share the next bit of information.

"Anything else here we need to know about?" Michael prompted.

"Well, just one thing seems out of place," Audrey remarked, her tone tinged with uncertainty.

"What's that?"

"The autopsy revealed one of them had a broken jaw and trauma to the larynx. Injuries consistent with a physical altercation, except they were shot in the back of the head."

"Okay, so?" Michael asked, his tone now bordering on dismissive.

"Well, if they were hit from behind, it remains unclear how there would have been an opportunity for that type of injury."

"Hmm. Okay. Not sure this is a thing. Guys like that get into scraps all the time, they're criminals," Michael retorted, in a tone meant to discourage further discussion.

"I suppose that's true. I don't know, it just caught my attention that's all. But we're all good here. We have enough on our plate," Audrey conceded.

"Agreed. Thanks for the update, Audrey." Michael picked up a piece of paper, indicating it was time to move on.

Despite Audrey's briefing raising more questions than answers, Michael attempted to close off any further consideration, hoping that this would mark the end of his involvement with the events at the Limelight.

He continued his stroll around the property, taking in the serene mountain air and picturesque surroundings searching for peace of mind. He found none.

\* \* \*

Dimitri Ivanov greeted Michael in the lobby sporting a white wool turtleneck and a brown double-breasted wool herringbone jacket with his trademark carnation affixed to the lapel. Michael wondered how he managed to find fresh carnations so quickly on arrival. Did he travel with them as part of his wardrobe, or did he order them from a local florist? He was tempted to ask him about the perennial accessory, but then thought better of it.

"Thank you for agreeing to meet with Tony. As you probably know, his illness has taken a toll on him. Gabriel and Rachel thought a private meeting before the celebrations would be a good way to get reacquainted," Michael offered.

"Yes, yes. Of course. The opportunity is most welcome. I have not seen Tony De Castro in many years and of course I'd like to meet Gabriel, after all he is marrying the woman we both treasure." Dimitri Ivanov put his hand on Michael's shoulder and smiled. Michael's muscles involuntarily recoiled at his touch. He offered a strained smile in agreement.

In response, Dimitri suggested a brief detour. "Michael, would it be alright if we grabbed a quick drink in the lounge before we left? Carlos is tending to some things upstairs and I have something I wanted to discuss with you before he joins us."

"Of course." Something in Dimitri's voice triggered Michael's defenses. *Why was Carlos tagging along to a gathering he wasn't invited to?*

"Michael, you remember the artist that calls herself Dallas, don't you?"

"Of course. I could never forget that performance."

"So much happened that night, we could be forgiven for not recalling the breathtaking beauty of her work," Dimitri said.

"I remember her," Michael said, taking a seat in a corner of the lodge.

"Well, it has been brought to my attention that she often travels with a team of photographers to capture images of life around her that she can later use in her work. It's part of her artistic modus operandi."

"Oh?" Michael said, tension coursing through his body.

"Yes, Amanda brought this to my attention."

"Why?"

"Because of *this*." The flame in the stone hearth behind Dimitri Ivanov appeared to grow in intensity as he spoke. He handed Michael an envelope as the waiter came by with their drinks.

Michael waited for the server to leave before opening the envelope. Inside he found images of the private party following Dallas's performance. He sifted through the photographs and eventually came across a series of pictures of himself striking the man who had insulted Rachel. Michael's face turned pale as he looked up to an expressionless Dimitri Ivanov, the fire now roaring behind him.

"What is this? Are you trying to blackmail me?"

"I don't blame you for drawing such a conclusion, I take no offense from your question. But I can assure you, my friend, I am not here to do harm. I did not cause these photos to be taken and I have no interest in blackmailing you. Amanda brought the photographs to me knowing the images had the potential to be damaging to your reputation should they fall into the wrong hands. She explained that Dallas was unaware of the nature of the images until she herself developed the pictures. Knowing how the evening ended, she brought them to Amanda's attention."

"This is a disturbing development, Dimitri. These pictures could do more than damage my reputation, they could put me in serious legal jeopardy."

"I understand, Michael. The envelope contains both the pictures and the original negatives. Dallas offered them willingly, in confidence and with no strings attached. She's a gifted artist who has no interest in playing games."

"And you, sir, what interest do you have in all of this?" Michael's face reddened and his heart quickened, fight or flight adrenaline surging through his system. *Keep all options open, don't overreact. Let Dimitri Ivanov play out his hand, must wait for the proper leverage before taking action.*

"Michael, have you ever heard of Nikolai Pavlenko?" Dimitri Ivanov's question pierced through the air, injecting a sense of intrigue into the conversation.

"No, I can't say I have," Michael replied, attempting to maintain a casual tone.

"Nikolai Pavlenko is a name revered around the world, particularly in Russia. Some consider him a mere lion tamer, but his craft transcends the taming of wild beasts; he is a masterful trainer and a captivating performer."

"I fail to see the relevance of a lion tamer to our discussion," Michael interjected, his curiosity piqued despite his efforts to remain composed.

"Allow me to elaborate," Dimitri responded, his voice measured and deliberate. "Pavlenko's approach to taming wild animals differs significantly from his counterparts. Unlike traditional methods that relied on violence to control the big cats in his show, Pavlenko employed a strategy rooted in patience and mutual understanding."

Michael's tension mounted, but he forced himself to stay attentive, realizing there was more to Dimitri's story.

"The first person to ever use wild animals in a performance was an American trainer, Isaac Van Amburgh, whose methods became the standard for animal trainers operating in the entertainment world during the 1800s. His techniques relied on fear and domination. Van Amburgh's tools included whips, chairs, and even guns to subdue his beasts."

"Ah, the infamous chair," Michael interjected, his curiosity overriding his frustration.

"Indeed," Dimitri continued, "the chair serves not as a weapon, but rather as a tool of confusion. Cats, you see, are single-minded creatures, the sight of a moving chair interrupts their thought process, it confuses them, allowing the trainer time to assert control."

Michael nodded, curious about the message behind Dimitri's intended parable.

"Pavlenko, however, revolutionized the art of animal training," Dimitri continued. "Through patience and positive reinforcement, he taught the beasts to trust him willingly, without the need for violence. He forged a partnership with the lions, based on mutual respect rather than fear."

"A remarkable feat," Michael acknowledged.

"Nikolai Pavlenko tamed the big cats humanely. Van Amburgh used violence and cruelty. At the end of Van Amburgh's performance the man would force the lion to lick his boots, displaying his total dominance over the creature. Nikolai Pavlenko's performances on the other hand are a thing of beauty, elegance and symmetry."

"And?" Michael said, betraying his waning patience. He had no use for stories about the subtle art of lion taming, he wished Ivanov would just get to the point.

"And? There is no *and*, Michael. The thing you must understand is that any working relationship must be built on trust. Without trust you have nothing. Nothing. Only violence and cruelty."

Dimitri Ivanov stood up, removed the envelope from Michael's hands and threw it into the roaring fireplace.

* * *

The analogy of being pulled along the crest of a careening wave Gabriel used earlier felt remarkably prescient. The perfect depiction of how Michael felt at this very moment. Once again he was forced to confront how an unexpected encounter can pierce the façade of randomness and expose unseen connections. Events intermingle and coalesce—fear, desire, regret, love, hate, trepidation.

He could feel it, the gravitational force of interwoven destinies highlighted so brilliantly on the night of the Dallas performance, tugging at him. He could see it clearly now. A humbling realization that he and those he loved were inextricably part of a connected tapestry. Causality. Cascading events ripple across time forming a swirling maelstrom.

Clarity. The inescapable nature of truth unveiled. The two men who twenty years ago murdered everyone involved in the JFK assassination were gathering at his best friend's home. He and his closest companions were integral players in an unfolding chronicle. Past, present and future. Everything Michael cared about was caught up in the advancing tide.

Michael strained to present an outward semblance of calm but the unaccountable effects of shifting realities now loomed. Lost in the corridors of growing doubt and uncertainty, Michael sought stability, yearning for the dwindling luxury of time. Too many variables hovered beyond his grasp. He needed space to recalibrate, to forge new pathways, to unearth hidden reservoirs of power. He chastised himself, urging restraint, imploring his mind to remain lucid amidst the swirling chaos. *Stay calm, think, don't give up. Stay in the fight.*

Dimitri Ivanov appeared to have destroyed evidence linking Michael to the two dead drug dealers: his true motivation unknown. The woman who owned his heart was about to marry his best friend. Had he made some kind of Faustian bargain by turning away from what he treasured most? Gabriel, his closest friend, an honorable man who built his career investigating the hidden secrets of powerful people, appeared willing to suppress evidence that could expose the greatest cover-up in American history. Allowing Tony De Castro's secrets to die with him, an inconceivable break with the standards that defined his life's work.

The key players in this bizarre game were about to cross paths in Gabriel's home this very afternoon. He had lost his queen, and his options for regaining his former life were dwindling. He played out endless scenarios, wrestling with a cacophony of conflicting internal voices, unsettling and dark. Out of the unrelenting discord, a familiar voice emerged, cutting through the chaos like a lifeline. It was a voice from a distance past, a past when he was still master of his own destiny. The voice offered counsel. He recognized it instantly, a reminder of who he once was, its empathetic intonations providing guidance out of the gathering storm.

*Bide your time, the path you are meant to walk will soon be made clear. Protect those you love.*

# 36

## BETWEEN PERDITION AND REDEMPTION

Michael paused at the door, mute, a proper greeting trapped in his throat, along with an intended warning. Dimitri Ivanov swept past him and enfolded Rachel in a paternal embrace, his face aglow with familial affection. Rachel reciprocated warmly with a gracious smile.

"It's good to see you, Dimitri. I fear that when I last saw you I may have been unreasonably hard on you. I'm so happy you decided to join us for our little celebration."

"Nonsense, my dear, it is an honor to be invited to your home and I assure you, you did not say anything at our last meeting that was not warranted. I only hope that whatever insight I may have proffered that evening lessened the pain caused by my not sharing it sooner. Most importantly, I hope that it helped you better understand your father's absence, and perhaps also helped you embrace him in his time of need."

"It did and it has. And although I may not have expressed it at the time, I'm grateful to you," Rachael replied tenderly.

Bright sunlight streamed through the long windows over the foyer's threshold, bathing the entrance in a warm glow. A whisper of cold Vermont air trailed the guests as they entered the home. Michael lingered behind seeking an appropriate opportunity to alert his friends, take them aside for a moment to share his concerns and strategize.

"You are most kind, my dear. I've brought along Carlos, my ever-present traveling companion and nephew. I would be lost without him. I hope it was not impertinent of me to have him join us."

"Of course not. I remember Carlos, the quiet one at the party, the one who came to our rescue when hell broke loose. Welcome to our home, Carlos. Let me introduce you both to my fiancé Gabriel, he is in the study with my father and very much looking forward to seeing you."

"I too have been looking forward to meeting the celebrated journalist Gabriel Hernandez. And where is that old Cuban? I am anxious to see him again after all these years."

"You know, Dimitri, I think I should mention that in addition to the cancer which continues to spread, my father is struggling with bouts of dementia."

Dimitri raised an eyebrow. "Oh?"

"Yes. His treatments seem to be aggravating what otherwise might have been a mild condition. He sometimes confuses where he is in time and place. He sometimes regresses and believes he is somewhere else and at times it manifests as delirium. He has just undergone his final treatment but he's still physically and mentally fragile."

"I see," Dimitri said, unconsciously rubbing his forehead. "I have heard of this in elderly patients. But Tony and I are more or less the same age."

"He is seventy, but this disease has taken its toll on him, you'll see. Sometimes he is as sharp as ever, other times much less so."

"It's difficult to imagine Tony De Castro as anything but in full command of his senses. Thank you for the warning," Dimitri said, and glanced briefly at Carlos.

Rachel guided the men into the study, her keen intuition sensing Michael's apprehension. She could guess as to its cause and wanted very much to alleviate his unease. The reconciliation with her father had infused her with a newfound hope for the days ahead, a belief that she was precisely where she was meant to be, a conviction she desperately wanted to extend to Michael.

The crackling fireplace cast a comforting glow on Gabriel's study, its flames dancing against the backdrop of limestone and granite. Two leather chairs, arranged to face the warmth, beckoned intimate conversations by the fire, hopefully the sort that helped rekindle old friendships. An ancient Underwood typewriter, once belonging to Gabriel's father, was displayed prominently on his desk which sat facing the French doors that framed a picturesque vista of the majestic Mt. Mansfield.

Tony occupied one of the leather chairs, his figure silhouetted against the flickering backdrop, while Gabriel sat perched close to the hearth, soaking in the warmth. Noting the arrival of his guests, he informed Tony and motioned them to enter. As they did so, a sudden chill filled the study.

"An old friend has arrived," Gabriel whispered to Tony.

"All my old friends are dead. Who is it?" Tony's voice, tinged with weariness, carried through the room.

"Dimitri Ivanov," Gabriel whispered, leaning in with a cautious intensity, seeking to gauge Tony's mental state.

"Who's that?" Tony's confusion was evident as his eyes darted between Gabriel and his arriving guests.

Rachel led Dimitri past Michael with tentative grace, her movements measured as she approached Tony, Helen following behind while Carlos lingered discreetly in the foyer, out of sight.

"Well, I do remember you, old man," Dimitri remarked with a hint of nostalgia. "And frankly I never thought our paths would cross again. How are you, old friend? Here we are, still standing after all these years, and blessed to be surrounded by loved ones. *¡Tanto tiempo, hombre!* Who could have imagined?"

Rachel introduced them formally, hoping to spark Tony's memory. "Papa, this is Dimitri Ivanov. He's been an enthusiastic supporter of my art, and he mentioned he used to work with you many years ago. I thought it would be nice for you two to catch up."

Dimitri stood by Tony's side, his usual loquacious banter subdued, as he quietly assessed the ailing man before him. Tony's hands clenched into fists, a futile attempt to quell the tremors coursing through him. As he met Dimitri's gaze with steely resolve, his lips remained taut and unmoving.

Gabriel stood up and extended his hand. "Mr. Ivanov, I'm Gabriel Hernandez. It's nice to finally meet you, sir. Rachel and Michael speak very highly of you. Welcome to our home. I understand you and Tony have some history together."

"Yes, in a manner of speaking, we do have history together. It is a pleasure to meet you, Gabriel. Please call me Dimitri. I too have heard much about you and have been following your work for some time."

As Gabriel held Dimitri's hand, distress swept over him, like a sudden gust of ill wind. The crimson bloom adorning Dimitri's lapel triggered recognition, a memory harking back to the morning of the arraignment. The impeccably dressed and seemingly out-of-place figure that caught his eye at the Courtland proceedings now stood within the gates of his home. Gabriel's thoughts careened through a maze of potentialities, piecing together the improbable sequence of events that led to this unsettling convergence. A sense of foreboding gripped him.

Though Gabriel had been slow to fully confront the linking threads woven beneath the surface, the gravity of the situation now loomed over him with an inexorable force. The surge of uncontainable circumstances threatened to upend everything he held dear, forcing him to seize a single urgent imperative. Protect Rachel.

A veneer of calm concealed the storm brewing within Gabriel, his senses attuned to the minutiae of the unfolding scenario. Every movement calculated, every word measured, as he strove to navigate a perilous game of strategy and survival. His exchanged glances with Rachel conveyed a wordless reassurance between them, even as he assessed the potential threat of Carlos lurking on the periphery. Intuition screamed— the man's presence was no coincidence. Should violence erupt, it would likely begin and end with him. Where was Michael? Instincts, honed in the trenches of investigative reporting, triggered silent alarms.

In that moment of uncertainty, Gabriel recognized that his actions in the next few moments could shape the course of their fates. With Rachel's safety as his guiding principle, he steeled himself for unpredictable encounters, potential outcomes set in motion long ago.

"Please make yourself comfortable." Gabriel pointed to the leather chair across from Tony. "Can I get you something to drink?"

"Yes, thank you, I would love a Scotch if you and Tony are inclined to join me? Tony, what do you say?"

Tony De Castro remained ensconced in silence, the fingers of one hand clenched tightly around a trembling fist. The toll of his recent chemotherapy treatments lingered, casting doubt over his situational awareness.

"Allow us to pour you both a Scotch, and then leave you to catch up," Gabriel suggested, his gaze sweeping the room before he locked eyes with Rachel, who stood nearby. Michael and Carlos hovered by the doorway, observing the proceedings. Michael looked distressed, as if he were reading his friend's thoughts. Gabriel's mind raced with urgency, seeking the right moment to apprise Michael of his disquieting discovery. Dimitri must be connected to the Courtlands somehow.

Rachel, attuned to the subtle shift in atmosphere, acquiesced to Gabriel's suggestion. "That sounds good to me. Helen and I can whip up a little something for us to nibble on while the men talk."

"Of course," Helen chimed in, her smile also masking a deeper concern. She detected the strain etched upon Tony's features, the unrelenting tremors betraying some inner turmoil. Ever vigilant, and aware of the fragility of his condition, she nodded her approval, but remained sensitive to the reaction his guests were provoking. She and Rachel left for the kitchen.

Gabriel quickly returned with a bucket of ice, a bottle of his best Scotch and two glasses. "Rocks or neat"?

"Ah, Macallan, an excellent Scotch, Gabriel. I will have mine neat. What about you, Tony? Neat? No point in watering down good Scotch."

Tony leveled a steely gaze at Dimitri. "Have a seat," he commanded, his voice suddenly cutting through the air with authority, some of the old fire returning. Memories of their encounter in Barcelona lingered, a reminder of the unfinished business that should have remained in the past. "Now would be a good time for you to explain exactly why you've decided to grace us with your presence."

He gestured toward the vacant chair, a silent insistence that Dimitri comply. "And who's the man lurking in the shadows?" Tony's eyes flicked toward the threshold where Carlos stood, a silent sentinel cloaked in ambiguity.

"Thanks for the Scotch, Gabriel," Dimitri acknowledged, adopting a gentle demeanor, a concerned look settling over him. He offered a nod to Gabriel, an unspoken acknowledgment of the fluctuating tension in the room.

Gabriel glanced at Michael and Carlos, silently signaling them to depart. Michael remained silent, alarm trapping words in his throat.

"Let's leave these two to catch up. We can grab a drink in the other room, and if Carlos is interested, I can show him around the property."

Carlos received a subtle nod of approval from Dimitri. The men exited the room.

Alone at last, Tony's eyes bored into Dimitri. "How much have you told them?" he demanded, his tone laced with anger.

Dimitri offered a faint smile, deflecting Tony's inquiry with calm indifference.

"You're looking well, Tony, given the circumstances. How are you feeling?"

"I'm feeling well enough, but I want answers from you," Tony retorted, his voice impatient.

"You have nothing to fear, old friend," Dimitri reassured him, his tone soothing yet evasive. "Please indulge me. How's your health holding up?"

"The doctors say I don't have much time. Ha! Not much time. None of us has much time, our lives are but a flicker of light. But there is no doubt that I'm dying. Tell me then, old friend, why are you here? I'm already dead, but I can still protect my family."

"I am sorry to hear of this, Tony. All the more important that you make the most of the time you do have. Your daughter is with you now. This is a good thing, isn't it? After all these years you now have Rachel back in your life."

"What do you know about it? I ask you again, tell me, Ivanov, why the hell are you here? Is my family in danger? Give me the dignity of an honest answer, you owe me at least that."

"Danger? From me? Of course not! Please, why would you think so? You saved my life." Dimitri looked at his old counterpart, frail and vulnerable; a shadow of the man he remembered.

"I've never breathed a word of our work to anyone. Our secrets remain locked away," Tony said, his voice quivering and hands trembling.

Observing Tony's frailty, the Russian pondered whether the man possessed the capacity to recollect their shared past, let alone discern what he might have disclosed to others. If Dimitri aimed to prevent Tony from divulging the buried truths, his efforts were likely in vain. This man who stood on the precipice of delirium, was likely incapable of remembering the details of what he did and didn't share. How much had he confided in Helen? How much had Gabriel deduced? It was likely too late to contain the fallout, too late to contain the burgeoning storm. The prospect of eradicating Tony's family now seemed pointless, a futile endeavor destined to attract unwanted scrutiny.

"Secrets? You needn't concern yourself with that any longer, Tony," Dimitri reassured him, his tone tinged with resignation. "What we did, we did out of duty to a higher calling. We sacrificed for the welfare of future generations, striving to rectify the errors of misguided zealots. But the tide has turned, and the current custodians of power care little for our past deeds. They have no time for fanciful tales, no inclination to discern truth from fiction."

"And what does my daughter know of our past doings?" Tony pressed, his voice laden with a father's concern.

"Your daughter knows you safeguarded her and her mother," Dimitri assured him, his words a balm to Tony's anxieties. "That's all she needs to know. I made sure she understood how your absence shielded them. She's here, and she's safe because of you."

Tony looked at Dimitri, unwilling or unable to acknowledge the truth of what he had just said.

"I am pouring you a drink, Tony, and I will answer all your questions. I just need you to relax a little. I don't want you over-agitated. You are among friends and family here."

"How did you come to know Rachel? How long have you been following her?"

"Following her? You make it sound as if I intend to do her harm. It is true that I have been looking after her in my own way, you would have done the same for me if you could have. You must know that if I meant to harm any of your people, we would not be having this conversation now. I found Rachel through her work. She is a wonderful artist. I kept an eye on her to keep her safe and provided some support so she could thrive doing what she loved. I owe you, Tony, you saved my life. Do you remember that?"

"No," Tony said taking a sip of Scotch. "I didn't save your life. I just got tired of killing. I couldn't do it anymore."

"You could have eliminated me in Barcelona, Tony, but you didn't. We were both tired, we both had seen enough bloodshed. We were both tired of cleaning up the mess zealots and misbegotten ideologues create; men who profit from creating chaos and rely on men like us to clean up after them. You saved my life by just walking away and letting me live."

Tony's hands trembled, his thoughts plagued by the persistent images that time would not erase. "We did terrible things and you don't know the half of it," Tony said, boring a hole in Dimitri, his eyes reflecting the inescapable weight of the past. He held his trembling fist tightly.

Helen entered the room with a plate of ham, cheese, olives and homemade knishes.

"You can't drink that stuff on an empty stomach, eat some food," she insisted.

"You are very kind, madam. I don't think we've had a proper introduction. I worked with your husband many years ago when we were both foolish idealists doing work for our governments. I have not seen him in nearly twenty-three years."

Dimitri stood up to assist Helen with the plate of food.

"It's a pleasure to meet you. I'm told you have been very kind to Rachel and that pleases me. Rachel and Gabriel have been very welcoming to us." She looked suspiciously at the Russian as if to let him know she would not be taken in by his charming ways. Dimitri could not help but wonder again how much Tony had shared with his wife.

"Twenty-three years?" Helen remarked. "This is right around the time Tony and I first met in Israel, shortly after my first husband died. Did you know my late husband Aaron?"

"No, I don't believe I knew your husband. Did he work for the Israeli government?"

"Yes, he also worked with Tony in private security."

"I see. No, I'm sorry, I have never met any of Tony's colleagues, we travelled in different circles."

"I will let you both get back to reminiscing. Please make sure he eats something and please try not to agitate him," Helen said sternly, "he has been through a lot these past few weeks."

"She takes good care of you," Dimitri remarked, his smile directed at Tony. "I'll be sure to enjoy some of this delicious food. Thank you," he added, addressing Helen, who remained impassive as she regarded Tony, whose mouth hung open in silence.

As Helen exited the room, Dimitri drew his chair nearer to Tony, lowering his voice to a conspiratorial murmur. "Please tell me she's not the wife of the man you eliminated in Paris, your second-in-command. He was Israeli, wasn't he?"

Tony's expression remained inscrutable. "I don't know what you're talking about. Just pass me a plate," he deflected.

"But she is, isn't she? An Israeli," Dimitri persisted, his tone edged with thinly veiled disdain. "This is why you fled to Israel, isn't it? You eliminated her husband and then sought solace in the arms of the woman you widowed. I'm not here to judge you, Tony," he continued, though skepticism colored his words. "I just want you to cease this charade. We've come too far to play games with each other."

"*Es la verdad.* It's the truth," Tony said, the Scotch loosening his tongue. "But she knows nothing of the work we did. *¡No sabe nada!* My family knows nothing! Our secrets die with us."

"Secrets? Again with this? My God, Tony, our secrets died a long time ago, the truth died a long time ago and we had nothing to do with it. Who would believe us now if we told the world all we know and exactly what we did? We could tell the world exactly what happened; we could tell them about the confounded Russian zealots, the rogue plot to kill the president of the United States, the patsy, the fixers, the wet-work, the elimination of all possible witnesses. Who would care? We would sound like all the other crazies who peddle conspiracy theories. No one cares about the truth anymore. Lies are easier to sell than the truth. Who would believe us? Khrushchev is dead, Johnson is dead; they are all dead. No, we don't have to worry about the truth anymore, Tony."

"So, you are not here to kill my family? Then what do you want?" Tony said, taking another sip of Scotch.

"No, Tony, I'm not here to kill anyone. I am here for your daughter's wedding. Like you, I'm seeking what redemption can be found in this crazy world, and seeing you reconnect with your daughter gratifies me. It fills me with hope."

Dimitri refilled Tony's glass and leaned in, hoping to reconnect with the only other man alive who knew what he knew. Men whose secrets, noble and otherwise, would perish with them. The only men left alive who knew what it meant to carry the burden of the untold deceptions that altered history.

"I chose a different path than you, Tony. I never had children of my own. I learned how to play the game. I learned how to use what I know to help people make money, lots of money. I have associates all over the world now and they all worship at the altar of the golden calf. They have no allegiance to cause or country, they just want to be rich as gods and I help make them rich. Greed knows no ideology, no national boundaries and no religion. Greed is the universal force that animates human progress. I admit that I've assisted some questionable people, but I've also helped some good people. Helping your daughter find success as an artist has provided me with my own path to redemption."

"I killed him, Dimitri. I killed him."

"Who?" Dimitri asked.

"Aaron."

Dimitri's forehead tightened in an involuntary flinch. "We did what we had to do. We had no choice."

"He was a good man. He did what I asked of him, and then I killed him."

Tony held his clenched fist, his hands trembling.

"We believed we were working for the greater good," Dimitri said. "Maybe we were. The truth would have set the world ablaze. We kept that from happening by burying it. We were given a mission and we accomplished it."

"I shot him in cold blood and then I went to Israel. I wanted to tell her everything, but I couldn't bear to speak the words. She was so kind and beautiful and honorable. I couldn't tell her. Instead, I fell in love with her. I married her and never told her what I'd done. I didn't have the heart to tell her. I didn't have the nerve. I didn't plan to love her, it just happened. I had nothing else left."

"Tony, that night in Barcelona, I thought if you didn't kill me, you'd surely end up killing yourself," Dimitri reflected, his voice tinged with compassion. "You were shattered, Tony. Yet somehow, you found the strength to carry on. You couldn't save Aaron, but looking after his wife, that was an act of compassion. Wasn't it?"

"At first, I saw it as penance, something I felt compelled to do," Tony confessed, his voice heavy with introspection. "But then I witnessed the work they were doing in Israel. I saw how they cared for their Palestinian neighbors, the displaced and mistreated. It took immense courage to stand up for these forsaken people. It reminded me of the things Castro said he wanted to do for the poor and dispossessed in Cuba, before his paranoia consumed him.

"She was a force of nature. Israelis tending to their sworn enemies," he continued, admiration coloring his tone. "She realized that the atrocities committed against her own people began with their dehumanizing. She refused to condemn an entire people for the horrible actions of a few zealots. She recognized that Israelis were also guilty of horrible acts in their systematic oppression. I admired her sense of compassion, her faith in the idea that Israelis and Palestinians could live side by side, her conviction that a peaceful and prosperous Israel required it. I admired her dedication and unwavering commitment to this idea. I wanted to protect her, I wanted to help. And yes, you're right, I was seeking redemption. I couldn't face my own child after all I'd done. I couldn't expect her to understand or forgive. Even if she did forgive, I couldn't risk putting my family in danger."

"You've paid a steep price, my friend," Dimitri commiserated, his gaze steady as he reached out to touch Tony's trembling fist. "What you did, you did in service to your country, in service to humankind. You were a good soldier with a noble heart."

"NO!" Tony raised his voice. Fear, pain and anger cast a ghostly shadow on his features. "It was a safehouse. He was supposed to be alone." Tony's eyes looked past Dimitri, his countenance tense and confused, the ghosts around him conjuring visions that had plagued his nightmares for too many years.

"What is this? Women's clothing, toys, this is not right!" he said, raising his voice as if transported to a different time. "I CAN'T DO THIS. I must do this. *Mierda*. This has to happen now. But what if he is not alone? WHAT IF HE IS NOT ALONE?"

Dimitri could see Gabriel, Michael and Carlos from the window walking back from Rachel's studio toward the main house.

"Settle down, old friend, settle down and please lower your voice," Dimitri urged him. "That happened a long time ago. You are among friends and family now, you are safe. Let us get our bearings here."

"I shot them, Dimitri. I shot them!" Tony's voice bellowed in anguish. "I shot Aaron, I SHOT A WOMAN AND A LITTLE GIRL. I killed a little girl and then I walked away as if nothing happened, just like they taught us. I killed them, Dimitri, I KILLED ALL OF THEM."

Tony wept uncontrollably like a man trying to purge himself of the poison inside him.

"Please lower your voice, my friend," Dimitri insisted. "Let us get our bearings."

Dimitri felt both pity and disgust: pity for the broken man wailing like a wounded animal, and disgust at knowing the work they did required accepting the blood of innocents as collateral damage. The murder of a dedicated soldier, a woman and a small child—the price men like him had no choice but to accept. Dimitri Ivanov was moved by the tortured soul of a man who committed to a mission that required him to sacrifice everything he loved and treasured. A mission that demanded nothing less than his very soul.

Dimitri did not want Rachel to see her father this way, not on the day before her wedding. He cared. He found solace in knowing, despite all he had done, he could still cherish something beautiful. Evidence that he not yet used up the man he once was, that some essential part of him still survived.

"Let it go, old friend. That time has passed. Please stay with me in the present. You have carried this burden long enough, stay with us here in the present. Let the nightmare pass…"

Helen's trembling voice rang out from the doorway, stopping Dimitri mid-sentence. "I didn't want to believe it!" Her voice was seething with rage. "Some part of me sensed it, his ramblings, I suspected there was more to them, that there were things, horrible things that he was holding back. Part of me just didn't want to know more. Maybe that's how I protected myself, I shut them out of my mind. His ramblings, I wanted to believe they were delusions, something he made up. But it's true, he said it himself. He murdered innocent people."

Helen stood in the doorway holding Tony's 9mm Beretta, pointing it directly at Tony's heart. Her eyes were ablaze with rage, fierce rage, the kind of rage that leads to madness.

"You weren't a fucking soldier, you crazy bastard, you were—and still are—A COLD-BLOODED MURDERER." Her voice seething with righteous outrage, the gun moved unsteadily in her quivering grip.

Dimitri stood up. He took two steps away from Tony and quickly glanced outside. Gabriel, Michael and Carlos were no longer visible through the study window. *Could they be in the house? Need to engage Helen, stall for time.*

"Think about what you're doing, Helen. You should know that gun has a very sensitive trigger."

"I'm an Israeli, you think I don't know how to handle a weapon? That man murdered my husband, my real husband. He murdered a woman and a child. Good people we rescued from the hell of occupied Palestine. The woman you killed had a name. Her name was Asima. Her daughter had a name. Her name was Amal. Her name was Amal!" she shouted. "We wanted to give them hope, we helped care for that child, for a time she was like a daughter to us. They were going to escape, start a new life, we were helping them do that. Aaron used his connections to help them get settled in France. We wanted to help them move past the abuse Amal and her mother had survived in their homeland and begin a new life in Paris." Helen howled in pain.

Tony wept inconsolably.

Dimitri attempted to stall for more time.

"A horrible tragedy, Helen. Horrible. Like you, I am just learning of these things now. But please listen carefully. This man is dying, make no mistake, he has held this horrible truth inside him for so long that it is consuming him from the inside. Your bullet will only hasten what is already his fate. He has already been punished. If you do this now, your fate will be tied to his. Your life will never be the same."

"Your fancy words won't change anything. He murdered my husband and two beautiful, innocent souls. For this he must pay."

As she spoke the front door of the house opened. Startled by Helen's frantic shouts, Rachel and Gabriel rushed into the study to find her pointing the Beretta directly at Tony, her expression fraught with tension and alarm.

"What is going on? Why are you pointing a gun at my father?" Rachel shouted.

"He's a murderer!" Helen said, the guttural sound of uncontrolled fury caught in her throat.

"What?"

"Rachel, STAY WHERE YOU ARE!" Dimitri commanded. "Helen, remember what I said. He's already dead. It would be very unwise to do this. Believe me when I tell you, there is no satisfaction to be found in killing."

Tony sat weeping, his hands trembling, his body convulsing.

"He IS dead and he will not see another sunrise, but before he goes he must pay, he will see his beloved daughter perish, just as Aaron must have seen Asima and Amal die."

Tony pleaded with her. "No! Please, Helen, pull the trigger. Take me, but please let Rachel…"

Helen cut off Tony's pleas with a swift motion, her trembling hands releasing the first shot aimed in Rachel's direction. The bullet missed its mark. Perhaps some part of her intended it to be so. Another round followed, this time directed at Tony from close quarters. Dimitri Ivanov staggered backward in a frantic attempt to evade the line of fire, his reflexive movement propelled by an instinctual desire to live. Meanwhile, the burning flames in the fireplace seemed to swell in intensity.

Rachel moved to protect her father, triggering Helen to raise the gun again in her direction. Without hesitation, Gabriel leaped to intercept, positioning himself between Rachel and the imminent threat. The gunshot echoed through the tainted air as the bullet found its mark, piercing Gabriel's knee, eliciting a sharp gasp of pain. Collapsing onto Rachel, his face pressed close to hers, he whispered, "I love you, Rachel." Helen, now possessed by irrepressible rage, fired randomly. Instinctively Gabriel shoved Rachel behind the couch away from Helen's line of fire, and a second bullet entered his abdomen. Bleeding profusely, he attempted to stand up in order to draw Helen's attention away from Rachel. Through the haze of pain, he watched as Michael lunged toward Helen, only to be halted by a bullet that tore through his leg, sending him crashing to the ground, his head colliding with a marble table.

Before Michael could gather himself, the next bullet from Helen's Beretta found its mark, piercing Gabriel's neck. His hands moved reflexively to cover the fatal wound. Beside him, Rachel lay motionless, a silent witness to the tragic chaos that engulfed them.

In the heightened state of perception that often illuminates the final moments of life, Tony watched the bullet, spinning at three thousand revolutions per second, making its fateful journey toward his heart, a heart already scarred by irreconcilable compromises made in the service of what he deemed to be a noble cause. Layer by layer the bullet pierced the veil of invulnerability that had long ago been exposed by his disease.

There was so much more he wanted to share. His heart, damaged as it was, remained capable of loving deeply. He understood now. In those fleeting moments of expanded awareness, he apprehended that the heart was more than a muscle, it was a portal, a pathway to the river that animates all things, an organ of divine purpose, the compass that directed his journey to this pivotal juncture. His heart still held the authority to illuminate his most reverent desires. It was the connective tissue that bound him inexorably to the embodiment of his highest aspiration, to the purest manifestation of his existence—to Rachel.

The bullet pierced the right ventricle, punctured the ventricular septum, penetrated the right atrium and traversed the aortic valve. It brought with it luminescent clarity and the promise of deliverance. *Forgive us now our trespasses as we forgive those who have trespassed against us. Deliver me, Lord, from evil.*

He saw Gabriel fall. Gabriel, the avenging angel, setting aside the flaming sword of his life's work to protect the one he loved. He saw the rage in Helen's face. The aggrieved, the innocent and faithful advocate of the powerless, succumbing to the poisonous madness that is retribution. Vengeance. The toxic seduction of reckoning and reprisal. He would not judge her. He wanted to explain that he really had no choice, though he didn't blame her for not understanding. The bullet was superfluous, his heart had already been broken, he bore the damage believing it was his duty. Her bullet released him from the prison that had confined him for so long. He had found redemption. He had seen his daughter one last time; that would be enough.

Michael attempted to stand and move toward Helen. He had lost a lot of blood; he couldn't feel his leg. He couldn't feel anything at all. He didn't see Carlos fire the shot that ended Helen's role in the great unfolding of things.

Tony muttered incoherently, his unblinking gaze fixed, as the life drained from his trembling body. *She didn't deserve this. The hate, the rage, the inconsolable grief, the cascading consequences of human folly. She didn't deserve this. Deliver us from evil, Lord.*

\* \* \*

"It's okay. The pain will soon be over. You did what you believed to be right, I know that now. You took no pleasure in it. Here, hold him, he'll help you on your journey." The little girl in the pink dress handed Tony a white teddy bear and pressed it against his bleeding chest. The bear turned red with blood as her dress transformed into radiant white.

"Who are you?"

"Evil men tried to break the world, you tried to fix it. Now you're broken too."

"He's been broken for a long time. Maybe now he'll find peace," Gabriel said, standing next to her.

"Gabriel? Who is this little girl?"

"Maybe you'll find peace too," she said, turning to Gabriel.

"I have found it," he said. "Will she be okay? Will she live a happy life?"

The little girl reached for Gabriel's hand. "Would you feel better knowing that Rachel will live a full and happy life?"

"Yes," Tony said, feeling the warm blood run down his chest.

"Yes," Gabriel said, holding the little girl's hand.

"She will be okay, Gabriel. She's hurt, but she'll recover. Rachel loves you, Gabriel, she won't forget you, your stories are forever bound to one another and there is much yet to be told."

"Who are you?" Tony reached out to the little girl as she continued her transformation, standing beside Gabriel holding his hand.

"You don't remember me? I am the silent watcher. Witness to the breaking of the world. I stood with you in the eye of the tempest. Witness to the breaking of faith and the impudence of men. I was there when your heart first shattered. I am light in the darkness. I am part of the endless and unfolding story that ripples through time. Some called me Amal, it means hope."

"I am so sorry." Tony clutched the blood-soaked bear and slowly slipped away to another time and place…

*And if I should die before I wake, I pray thee, Lord, my soul to take.*

# EPILOGUE

Michael released a sigh of resignation as Jeremy Wolfram closed the door behind him, assessing the Senate office as if it were one of his investment properties. He was clutching a leather briefcase in one hand and an elegantly wrapped gift box in the other.

"Please, have a seat," Michael urged, gesturing toward the couch. "It's more comfortable here. My old war wound has been acting up lately, so I'll be stretching out my leg while we talk."

"I appreciate you taking the time to meet with me today, Senator," Wolfram replied, but remained standing.

Navigating through armies of high-priced lawyers representing one special interest or another remained a routine aspect of the job, notwithstanding the numerous efforts to rein in the corrupting influence of money on public policy. Many of his old law school chums, Michael reflected, those with the right connections, were raking in exorbitant sums of money advocating for America's corporate elite. Lobbying was a game of leveraging connections, trading favors, and, when necessary, wielding carrots and sticks. Though lobbyists in expensive suits maintained a façade of civility, they were capable

277

of persuasive tactics that would make even Machiavelli blush.

"What can I do for you, Jeremy?" Michael inquired.

Wolfram took his time, meticulously arranging his belongings before finally settling into the seat. Adjusting his tie, crossing his legs, and folding his hands in his lap, the lobbyist met Michael's gaze, his smile betraying only the slightest hint of condescension.

"Senator, I'm told you're a straight shooter who has little tolerance for lobbyist spin."

"Guilty as charged," Michael said.

"Then please allow me to get right to the point of my visit. Our firm represents a consortium of energy interests."

"You represent a cartel with fossil fuel interests," Michael interjected.

"We prefer the term consortium. A consortium of coal and oil producers, although in the coming decades, our clients do plan on expanding into other energy sectors."

"Decades?"

"Yes, there is still plenty of upside to coal and oil, and Americans consume more oil, coal and gas than any other country on the planet. But I'm here to talk to you about our current business objectives. I represent an economic sector responsible for providing energy to ninety-nine percent of the American economy."

"Go ahead, I'm listening."

Michael's leg throbbed. He didn't care much for the man in the Armani suit. Today's meeting was not a perfunctory lobbying effort. Both men knew Wolfram represented one of the most powerful industries in the country. Still, they danced.

"We are asking you to make a statement in support of an industry currently employing thousands of Americans in good-paying jobs. In your statement, we'd like you to make it clear that you have reconsidered your position on the Hamburg Protocol. Your statement will indicate you now believe it will be ill-advised for American companies to be tied to any limitations imposed by an international energy agreement."

Michael flashed a cold smile. "Jeremy, you realize I've been an active participant in developing these protocols? My commitment to establishing energy independence for this country through the development of new sources of clean energy is well documented."

"I do, Senator. That's why it's so important the statement come from you."

"Alternative energy is the pathway to a competitive and adaptive twenty-first-century economy. It is the cornerstone to building sustainable growth for our country. The science pointing to the catastrophic impact of accelerated climate disruption is undisputed. Our global competitors are beating us to what will eventually become a very lucrative new energy market. This isn't an American problem, it's a global problem. The Hamburg Protocol is a significant first step in addressing this issue."

Wolfram leaned forward toward Michael and smiled.

"Senator, I'm told you're a man of principle but also a practical politician. Our consortium is investing in new technology that will allow us to efficiently extract oil from shale rock, we will develop new sources of oil right here in our own backyard. The United States will become an exporter of oil again. Hamburg will discourage the capital investments required to introduce this new technology."

"I'm aware of shale extraction technology and it does nothing to diminish the carbon we release into the atmosphere; on the contrary, it exacerbates the problem. It's the wrong investment at the wrong time."

The empty suit continued, unfazed. "Codifying the standards outlined in the Hamburg Protocol into law will be perceived as a deterrent to growth. An initiative that will usurp American interests in favor of a globalist agenda."

"What part of 'it's a global problem'—a threat to life and commerce on the planet—do you not understand?" Michael gave Jeremy a hard stare, looking for any sign of an internal moral compass.

"We do understand, Senator. We have our own studies and we realize pulling back on alternative energy investments for a time will have some negative impact on the planet's ecosystem. But our scientists have faith the ecosystem will adjust. We plan to gradually and methodically shift to alternative fuels in a decade or two. A plan that won't adversely affect shareholder value."

"Since when do scientists act on faith? Adjust? We don't have a decade or two, Jeremy. We are already arriving late to the game."

Shaking his head, Michael did little to hide his disdain.

"I was told you might need time to process our request. Nevertheless, we are asking you to withdraw your support for any legislation that would give teeth to the Hamburg Protocol. In addition, we'd like you to release a statement affirming that underwriting risky investments in unproven alternative technologies would not be prudent at this time."

"You were told? Who is sharing such brilliant insights with you, Jeremy?" Michael moved aside the support for his aching leg and stood up, signaling he had heard enough.

Wolfram stood up and shook Michael's hand, indicating he understood it was time for him to go.

"Oh, I almost forgot," he said unconvincingly. "Dimitri Ivanov, one of our directors, requested I deliver this personally." Jeremy handed Michael the beautifully wrapped gift.

"It's a birthday gift for your daughter Gabriella. She'll be ten this week, right? He asked me to send his warmest regards to you and your beautiful wife Rachel, and he asked me to extend his regrets for not being able to deliver the gift himself. He said he thinks she'll enjoy playing the game."

Jeremy held Michael's gaze to ensure he had communicated the message properly.

Michael winced at the gut punch. The coded message delivered with tactical precision, his muscles coiled, and his face became a steel grey mask of icy control. *I could snap his neck right now without breaking a sweat.*

He shook off the thought and offered a disparaging smile. "I haven't seen or spoken to Dimitri Ivanov for some years. I heard he was having health issues."

"Mr. Ivanov is fine. He's semi-retired but he maintains an active role in managing his portfolio. Our company represents many of his business interests around the world. Not sure if you heard, part of his considerable art collection is on loan to the Whitney in New York and the MFA in Boston. My understanding is your wife's work will be featured as part of the Ivanov exhibit."

"I'm aware," Michael said, still processing the brazen message Jeremy had come to deliver.

"Mr. Ivanov thinks very highly of you, Senator. He insists you're destined to become a great president one day. I don't need to remind you, Senator, how expensive it is to run for president."

"No, you don't." *Here it comes. The carrot that abates the stick.* Michael reflexively rubbed his leg, fighting off a surge of unpleasant memories.

"We understand supporting our position on Hamburg will cost you some support, but I am here to assure you, you will never lack the resources you need to achieve the capstone of your career. You have Mr. Ivanov's word."

"What are you saying, Jeremy? There are laws governing quid pro quo."

"I wouldn't worry too much about that, Senator. Laws change, and even if they don't, there are always ways to make sure you have all the funding you need. My firm specializes in facilitating such things, Senator, this is why I was asked to come see you. You can count on our support whenever you need it."

*Checkmate! We have him. But at what cost? The implied threat to Rachel and Gabriella was unmistakable.* Michael could not help but wonder what Gabriel would do if he were here.

"I see. Well, thank you for coming by, Jeremy. I'm sure you have other things to do, but before you go I'd like to introduce you to an old friend."

Before Jeremy could answer, Michael reached for the intercom on his desk.

"Please say hello to Audrey Zornberg, the newly appointed director of the FBI," Michael said as Audrey burst in with her distinctive energetic prowl.

"Pleased to meet you, Madam Director, and congratulations," Jeremy said, a twitch in his left eye suddenly noticeable.

"Nice to meet you, Mr. Wolfram. Tell me, are you familiar with U.S. Code Title 18 Part 1, Chapter 11 Section 201? The statute designating it a federal crime to attempt to influence the conduct of a public official through the direct or implicit exchange of something of value."

Wolfram picked at an invisible piece of lint on the sleeve of his suit. "I am familiar with it, Madam Director. It keeps all of us who have an interest in public policy honest." His façade of composure eroding, Wolfram's eyes darted back and forth between Michael and Audrey, his twitch growing ever more prevalent.

Audrey Zornberg flashed a hard smile and waited for Michael's signal to escalate the exchange. It didn't come.

After a long uneasy pause, Audrey offered a slight nod to Michael and softened her tone. "Don't take offense, Mr. Wolfram, it's my standard opening line when meeting a lobbyist in a senator's office. It comes with the territory."

Wolfram's eye continued to twitch, but his shoulders slumped in relief. "No offense taken, Madam Director. It's been very nice meeting you." He turned abruptly to Michael. "Senator, please extend *our* fond wishes to your wife and daughter. I know the way out." Wolfram picked up his briefcase and briskly exited the room.

"What an asshole," Michael said, chuckling at the way he scurried out of the room. "Nicely done, Audrey."

"I had a good teacher. What's our play here? How do you want to deal with this scumbag?" A mixture of confusion and anger flashed on her face. Michael was more than a mentor, she cared about him deeply.

"It's not him, he's an expendable mouthpiece." Michael took in a deep breath and exhaled forcefully. "I'm not exactly sure what our next move is, Audrey, but sit down, let me tell you about the night I first met Dimitri Ivanov."

\* \* \*

"I thought I might hear from you today, Michael. I take it you met with Jeremy?"

"He's a soulless Ivy League asshole," Michael said, his displeasure evident.

Dimitri Ivanov's laughter erupted through on speakerphone. "A quality considered an asset in his profession. Not every Ivy League graduate can have your scruples, Michael."

"This is a big lift, Dimitri. Your friendship and support have been invaluable over the years, but reversing myself on this important climate initiative would be career suicide."

"It won't be, I promise you. I know the climate initiative is important to you and I understand the importance of limiting carbon emissions," Dimitri said, acknowledging Michael's frustration. "My partners also understand there are significant business opportunities in alternative energy. But these things take time, and investments have already been made, commitments must be honored."

"How could I possibly win reelection to the Senate in three years if I turn my back on my constituents now?"

"What have I always counseled you? You have to play the long game, Michael. You are not seeing the entire chessboard. Short-term compromises handled properly can yield long-term gains," Dimitri explained in a familiar pedantic tone. "Let's play this out. Say the agreement gets through the Senate, you don't have a veto-proof majority. What are the chances the president will sign it? I'll answer for you. Slim and none. He won't sign the bill, he'll say his predecessor gave away too much. He'll say the agreement is a threat to American sovereignty, bad for the economy. The usual jibber jabber for mass consumption."

"I understand how he might push back, but we can pressure him. What makes you so sure he'll kill it?"

"I'm sure he'll kill it, Michael."

"If I support the legislation, at least my constituents know I am fighting the good fight. That's what they elected me to do. If I switch positions now, I lose my Senate seat."

"You're not going to run for Senate in three years, Michael."

"Says who?"

"Says you. You are going to run for president. And when you win the presidency you'll sweep in majorities in the House and Senate. You'll introduce new climate legislation that will go further and faster than the Hamburg Protocols. The climate package will have generous incentives for the private sector to support the transition to alternative fuels."

"Incentives that will benefit your energy consortium," Michael interjected, reading the larger play for Ivanov and his partners.

"Is that so bad, Michael? The private sector will help lead the way and the United States will lead the world. You won't stop at climate change, you'll take on prison reform, healthcare, and tort reform, invest in education, and help advance major technological breakthroughs. You will inspire a new generation of scientists who will do miraculous things, on earth and in space. You will become the most consequential president in history. You will take up the forward-looking mantle of John F. Kennedy, and Rachel will be this generation's Jackie."

Michael's head was spinning. The possibilities were intoxicating. But the mention of the fallen president triggered old questions. It opened up a floodgate of memories.

Questions unanswered and entombed. A stunning performance in a dark theater. The altercation. His first night with Rachel. His final days with Gabriel, the things they learned from Rachel's father, revelations they both agreed to suppress. Secrets he kept hidden, even from Rachel. The returning memories seared through him.

"I don't..." But Dimitri didn't let him finish.

"The long game, Michael. Focus on the long game. I'm not going to be around forever, but the consortium will be. Some version of it anyway. Your future will not mirror that of another idealistic Harvard man—one destined for transformative greatness, had his intransigence not sealed his fate. He and his brother didn't play the long game. They moved too quickly to upend the order of things. They failed to honor commitments made by the father. You'll be different. The progress you usher in will last for generations."

Michael flashed back to the conversations with Gabriel years ago. Things he never discussed with anyone. The secrets they were complicit in burying. The things Gabriel suspected but chose not to pursue. Dimitri's connection to Tony. The secrets Ivanov knew remained hidden, he was an architect of their concealment. The last man alive. The one man who could fill in the missing pieces of the story. Dimitri Ivanov, an engineer of altered history, still moving pieces on the board, still shaping events. Ripples continued moving through time.

Michael would do whatever he had to do to protect Rachel and their daughter. He could access the power to make the world safer for Gabriella and her own children. Using power wisely was the long game that justified the short-term compromise. Wasn't it?

"Dimitri." Michael struggled to form a cogent thought from the conflicting inputs clouding his thinking.

"You don't have to say anything, Michel. The decision is yours and yours alone."

"Dimitri, I have to ask you about Dallas."

"You don't have to ask anything, Michael. You already know the answer. Camelot was a beautiful dream. And we all did what we had to do. The past is the past, faded and irretrievable. The future is your canvas. This is your story now."

*"We are not here to curse the darkness, but to light the candle that can guide us through that darkness to a safe and sane future."*

*John F. Kennedy*
*Accepting the Democratic Nomination for*
*President of the United States*
*Memorial Coliseum, Los Angeles – July 15, 1960*

*"But however close we sometimes seem to that dark and final abyss, let no man of peace and freedom despair. For he does not stand alone."*

*John F. Kennedy*
*Address to the U.N. General Assembly – September 25, 1961*

# MY THANKS AND A SMALL REQUEST

Thank you for reading *After Dallas*. I hope you enjoyed reading it as much as as I did writing it!

If you did enjoy this book—and you purchased it online—please consider leaving a review on the book's purchase page. Reviews are incredibly useful feedback for both prospective readers and the author.

My thanks in advance for doing so!

*Louis A. Rivera*

# ACKNOWLEDGMENTS

Writing this book has been a circuitous journey, a rewarding and unparalleled learning experience.

The desire to write was embedded in my DNA by my father and grandfather. Becoming a novelist, however, required a commitment that I was only able to access later in life. Though it arrived late, I am eternally grateful it arrived. A fortuitous two-martini lunch with best-selling author and former CBS colleague Casey Sherman, coupled with the inspiration from seeing *Hamilton* on Broadway, provided a much-needed kick in the ass and the resolve to complete my first draft. *I'm not throwing away my shot.*

I firmly believe a work of art can change the trajectory of someone's life. For me the Beatles' *Sgt. Pepper's Lonely Hearts Club Band* was one such example, as was the Allman Brothers *Live At Fillmore East.* Reading Tolkien and Hermann Hesse in high school had a profound effect on my love of words. Later in life, the works of Kurt Vonnegut, Tom Wolfe, Don DeLillo, Salman Rushdie, Doris Kearns Goodwin, William Manchester, Ernest Hemingway, Philip K. Dick, Gabriel García Márquez, Stephen Kinzer, among many others, provided inspiration and insight into worlds of infinite depth and beauty. In a way, these artists and writers have been my mentors and spiritual guides, demonstrating how forms of expression can transform and illuminate our reality.

Two books I recently read were instrumental in overcoming self-imposed limitations and resistance: *The War of Art* by Steven Pressfield and *The Creative Act: A Way of Being* by Rick Rubin. They helped me understand how the desire to channel one's creative energy is an act of grace. How I was obligated to respect my muse and recognize that my own development was tied into my willingness to do the work. I recommend these books to anyone who has ever felt a creative impulse, especially those who have hesitation around sharing the work so inspired.

As this story evolved it became about so much more than a narrative around the JFK assassination. Earlier drafts had lengthy exposition about the early days of the Irish in Boston, the Vietnam War, the failings of the Cuban Revolution, the emergence of Rock radio, the causes of the Iranian revolution, the 'greed is good' decade, the punk scene in New York City in the '80s and a lot of other things that interest me, but were not necessarily germane to the story at the core of this novel. I am grateful to my editors for their advice on how to focus the narrative in order to keep readers engaged.

While the story quickly moves past the conspiracy to assassinate JFK, I felt I had to remain faithful to what my characters were trying to tell me. We all make compromises of some sort, and sometimes those compromises generate unexpected consequences for those we love—and in some cases, for people we've never met. The burden of holding on to a lie can be fatal, while facing a painful truth can be redemptive—but both carry unpredictable costs. I'm not sure who assassinated President Kennedy, nor was it my intent in writing this book to present a plausible theory about the assassination and the secrets associated with it. But what I am sure of is that JFK's assassination unleashed a series of connected events that continue to manifest in our present reality. The forward trajectory of our country was irrevocably altered. While none of the fictitious characters in my book were based on actual individuals, my guess is, we have some version of Tony, Dimitri, Gabriel and Michael walking among us doing and undoing, and influencing outcomes from the shadows. I hope to continue exploring that dynamic in future work. Stay tuned!

\* \* \*

I am indebted to William Boggess and Robert Astle for their insight and thoughtful critiques as the novel began taking shape, as well as editor Robin Seavill who helped me bring the work across the finish line, dotting i's and crossing t's. My designer Mark Thomas's insight into independent publishing has been as valuable as his intuitive cover design and formatting. I am also very grateful to my early readers who offered feedback and, most importantly, encouragement. This was particularly helpful when the prose was still quite rough. The feedback from early readers who connected with the novel's characters inspired me to keep working. A special thank you to: Lauren Chiaramonte, Mark Hobbs, Melissa Mangino, Brenna Shannon, Marc Kaplan, Karen Miles, Marissa Mediate, Toni Balcarcel, Julie Redd, Frank Galalis, Angela Stern, Michael Stolper and a special thank-you to my sister Laura for her detailed insights and suggestions.

I hope this book brings as much joy in the reading as it did to me in the writing.

> *"Language is a cracked kettle on which we beat out tunes for bears to dance to, while all the time we long to move the stars to pity."*
>
> Gustave Flaubert, *Madame Bovary* (1857)

# ABOUT THE AUTHOR

Louis Rivera grew up in a rambunctious New York City household, surrounded by four sisters who ignited his love for books, The Beatles, Star Trek, and Sabrett Hot Dogs. His appreciation for social commentary blossomed at an early age thanks to the insights of Kurt Vonnegut, Don DeLillo, Philip K. Dick, and George Orwell.

He studied media and politics at the University of Maryland, sparking a lifelong interest in how media influences our civic dialogue—a tenacious endeavor in a world where cat videos, conspiracy theorists, and thoughtful political commentary share the same digital stage.

Pursuing an unconventional career path, Louis dabbled in concert promotion and artist management before embarking on a successful career in media advertising—encompassing roles at legendary Boston radio stations WBCN and WFNX, as well as Viacom/CBS, NESN, and NBCUniversal. In 2022, he put away the corporate suit and tie to focus on writing.

Proud father of two accomplished young women who inspire him to live joyfully every day. When not crafting stories or unraveling historical paradoxes, he can occasionally be found wielding a Fender Stratocaster at local blues jams in the Boston area. On special occasions, you might spot him at a Sabrett Hot Dog stand in Manhattan, extolling the virtues of the perfect blend of mustard and sauerkraut to the uninitiated.

To discover more please visit Louis' website:

*louisarivera.com*

You can also connect with him on the following social media.

*facebook.com/AfterDallas1963*

*x.com/LouistheAuthor*

*instagram.com/LouistheAuthor*

*linkedin.com/in/louisriveraboston*